Clark Reeper Tales

Clark Reeper Tales

The Truthful Telling of the Adventures of the West's Wildest Bounty Hunter

Michael Panush
to Cousin Bob

Happy trails!

Written by Michael Panush and Illustrated by Jake Delaney

2008

Clark Reeper Tales

Tables of Contents

To my Family

An Opening Word from Clark Reeper

All right, Mr. Fancy Big City Dime Novelist, I'll tell you my story. I'll tell you about my time out in the West, and the strange things I saw there. I'll tell you how I battled dead folks that were still living, creatures from other worlds, and others horrors that I still cannot describe. I'll tell you of the men and women that I fought beside and against, rogues and heroes both. I'll tell you how I died and came back to life. And most importantly, I'll tell you how I became a father. So pull up a chair and take off your boots, cause it's a long story. Figure I'll start where it all started, a little town name of Dead Man's Gulch...

Dead Man's Gulch

Now, I ain't no resident of Dead Man's Gulch, no sir. That town had something queer about it, like something important was missing and you couldn't figure out what exactly it was. The people was always staring at you out of the corner of their eyes and seemed to be talking about you behind your back. I didn't like going to Dead Man's Gulch, but men in my line of work don't often have a choice in where they get to go. The name's Clark Reeper, and I'm a bounty hunter.

I reckon I've heard and seen my fair share of strange things out in the wild prairies that make up most of this old country, but that was before I went to Dead Man's. Things changed me there, and there weren't no going back. This all happened a couple of years back, just when it seemed like everyone with money to spare was headed out west.

I was chasing a two-bit gunslinger by the name of Fire-Eyed Dick, and word had it that he was holed up in Dead Man's. Kind of a funny story about who exactly Fire-Eyed Dick was, and I think now would be a good time to tell it you. Dick's bounty was two hundred dollars in pure gold dust, to be paid out in full to whoever brought him in, dead or alive. The bounty was leveled on Fire-Eyed Dick by an old scientist named Doc Torrent.

Torrent, who operated out of a lab in a particularly desolate part of the Dakotas, had heard about my success putting down the monstrous Jackalope nicknamed 'The Ricochet Rabbit' that had been terrorizing the Nevada-California border, and knew I was a feller that specialized in jobs of a strange and unnatural nature. He told me some bull's crap of a story about how a gunman with piercing eyes had attacked his lab, killed a few of his assistants, stolen his prize experiment and ran off. He wanted me to find this gunman, Fire-Eyed Dick, and bring him back. I knew the Doc wasn't telling me the whole story, but I needed the money and took the job anyway.

Dick's trail was as wild as a drunk man's wanderings. I chased him all over North Dakota, across desert and forest, until I caught up with him in a saloon in Deadwood. He was a thin rod of a man, completely covered by a black cloak and wide-brimmed hat. Black leather gloves even covered his hands. A burning light seemed to shine through his hat brim, and I began to think he weren't all human. I decided dead was better than alive in this situation.

I fired at Fire-Eyed Dick from behind with a trusty twelve-gauge, and that should have torn the feller apart. Instead, the gunman swung around and laid into me with a fist made of solid steel. But when he hit me, his entire body spun completely around, so that the tips of his boots were pointed the opposite way as his blazing eyes! He got up and ran out of the place, his feet still pointed backwards.

After I had picked myself up off of the floor and wheezed for a minute or two, I was hot on his trail. I caught up with Fire-Eyed Dick and shot off his hat with my Colt Peacemaker as he was riding out of town on a stolen horse. Without his hat, I saw that Fire-Eyed Dick didn't have much of a face at all. It was a metal rod with two light bulbs sticking out, and it was the light bulbs that gave him that glow.

See, it turns out that Fire-Eyed Dick didn't steal Doc Torrent's experiment. He *was* the experiment. Torrent had been trying to make a mechanical man with something like a clattering cash register for a brain and a steam engine for a heart. He had succeeded a little too well. That was why Doc Torrent was paying so much for me to kill the mechanical man. He knew that Fire-Eyed Dick would wise up quickly. Someone had to shut him down before he caused too much trouble. I reckon I was being paid to be that someone.

I tracked Fire-Eyed Dick out of Deadwood, but he was getting better and better at hiding. I would have to finish him quickly, before he got wise enough to finish me. I found out he was heading straight for Dead Man's Gulch.

A wagon train was leaving Kansas City on its way to Dead Man's Gulch, and I was able to tag along, the pioneers thankful to have a man of my skills riding with them. There are all sorts of outlaws, Indians, and other dangerous critters running amok in the frontier prairies, and that's not even counting some of the stranger things I've seen, like a train-hijacking crew of circus freaks, bloodthirsty cults, and a hairy giant the Indians called Sasquatch. The wagon train was filled with your typical number of immigrants to the west, thin-skinned pioneers looking to strike gold with their first footstep, and nervous families forced to move out to find work and new lives. I preferred walking with the latter.

I found myself beside a wagon belonging to a greenhorn from Baltimore by the name of Oswald Green. He was a little feller with a bowler hat and a thin moustache, the kind you would see toiling away in any big business. He didn't have no place out here and seemed drawn to me. Plus, he had this little boy who was riding along in the wagon, by the name of Charles, and the boy seemed real excited when I mentioned that I was a bounty hunter. Charles Green was a nice little kid, decked out in a Norfolk suit and peaked cap, and had a full head of curly brown hair, thick spectacles, and freckles on his face. Didn't have the heart to leave him hanging.

"So, you're saying the people in charge of United Coal are giant lizards?" Oswald asked me after I had mentioned my crusade against the cold-blooded reptilians that controlled the United Coal Company to his son.

"Shape-shifting lizards," I said. "You wouldn't know it to look at them."

"Wow!" Charles said, completely amazed. I couldn't help smiling, even though I could tell that his father didn't believe a word I had said.

"Well, enough about me," I said. "You folks gonna settle down in Dead Man's Gulch?"

"Oh no, we're just passing through on our way to California." Oswald seemed glad to get away from the subject of giant lizards. "I wouldn't want Charles to grow up in that town. His mother would have wanted the best for him, and right now that's in California."

"His mother is—"

"Dead." Oswald sighed and Charles looked away. "A couple of Confederate renegades who didn't realize the war was over attacked our home a couple years back. Charles was just born then." Oswald fixed me with a look a few miles from kindly. "What side were you on, if I may ask?"

"Both," I said simply. It was true enough. "But why don't you want to settle in Dead Man's?" I asked, trying to change the subject. "It ain't the most friendly town, but there are worse places."

Oswald shook his head. "You haven't heard about the Englishman who bought all the land on Blackpine Peak last year? Lord Dark-something, I think his name is. They say he's ruling the whole region like a king, and a depraved king at that. Also, rumor has it that the local residents are getting into arguments with the nearby Indians, and I really don't want to wait around to see what the outcome's going to be."

"Darkmoore," I whispered to myself. If Lord Darkmoore was here, that meant this was a place with a real presence for the supernatural, and it wasn't a good presence.

"You know him?" Oswald asked.

"Yeah. I know him. Had a run in with his men, Noah Feratu and the Midnight Gang a while back—" My voice died away as I saw what was ahead of us.

The wagon train turned around yet another curve and I saw a sight that will stay with me until my dying days. I gulped and held out my hand for the wagon to stop. "Charles, you should get into the wagon and close your eyes. And probably cover your ears too."

"Why?" Oswald asked curiously. He peered ahead around the bend and gagged. After he had finished retching, he ordered his son to get into the back of the wagon. Charles must have realized how serious things were because he obeyed his father and didn't even complain.

Some things are just so dead wrong that all the words in all the fancy-pants books in the world can't do them justice, and this was one of those things. I had known that Lakota sometimes passed by this area, and the townsfolk battled with them, but I couldn't imagine nothing like this.

The people here had been a Lakota tribe. Well, mostly women, old folks, and little kids that made up a Lakota tribe when the men weren't around, before the townsfolk of Dead Man's Gulch had finished with them. Now they was just pieces, dripping and draining in the dusty dirt.

Some of them were still alive, horrible as it may seem, but vultures, coyotes, and desert critters were finishing them off the painful way. I spotted a dying old man whispering words in his own language over the bodies of a couple of young children, and I knew he was having the most painful moments of his life. I took out my Peacemaker with a practiced spin and walked over to ease his passing.

"Easy there, old man, just performing the Good Lord's mercy," I said, pressing the Colt's muzzle to the back of his head. His arms and legs were twisted around like broken twigs and he was covered in blood. Even so, he turned around and started shouting furiously in his language, a lot louder than someone in his position should be able to shout.

I put one round in his skull right when he was in the middle of his chant, and the old man keeled over. I returned my Peacemaker to its holster and walked back to the wagon train.

Most of us holed up in the Killgrave Hotel, a two-bit dump that suited the two-bit town of Dead Man's Gulch. I got a room next to Oswald and Charles Green, and then went off to see if I could catch Fire-Eyed Dick's scent.

I didn't see the mechanical man, but I did figure out the reason why he came to Dead Man's Gulch. Lord Darkmoore was looking for bodyguards, and he had put up posters advertising his need for guns and muscle all over the town. It didn't take me long to figure out why Darkmoore needed hired guns. He was a Vampire, a Vampire Lord, if you want to use their bloodsucker terminology, and he needed folks with guns to watch over him while he slept during the day. I didn't have any reason to pick a fight with Darkmoore, and I hoped I wouldn't even run into him.

With no sign of Fire-Eyed Dick, I headed to the local saloon to knock back a few. Alcohol has always been my vice of choice, and I haven't found any reason to stop yet. But on the way to the saloon, two things happened that would make my stay in Dead Man's Gulch a lot less easy.

First, Charles Green ran up to me, crying and afraid. He shivered all over like he had been out in the cold for too long. His father wasn't anywhere to be seen.

"Mr. Reeper! Mr. Reeper!" he cried. He would have collided with me if I hadn't caught the little feller in my arms.

"What's wrong, son? Where's your pa?" I asked, kindly as I could.

Charles cried for a few seconds, but I calmed him down and got him to talk. "I wanted to see what you wouldn't let me see, the dead Indians! So, I headed out while my father was checking in at the hotel, and then he went after me. And I saw the Indians, and they were dead, but they were also...alive!" He burst into tears again.

"Don't worry, son," I said to Charles. "Corpses can stiffen up sometimes. It happens a lot. They ain't really alive though. Now, where's your pa gone to?"

"They got him!" Charles cried. "The dead Indians came and ate him up!"

I stared at Charles. I had seen a heck of a lot of strange things, but I wasn't inclined to believe a crying boy's story about the living dead eating his daddy. I was about to say something else that would ease Charles's fears, but then a bullet whizzed by my head and clipped my hat.

"Son of a gun!" I shouted. Sure enough, Fire-Eyed Dick stood right in front of me, a Winchester Rifle in his iron hands. "Charles, you better get behind me," I said. "Things are about to head straight for Hell." Even I didn't know how right I was.

The boy seemed too scared to move. He stood still, like he was rooted in the ground, right in the path of Fire-Eyed Dick's bullets. I ignored Charles's squeal of terror, roughly picked him up and tossed him to the side. I wouldn't have tossed him around normally, but I didn't have much choice in the matter.

Fire-Eyed Dick fired again, but the mechanical man's shot went wild and kicked up dust near my right leg. I drew out both of the Peacemakers and let him have it. My two shots caught him straight in the chest, tearing off his black coat and letting me get a look at him. He weren't nothing more than arms, legs, a head, and a body made out of thin medal rods with a couple smoking machines welded onto him. Having a chest about as wide as a stack of nickels meant that he was a lot harder to hit.

Well, we exchanged gunfire for a while, his bullets hitting close but always missing, and my shots not even grazing his metal stick of a body. Those twin light bulbs were glaring at me like two little suns, and I got myself an idea. I fanned one of my revolvers, the bullets rapidly flying around Dick and driving him back. Then I holstered one six-gun, grabbed the other one with both hands, closed one eye to aim, and put a single bullet into one of his light bulb eyes. The glass shattered and Fire-Eyed Dick let out a loud whining sound, the first sound I had ever heard him make. I tried to shoot out the other light bulb eye, but Dick scampered down an alley and leapt over a water trough, running like a wounded antelope. He was gone. By now it was nearly dark, and the pale moon had crept out of its hiding spot.

Then something else caught my attention.

See, Charles weren't lying about the living dead Indians. They really had gotten up, still rotting and spilling out every which way, and were coming into town. The townsfolk started screaming and running around in circles, hollering about 'dead walking,' and other such things.

I turned to Charles, still crouched on the ground. He had stopped crying, and stood very still. Slowly, he raised his little arm and pointed behind me. I looked, and there was a large mob of corpses, men, women, and even little kids, all heading our way.

"Ah hell," I muttered. "And I thought Dead Man's Gulch was just a colorful name! What do these dead folks want?" I soon got my answer when a gaunt-looking Lakota maiden with only half a face grabbed the town banker and bit straight into his skull. The poor feller let out a piercing cry and doubled over on the ground, clutching the gaping hole in his head. Then, in a few seconds, he came to his feet and let out a low, hungry, moan. It didn't take long for me to put two and two together and realize Charles and me had to get out of that place fast.

..."still rotting and hanging out every which way..."

"Can you walk?" I asked Charles, pulling him to his feet.

"I...uh...I guess so," he stammered. I was probably being a little too hard on a boy whose own father had just been eaten, but I didn't have much of a choice. I was having a lot less choices lately.

"Well, we're gonna have to run. Those dead folks don't look too fast, so it shouldn't be no problem to outrun them. Follow me, we'll get to the stables, get a horse, and leave this town to the corpses. Come on!"

We took off running. To his credit, Charles managed to keep up with me, even though he began panting and wheezing after a couple minutes of sprinting. He followed me down the dirt main street and round the corner to the stables. But then I stopped.

A large army of those dead folk blocked our path, and they weren't just Indians. Nope, it seemed that most of the citizens of Dead Man's Gulch had got bitten, and had turned into the same flesh-hungry creatures as their attackers. I turned around and found more hungry corpses drooling over my flesh. We were surrounded.

"Son of a gun!" I shouted, drawing out my Peacemakers. I blasted the first dead feller, an overweight man in a butcher's apron, but the bullets just sent him rocking on his feet. Fighting Fire-Eyed Dick gave me another idea, so I tried shooting the dead man in the head. His brains splattered on the dirt road and he toppled over. I reckon even dead folks can't go on when they're missing a brain.

Well, there was only option open: the Killgrave Hotel. "Charles," I said, "we're gonna have to go inside and stay there until we can leave this town for good. How you getting on?"

"Uh...okay," he wheezed. He was doubled over and his face was red. Poor kid.

"All right, now you just stay near me and I'll keep them dead things away from you. Don't worry, son." I blasted another walking corpse and started walking slowly backwards to the hotel, Charles right next to me.

Then a dead boy only a little older than Charles lunged out and grabbed him. I blasted the dead kid's head off with both my Peacemakers, but not before he had sunk his teeth into poor Charles's arm. I holstered one of the revolvers, picked up Charles, who was crying piteously, and threw him over my shoulder. Then I raced backward into the hotel. I kicked open the door and slammed it behind me, then found myself looking down the barrel of a wide-mouthed shotgun.

"I ain't no dead man!" I cried, "and there's no need to make me one!"

"The kid's been bit," the man with the shotgun said. He was a short feller with thinning hair and spectacles. "The name's Murphy, I own this place, and I think we're in the last building not overrun. I'll be damned if I let some kid turn into one of those things on us!"

"If he does, then I'll put him down myself!" I shouted. I drew out one of my revolvers and pointed it at Murphy. "Now let me pass or I swear I will blow your goddamn head off!"

I reckon he knew I weren't kidding, so he lowered the shotgun and let me in, but glared at me as I headed upstairs. There was about ten or so townsfolk hiding out in the hotel, and they had barricaded the pathway to the upper story pretty well. I laid Charles down on a bench and looked him over.

"Does it hurt?" I asked. He was very pale and wasn't crying too much. Even though I didn't want to admit it, I knew he was gonna change.

"It hurts," he whispered. "Am I going to be one of those things that ate my father?"

"I don't rightly know," I whispered.

"I do," Charles said. "I can feel it happening to me right now. I'll be one of them soon." He was very quiet for a few moments. "Can you make it painless?"

"That I can," I said, feeling sick to my stomach with what I was gonna have to do. I gently pressed the muzzle of my revolver to the boy's forehead. "You won't feel nothing until you reach the Gates of Heaven." I was going to wait for him to change, wanting to give the kid as much life as possible before shooting him, but then something distracted me.

"Hey, look at this!" Murphy shouted, pointing out the window. I left Charles lying on the bench and went to see. A youngish man in a striped shirt, vest and bowler hat decorated with feathers stood on the roof of the one-story general store across the street. By his browned skin and face paint, I could tell he was a Lakota. He took out a bow and arrow, tied a rope to the arrow, and shot it straight at the roof of our building, so that the rope hung down like a vine in a jungle. Then, he gave the rope a test pull, and leapt into the air, swinging on the rope like he was some kind of monkey.

Much to my amazement, the Lakota made it all the way across. He swung low, and some of the dead people reached up to try and grab him, but he swatted away their hands. Once he had made it across, he climbed up the rope until he got to the window and leapt inside.

"My name is Running Dog. You are the last living people in this city," he said, not sounding tired or short of breath at all. "I am here to help." He had a real strange accent, almost like a stuffy old Easterner, or even an Englishman straight out of Victoria's Britain.

The survivors gasped in horror and surprise, scared out of their minds when they heard that they were the last ones left alive.

"Now hold on!" Murphy said, swinging his shotgun so it pointed to the Lakota. "Indians were the first ones to stop being dead and start eating people after we killed them all! I say we can't trust any heathen dirt worshipper!"

Faster than I could see, the Lakota grabbed the shotgun and tore it out of Murphy's hands. "You foolish paleface!" he cried. "Even Sitting Bull would not wish this on you! If a Lakota Burial Chant is interrupted, then the dead are not yet dead, and they become hungry. They spread that hunger to everyone else they bite, unless the proper rites are preformed. Or the head is removed." I swear he looked straight at me, like he knew what I did. "Someone must have interrupted an elder's Burial Chant."

"Well," I said, "that don't matter none. You can finish the chant and send all of those corpses back to being dead, so why don't you do it?"

Running Dog shook his head. "It is not that easy. I only know a few chants and rituals." He sighed. "I was the son of our tribe's medicine man, but I preferred the paleface's ways to our own. I left my tribe for what I thought were greener pastures, even attended Oxford, and I just returned yesterday. I wish I had never left my people."

"So do I," I said. "Don't you remember any chants?"

Running Dog nodded. "I know one that can stop someone who is bitten from turning."

My eyes instantly went to Charles. "That boy over there, he's been bitten. Can you save him?"

The Lakota walked over and gave Charles a quick look. "I believe I can. Bring a bucket of water and some tobacco, some bandages if you can find them, and I will try my best."

We gave Running Dog the materials he wanted and then he set to work. Now I had seen Lakota fighting, and I knew they were fierce warriors. But I had no idea they could be so tender. Running Dog wiped Charles down, gently caressed the wound and burned some tobacco next to him, all the while chanting in a low voice. When he was finished, some color had returned to Charles's cheeks, and Running Dog had also wrapped and bound the wound.

"Thank you," Charles whispered softly, wiping the tears from his eyes.

"You are welcome, dear boy." Running Dog came to his feet. "It is done. The child is saved. Now we have to save ourselves." He went over to the window and looked down at the walking corpses. I walked over to Charles, figuring I was the closest thing he had to a father in this town.

I took off my long brown coat and wrapped him up in it. "You feeling better, son?"

"Yes," Charles said weakly. He smiled. "I can't believe I met a real Indian! And a British one too!"

I chuckled and ruffled his hair. Then I went over to where Murphy and Running Dog were talking. It was time to get out of here.

"The stables are our best bet," Murphy said. "The only problem is that the dead have clogged up the streets!" A lot of time had passed, it was almost midnight, and us survivors had realized that we didn't have enough food to hold out for more than one or two days. It was time to leave, but that presented a bit of a problem.

"If we just had something to clear the way," Running Dog whispered. "It wouldn't be a stroll through Hyde Park, but maybe we could get through."

Running Dog's words gave me an idea. "My tools! They must still be here. You guys just wait here a second or too, and I'll give us something to clear the road." I ran out of the room and headed for my room on the bottom floor. I jumped over the barricade and then stopped dead in my tracks.

The walking corpses had torn down the door and they were walking around inside the hotel lobby. A thin woman with smashed glasses and a tall young man with no left leg fixed on me with hungry gazes.

"Uhhhhh," the young man said. He reached out with one hand and grabbed on to my collar. I went for my Peacemakers, but they were plumb out of ammo.

"Son of a gun, son a gun," I said, kicking the dead man away and stumbling backwards. "Son of a gun!"

I came quickly to my feet and picked up one of the saloon chairs. I had been in plenty of barroom brawls before, but never one against rotting corpses. The woman came at me, and I slammed the chair into her head. It broke apart and sent her sprawling, her brains spilling out on the floor.

Then I grabbed a chair leg and swung it into the one-legged corpse. His skull was soft and spongy, so I whacked him again and again until he stopped moving. I dropped the bloody chair leg, gave the corpse a final kick, and headed to my room.

The tools were right where I had left them. There was my twelve-gauge, a scoped Sharps rifle from the war, and a few more Peacemakers. I reloaded, grabbed all of the guns, and then found what I had been looking for—a dozen sticks of candy-red dynamite.

Yes sir, Alfred Nobel had outdone himself with the dynamite, and I was happy to have it along. I went back into the lobby, and saw a couple more corpses. After easily blowing their heads off with the twelve-gauge, I headed upstairs.

Murphy, Running Dog, and the rest of the survivors were as happy as I was to see the dynamite.

"Now we can finally bust out of here!" Murphy said. He picked up one of the dynamite sticks like he was a kid on Christmas morning.

"Not so fast," I said. "This stuff is just as likely to blow us to smithereens as it is the dead folks, so we're gonna play this careful." I turned to Running Dog and handed him a stick. "You got a good arm on you?"

"I was a champion horseshoe thrower when I was at Oxford," Running Dog said with a smile.

"Good, here's the plan. First, we split into two groups, each with a couple of sticks. We'll have to leapfrog our way to the stables. First group throws, the second group runs, and then the second group throws while the first one runs. I'll take one group, Running Dog takes the other, okay?"

Running Dog nodded. "And who takes the wounded child?"

"I reckon I will." We all stared at each other, as did the other survivors. Some of them had pistols on them, but we didn't have nearly enough ammo to hold out against all the hungry dead for too long. This would have to be quick.

While they were all getting ready, I walked over to Charles. He was looking a lot better, but still pretty weak. "We're gonna get out of here now," I said. "I'm gonna put you on my back. You just hold on real tight and we'll make it. Okay?"

Charles nodded. "Um, Mr. Reeper?" he asked.

"Yeah?"

"Those dead people, are they going to eat us?"

"Don't you fret, son," I said simply. "I won't let them". Charles looked a little bit better, but he didn't say anything. I picked him up and set him on my back, and he held on as tight as he could. I drew out one of my revolvers and looked it over. It was almost time.

I picked up my Sharps rifle and offered it to Running Dog. "Need some firepower?" I asked.

"I'm fine, thank you." Running Dog tapped the bow and arrow on his back. "You never forget how to use a Lakota War Bow. Let us begin."

I lit a match on my boot heel, lit the first dynamite stick and tossed the dynamite down the stairs so it could clear out the barricade and any dead people that had walked in. There was a lot of smoke and noise and the way was cleared.

My group, of about five folks besides Charles and me, ran out of the Killgrave Hotel and into the street, blasting away with every gun we had. I had given my twelve-gauge and Sharps rifle to two of the townsfolk, and while they weren't no Annie Oakley, they held their own. Just as the crowds of dead folk were about to overwhelm us, Running Dog blew apart another hole in front of us and we ran into the general store, and then blasted a path for him.

Using this pattern we slowly made our way to the stables. It took a long time, a lot of ammunition, and every single stick of dynamite, but we finally made it. Charles hung on like a limpet and I was mighty proud of him.

But just as I shoved open the door of the stables, I thought of something. What if the dead folks liked horsemeat just as much as human flesh? With a sinking feeling in my chest, I peered inside.

I was right. The walking corpses had gotten there first, and every horse in the place had been chewed up good. Running Dog and his group ran inside the stable and then they saw what had happened.

"Well that does it!" Murphy cried. "I've had it with running! Those goddamn red heathens ate everything!" He swung around and aimed his shotgun at Running Dog. "This is all your fault!"

"Now calm down Murphy," I said. "It ain't nobody's fault, so just calm the hell down!"

Murphy shook his head. "No, this goddamn dirt worshipper did it, and I'm gonna do him in!" He was about to fire, I could tell, and there weren't nothing Running Dog or I could do. But then a hand grabbed Murphy from behind and pulled him backwards. It was a young woman, a Lakota by the looks of her, with a bloody slash in her tan buckskin dress. Running Dog stared at her and watched silently as she tore the screaming Murphy apart. Then Running Dog notched an arrow to his bow and shot it straight into her head. After he had put another one in what was left of Murphy's head, he turned back to me.

"That was my sister," he said simply. "I would recognize those eyes anywhere." We said no more about it.

"There's a train refueling depot a little ways from town," I said, trying to change the subject. "If we can get out there, we'll be safe. Once we explain what happened to the train's engineer, I'm sure he'd give us a ride out of here."

"But how are we going to clear away the dead people?" Charles asked, still on my back. "We don't have any more dynamite, and all the horses are dead."

"Maybe dead." I walked over to one of the horses, a big feller with his legs all chewed to the bone, and put my hand next to his muzzle. I wasn't completely surprised when he lunged for it. "But the folks outside are dead, and that doesn't slow them down none."

It took us a while to saddle up the dead horses, but we did it. We took some pieces of flesh from the dead people outside and hung them from some poles we found in the stable. We used those to lure the horse corpses forward. It was probably the most stinking ride I ever had, but I was sure grateful for it. Then, with me on the horse and Charles on the back holding onto my waist, we rode off.

"Yeee-haw!" I couldn't help shouting as my horse pounded out of the stable. One of its back legs tore off but the animal managed well enough with the other three. The survivors rode after me with Running Dog bringing up the rear. The corpses blocking our way were trampled under the hooves of the dead horses, and we left that stinking town to the flies, the vultures, and the living dead.

We rode the dead horses until the sun rose and Dead Man's Gulch disappeared behind us. Then, we carefully blasted apart each one of the horse's heads and buried the bodies. We walked the rest of the way to the train depot.

It wasn't until I was waiting for the train that I realized just how tired I felt. I fought to stay awake until the train arrived, but there was some nagging sensation in my mind that there was still something I had to do. I shrugged it off and sat down next to Charles. He leaned against my shoulder and closed his eyes.

"Where am I going to go now?" he asked in his quaking little voice. "My father is gone, and I don't have any other relatives."

I thought for a while and then said, "I reckon I'll send you off to a boarding school. You'd get yourself a first-rate education there."

Poor Charles didn't seem to share my opinion of being packed off and sent away. "I don't want to go to boarding school," he whispered, leaning his curly-haired head against my shoulder.

"It ain't gonna be that bad," I said hopefully. "Teachers might beat you a few times, but you'll get a good schooling, and you'll be safe."

"I don't want to go to boarding school," he repeated. "I want to be with you."

"Uh, well, I don't know if I'd be a good father," I muttered. "I've never had much of anything to do with wives and children and such. Sorry son, I'm just not cut out for it."

Then Running Dog kneeled down next to me. "But you were a good father," he said. "When the lad was scared you comforted him and cared for him. I think you did a capital job."

I looked at Charles and he looked at me. His eyes got all big and he was looking small and helpless. I gave in. "Ah hell," I muttered. "Fine, you can stay with me for a bit. Until I figure something else out."

"Thank you, Mr. Reeper!" Charles cried, beaming.

"But I'm warning you, it's gonna be dangerous. I don't even understand half the outlaws and beasts that are trying to kill me these days, or the outlaws and beasts that I'm paid to kill."

"It can't be that dangerous—" Charles was interrupted when a metal stick figure with one light bulb still shining from his tiny head burst out from behind a coal pile and fired at me with a Winchester Repeater. I hadn't finished off Fire-Eyed Dick and now he was here to finish off me.

The bullet went by my shoulder, and I went for my Peacemakers. The mechanical man was working the lever of his rifle when I had his last light bulb eye in my sights. I fired, but the bullet neatly missed. He seemed to gloat at me as he finished working the lever and went for the trigger. But with all his cash register brain-powered intelligence, Fire-Eyed Dick had forgotten one thing. He was standing on a railroad line, and railroad lines are home to trains. Doc Torrent must have forgotten to put ears onto Fire-Eyed Dick, because the mechanical man didn't hear the train coming until it was too late.

The train plowed straight into Fire-Eyed Dick and when it came to a stop, only shards of glass from his light bulb eyes remained.

"Like I said," I told Charles as we boarded the train, "it's dangerous."

"Oh," Charles said slowly. "Uh, where are we going to go now?"

"Now? Probably a little town in New Mexico by the name of Roswell. Heard on the grapevine a while back that they've been having some trouble with hovering discs and bigheaded babies that can shoot lightning bolts or something. Probably need a feller like me around."

"I'll go with you," Charles assured me. And he did.

The Showdown at Roswell

Now I've seen my share of strange things. After I had rode a dead horse out of a city filled with walking corpses who wanted nothing more than to snack on me, I figured I had seen all there was to see. I couldn't have been more wrong. You see, my name's Clark Reeper, and I'm a bounty hunter.

It's my business to deal with strange things, and one of the strangest had just happened in the little town of Roswell, New Mexico. The town had been founded a while back in 1871, a little settlement surrounded by desert that no one would think twice about. But lately, some mighty odd events had made Roswell the center of the nation's attention.

First of all, a couple of farmers began losing their cows. One of the farmers said he had spotted a big metal disc flying in the sky, and that it grabbed his cow in a kind of green light, and flew away with it. Most of the normal people in Roswell figured that he had been hitting the bottle a bit too hard.

Events got stranger when one of those flying discs, supposedly one as big as a mountain, crashed into the desert outside of Roswell. The townsfolk sent out a few men to look at it, but they didn't come back. It didn't take long for the army to get wind of what was going on and evacuate the whole town. According to the papers, Roswell was now just a ghost town, with a giant flying metal disc lying smashed somewhere on the outskirts. I had a good feeling that my services would soon be needed, so there I was, sitting on a train headed for Santa Fe, with my Colt Peacemakers in the holsters at my waist and God only knows how many other guns tucked away in my baggage.

Soon as I got off the train in Santa Fe, I received a letter delivered to me by a Western Union Telegram boy. It was asking me to meet a client in the fanciest hotel in Santa Fe in two hours. I gotta take any job I can get these days as I sure do need the money.

You see, when I was fighting those living dead way up in Kansas, I found myself looking after a curly haired little boy by the name of Charles Green. Poor little feller's father had been gobbled up by those dead folk, and I decided that since I was the only person he had in the whole world, I ought to look after him.

When I got the telegram, Charles was sitting on a bench in the train station next to my luggage, his legs idly kicking in the air. He was small for his age, had curly brown hair, freckles and was dressed in a little suit and peaked cap. With my weathered face, crumbling Stetson and dirty tan duster, we could have come from different worlds, just like what some people were saying about the flying disc that had crashed in Roswell.

"Well, will you look at this?" I said, sitting down next to Charles and showing him the papers. Charles was working on a math problem in a composition book, on account of I figured a boy should learn his reading and his ciphering. Charles had taken up the book without complaint.

"What are those?" Charles asked, closing the composition book.

"I got this here letter asking for my help, and would you believe who sent it?"

"Who?" the little feller asked curiously.

"P.T. Barnum," I said, not quite believing that the great eastern showman had dragged himself all the way out here, or that he was asking for my help. "You know, P.T. Barnum of Barnum's Grand Traveling Museum, Menagerie, Caravan, and Circus."

Charles perked up. "Wow. My father always talked about taking me to see one of his shows, but..." He drifted off and fell silent. Poor kid.

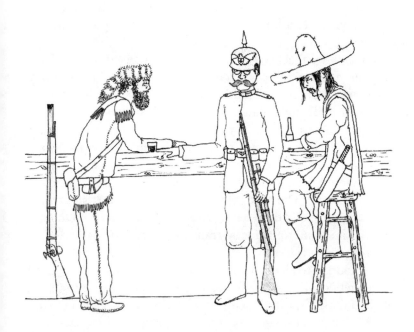

I put a hand on his shoulder. "Well, now we're gonna see the man himself. Come on, I don't want to keep him waiting." I checked our luggage in a place at the train station and followed the directions of the letter. It didn't say what he wanted me for, but I could figure it out easily enough.

The hotel was near the train station, so Charles and I didn't have to walk that far. I kept my coat open so passersby could see the shiny Colts in my holsters. Santa Fe is a tough town, and I didn't want no two-bit thug to try and rob me, or put Charles at any risk.

When we reached the hotel, I was surprised to see a large number of men I recognized standing around in the lobby. There was Werner von Humboldt wearing a blue uniform and a pointy pickelhaube helmet. He was the Prussian sharpshooter who had come out to America looking for work and found it in killing. Trapper Jack was there, dressed in a fringed deerskin jacket and fur cap. He was a noted mountain man and slayer of the famed Beast of Bray Road. Rounding out the crowd was Hugo Montez. The wild Mexican bladesman was sporting a torn sombrero and dusty poncho. He was the only man to have braved the numerous booby traps in the fabled Montezuma's Fortress and survived.

I nodded to all of them as I walked in, not having a quarrel with anybody. But as I was heading to some seats in the back of the lobby, I spotted a cluster of people that made me stop dead in my tracks. Charles saw my surprise and stopped too. He pointed at the strange group of individuals, one of them as small a desert mouse, another as big as a building from a back east city.

"Who are they?" he asked. "Friends of yours?"

"Nope," I said, anger sneaking into my voice. I went for my guns, and when the group of strange folk saw me, they went for their guns too, until we had a Mexican standoff going. This was the notorious Sideshow Gang, former circus freaks, and now the terror of the West. I had been paid considerable sums of money to kill them, and we had a running feud that made the Hatfields and the McCoys look like peaceful neighbors.

We stood there looking at each other, still as statues. "Howdy Sideshows," I said. "Still got the same number of freaks?"

"You better believe it, buster," shouted a squeaky voice about an inch above the floor. It belonged to Little Napoleon, a midget dressed in a dark suit and a stovepipe hat about three times as big as he was.

Standing behind him was the Sideshow Gang's strongman, Pantagruel Johnson. The massive giant had twirled mustachios and was covered in muscles from head to toe. A long barreled revolver looked small in his huge hands, while Little Napoleon's derringer looked huge. Behind them were Jacob Haff and Nick Haff, a pair of Siamese Twins known as the Haff and Haff Bros. Each one of them had a sawed-off shotgun aimed at me. Standing near them was Beardita, an overweight bearded lady in a tight dress armed with a Springfield, and sitting on the floor next to her was Armless Hans, whose lack of arms didn't prevent him from aiming a Colt at me with his feet. The final member of the gang, and the ringmaster of their little circus, was Mr. Adagio, a lithe gent with a curled black moustache decked out in a crimson tuxedo.

"I can't help but notice," Adagio said as he leveled a revolver at me, "that we have you outgunned."

"That depends on what you mean by outgunned," I said, keeping my hands steady on the triggers of my pistols. "I can still blast two of you before your bullets bring me down. Y'all wonder which two it's going to be?"

"That may be so," Mr. Adagio spat back, "but your midget assistant will also perish in the gunfire." I looked to Charles. He looked very small and thin, like I could pick him up and put him in my pocket if I wanted to. I knew we couldn't both get through a gunfight alive. I holstered my Colts.

"I don't want no trouble," I said. "Just let me hear P.T. Barnum's proposition and I'll be on my way."

"Don't want trouble, eh?" Little Napoleon said, stepping forward. The little guy was easily the most aggressive of the whole Sideshow Gang. "Well, listen here bub, we are looking for trouble! You're gonna get it, and so is that stinking midget you have licking your boot heels!"

"I'm not a midget," Charles said. "I'm only nine. I'll be ten in a few months."

"Is that a fact?" Little Napoleon snarled.

Then, the devilish dwarf's insults were interrupted when P.T. Barnum himself marched into the lobby. The Master Showman was dressed in a striking black cape and three-piece suit with a black top hat set jauntily on his head. His red face was clean-shaven and his straight black hair reminded me of a scraggly tumbleweed. Barnum was followed by a trio of assistants, nervous-looking young men in their shirtsleeves, who had to turn him around and point him in the right direction, as well as straightening his tie and adjusting his cap.

"Ladies and Gentlemen," Barnum shouted out in a booming voice, "Children of all ages! You are about to witness the greatest—" One of his assistants leaned over and whispered into his ear, and Barnum suddenly stopped shouting like he was opening one of his shows. "Oh, excuse, me. I always forget when I'm not supposed to be performing. Light me a cigar, will you?" he ordered his assistant as he plopped unceremoniously down in a nearby chair.

The assistant lit and placed a large cigar in Barnum's mouth, and the circus owner turned to the collection of bounty hunters and ruffians he had assembled in the hotel lobby. "Ladies and gentleman, I'm sure you all know what happened in the town of Roswell recently, and have heard rumors about what exactly fell out of the sky. Some of my advisors have told me that the metal disc contains the body, or bodies, of creatures from another world."

We all gasped. P.T. Barnum smiled at his audience and continued. "That's right—Martians! They're here, they're real, and I want one. I will pay four thousand United Sates dollars for a dead one, and six thousand for each living specimen. The Martian will be put on display at my circus, and every American who coughs up a nickel can gaze at its alien strangeness!"

We all stared at him. That was the kind of money you could live off of for the rest of your life. Putting down my Colts for good and spending my life in a comfortable cabin somewhere was starting to sound mighty good to me. After all, I wasn't getting any younger, and I could give Charles the childhood he deserved.

"Now, whoever brings the Martian back first gets the money," Barnum said. "Let the race begin!"

Well, we all bolted after we heard that. Time was ticking, and I knew that every second I wasn't looking for that Martian was counting against me, especially with folks like Hugo Montez and Trapper Jack on the trail. As for the Sideshow Gang, they didn't give Charles or me a second look as they dashed out of the hotel.

Not having a horse or very many supplies, I hightailed it to the local stables to procure us some transport. Charles tagged along, and as I was checking the teeth of horses to find the best one, I noticed the boy looked kind of forlorn.

"What's eating you, son?" I asked. "Don't you want to find the Martians P.T. Barnum was talking about?"

"I guess so," Charles said, looking at the floor. "It just seems kind of cruel to capture the Martian and have him be sent to a circus. I mean, people will just stare at him all day, and he won't get to go home to Mars..." Charles trailed off. "It just seems mean."

"Ah hell," I said comfortingly. "Martians ain't got no feelings. They're probably just like big rocks, or big brains, or something."

"Really?" a strangely cool, almost metallic voice came from my side. I spun around and saw a feller all dressed up like an Undertaker. He had a black top hat, black suit, black tie, black gloves, and smoked glasses resting on his thin nose. His appearance seemed kind of unearthly, and I noticed he was standing next to a horse that was as black as his clothes "Are you an expert on the creatures that fell from the sky, then?"

"No, sir," I said, a bit taken aback by this mysterious feller. "Just got myself an assignment from P.T. Barnum to capture one of them is all. I reckon I can do it."

"Are you potent with those pistols?" the Undertaker asked. "I see six-guns on everyone in this day and age. Some people know how to use them. Most don't."

"I'm a good shot," I said. "Wouldn't last long in my line of work if I weren't. Why you asking so many questions anyway? Is P.T. Barnum paying you money to go capture the Martians too?"

"First of all, they might not be from Mars," the man in black said calmly. "Secondly, I serve a far higher authority than any trumped-up ringmaster—the United States Federal Government to be exact. And if anybody gets in our way, I'll be glad to have them executed for treason."

"I didn't mean no harm," I started to say, but the Undertaker turned around and led his horse out of stable without giving me a backwards glance. I turned to Charles and shrugged. "Do you think a crazy feller like that could be a federal agent?"

Charles shrugged.

After I had purchased a good palomino mare, I went to the general store and got two bedrolls, enough food to last us for five days, enough water for ten, a couple more rounds of ammunition, and a bunch of bear traps. I figured that no matter how many arms or legs the Martians had, one of them would get stuck in the iron jaws of the trap. With all of that packed up in my horse's bulging saddlebags, and little Charles seated on the back of the horse with his arms around my waist, we set out.

For the first day, we didn't see nothing but the rising sun, the empty stretch of desert and an occasional cactus. New Mexico is a pretty barren part of the country, and sometimes there weren't even a patch of grass taking up the space between the sky and the ground. I drank a lot of water, and I urged Charles to drink even more. Being so full of liquid that it sloshed inside of you whenever the horse bucked wasn't no fun, but getting dehydrated out in the deep desert was even worse.

It wasn't until late in the evening, when the sun went down and a moon that looked three sizes too big peeked out of the darkness, that we saw a sign of life. Way out near a rocky outcropping was a little fire, but I couldn't see a soul around it. Kind of confused, I urged the horse towards the fire. Charles had fallen asleep in the saddle, and his regular breathing was comforting in the night. As I got closer to the fire, I heard someone shouting, begging for help in what sounded like Spanish. I spurred my horse to a light trot and cupped my hand to my ear.

"Ayuda! Ayuda!" someone cried. It sounded like Hugo Montez. I didn't speak much Español, but I had spent enough time south of the border to know he needed help. I turned my horse's trot into a gallop until I reached the outcropping.

Sure enough, Hugo Montez was hogtied and lying on the ground next to the crackling fire. Looked like there had been a real scrap around his campsite too, with a collapsed tent, a couple of spent shells lying on the ground, and a long-bladed Mexican machete jabbed into the dirt.

"Hugo?" I said, stopping the horse next to me. "Que Pasa?"

When he saw me, he gulped and wouldn't meet my gaze. "Oh, Clark Reeper," he said. "Lo siento. Los ejemplares anormales, they snuck up on me, tied me up, made me yell. I am very sorry."

"Ejemplares anormales?" I said, mashing up the Spanish words with my bad accent.

"In English," the nasally voice of Little Napoleon said from behind me, "freaks!"

I turned around and saw the entire Sideshow Gang aiming their weapons at me. They stepped out from behind the rocky outcropping where they had been hiding, after they had used poor Hugo as bait. Now I was trapped.

"Well, well, well," Mr. Adagio said in a soothing voice as he walked next to me. "If it isn't Clark Reeper, with his pistols so very far away from his hands."

"That can change real fast," I said, but didn't make no move.

"Perhaps," Mr. Adagio said. He nodded to the Sideshow's strongman. "Pantagruel, kindly disarm Mr. Reeper." The muscled brute stepped forward, twirled his moustache and lifted me off my horse with one hand.

The Haff and Haff Brothers stepped forward, relieving me of my pistols. "I'll take that," they said in unison.

I was getting a little bit upset, not for myself, of course, as I had been in several worse scraps than this, but for Charles in the saddle.

"Y'all can beat up on me as much as you want," I told Mr. Adagio, "but I'm gonna have to ask you not to hurt the boy. He didn't do no one any harm."

Mr. Adagio merely smiled. "Quite the contrary," he said, leaping next to me with a practiced somersault. "Doing harm to him will do harm to you." He pulled a thin stiletto knife out of his jacket.

I felt my heart stop beating as he approached Charles. I had saved the boy from flesh-eating walking corpses, and I didn't want to see him done in with a letter opener.

Charles awoke as Mr. Adagio leered over him. The aggressive acrobat seemed a bit surprised, but he wasted no time in pulling Charles off of the horse and putting the blade to his throat.

"Mr. Reeper?" Charles asked, his voice high and nervous. "What's going on?"

"If you touch a hair on that boy's head I swear on my own soul I will kill you in ways that would make a murderous Comanche look like a saint," I snarled at Mr. Adagio as my throat went cold. I took a step forward. Little Napoleon ran over to block me, but I kicked the midget backwards and stepped over him. To my horror, I realized I wasn't gonna be fast enough to save Charles. The grinning Mr. Adagio was already bringing down the knife.

A shot rang out and a single bullet shattered the stiletto. Mr. Adagio violently shoved Charles to the ground and gracefully flipped backwards. For a single second, everything was silent except for the chirping crickets and Charles's nervous teeth chattering. I took a step towards Charles.

"Nobody move or I shoot!" a bass voice called out from a nearby cactus. But it weren't no cactus. It was Trapper Jack, wearing a strange green spiky outfit that disguised him real good. He was armed with the biggest muzzle-loading rifle I had ever seen. It was as big as a cannon and had a muzzle that looked like an endless black tunnel you could get lost in.

"Trapper Jack!" I exclaimed, "You, uh, you surprised me."

"That's what I do," the mountain man said gruffly, shaking off his costume. "Now, let's all drop our guns and lie down like good boys and girls. I'll tie you up like the Mexican and get the Martians for myself."

"What about the Prussian?" Beardita asked in a voice a little deeper than Trapper Jack's. "He still hasn't shown up."

"Let the kraut come," Trapper Jack said haughtily. "I can take him!" As if on cue, a shot rang out and blasted the trapper's hand-cannon from his hands. Werner Von Humboldt galloped in on a large Clydesdale, a scoped rifle held in his hands.

"Foolish American," he said with his strong German accent, "you cannot outwit the favorite son of Prussia! Are you willing to test your weak American reflexes against the height of Teutonic breeding?"

Before anybody could answer, we all heard a great whooshing noise, and something, very large, very silver, and very fast zoomed over our heads. It fluttered the tent and blew out the campfire.

I'm still not sure what exactly happened after that. All sorts of guns seemed to go off, Pantagruel picked up a rock and threw it at Trapper Jack, who smashed the strongman on the head with his rifle. Humboldt was thrown from his horse, which I think was trampling Little Napoleon, and Hugo Montez managed to free himself and jumped into the fray with his machete. I punched and kicked, giving a good account of myself, all while waiting for my eyes to adjust so I could find Charles, who was still on the ground somewhere. I managed to punch out the Haff and Haff brothers and retrieve my Colts. Then, through the dust, I spotted Charles.

He had crawled to the very edge of the outcropping, and was covering his ears. I noticed Armless Hans tiptoeing toward the boy on one foot, a Bowie knife clutched in the other. My heart stopped beating again.

Suddenly, the whooshing silver disk came back, but this time, it hovered above the outcropping and was still. Everyone stopped fighting and stared at it. The first thing I noticed was how reflective it was. Looking into it was like staring at a circular mirror. It was about the size of a large carriage, and had a small bulge on the top that seemed to be made of darkened glass.

"What in holy hell—" I started to say, but then things got even stranger. The hovering disc got a bit lower, and the bottom part of it opened up. A strange green light flared out, focusing on Charles. He was completely bathed in it, and he stood up and opened his eyes.

"Mr. Reeper?" he gasped. "What's happening?"

"I don't rightly know, son," I shouted. "But I aim to find out. Just stay still and don't go anywhere."

"But I can't help it!" Charles said and he was right.

Before my eyes, the boy seemed to lift into the air. He was headed for the opening in the flying disc. I ran over and jumped, grabbing onto his legs, but the light was too strong, pulling me about a foot into the air before my grip loosened and I fell down. All I could do was watch as Charles disappeared into the middle of the flying disc just as the fight started up again.

The disc started slowly to move away, but I figured I might catch it if I was fast enough. I ran through the battling group of circus freaks and gunmen, and leapt onto my horse. I dug in both spurs and galloped after the flying disc. I had been in chases before, but this one was probably the most one-sided. The disc cut effortlessly through the air, and it was all my poor horse could do to keep up with it.

Then the disc hovered lower and lower, closer and closer to the ground. I spurred the horse on, hoping to get close enough to stop it somehow. There was nothing ahead of us but flat ground, so I figured I could stop checking where I was going and start shooting.

I stood up in the saddle and drew out both my pistols, aimed them at the flying disc, and fired. I might as well have not bothered. The bullets just pinged off of its reflective sides without leaving a hint of a mark.

"Why don't you just stop flying and fight me!" I shouted at the flying disc. It flew a little bit ahead of me, stopped, and turned around. I began to wish I hadn't yelled at it.

"Son of a gun," I muttered as the flying disc dived close to the ground and zoomed straight towards me, its mirrored sides looking hard as diamonds. "Son of a gun!" I stood up on the horse, and without thinking, jumped. I landed right on top of the flying disc.

The disc went off faster than a bullet from a gun. I hung on to the sides, but I could feel myself slowly slipping off, ripped apart by the crushing wind. I pulled my Bowie knife from my boot and slammed it into the hovering disc. That knife might have cut through bone with ease, but it became as flimsy as uncooked bacon soon as it touched the surface of the speeding saucer.

After that, I don't remember too much. I guess the wind got to me, because I slid backwards faster and faster, until the hovering disc seemed to have passed me up completely and I fell off. I hit the ground screaming like all hell, and after that I didn't see much more for a while.

When I woke up, I found myself looking into the face of a nightmare. A feller with pale pasty skin dressed all in black with a pair of smoked glasses over his eyes leered at me. It took me a while to realize it was the Undertaker from the stables, or someone dressed just like him.

"I see you're awake," the Undertaker said.

I sat up, even though it seemed like some miners were blasting off dynamite in my head.

"You know," the Undertaker said. "You are the only gun-toting rogue to make it this far towards Roswell. I feel I must congratulate you."

"Where the hell is my boy?" I said. We were in some kind of tent made of a black material that made it look like it was still dark outside.

The Undertaker shook his head sadly. "You seem so promising, and yet, you seem to have the same feelings as every other sap and sucker out here. You are going to make history today, Clark Reeper, and all you can think about is your pathetic offspring who is not even your own."

"Now see here," I said, coming to my feet. Despite my aching body, I found myself getting angry. "Charles is a good boy, and I'm the one looking out for him. I don't want any stinking Martians taking him away to Mars or wherever they came from."

"Then perhaps you shouldn't have made this journey," the Undertaker shot back, still keeping his tone of low malevolence. "Come outside, Clark Reeper, and see what glorious events will soon transpire."

I followed him out of the tent and into the blazing New Mexico sun. I gasped at what I saw. The Undertakers, and there were a hell of a lot of them, had set up camp, and they hadn't wasted any time doing it. Black tents stood in rows, and a large number of black carriages pulled by black horses stood at the ready. But the strangest part was that a whole mess of black hot air balloons with black baskets hanging from them filled up the sky. Each one had an odd insignia on the gasbag, a pyramid with an eye in the middle.

"Quite impressive, isn't it, Clark Reeper?" the Undertaker next to me said. A number of other men in identical dress joined us in the center of the camp.

"How do you know my name?" I whispered.

"We've read your file, Clark. Reeper. We know all about you."

I couldn't help gulping. My hands went to my Peacemakers, and I was pleased to see they were still there, but then I realized that if the Undertakers had let me keep my weapons, they must not be afraid of them.

"What government do you black-covered folk work for?" I asked.

"The United States. The Kaiser. The Tsar. The Mikado of Japan. Or perhaps our own. After today, we shall decide what government serves us."

I felt a little weak in the knees. My whole body still felt like jellied pig's feet from the fall, and just as I really began to feel sick, a familiar whooshing sound filled the air.

"They are coming!" the Undertaker suddenly shouted. "Clark Reeper, help us destroy them, and we may let you and your offspring survive the day! We have made sorties against them, and now they try to test us!"

The Undertaker was right. Four of them flying silver discs were headed straight for the camp, and a whole bunch of strange looking creatures were flying next to them. They had bulbous heads, spindly bodies, and huge black eyes that didn't look like anything found on earth. They wore silver suits that glimmered just like the hovering discs, and they had on backpacks with tiny rockets that kept them in the air. But what worried me was the strange looking pistols with pie-plates stuck on the end that they all carried.

"Martians!" I shouted. "Honest-to-God Martians!"

"To your guns, Clark Reeper!" the Undertaker ordered me. "The enemy draws nearer!"

"What about you guys?" I said, dropping to my knee and drawing out my Peacemakers with a spin. "You got any shooting irons?"

The man in black laughed without humor. "You have no idea." He reached into his coat and drew out a Gatling gun, only small enough to fit his hands, and began working the crank while holding on to the trigger. All of the other Undertakers drew out either handheld Gatlings, or long barreled silver pepperbox pistols that seemed to fire explosive bullets. The flying discs got closer and the battle was on.

Now I'm not a stranger to conflict, having fought on both sides of the Civil War, and being a veteran of countless shootouts and gunfights, but this was like nothing I had ever seen. The flying discs shot out huge blasts of red light that burned my eyes if I just looked at them. The red beams set fire to the black tents, and when it passed over an Undertaker, it fried him up just like a magnifying glass to a bug. The little Martians shot smaller red lights out of their pie-plate guns, and they burned holes straight through some of the unlucky Undertakers.

But the men in the black clothes fought back hard. The tops of the carriages opened up and a swarm of rockets flew out of them, crashing into the flying discs. The black hot air balloons blazed away with miniature cannons and rockets too, and one by one, the flying discs

became blackened and burnt. One of them exploded in the sky and was nothing more than dust, and another one sunk lower and lower until it stopped moving and smoldered in the dirt.

I blazed away at the flying Martians, but my bullets all seemed to fall short. The Undertaker next to me worked the crank of his hand-held Gatling gun fast as lightning and tore the oncoming Martians apart, and the strange pepperbox pistols seemed to blow flying Martians into tiny pieces. One of the hovering creatures came straight for me, but I brought up both my Peacemakers and shot it twice in his bulbous head. It let out a screech, bled blue blood, and collapsed to the ground.

I reckon that Samuel Colt made Men and Martians equal.

After the battle was over and all the flying discs lay burning on the ground, I walked over to them to see if I could find any trace of Charles Green. The Undertakers were stripping apart the crashed silver discs like vultures eating up a corpse. But there weren't nothing in the first two I looked at.

But then, I heard a high-pitched voice piping out my name, and I felt my heart beating back to normal. Charles Green had crawled out of the smoking wreckage and didn't look no worse for wear, if a bit scared. He ran towards me across the dusty desert and we embraced.

"Mr. Reeper," he said, after he had calmed down a bit, "the Martians, why were you shooting them?"

"I don't rightly know. The Undertakers, the men in the black suits, they were shooting at them."

"But the Martians are nice," Charles said, and I could hear the conviction in his voice. "They saved me from that guy with the feet. And they talked to me, or well, thought to me on the flying ship, and they're not even from Mars! And—"

"Slow down, son," I said. "What exactly happened on that flying ship?"

"Well, it was very bright, and there was a bunch of those bigheaded beings in there." A small group of Undertakers had silently surrounded us. Charles didn't seem to notice and continued. "They thought to me, talking without moving their lips. I could hear their voices in my mind."

"What did they say?" I asked curiously.

"They told me that they came from a planet far away, not even in the same universe as earth! They are on a research mission to find out what kind of life was living here. They never wanted to hurt anybody, but then their mother ship, that's the big one, crashed outside of Roswell, and they had to wait to repair it. Some people from Roswell came, and tried to attack them, and they defended themselves and the people got killed."

"They don't seem to have much qualms about blowing up folks," I said. "You sure they're nice?"

"Well, not nice. They think humans are like animals. 'Lower life form' is how they referred to me. But they want to research us, not to hurt us! Then they found out that these men in the black clothes were trying to capture them, so they flew out to talk with them, and I went along. And you guys shot at us!"

One of the Undertakers, looking identical to all of his brothers, stepped forward and put a hand on each of our shoulders. "We've just received a telepathic communication from the mother ship," he said coldly. "They want to meet with us, to discuss things. They are sending an emissary and we will meet in the abandoned town of Roswell."

"Well, that don't sound too bad," I said. "You can apologize to them, they can apologize to us, they can repair their ship, and we can all go home happy."

"That's not the way it's going to be, Clark Reeper." His grip on my shoulder seemed to tighten. "They have requested you as our emissary, because your child told them good things about you. They trust you, and that will give us the opportunity to strike."

"How do you figure?" I said, not liking at all where this was headed.

"You will shoot the alien emissary, and we will be in the buildings of the abandoned town, ready to ambush them. The aliens will be overwhelmed and destroyed. Then we will go and capture their main ship. All the technology will be ours."

"Don't do it!" Charles cried, but then the Undertaker tightened his grip and made Charles cry out in pain.

"Son, I don't reckon I have much of a choice. Not if we want to keep on breathing." I came to my feet, straightened up as best I could, and with my body still aching, I went out to meet the Martians, or whoever they were, and have a showdown at Roswell.

Roswell had been abandoned long enough to look like a ghost town. It had one main street and only a few two-story buildings. Some of the glass had been shattered in the windows, but other than that, there was no sign of disturbance. Some of the rocking chairs on the porches of the abandoned houses even rocked eerily in the light wind that blew through the town.

The Undertakers scurried into the buildings, doing their best to hide themselves. Though they told me they would pop out and save me before the alien emissaries fried me up like Kentucky Chicken, I had a feeling that the only way for me to survive this showdown at Roswell was for me to keep a firm grip on my Peacemakers.

Poor Charles was rudely grabbed by an Undertaker and taken to the roof of Roswell's general store, where I could see the outline of a man in black clothes behind him. The meaning was clear: if I messed up, Charles would pay.

The main street of Roswell was completely empty, except for me on one end, and a group of those short, bigheaded aliens on the other. The low wind running through the abandoned town, made my duster flutter and the alien's silver clothes shimmer. Slowly, we approached each other. One of the aliens walked in front of his friends, and I figured him for the leader. He was a bit taller than all the other bigheads, and he had two pie-plate guns in a slim medal belt around his waist. We faced each other.

The wind blew again and a thin stream of dust floated into the air. My hands stood inches above my Colts, my legs spread out, my eyes narrowed. The alien rested one hand on the top of one of his pie-plate pistols. His giant black eyes were fixed on me. It was clear what was going to happen next.

Then I turned my head and spotted Charles standing up on the top of the general store. His story about the aliens being just explorers whose ship had crashed sounded right. They didn't mean anyone no harm, unlike the black-clad men who had attacked them. If I killed those aliens, Charles would be heartbroken; but if I didn't, then the Undertakers would break more than his heart. There was nothing for me to do but shoot the bigheaded feller in front of me and hope for the best.

Unless...I looked up at the Undertaker standing behind Charles again and narrowed my eyes. It was a crazy shot, and an impossible angle, and even if I made the shot, I would have to survive the Undertaker's volley. But I was going to do it.

Wait, something in my brain said, like someone was talking to me. But no one's lips were moving; instead the bigheaded alien was thinking to me, just as Charles had said

The voice in my head continued. *If you move against us, you will be terminated. You are fascinating specimens, but we have already lost too many researchers on this world.*

"I ain't got no quarrel with you," I whispered, every aching muscle in my body prepping for what I was about to do. "Just follow my lead."

I leapt backwards, spinning my body around in the air as my hands went for my Peacemakers. The Undertaker behind Charles made an 'O' with his mouth before I blasted him straight in the forehead. The man in the black clothes wavered, and then his smoked glasses fell off and I looked at his eyes. They were segmented and red and certainly not human. I had about half a second to leap for cover before handheld Gatling gunfire and explosive pepperbox rounds filled the air. I ducked behind a bunch of barrels, blasting at the Undertakers who were taking cover behind the windows of Roswell's only hotel. I shot one of them and he shattered the window as he fell. I dodged across the street and headed for the general store where the bastards in black had taken Charles.

The aliens were holding their own too, but instead of taking cover, they stood in the street and simply fired away with their pie-plate guns. Loads of bullets were fired at them, but the aliens were kept safe by some sort of shimmering shield that appeared to protect their bodies. I found myself glad that I hadn't tried to shoot it out with the bigheaded creatures.

The Undertakers were waiting for me when I kicked down the door of the general store. A pepperbox round crashed into my shoulder and nearly knocked me over with its small explosion. I gritted my teeth with pain, then fanned out my revolver and blasted all of the Undertakers in there. Before their bodies had even hit the ground I was running to the roof.

When I got there, I saw Charles cowering on the ground, scared as hell and covered with some of the Undertaker's blood, but alive and unhurt. I kneeled down next to him.

"I guess you were right about the bigheaded folk," I said, helping Charles to his feet. "Why didn't they set up one of them shields when we were fighting them earlier?" I wondered.

"Maybe they needed time to set it up," Charles suggested. "They were here for a while, so maybe they created the shield."

"Well, we'd best get the hell out of this town before the aliens or the Undertakers bring in the big guns."

"Oh no," Charles said, pointing behind me. "They already have!" I turned and saw an ominous sight. The black hot air balloons were heading straight towards Roswell, and they were bristling with cannons and rockets.

"Son of a gun!" I shouted. "We better get in a storm cellar and hide this one out."

Just then, an Undertaker charged up the stairs at us, but before he could begin cranking his handheld Gatling gun, I blasted him in the chest and watched him sink down the stairs. His smoked glasses fell off and I got another look at segmented red eyes.

"Who are those people?" Charles asked. "Are they also from another planet?"

"Could be," I said. "Could be they come from holes in the ground. But we'll never get a chance to find out if we don't get out of here."

As I was heading down the stairs, a strange noise made me stop. A tinkling horn played a circus band's tune. I perked my head up, stared off into the distance and saw the strangest looking vehicle I had ever seen; something like a train car mixed with a tricycle being driven by a man with no arms. The Sideshow Gang had arrived. The cart plowed into Main Street, and I could see not only the entire Sideshow Gang riding in it, but also Trapper Jack, Hugo Montez, and Werner Von Humboldt. I figured they must have made some kind of deal to get to Roswell as fast as possible.

Suddenly, an idea gripped me. "Hey, freaks!" I shouted. "You feel like giving me a hand here?"

"You?" Little Napoleon yelled. "I thought the flying saucer splattered you! Well, I'll be glad to do the splattering myself."

"Hold," Mr. Adagio said, restraining the Sideshow's most angry and diminutive member. "Reeper, who are these people all dressed in black?"

"They want the fortune from capturing the aliens, Martians, I mean," I said with a smile. "Looks like they might just get it too."

"Things like that have a way of changing," Mr. Adagio said. He turned to his menagerie as he drew a Remington shotgun out of the cart. "Freaks, let's put on a show!"

The Sideshow Gang sprang into action, and the three gunmen along for the ride joined in. Pantagruel picked up two unfortunate Undertakers and smashed them together; Limbless Hans kicked one of them into a water trough and drowned him with his feet; and Mr. Adagio spun around like a top, spitting out bullets everywhere.

And the balloons? Well, those black-painted flying machines didn't cause too much trouble. Trapper Jack aimed his giant hunting rifle and fired a ninepins ball that blew one of the hot air balloons in two; Werner Von Humboldt whipped out a shot with his sniper rifle that set off the ammo in one of the other balloons; and Hugo Montez climbed to the roof of a building, leapt into the basket of an oncoming balloon, and gutted every Undertaker inside with his machetes.

With the aliens still blazing away from behind their invisible shields, the Sideshow Gang and their friends shooting everything up, and yours truly blasting the occasional Undertaker with his Peacemakers, the battle didn't go on for much longer. The men in black fought a running retreat through the town, and then piled into their black carriages. Some of the Sideshow Gang wanted to run after them, but Mr. Adagio said that we had won, and I believed him.

With the dead Undertakers still draining their blood in the street, I figured it would be a good time to leave, but the aliens had other ideas. A nagging feeling made me walk over to where the bigheaded ambassador and his friends were still standing with a small hill of bullets in front of them.

"Howdy," I said. "So, I reckon y'all will be heading back home right? We can part as friends, or at least not as enemies, right?"

Perhaps, the bighead thought, and I heard him loud and clear in my mind. *But we still have not fulfilled our mission.*

"And what would that be?" I asked, not liking the sound of what the alien was thinking.

We need specimens to bring back home. To display for our people, and to do research on. Then we can plan further action or inaction for the planet. We need specimens.

"Uh, what exactly did you have in mind?" I asked. "Like, plants or something?"

Humans. The emissary stared at me with his cold black eyes. *Accurate representations of what the average dominant creatures are on this planet. They will be cared for quite kindly, and only dissected when they die. We are not cruel researchers.*

Now, I really didn't like the way this was going. These aliens wanted to take back some souvenirs, and if I wasn't careful, I was liable to be one. I took a step backward and turned to run, but found myself looking straight at the large muscled chest of Pantagruel. He and the rest of the Sideshow Gang were blocking my only exit.

"So," Mr. Adagio said, pointing his Remington at me, "I see you've wasted no time in trying to get P.T. Barnum's reward. You're so greedy, Reeper, that's your weakness."

"I guess so," I said. "But I always thought it was lack of foresight. I'm thinking of taking this bunch of Martians back to see P.T. Barnum and getting some of the reward money, but I don't think I'm gonna go for the jackpot."

"Jackpot?" Mr. Adagio asked.

I smiled convincingly. "You know, the mother ship. There's supposed to be hundreds of Martians crawling around on that. It's the big one that fell from the sky. An enterprising feller with a few friends could capture them all, fly it back to P.T. Barnum and get enough reward money to become the next Vanderbilt."

I could see Mr. Adagio's black eyes get bigger. "Step aside, Reeper," he said. "Let me follow the Martians back to their mother ship." He stood up and locked arms with the lead alien. "Lead on, my bigheaded friend," he said.

Specimens, the emissary thought, and I could swear that the edges of his tiny mouth turned up in a smile.

"They're all yours," I told him.

Mr. Adagio must have thought I was talking to him, because he frowned and pointed to Little Napoleon. "You, guard him and the other ones until we get back with the mother ship. Don't hesitate to shoot if they make a move on you."

"It would be my pleasure, boss," Little Napoleon squeaked with joy. He stepped forward and gestured at me with his derringer. "Up against the wall, and the same with the mountain man, the greaser, and the German."

Trapper Jack, Hugo Montez, and Werner Humboldt looked like they were going to start a fight, but I shook my head and raised my hands, winking. I guess they figured it wasn't worth a brawl, because they followed Little Napoleon's orders without complaint.

"I guess Barnum was right," Mr. Adagio said with a laugh as he walked off with the aliens. "There's a sucker born every minute."

"I reckon he was," I said, still raising my hands.

I don't know if P.T. Barnum actually said that, but I was disinclined to put up any argument. Adagio and the Sideshow Gang disappeared into the desert, and after they were just tiny specks on the horizon, the three ruffians and I made our move.

Trapper Jack took a step towards Little Napoleon, causing him to wave his little gun around and shriek. Then Hugo Montez took him from behind. When the dust settled, we had tied up the pipsqueak and were wondering what to do with him.

"I say we cut him into strips and roast him like bacon," Hugo Montez said, cleaning his teeth with his machete, or maybe the other way around.

"We could always use him as bait," Trapper Jack suggested.

But it was Charles Green who had the best idea. He was digging around in the Sideshow Gang's trailer, and came out holding Trapper Jack's cactus costume. "Hey, look at this!" he piped. "We can dress him up as a cactus!"

"Or a Martian," Montez, Jack, Humboldt, and I said at the same time. I guess great, or greedy, minds think alike.

In the background there was a great rumble and a huge, round mountain of metal flew into the air. It was as big as a city and covered in blinking neon lights like a second sun. I couldn't help taking off my hat and letting out an awed "Son of a gun," as it went up and up until it was just a speck in the sky.

We rode the Sideshow Gang's bicycle contraption back to Santa Fe, and found P.T. Barnum excitedly waiting for us. When we showed him the hogtied form of Little Napoleon trussed up in the green cactus costume, he nearly burst his britches with joy. We all split the money and then headed in separate directions. Barnum was a smart man, and I gave him about a week before he found out his 'Martian' weren't nothing more than a midget in a costume. By that time, I would be halfway to California, far out of reach of Barnum or any agent he could hire. Hugo Montez planned to head south to Mexico; Trapper Jack, north to Canada; and Werner Von Humboldt, east to the big cities. P.T. Barnum would have to split his efforts to track us four ways.

As I plopped myself down in the train, my wound from the battle dressed and bandaged, and my aching body nearly back to normal, I wondered aloud if we would ever see those Undertakers again.

"I think so," Charles said. "They seem like they can hold a grudge."

"That they do," I said. I flipped through a few telegrams that were waiting for me when I came to Santa Fe. Somebody in Kansas was having vampire problems; some Americans were having a range war with a Rancho in California, and there were rumors of prehistoric creatures in an Arizona Canyon.

All of those happenings would mean a job opening for a feller like me, and I still needed work that paid. But for now, I put my hat over my face, closed my eyes, and took a well-deserved rest. I had a feeling I would need every second of it.

Hell on the Range

Now I've been in quite a few range wars, and have always found them peculiar conflicts. They normally are fought between two ranchers over a bit of land; the normal cause is too much strong talk and whisky and too little sense. Before anyone knows what's happened, battle lines have been drawn and the two sides are blowing each other away with six-guns, rifles, and dynamite. Ranchers hire all kinds of folk to do the shooting, and I am often one of them. You see, my name is Clark Reeper and I am a bounty hunter.

I don't like fighting range wars. Seems to me both sides are just variations of the same tweed-clad, fat cat who sits at home and drinks whiskey out of a gold cup while folks he paid a half-cent or two go off and die for him. But when times are tight and I'm in the need for money, I'll hire myself and my Colt Peacemakers out to the highest bidder. And that's just how it happened: times was tight, and I needed a job.

You see, I had a little boy in my care by the name of Charles Green. I saved him from a bunch of flesh-eating corpses in Kansas, and he's been along with me ever since. Raising a kid makes everything I do a heck of a lot harder, but I just ain't got the heart to get rid of him. His father got eaten by the hungry dead, and I figure I'm just about the only person he has. That's why when I got a telegram from the Cormrick Ranch way out in California asking for my help, I got on the first train to Sacramento.

Charles is a nice little feller. He's got brown curly hair, thick spectacles and he always wears a brown Norfolk suit with a peaked cap. I'm a tall gent and I wear a long khaki duster and a crumbling Stetson. A belt with two Colt Peacemakers is never far from my grasp. When we sat together in the lower class compartment of the train to Sacramento, we must have looked as different as an ornery mustang and a little pony.

I had been mulling over some thoughts during the long train ride, and just as we were nearing the end of our journey, I reckoned it was the time to let Charles know. He was reading a book, some cheap dime novel I had bought him at the last train station, and he was kicking his little legs idly as the train pulled in to Sacramento. I put my arm on his shoulder and he looked up.

"What is it, Mr. Reeper?" he asked curiously.

"Well, son, I gotta tell you something." I gulped. I had grown quite fond of Charles lately. He was very polite and shy, and he always seemed eager to help me out and watch my back. In fact, I was wondering if maybe him and me weren't too different from a father and a son.

"Sure, Mr. Reeper. What is it?"

"It's about this here job I'm about to do. The one for the Cormrick Ranch. There's gonna be a whole lot of shooting and other violence, and I want you to stay clear of it. I'll go out and fight the war. You stay back in the ranch and keep your head low. You understand, son?"

Charles shook his little head. "But I can help, Mr. Reeper! I want to be with you! I've been on your adventures before!"

I didn't let up. "Sorry, Charles. Those last times you got hurt, and I couldn't forgive myself if something worse happened to you. During this job, you've got to hang back."

Charles nodded reluctantly. "Well, I guess so, Mr. Reeper. But it can't be that dangerous, and I'm sure you can keep me safe."

"I wish I shared your confidence, son." I looked out the train window. We had just pulled into the station and passengers were already disembarking. "Well, we'd best get ourselves into town. I'm sure whoever owns the Cormrick Ranch will be waiting for us."

After getting our luggage, we walked out onto the platform. Sure enough, a portly feller in a black and white, checkered tweed suit ran up to me. A revolver was holstered on his waist, and a gray upturned moustache covered most of his face. He grinned at me and held out his hand.

"Jasper Cormrick, owner of the Cormrick Ranch. Mr. Reeper, it is a great pleasure to meet you!" He pumped my hand fiercely and then looked down at Charles. "And who is this?"

"My boy, Mr. Cormrick. His name is Charles Green, and he'll be staying back at your ranch while we do the fighting."

Cormrick nodded. "Whatever you say, Mr. Reeper. My, I am glad to have someone of your expertise along with us! We are going to blow those filthy greasers right out of the water!" We walked down the streets of Sacramento to a parked carriage.

"Greasers?" I asked. "You mean, Mexicans, right?"

"Rancheros. I've recently purchased a sizable area of fertile land, perfect for my herds, but a pack of greasers was already occupying the area. They call themselves the Juevos Rancho. The sombrero-topped stinkers raise a few scraggly head of cattle, and they simply refuse to leave, even after I politely told them to get the hell off of my land! The nerve!"

"Any reason why?"

He shrugged. "Something about them having nowhere else to go. A shooting war has just recently broken out, and with my resources, I will surely come out the victor. I've brought in some powerful artillery from San Francisco. To assure my success, I've hired another master gunfighter, besides you, to lead the charge against the greasers!"

"Another gunslinger?" I looked up at the carriage. Sure enough, a familiar looking feller was sitting on top of it. "Who is it?"

The man on the stagecoach roof dropped down in front of me. He was a tall, thin, gunman, dressed in a black cloak topped by a wide brimmed black hat. A silver pentagram glinted in the hatband. A long barreled Colt Buntline Special was at his waist, as well as one of them long knives called an Arkansas Toothpick.

His dark eyes stared out at me from a head of tangled black hair. He looked crafty as a cougar and twice as hungry.

"Clark, this is Brimstone Brown," Cormrick said, pointing to the other gunslinger.

I drew my Colt out and pointed it at him before I knew what was happening, and soon was seriously considering pulling the trigger. "We've met," I said.

Brimstone Brown held out his hands. "Please, Clark, there's no need for you to bring up old grievances. Let's forget the past for now. We can be friends."

"The last time we saw each other, you had tied me to a steamboat heading off the edge of Niagara Falls." I kept my pistol leveled. "We ain't friends."

"Well, honored foes at least." He held out his hand. "Please, Clark, give it a shake."

I shook my head. "That last time I shook your hand, you reached around and tried to stab me in the back. I've still got the scar."

Jasper Cormrick quickly intervened, stepping between us. "Now, Mr. Reeper, Brimstone Brown has been a very good employee! In fact, it was he who pointed out the patch of fertile ground that we're fighting over. You work for me now, Mr. Reeper, and I won't have you starting fights with my men."

I stared at Brimstone for a long time before holstering my six-gun with a practiced spin. Brimstone was a bastard of the first degree, a cultist always on the lookout for arcane power, and willing to do almost anything to get it. Ignoring him would be tough, but I reckoned I needed the money more than I needed to settle a score.

We got into the stagecoach. Charles was a mite tuckered out from the train ride, so he climbed inside the coach and tried to get some shuteye while me and Brimstone sat on the roof and Jasper Cormrick drove. Cormrick cracked the whip and we started off down the road, soon leaving Sacramento behind and heading out into the country.

"So, Clark," Brimstone said after a while. "I didn't know you had a son."

"He ain't mine," I explained. "I've been taking care of the boy after his parents were killed. Charles is near and dear to me, so don't you go hurting him or you'll answer for it."

Brimstone shook his head and laughed. 'Please, Clark. Are you making me out to be some kind of monster? I love children. Always good to have a little lad running about. Makes everything a little bit easier." That was a queer thing for Brimstone to say and it made me a mite uneasy.

Apparently, Jasper Cormrick really trusted Brimstone Brown, and valued his advice. But Brimstone would rather look for occult knowledge than take sides in a petty range war. Something was amiss, and Cormrick and Brown weren't telling me the whole story.

By and by, we came to Cormrick Ranch. It was a nice place, with a large number of barns and houses, some crops growing, and herds of cattle grazing peacefully away. A score of ranch hands and cowboys were waiting for us, all armed with pistols, rifles, and shotguns. Guess they had been waiting for their boss to come back before they made their move.

"Hello boys," Jasper Cormrick said when he saw his men. "I'd like you all to meet Clark Reeper, one of the best guns in the West!" He stood up and pointed a pudgy finger at me. "He's my new top shooter!"

I touched the brim of my hat and they all cheered like I was a hero or something.   "We'll be attacking the greasers in a little while, so don't get lazy, and don't get too drunk!" Jasper commanded.

The men grumbled, but they were in good spirits, shouting out battle cries and waving their guns around. Jasper took me, Brimstone and Charles to the ranch house to get our bearings and prepare for the attack.

He had a nice little cabin, filled with furniture and adorned with bull's horns on the wall. Several maps of the surrounding area had been spread out on a few tables, and Cormrick bent over one like he was Napoleon. Charles was snoozing away, so I carried him inside and laid him down on a comfortable looking chesterfield in the corner.

"Very well!" Cormrick said, plucking his white moustache. "Let's see how things lie. Here is the Cormrick Ranch." He pointed a thick finger at a large brown square on one side of the map. "Here is the Juevos Rancho." He pointed at another smaller square. There was a small amount of land between them, and I noticed a small white square filling up some of that.

"What about that one?" I asked, pointing at it.

"Oh that," Jasper said, as if it weren't of any importance. "That's San Diablo, an old Mission from the Spanish days. It's just a ruin. We may use it as cover or something, but we probably won't have cause to go there."

"It's nothing to get excited about," Brimstone Brown added, staring at me with hard black eyes. I shrugged and said no more about it.

"Everything understood?" Jasper said. Brimstone and I nodded. "Excellent. Get your guns ready, and we'll ride out. The greasers might send an advance force to head us off, but we can cut through them with ease. Those lazy Mexicans are good at one thing and that's taking siestas. Consider this an evening in the park, shooting very lazy deer."

I checked my weapons: my trusty Colt Peacemakers, my Bowie knife in my boot, and for long range work, a borrowed Winchester Repeating Rifle. After getting everything ready, I headed for the door, but a small hand grabbed my duster.

Charles tugged at my jacket. "Mr. Reeper?" he asked plaintively. "Can I come with you?"

"No, son, you stay here. I won't be that long."

"Are you going to fight?"

"Reckon I am." I didn't see no point in lying to Charles.

"Well, then be careful. Please." He looked up at me with big eyes and I couldn't help but smile.

"Son of a gun, Charles, I'll just be fighting some stuck-up Rancheros. No need to be careful." I couldn't have been more wrong about anything.

Jasper Cormrick and Brimstone Brown had the cowboys assembled outside. Whooping and hollering, they got on their horses and rode out to battle. I rode next to Cormrick, with Brimstone nearby.

"We'll get to the outskirts of the Rancho soon," Jasper said as we rode towards the horizon. The landscape was mostly fields of tall grass. "When we get close enough, we'll dismount and proceed on foot. I've brought some surprises for the greasers."

The surprises were four honest-to-god Hotchkiss Guns, machine guns just like the kind that were used by Federal Troopers. Jasper Cormrick must have had even more money than he let on. A wagon carrying the machine guns brought up the rear.

After only a couple of minutes of hard riding, we came to some hilly territory. It was typical California ground, short grass, hills and the occasional tree. Fine land for ranching. I could see the Juevos Rancho in the distance. It was like a mouse compared to the monster of Cormick Ranch, made up of only one barn, a collection of adobe huts, and a few sparse fields of crops. We got off of our horses and some of the ranch hands set up the Hotchkiss guns. It didn't take long for the Rancheros to come.

"There they are," Brimstone said, pointing to the Juevos Rancho. Sure enough, a small army of sombrero-topped men on horses rode straight for us.

"You think we're in for a tough fight?" I said, crouching down and taking my Winchester off the sling on my back.

"No problem, no problem at all." Cormrick grinned. "They're lazy greasers! They can't even ride right!"

Suddenly a lariat snaked out from one of the oncoming Rancheros, wrapped around my Winchester, and pulled it right out of my hands. The man stood on his horse like a professional rodeo star, expertly dodging the bullets the cowboys blasted at him. Then he grabbed the Winchester and blew a hole in the head of the ranch hand next to me.

The Rancheros rode straight into us, and the battle was on. Those Mexicans may have been a lot of things, but they sure as hell weren't lazy. They used old breech-loaders that wouldn't have been out of place during the Mexican War, but guns weren't the only weapon they brought, no sir. The lariats they carried lashed out and fastened around the necks of the cowboys, strangling some of them where they stood, or dragging them behind the Ranchero's horses, and crashing them into the rocks and such.

The Rancheros also wielded lances, impaling some ranch hands, or throwing the lances like javelins. Cormrick's men tried to blast them with their guns, but the fighting was up close and bloody, no time to aim carefully or reload. Horses kicked around, trampling everybody, deadly lances were flying through the air and an occasional gunshot went off. It felt like Bedlam itself.

My Peacemakers came in handy, and I fanned them off at the oncoming Rancheros as fast as I could. A couple of the horsemen went down, but not enough. Soon my revolvers were empty. I didn't have time to reload, and found myself drawing the Bowie knife out from my boot, but I knew that it wasn't going to help much. I hid behind a dead horse and reloaded my revolvers as Jasper Cormrick crawled over to me. His hat was gone, but he didn't look too beaten up.

"Goddamn greasers!" he cursed. "This wasn't what was supposed to happen!"

"Well, what do you figure we should do?" I demanded. Before Cormrick could answer, I stood up, and shot a charging Ranchero off his horse. The lance he threw landed in the dirt a few feet from us.

"The Hotchkiss!" Jasper Cormrick cried, pointing to a hill that might as well have been miles away what with all the Rancheros riding around it. "The greasers killed the crew, but if you can get to it and set it up, we can mow down these lazy Mexicans!"

"I don't think I'd call them lazy," I said, ducking back down. "And I'll tell you something else. It takes two to fire a Hotchkiss, and I'm just one feller."

"I'll help," Brimstone's eerie voice echoed in my ear. I spun around and found him staring at me. His Arkansas Toothpick was out and bloodied, as was his smoking Buntline Special. "That's what friends do. Isn't it?"

"I reckon so," I muttered. Without giving Jasper Cormrick a backwards glance, I ran for the downed Hotchkiss. Brimstone Brown was running right next to me, and our pistols seemed to shoot out lead in tandem. A group of Ranchero horsemen started stampeding towards us, but we gunned them down quick enough. After a time that seemed longer than all of creation and a half, we reached the hill.

A couple of Rancheros looked our way. I stood back and fired at them while Brimstone Brown charged in for the kill. He leapt into the air like a mountain cat and drove his long Arkansas toothpick straight into the skull of the unlucky Mexican, then pulled it out and neatly slit the throat of another. I wouldn't want to be on the opposite side of Brimstone in a knife fight, that was for sure.

After the Rancheros were dispatched, we set the Hotchkiss up and put a string of bullets inside. "You want to fire?" I asked Brimstone.

"It would be...a pleasure," he whispered slowly. I started threading the ammo belt and Brimstone began to work the crank of the Hotchkiss. Soon a stream of bullets flew out, tearing apart the Rancheros and their horses. The poor Mexicans didn't stand a chance. It was a miserable way to fight, and I didn't like it one bit, but I still kept the bullets coming. Brimstone Brown, on the other hand, was grinning ear to ear.

The Rancheros tried to retreat, but the Hotchkiss gutted them as they rode away. It wasn't long before the ground was covered with the bodies of men and horses, and there weren't nothing left to shoot. Brimstone stopped working the crank. We both stood up and looked over the carnage.

Jasper Cormrick and the surviving cowboys raised a ragged cheer. Cormrick ran to our side. "We sure showed them!" he exclaimed.

I looked at the dead bodies, cowboy and Ranchero, that littered the ground. He was right, but for some reason I weren't glad of it. "What now?" I asked.

"Well, I'd suggest repairing to my ranch for victory drinks." Jasper Cormrick put a hand around Brimstone's shoulder. "A congratulations for a job well done."

Brimstone Brown shrugged off Jasper's hand. "The job's not done yet. More Rancheros must be out there, waiting to attack again. With most of our men dead, we won't be able to hold them off, even with the Hotchkiss."

"More?" Cormrick looked surprised. "But the Juevos Rancho is just a small place! We must have killed all of their men and boys!"

"But the Mexicans breed like rats." Brimstone clasped his hands together. "You know that, Jasper. Perhaps even as we speak, an army of horsemen even bigger than the one we slaughtered is coming straight towards us."

Something wasn't right here. I didn't know the situation too well, but I figured Brimstone was spitting out hogwash and Cormrick was buying it.

"What should we do?" asked Cormrick, his voice wavering.

"The Mission San Diablo." Brimstone Brown jabbed a thumb behind him. "We can fortify it, mount the Hotchkiss guns and take up firing positions along the walls. No Rancheros will be able to get close."

Jasper nodded. "A decent idea." He raised his voice, ordering his men. "Come on, boys! Let's head on down to the Mission San Diablo!"

We rode in a grim silence. I was wrapped up in my own thoughts about what Brimstone Brown could be planning. He had some sort of hold over poor Jasper Cormrick, but I still couldn't figure out his purpose. The Mission San Diablo seemed to play some role in it.

Now, I ain't exactly a Spanish speaker, but I know that San normally means Saint, and Diablo is Devil. Missions, being Christian institutions, would not normally be named after no devil. There was some sort of story behind the name, maybe explaining why it had been abandoned. But none of the cowboys, ranch hands, or Cormrick seemed to know anything about it.

We finally got to the Mission. The place was just wrong. There ain't exactly a way of describing it to get the feeling across: A certain heaviness in the air; a stale, rotten scent filling up your nose; the sun burning a little less bright overhead. The Mission looked all wrong too. Odd stains covered the outside walls, chains dangled every which way, and the big cross on the main entrance was turned completely upside down.

I weren't the only one who felt it. The ranch hands fidgeted in their saddles and even Jasper looked a mite flustered. But not Brimstone Brown. He smiled wide as an alligator as he looked San Diablo over.

"Brimstone?" Cormrick asked. "Are you sure this is really necessary?"

"Absolutely." Brimstone turned to Cormrick. "Come on, Mr. Cormrick, or do you want to let the Mexicans win?"

"I-I don't!" Cormrick stammered. "Those greasy greasers! Come on boys, let's fortify the place!" We rode inside, and it got even worse. The sides of the place seemed to close in, and there were odd carvings and words etched onto the wall, images that made you want to look away as soon as you saw them.

Brimstone was the last to enter the Mission. After he trotted his steed into the courtyard, the doors slammed shut with a bang.

"W-what was that?" Cormrick demanded. "Brimstone?"

But Brimstone Brown was busy. He bent low over his horse, whispering something very low and very fast. I couldn't make the words out, but something about them syllables was wrong, and I felt a shiver pass through me. The walls of the Mission seemed to get a little bit closer, and a deep rumbling sound came from somewhere deep below our the hooves of our horses.

"What's going on?" Jasper Cormrick asked, as the horses began to whinny in panic. The cowboys fidgeted and clutched their weapons, and I had an urge to turn tail and flee. "What is this?" Cormrick cried again. "Judgment Day?"

Brimstone Brown grinned rakishly. "Close," he said. Then he whispered a few more words in that strange language. A red mist-like specter came out of the ground, seeping up like smoke. The rotten egg stench of sulfur filled the air. The mist floated toward an unlucky ranch hand, completely surrounding him and forcing itself into the poor feller's mouth. The ranch hand went into spasms and fell off his horse. When he stood up, his eyes weren't his own. They was blood red and bulging out of his skull. His skin looked like it was melting from the inside.

Cormrick seemed to have recovered some of his wits. "Brimstone!" he shouted, rage in his voice. "I demand you to stop this at once! If this is some kind of trick or practical joke, rest assured that I am not amused." Brimstone ignored him and Jasper got even more flustered. "Damn it Brimstone, you're fired! You are no longer in my employ!"

"Thanks for accepting my resignation." Brimstone leaned forward on his horse. "Matter of fact, you'll have to accept the resignation of all your other cowboys as well. They've got a new master." With that, Brimstone snapped his fingers, and more of that red mist filtered out of the ground. It flew into the mouths of the other ranch hands. The unfortunate cowpunchers tried to stop it. Some of them fired into the crimson clouds, others tried to run away. One man managed to blow his own brains out before the fog got him, but the others had no such luck.

Soon each one of the ranch hands had red glowing eyes and slightly melting skin. They all aimed their weapons at Cormrick and me.

"Stop it! Stop it, please!" Jasper pleaded, waving his arms and crying. "I'll give you my ranch, my fortune, just please make it stop!"

"You fat little puss." Brimstone drew out his long barreled pistol and aimed it leisurely at Jasper Cormrick. "And Clark Reeper, idiot amongst idiots. It's been a pleasure."

They opened up like a firing squad, cracking away in unison with military discipline. I jumped off my horse and hit the dirt, covering my head as the bullets whizzed by. But poor old Jasper was not quick enough and caught most of the slugs. He was soon shot full of holes and slumped backwards on his horse as his blood dripped out of him.

As soon as I saw an opening, I came up firing. I shot one of the possessed ranch hands off his horse as I ran backwards, distracting them long enough for me to reach the walls. Some of them big chains were hanging down like the limbs of a tree, and I scrambled up, nimble as a monkey.

"Kill him!" Brimstone ordered, and the ranch hands opened fire on me with everything they had. But the Good Lord seemed to have me on his mind, or maybe the ranch hands just had bad aim. Whatever the case, I avoided the shots and climbed to the top of the Mission.

"Missed me, you dumb demon-lover!" I shouted down, as I climbed up to the parapets of the Mission.

"You fool, Clark, you damned fool." Brimstone snapped his figures. "A death from a bullet would be a mercy considering what your asking for now. Hell hath no fury like my own, and you've gone and pissed us both off." The ground rumbled again and the dirt began to seethe. Odd-looking critters burrowed out of the dirt, sticking up their heads like prairie dogs before they crawled out.

The creatures were short and spindly little beasts with electric blue skin, long pointed noses and tiny sharp fangs. Each one was vaguely bipedal, and they were all dressed in neat little sailor suits. I figured they were imps and they served as lapdogs for Brimstone and his demonic masters.

"Go, my minions!" Brimstone commanded. "Bring him to me alive, but feel free to have a little fun with him."

The imps chattered in high-pitched voices like laughing children, and then they came after me, climbing the walls of San Diablo. I fired downward with my Colt, picking the little critters off, but there were just too many of them. One of them leapt up and scratched my leg with its claws. The cuts burned like I had been branded.

"Son of a gun!" I cursed. I toppled over backwards, teetering over the edge of the wall, and then I fell. I fired upward and killed the imps leaping after me, but soon I crashed down hard on the ground below, just outside the Mission's walls. Some leafy desert bushes broke my fall, but I was still pretty banged up. As I tried to gather the strength to stand, I could hear Brimstone talking inside the Mission's walls.

"He fell? How poetic. Oh well, I'll have myself a time nonetheless."

I finally got to my feet. I wanted to kick those big wooden double doors open and send Brimstone to meet his maker, whoever that was. But I knew I couldn't win against the Hosts of Hell, not all by my lonesome. I needed help, and I was too weak to go far to find it.

I turned around and spotted the Juevos Rancho in the distance. The Mexicans had no love for Brimstone Brown, and I reckoned maybe they could lend a helping hand. Wincing with every step, I started to walk to the Rancho.

By the time I got there, the sun was already setting. I stumbled into the outskirts of the Rancho, leaning against one of the adobe building to rest a little. There weren't a single guard patrolling the perimeter of the Juevos Rancho. Not a single Ranchero in a guard tower, or even a guard dog on a chain. With the Juevos Rancho in the middle of a range war, the lack of any guards was mighty peculiar.

The biggest building in the place was a stone church in the center of the Rancho. There were lights in the building, and the sounds of voices as well. I figured that's where the people were, and that I ought to go there.

I walked over to the door, and I was about to push it open and walk on through when I noticed something. The voices coming from the church weren't the voices of men. They were speaking Spanish, and some of them seemed to be crying, and they were all high-pitched. I stood on tiptoe and glanced in through a nearby window. Just as I had thought, there weren't a single man of fighting age in there, just little boys, girls and women.

Then I heard some footsteps behind me. I spun around, a revolver already in my hand, and there was a little dark-haired boy a year or two younger than Charles. He was dressed in a shiny dark suit with silver embroidery on it, and had a small sombrero on. We stared at each other for a while, and then he spoke.

"Are you here to kill us, mister?" he asked, his little voice high and nervous.

I shook my head. "I'm looking for help. Any men around here? Like them tough fellers that went out to battle?"

Tears welled up in the kid's eyes, and I felt worse than the devil himself. "My father and my older brothers died today. It is a bad day and we're crying over them."

Suddenly, I realized that there weren't no men in the Juevos Rancho, on account of Brimstone Brown and me had killed every one of them. Now I normally try not to regret the lives I've taken, but this was too much. Brimstone had made me shed innocent blood, and now I was aching to shed some of his.

"Sanchito?" a woman's voice called. "Where did you get to?" A young woman with short brown hair in a loose dress and a vest came walking out of the church, probably looking for the little boy. She had an old Schofield revolver in her belt, and pulled it out lightning quick when she spotted me. "Gringo! Trying to kill us while we pray!"

"Now that ain't quite true—" I started to say, but the woman stepped forward and shoved the revolver in my face.

"Dirty, rotten gringo! The fat one from the ranch must have sent you! Murdering our men is not enough, eh? You must kill women and children too! Well, I am Valentina Valdez, and I shall enjoy killing you!" She was full of anger and fury, and I guess she had her reasons.

"Wait, before you kill me, let me just tell you something," I begged. "I'm a hired gun, I just do what I've been paid to do, and I never wanted to hurt any women or kids. I reckon I'm a decent feller, and most of the time, I try to act like one."

"A mercenary!" Valentina spat. "Oh, we will bury your head in the sand and let the fire ants feast on your eyeballs! We shall tie you to four horses and send them all off in different directions so you are torn apart! We shall burn you alive and step on the ashes!"

A few more people came out of the church. Most of them were women in shawls, but one was an aged preacher, bent over and dressed in a black robe. They looked at Valentina Valdez and me. I smiled sadly at them, wondering how I was going to get out of this alive.

"Well, at least we can get some information out of you before we kill you!" Valentina snarled, shoving her revolver nearly up my nose. "Tell me, what are the gringos doing now?"

"Nothing much, and that's on account of there ain't none of them left." I gulped as I thought about the horrible events that had gone on in the Mission. "Brimstone Brown done tricked us! Led us right into the Mission, and then—"

"The Mission?" Valentina asked. "You mean—"

"Yeah," I said. "San Diablo."

As soon as I mentioned the name, the old priest let out a cry in Spanish and fell backwards. Some of the women caught him, and all eyes turned to the old feller. I had a sinking feeling in my chest.

"San Diablo!" The old priest cried. "San Diablo!"

"Sorry, sir, but that's what it is. Now, you mind letting me know what in heaven, or hell's name was going on back there?"

I was a bit rude maybe, but I was still aching from my fall, and mad as could be about Brimstone's trickery.

"Follow me, all of you!" the priest said. He turned and entered the church. Not knowing what else to do, I followed him, and so did Valentina, Sanchito, and the other Rancheros. He walked into one of the backrooms of the church, came out with a book the size of a small mountain, and plopped it down on the podium. We all gathered round to look at it. Valentina seemed to be less focused on torturing me, though she did send me the occasional menacing glare.

"All right, Padre, what is San Diablo?" I asked.

"Do you not know the name of it? In English, I think it is called St. Devil. Do you not know the meaning of that?"

"I thought it was just a colorful name."

The preacher shook his head. "There are no colorful names out here. San Diablo started out as just another Mission. It had a small number of devoted priests in charge of converting the Indians to Christianity, and a small band of soldiers to protect them." As he spoke he flipped through the large book and showed a few stiff-looking woodcut pictures. They showed Indians working while a few bald priests in brown robes looked on. "The priests believed in total discipline from the Indians, and there was much punishment." He showed a rather terrifying picture of a few Indians being burned at the stake, while others were whipped.

"So what makes it St. Devil?" I wondered.

"An earthquake occurred, cutting off the Mission from the supply routes. The same year, a drought came and the crops were very poor. The priests became more and more violent towards the Indians as the food supplies dwindled. Then utter savagery occurred." The Padre turned the page and showed me a picture straight out of an Edgar Allen Poe story. The priests had apparently resorted to cannibalism, and were munching on the Indians, and other pictures showed the priests and the soldiers doing terrible acts to the Indians, well, I can't mention it even now. The woodcuts made shivers run down my spine.

"And that is only the half of it!" the Padre explained. "The priests believed that God had forsaken them and began to worship El Diablo! They made sacrifices of human flesh to him, forever binding human suffering into that cursed Mission. One soldier managed to escape before the final orgy destroyed all—even the fallen priests! The surviving soldier made these woodcuts to warn other priests never to venture into San Diablo. No one has entered that Mission for centuries."

"This connection to Satan," I said, thinking about Brimstone Brown, "could someone, like a devoted servant of the occult, set it up again?"

The Padre looked at me, pure horror in his old eyes. "Sí."

Everything fell into place. Brimstone Brown had come here to access the demonic power in San Diablo, and finding it owned by the Juevos Rancho, had sided with Jasper Cormrick to take the Mission over. He had known that Comrick's men had killed every able-bodied man working for Juevos Rancho, and he had exploited Cormrick's hatred of the Mexicans to get him and his men into the Mission, where he could access its dark power.

"What exactly would making the connection work do?" I asked, not sure if I wanted to know.

"Open a portal to Hell itself and unleash the demonic hosts upon our world."

"Hell? Ah hell," I muttered. I came to my feet and headed for the door. "I better go shut Brimstone Brown down. Maybe I should get some rest before, but I don't reckon I got much time."

As I started for the door, a horrible thought entered my mind. There was one thing that hadn't been accounted for: Brown's pleasure at seeing Charles. "Say, Padre, what kind of ritual needs to be done to open the portal?"

"A sacrifice. Unjustly spilled blood, such as the blood of the poor Indians, to touch the stones of San Diablo."

"Would a child's blood work?"

"That would be perhaps the only thing that would work."

That was all I needed to hear. Brimstone was probably planning to use one of the Juevos Rancho's children, but when he saw Charles, he would have changed his mind. Cormrick Ranch was now defenseless, and closer to San Diablo. And Brimstone would go out of his way to hurt Charles just to spite me.

I ran out of there as fast as I could, leapt on the first horse I could find and pounded off towards Cormrick Ranch. Charles Green had stayed at the ranch because I wanted him to be safe, and now it seemed that he was going to be sacrificed.

Whatever was gonna happen, I knew that all hell was gonna break loose, maybe literally.

But the Priest ran after me. The old Padre nearly knocked himself over, but he kept on running. He was holding something in his hands and urged me to stop. I forced myself to obey.

"Gringo!" he cried, pushing a small cluster of prayer beads at me, "Take this! Wear it, and the evil spirits will not be able to take you!"

"Thank you kindly, Padre." I grabbed the beads and put them around my wrist without thinking, then continued pounding on.

It was dark when I got back to the Cormrick Ranch but I was too damn late. I leapt off of the horse and ran into the ranch house, looking for Charles. I could tell there had been some kind of a struggle. There were windows broken, and the body of a ranch hand lay on the floor with cuts that could only have come from Brimstone Brown's Arkansas Toothpick. Most of the furniture was overturned. Worst of all, there was no Charles. I let out every curse word I knew.

Brimstone Brown must have captured my boy, and was possibly carving up poor innocent Charles and feeding his bits and pieces to Satan himself. Charles was such a good kid, not an ounce of malice anywhere in his little body. It made me sick just to think about the lad in the clutches of a man like Brimstone Brown. Right there I resolved to get him back or lose my own wretched life in the attempt.

It didn't take long for me to find the armory of the Cormrick Ranch. The place had all kinds of weapons ripe for the taking. I loaded up with a couple of pistols, including a few quick-firing Colt Lightnings, two repeating rifles, a coach gun, and as much dynamite as I could stuff in my pockets.

I walked out of the armory armed to the teeth, and then it hit me like a punch to the jaw. Brimstone must have been summoning demons all night long. He probably had an army of them there, not counting the possessed ranch hands. No matter how well armed I was, I couldn't win.

"Son of a gun," I cursed. "There's no way one feller can win against everything Brimstone's brought up from Hell!"

"What about two?" a woman's voice asked. I looked up and saw none other than Valentina Valdez smiling at me. She was holding the reins of a train of three mules. I took a closer look at the mules and found that each one had a sack of dynamite stuck on their back. "Cormrick had these mules loaded up with explosives," she explained. "The fat gringo was planning to demolish the Rancho. Maybe we can use these to our advantage."

I smiled at her and doffed my hat. "I thought you were trying to kill me."

"That can wait until El Diablo is back in Hell," the fiery Latina answered. "I can kill you then, but maybe I won't. You don't seem that bad for a gringo."

"I guess that's the only compliment I'll get outta you," I said. "Well, let's load up and head on out. We've got a long day ahead of us."

We decided to risk it all on a frontal assault, not wanting to waste the time that Brimstone Brown could be using to spill more blood and summon more demons. Valentina and I hunkered down behind a large rock and watched the San Diablo Mission. It was built like a fortress, armored doors, high walls, and small narrow windows. The round muzzle of the Hotchkiss gun stuck out of the window above the main double doors.

The ranch hands stood on top of the wall like statues, their eyes wide and completely red, with thin streams of spittle hanging off of their mouths. It was quite an eerie sight, and a distinct scent of sulfur floated in the air.

But there was one thing that would blast apart those big double doors and give Valentina Valdez, me, and our guns enough time to do what needed to be done, and that was the mule hunched next to us with a bag filled with dynamite on its back.

But there was one problem. "We gotta take out that Hotchkiss," I said. "It will shoot the mule before it gets even halfway to the door, and then we might get ourselves caught in the explosion."

"Could you pull off a shot?" Valentina asked.

I narrowed my eyes, but shook my head. "Nope. Too damn far away."

Valentina stared at the Hotchkiss and her fingers went to the coiled lariat at her hip. "I think I have an idea," she said, a cruel smile on her face. "Give me some covering fire."

Without even waiting for me to agree, she took off running. I stood up and opened fire with both of the Colt Lightnings. The favorite guns of Billy the Kid did their job, shooting out bullets lickety-split. I blasted one of the possessed ranch hands off of the wall and watched his body tumble to the ground. Soon as he slammed down on the hard California dirt, the bloody red mist floated out of his body and disappeared into the walls of the Mission.

Valentina took advantage of my firing and ran ahead, her lariat in one hand and her revolver in the other. She fired at the Hotchkiss, spinning and jumping to avoid getting shot, and then, right when she was just under the rapid-firing gun, she lashed out with her lariat. The strong Rancho rope fastened its lasso right on the muzzle of the Hotchkiss. Valentina gave it a quick pull and the gun came tumbling down.

I grabbed reins of the mule and pointed it in the direction of the door. Then, I lit the fuse on its back and gave the animal a quick stab in the rear with my Bowie knife. The mule let out a bray of pain and ran screaming towards the gate. The dynamite fuse worked perfectly, setting off the candy-red explosives just in time. The mule exploded in a red fireball and blasted a huge hole in the gate. Some of the defenders flew into the air and fell to the ground with sickening crunches, their misty spirits disappearing into the walls after they died.

It was a cruel thing to do to a harmless animal, but I reckon it was the quickest way inside the Mission, and I don't think I'll regret it. Not wanting the mule to die in vain, I began running towards the opening in the wall, dropping the emptied Colt Lightnings and going for my trusty Peacemakers. Valentina was right behind me. We blasted a few more ranch hands and soon found ourselves standing in the courtyard of the Mission San Diablo.

"Brimstone?" I asked, spinning around and looking for a sign of him. "Where you hiding? What have you done with my boy?"

"He's here." Brimstone Brown's cold voice came from nowhere and everywhere at once. "And he's safe. I was waiting for the right moment to gut him, and I'd like nothing more than for you to watch his lifeblood trickle out of him."

"Mr. Reeper?" Charles's high voice suddenly shouted from the same impossible direction as Brimstone's. "I think he might do it! I'm scared..."

That was something I would never allow to happen. "Where are you Brimstone? You yellow-bellied varmint! Come out so I can shoot you!"

"I'll do you one better," Brimstone's voice taunted. "I'll give you some other things to shoot. We have plenty of time. No point in rushing things." Mists started to course out of the walls, and my mind went to the prayer beads that the old Padre had given me.

"Quick!" I shouted, tearing the beads off of my writs. "Grab on to these! We don't want no spirits setting up camp in our minds!"

Valentina grabbed onto the beads and we stood together as the mists churned around us like waves in a sea. The evil vapor tried to get into our mouths or sneak up one of our nostrils, but each time the dark power stopped like something was holding it back.

Pretty soon, the mist disappeared all together.

"Yeee-haw!" I shouted with joy. "Looks like the old Padre was right!"

"I suppose I can't have your minds," Brimstone shouted. "But the imps can at least have your bodies!" Soon as he said the words, a bunch of burrows appeared in the ground, and more of them little creatures came crawling out.

Their sharp claws glinted in the morning sun, and they surrounded us. I drew one of the Winchesters and tossed the other to Valentina. "Shoot them dead as they come!" I shouted.

Valentina nodded. She fired, worked the lever and fired again. Two imps flopped backwards, dead. "Vaya con Dios!" the Rancho girl shouted as both of us started shooting away.

Back to back, we gunned down the charging imps, and when the little buggers got close enough, we crushed their heads with our rifle butts and stomped them under our boots. Soon the last imp was destroyed.

"The little ones always die first, I suppose." Brimstone's disembodied voice came from all directions. "But the Hosts of the Inferno have yet to truly come forth." After he said that, things got considerably more like Hell.

Other creatures emerged snarling from the ground. Giants with bull's heads and cannons for arms, and bigger imps dressed up like Confederate soldiers and armed with rifles, and many other horrors too damned numerous to mention, all came pouring out of the earth.

"And these are the just the welcoming committee!" Brimstone's voice let out a ragged laugh. "Just wait until I bleed your little boy dry and summon the Lord of Hell himself!"

I had to stop Brimstone Brown before he did that, but I just didn't have enough time or bullets and I didn't know where the bastard was. The demons let out a thunderous roar, and started firing. Valentina and I just had time to dive for cover before they crashed down on us.

Luckily, we had plenty of guns and ammo, courtesy of Jasper Cormrick. Valentina and I stood up and fired together, driving the demons back. One by one, the terrible creatures keeled over and fell into the dirt, but each time one died, another one jumped up and took its place.

"We can't hold forever!" I shouted. "Not enough bullets to kill all of them!" I dropped the empty Winchester and blasted an incoming demon with my Peacemaker. "We gotta find out where Brimstone is and shut him down! But his damn voice just seems to come from everywhere!"

Valentina looked at me thoughtfully, after she had warded off a demon's bayonet and blown apart its spongy skull. "What about your boy? Why don't you ask him, you stupid gringo?"

That sounded like a good idea, so I took a deep breath and shouted as loud as I could. "Charles! Tell me where you are!"

There was a few seconds of deep silence when even the demons seemed to stay quiet. Then, just as I was wondering if the boy was ever going to answer, there was a loud yelp that could only come from Charles, followed by a wet slapping sound.

"The tower!" he yelled, and I looked directly at a tall bell tower at the opposite side of the Mission. "I'm in the tower, Mr. Reep—" Another wet slap interrupted him.

"I'll be back in a spell," I said, and started running straight into the crowd of demons. They came at me from all sides, raking me with iron claws, firing at me with insane weapons, and snapping at me with pointed teeth.

My Peacemakers were out and blazing away, keeping the demons back long enough for me to make it all the way across the courtyard. I got to the entrance of the church tower just as I fired the last two bullets from my Peacemakers. I chucked the empty pistols at the demons and ran inside.

As I ran up the winding steps, I took out my Bowie knife. I reckoned there was gonna be some knife music before the day was out.

When I got to the top of the bell tower, I found Brimstone Brown standing next to Charles, who was hogtied and lying on the ground. The satanic snake-in-the-grass had a mad light in his eyes and was holding out his Arkansas toothpick, and he had it pointed right at Charles's throat.

"Ah, Clark," he said, "so good of you to join us. I was just about to make the first cut and open up the portal for good."

"You touch him." I took a step forwards. "You die."

"Fool." Brimstone laughed his cold laugh. "You think such pathetic concept as death scares one such as me?"

"Well," I said with a shrug, "maybe not dying. But I bet you think getting carved up like a prize pig is pretty damn scary." I jumped on him. Brimstone tried to stab Charles, but I grabbed his wrist and dragged the blade away.

We fell to the ground, each of us trying to drive his blade into the other's chest. My Bowie knife was shorter than Brimstone's long-bladed pig sticker, but I pushed forward with all my strength. Brimstone snarled at me and his eyes turned white.

"You have no chance!" he cried. "All I have to do is spill a drop of the child's blood and the Lord of Hell will come forth to claim him!"

"A drop of blood?" I said. "Just one drop?" I stabbed forward with all of my might, nicking the tip of Brimstone Brown's chin.

A single drop of crimson blood fell onto the tip of my blade, and I turned it over.

"Oh no," Brimstone said, fear suddenly very real in his voice. "Not my blood. Not my blood!" The drop fell and Brimstone's blood fell to the cursed stones of the church tower with a plop. As soon as it fell, the ground itself seemed to shake.

Something exploded outside, and a gigantic figure appeared in the courtyard, crushing all of the smaller demons under its feet. It was dressed in a dark robe and had nothing but a gaping hole for a mouth. It struck out with a claw the size of a horse, reached into the church tower and grabbed Brimstone Brown.

"Alas," it said, in a voice somewhere between screaming and laughing. "For this blood is not what I desire. Still, it shall suffice." He pulled the screaming Brimstone away and shoved him inside his mouth. Brimstone's horrible cries grew softer and softer as he slowly vanished, and in a few seconds he was gone. The giant Lord of Hell and all of his minions vanished as well, sucked down into whatever netherworld they had come from.

We all hightailed it out of that Mission as fast as we could, and Charles was never more grateful to have me around. I think he understood how dangerous my job was now, and I think I understood how dangerous it was for me to let him out of my sight.

I got paid in full, even though Cormrick Ranch closed down on account of there weren't no one alive to work it. I found Jasper's safe deposit box, blew it open with some of the dynamite, and took my fair share of dollars from it. I figured the poor feller owed me that much at least.

As for Valentina Valdez and her Ranchero family, well, she ended up owning not only the land of Juevos Rancho, but also taking over the entire Cormrick Ranch as well. Even with all the men folk dead, they were set to rake in a pretty profit from all the cattle they got.

Valentina wanted me to stay and help work the land, but I told her I had other jobs to do. She was a wild one, tough as nails and feisty as could be, but I don't think I was ready to settle down just yet. Maybe, someday way in the future when I was all old and gray, and I wanted a break from bounty hunting, I would return to the green grass of California and settle down on that ranch or in some town nearby. But I am a long way from old age, and as long as I have Charles to support, I will continue my career.

The Mission San Diablo went back to being abandoned for a bit, but soon, thanks to me and Valentina, word got out about the kinds of spirits that were lurking there. The famous scientist Charles Fort, Theosophist cult-leader Helena Blavatsky and even the Reverend Doctor John Scudder, a British Missionary from India, came down to San Diablo to do what they could. For a full week they studied and preformed spells and exorcisms, and finally, they all decided to dynamite the place and move on. I had already left town when they blew it up, but I hear some of the surrounding country still ain't all earthly.

But I was already heading out. There were reports of disappearing ships way down in Bermuda, and I had heard that someone was thinking about uniting all of the gangs of New York and taking over the city. Both of those jobs seemed like they would be something right up my alley, so I returned to Sacramento and boarded the train, not sure where I was gonna end up next.

Charles and I sat next to each other on the train. Charles smiled up at me. "See, Mr. Reeper, I knew you would always be there to save me."

"Sure, son, I'll always be there." I squeezed Charles's shoulder. I may have been worried about the kid's safety in the long run, but for now, I was just glad to have him safe, sound and by my side.

The Man with No Face

Now I've never had much truck with politics, on account of a man in my line of work can't afford that. You see, I'm a bounty hunter, specializing in the odder jobs that are out there. If a hired gun starts worrying about who does the hiring, the number of jobs available gets smaller and smaller, until there ain't none left.

My name is Clark Reeper, and I've found myself fighting on every possible side that a feller can think of. I've fought on both sides of the Civil War, been stuck in range wars and family feuds, and I've done a little work for Mexico and Her Majesty's Empire. A few times, I even worked for clients who probably shouldn't even be considered human.

Well, one time I found out that politics have a bad habit of latching on to a feller, even if you don't want them to. Then they get you in the worst possible place you can think of.

In my travels, I happened to become the adopted father of a little ten-year-old boy by the name of Charles Green. We couldn't look more different. He is a short feller with curly dark hair and thick glasses who always wears a miniature Norfolk suit, thin tie and a peaked cap. I'm a gaunt gentleman dressed in a long brown duster and a crumbling Stetson.

I like Charles a lot, him being the closest thing to family I've ever had for any discernable amount of time, and also being one of my truest friends. We went together like a cigar and smoke. But the life of a bounty hunter ain't one that calls for partnerships, particularly when one of the partners ain't past puberty. Truth was, it was getting mighty dangerous for poor Charles. Being around me led to him almost being munched on by the walking dead, drained by vampires, sacrificed to the devil, and even sent to another world.

I began to realize that if something happened to Charles, there wouldn't be no forgiveness for it. So I decided it would be best if we went our separate ways. I needed a place for him to stay safe and be cared for, and I soon found an arrangement that would do all that and more. It was a private boarding school called St. Walpurgis Academy, and it was one hell of a nice place. The tuition cost a small fortune, and the teachers and students were all the best, brightest, and richest of the entire nation. It went from third grade to ninth, and it taught ciphering, reading, Latin, and Greek, and plenty other useful disciplines for a growing boy. I reckoned it would be the perfect place for young Charles.

So, I cashed in a couple of checks, and came up with enough money for one year. I figured that I'd be out west taking expensive jobs and sending the dough back to Charles for a while, and I did have a good amount saved up, not needing to spend too much on myself, so that was taken care of.

We took the train back east to the area around Boston, and then he began to wonder what exactly we were doing. We were having breakfast in a little café in the center of town and were facing each other across the small table when he brought it up.

"Mr. Reeper?" Charles asked, his voice squeaking like it did whenever he asked me a question. "What kind of job could you be doing around here?"

"There's no job, son. We're here on account of you." I looked the boy in the eye. "You see Charles, my side ain't no place for you. It's too dangerous, and it's probably an act of whatever God watches over me that you haven't been hurt too badly. So you see, I want you to be safe, and I want you to get an education."

The boy looked crestfallen. "Are you sending me away?"

"I'm sending you to school. There's this expensive boarding school called St. Walpurgis Academy, and I think you'd like it there. I already paid for one year, and we're here to get you all squared away and ready for the school year."

"I like being with you, Mr. Reeper," Charles said. "Don't send me away! I learn lots of things being with you! Please, Clark!"

He pleaded with me, but I was stubborn. "Charles, this will be what's best for you. There won't be no chance of you getting hurt." I reached across the table and squeezed his shoulder. "I'll visit you every chance I get, I promise."

"But I won't get hurt!" Charles begged. "You always protect me!"

"I've been lucky so far." I gulped. "Charles, if you got yourself hurt, or worse, I don't know what I'd do. Drink or opium couldn't take away that pain. Please, son, for me, can you at least give this academy a shot?"

I guess he saw how serious I was, because he relented. "Okay, Mr. Reeper. I'll see how I like it. But you have to visit me—"

"I will. And I am very much obliged to you, Charles." I drained my coffee and stood up. "Come on, son. We've got a lot of shopping to do."

I weren't kidding none. We spent the rest of the day getting schoolbooks, a uniform, a complicated abacus that could have been a damned difference engine calculating machine judging by how expensive it was, and a selection of caps and scarves bearing the school seal—some combination of trees, a lion, and some Germanic runes.

Then we took a coach out into the countryside to get a look at the school. St. Walpurgis Academy looked a little like an ancient temple mixed with a European castle. Everything was built of stern, gray stone, with minarets and towers. Charles took off his cap and scratched his curly dark hair.

"I don't know if I'll like it here," he said.

"You ought to give it a try," I urged. "Come on. Let's go get you signed up."

A lot of the other students were arriving, and I could see that they were certainly from the diamond waistcoat part of the country. They came in the fanciest carriages, all gilded and expensive-looking. They and their parents were dressed in rare furs, with rings sparkling on their white-gloved hands and top hats on their heads. As we were waiting in the line for registration, some of them stared at me like I was something they found squashed on their boot-heels.

One portly gent with a top hat that nearly brushed the ceiling and a thick moustache worked up the gumption to talk to me. "So," he said in a resonant voice. "Your employer didn't decide to come out here for the enrollment of his son?"

"No, sir," I said. "This here boy is my adopted son and I'm giving him a better home." I held out my hand and he stared at it. "Name's Clark Reeper. My boy's name is Charles."

"Charmed," he said, sounding anything but. "I am Eldridge Drump, of the Drump's Rumps and Shoulders Slaughterhouse and Stockyards of Chicago." He looked me over again. "You don't seem to be St. Walpurgis material, my good man."

"No, sir. I'm a bounty hunter," I explained. "You need someone hunted down, you send me a telegram."

"Ah. And I suppose you carry a six-shooter with you?" he asked incredulously.

I pulled aside my duster and showed my two Colt Peacemakers. "I carry two, actually."

Eldridge Drump's son, a freckle-faced boy of around eleven or twelve with thick brown hair, gasped in joy when he saw my irons. "Wow!" he exclaimed. "Guns! Can I fire them, mister, can I?!"

"My son, Darby Drump," Eldridge said coldly. "No Darby, you may not touch those firearms, pugnacious as you may be."

"Father…" Darby moaned.

By then we had reached the desk, and it took me a while to make my signatures and get all the paperwork done. Then I had to say goodbye to Charles. He looked very small in his school uniform, checkered tie knotted loosely around his neck and hanging down the front of his gray uniform with the crest over his heart.

"Well, I'm gonna head out now," I said. "You take care of yourself, Charles, and I'll come back and visit you."

"Okay, Mr. Reeper," Charles said softly. "Goodbye." He blinked several times, and so did I. Then I bent down and embraced him. I walked away facing him, waving several times and promising to write him every week.

Then I got back on the carriage and headed back to Boston. The sun was setting and I could see a few stars peeking out at me. When I got back to the hotel, I ordered a bottle of whiskey and had a couple of drinks to settle my nerves. I was about to hit the sack and get some shuteye, when there came a knock on the door.

It was a uniformed officer, a roundhead policeman. "Clark Reeper?" he asked me. "Guardian of Charles Green?"

"Yes?"

"The police would like to see you. It's about your son."

I didn't know what to think when they took me to the station. Had Charles been harmed in some way? Or maybe he had done something wrong? When I saw all of the other parents who had taken their children to St. Walpurgis waiting in the police station's lobby, I felt a bit better. At least whatever was happening to Charles was happening to all the other schoolboys.

"Ladies and gentlemen," announced the police chief, an overweight feller with a red face and a balding head. "I really don't know how to tell you this. In fact, this is one of the hardest things I've ever had to say." He gulped. "We've just received a telephone call from the headmaster of St. Walpurgis Academy. Apparently, the school has been occupied by several heavily armed men, and they are holding every student and faculty member hostage."

I gasped and all the parents did too. I couldn't believe this. A school ain't no place to be attacked, not with youngsters running around in it! Infuriated, I almost yelled out my question. "Who the hell's doing this and what do they want?"

"They have yet to issue any demands," the police chief said. "Already, officers under the command of Isaac 'the Eyes' Eisendrath from the Diamond Detective Agency have surrounded the school. Nobody's been hurt, and no shots have been fired, as far as we know."

"Who are the ruffians attacking our children?" a well-dressed woman asked.

"We have identified one of them," the police chief said. "Notorious Mexican gunman Hugo Montez."

I knew Hugo Montez. He was a desperado from down south, and the only man to have braved the fabled Montezuma's Fortress. We had parted last on decent terms, but I had no idea what he was doing threatening a bunch of wealthy children.

"I know him," I said. "I'm going over there to have a talk with him and get those kids out safe."

"We cannot guarantee your safety," the police chief warned.

"Fair enough." I drummed my fingers on my six-guns. "I can guarantee it fine myself."

"I will go as well," Eldridge Drump declared. "If my Darby is in trouble, I have to be there."

"Very well," the police chief agreed. "Rest assured, we will do everything possible to ensure the safety of your children."

We took a police carriage out into the countryside. It was the darkest that night could be. Now that Charles was in danger, even the stars shone a little less.

St. Walpurgis Academy was surrounded by police vehicles, and they seemed to have camped out a few feet from the walls of the school. Tents had been set up, making for a small command station. Searchlights continuously raked the sides of the building, and police snipers in their round helmets aimed their Springfield rifles at whatever was caught in the light.

Isaac 'the Eyes' Eisendrath was waiting for us. "Clark Reeper?" he said in a thick New York accent when he saw me. "I've heard of you." He wore a trench coat and fedora, squared spectacles covering his eyes. He was a short feller and it looked like he could roll up in the trench coat and go sleep if he wanted to.

"Then I reckon you'll let me go in there." I gestured to the fortress-like academy. "My kid's in there, Mr. Eisendrath, and I'm damn scared about what's going to happen to him. Have they asked for anything?"

"Nothing. And none of my bruisers want to go ask them." Isaac Eisendrath smiled at me. "You want to waltz in there, you be my guest."

"Much obliged," I said.

Before Eldridge Drump or anyone else could say anything, I was heading for the school. I took out my two revolvers and held them over my head. "I ain't coming in armed!" I said, setting them down on the ground. I tried not to quake in my boots too much when I did it. "There's no reason to shoot me! I just want to figure out what's going on!"

The two wooden doors to the school were cranked open, and I walked inside, my hands still over my head. Waiting for me were two fellers dressed in black greatcoats and trousers, with bandoleers around their shoulders. One of them was Hugo Montez, with his weather-beaten brown face and unkempt black hair. He held a machete and idly caressed the sharpened edge.

The other feller wore a black balaclava and smoked glasses that completely obscured his face. He was armed with twin Winchester Volcanic Ten pistols and I could see candy red sticks of dynamite on his belt.

"Howdy. Name's Clark Reeper. " I said pleasantly. "Y'all mind telling me what you're doing here?"

"What does it look like, gringo?" Hugo Montez asked. "We are holding hostage the children of the wealthy."

"I can see that, and I don't like it one bit. Threatening a bunch of students and scaring their parents. Hell, my own kid is here and I'm worried sick about him."

"We have our reasons," the masked feller said, walking over to me. He pressed a piece of paper into my hands. "This is a written list of our demands, but I will say them for you verbally right now. First of all, we require twenty horses to escape and twenty thousand dollars, and that

would be easy to achieve if a paltry sum is donated by every wealthy parent. Furthermore, we demand that a number of intellectuals currently unjustly imprisoned be released."

I looked over the list. "Eugene Debs. Red Emma Goldman," I read. "Alexander Berkman.... These here are anarchists."

"So am I." There weren't a mite of emotion in the masked man's voice. "They will be released. Also, I demand a full scale federal investigation into the operating practices of Drump's Rumps and Shoulders Slaughterhouse and Stockyards, as well as several other major businesses and factories identified in the paper. The investigation will be independent and not influenced by any amount of money given to it by the Drump Family."

"That's an awful lot of requests," I said.

"There's an awful lot of children in this school, including your own, Mr. Reeper, and if my demands are not met, we will execute them. Nobody must die today, but we are prepared to end lives." He took off his smoked glasses and I stared into harsh blue eyes. "If the police attempt to storm the school, they will find that my associates and I have planted several tons of dynamite at strategic places around the building, including the school chapel where all the schoolboys are being held. We will not hesitate to detonate it."

I began to shiver, partly because of what this feller was talking about, and partly because of the deadpan way in which he was talking. "I gotta ask," I said. "Who the hell are you, and why are you doing this?"

"My name is Franklin Franks," he said. His hands moved to the bottom of his balaclava. "Let me show you why I am doing this." He tore off his balaclava in one smooth motion, and I nearly puked when I saw what was under it.

His eyes, nose, and mouth were all where they should be, but nothing else was. There weren't no skin on his face, just his red flesh, moving muscles, and even the pale white of bone. The Man with No Face gave me a good look before replacing the balaclava and hiding his mutilation.

"This grievous injury was dealt to me when I was seven years of age. It was a result of an accident in the Drump's Rumps and Shoulders Slaughterhouse where a malfunctioning piece of machinery literally ripped away my face. I soon discovered that the machinery could easily have been repaired, but the Drump Corporation was more concerned with profits than workers. I am the result of that decision." He jabbed a Winchester pistol at me. "Leave me, Mr. Reeper, and tell the world that the Man with No Face will not take no for an answer."

I headed outside with my hands reaching for the sky. I didn't glance back. Detective Eisendrath waited for me, tapping his loafers on the manicured grass and smoking a stubby cigarette. He handed me my revolvers and I set them in my holsters with a spin.

"Well, who are they and what do they want?" he demanded.

"Anarchists."

The word made everyone stop, and Eisendrath let out a long puff from his cigarette. "I should've known. Damn bomb-flingers only understand violence."

"Oh heavens!" Eldridge Drump cried. "My Darby in the hands of salivating communards! What do those fiends want?"

I handed him the note, and Drump stared at it while Eisendrath read it from over the meat tycoon's shoulder. "A full-scale investigation!" Drump moaned. "Those beasts!"

"This list has every Red wanted for mayhem, murder and subversive thought," Eisendrath mused. "There's no way we're agreeing to any of these demands, I guarantee it."

"But all those kids..." I said. "It ain't right to let them die like that. My little Charles is in there..." I felt kind of weak in the knees and had to shake the feeling of helplessness out of my head.

"Darby is very important to me," Drump said uncertainly. "But so is the business. A federal investigation is quite out of the question."

"No need to pander to these Reds!" Eisendrath said with a cheerful grin. "I've done some talking with some friends of mine. We're going to bust in there and break those kids out—after breaking a couple anarchist skulls, of course."

I looked at the fortress-like private school. The mammoth gate that I had walked through was closed and doubtlessly bolted shut. "I reckon it would be mighty hard to go strolling in, detective."

"We've just got to make an entrance." Eisendrath raised his hand and signaled to some of his men in the telegraph tent. "Just wait, Mr. Reeper. Help is on the way."

A few minutes later a buzzing sound filled the air. I looked up to see an honest-to-god aeroplane soaring down. It was like one of those newfangled Wright Flyers, a whole bunch of separate wings and fins stuck together, with a spinning propeller at one end and a swiftly moving tail at the other.

"Heavens!" Drump cried. "What is that contraption?"

"Meet the Diamond Air Service," Eisendrath said. "Go get them, boys!" He pumped a fist into the air.

The aeroplane swooped low, and let a small package fall from its underside onto the bolted gate. The stone entrance exploded, sending rocks and debris flying everywhere. Eisendrath had drawn one of them newfangled automatic pistols out of his shoulder-holster and was waving it at the school. "Come on, men!" he cried. "Let's do this!"

Two dozen police officers charged into the breech, rifles lowered, and Eisendrath smiled at me. "Move it, cowboy!" he shouted. "Let's kill us some anarchists!"

Not knowing what else to do, and thinking of poor Charles, I drew my own revolvers and followed them into the school.

The Police Officers stopped and lowered their weapons as soon as they reached the main courtyard, and I soon saw why. Frank Franklins, the Man with No Face, and Hugo Montez stood in the darkness, an electric light from the school eerily highlighting their faces.

The police officers shouted and yelled and gestured with their bayoneted rifles, while Montez and Franks stood there in cold silence. Finally, Eisendrath spoke up, his rasping voice louder than any other.

"You two! Where are the hostages? Answer now or we'll plug you!"

Franklin Franks and Hugo Montez exchanged a glance before Franks spoke. "It seems imbecilic for you to terrify a bunch of already frightened schoolboys with your aircraft-dropped bomb. I'll have to spend a great deal time calming them down and assuring them everything will work out all right after this." Not a drop of emotion crept into Franks' voice. He calmly took off his shaded glasses and held them in one hand, then removed his mask.

The officers gasped as they saw his bloody features, but they kept their rifles leveled. Slowly, the Man with No Face replaced his smoked glasses, a spurt of blood reddening one of the lenses.

"Wise up, faceless freak!" Eisendrath taunted. "We've got you and your greaser buddy surrounded!"

"And yet, you have not bothered to examine your own surroundings." The edges of Franklin Franks' mouth curved upwards as he drew out a small detonator from the folds of his dark greatcoat. Before any of the policemen could fire on him, Franks clicked it down and everything went to Hell.

The ground shook under me and I went down, debris, dirt and body parts soaring over my head. The damn anarchist must have had dynamite planted right under our feet! I was knocked onto my back and it took me a while before I felt well enough to stand back up. By then the battle had already begun.

The surviving police officers charged, rifles blazing, bayonets poised. The Man with No Face spun around, his cloak flying as he drew out twin Volcanic 10 pistols and opened fire. The oddly shaped weapons with their long barrels and curved handles spit out lead messengers lickety-split. He spotted a bunch of huddled officers and then hurled a lit bundle of dynamite towards them, the bundle's flimsy bindings coming apart and sending out a barrage of explosives.

I ducked down and fought through the smoke, trying to get a clear shot while I hunkered down behind a stone bench. The other anarchists in the school buildings started firing, hidden from the policemen in their cover. Bullets whizzed every which way, dynamite was going off, and I was wondering if anyone was thinking about the safety of those poor kids.

Hugo Montez spotted me. He had drawn out two machetes and was hacking through several police officers when he caught my eye. Then, the Mexican hurled one of his machetes like it didn't weigh no more than a tooth-pick, catching a roundhead straight in the face. I popped up from behind the bench and fired a shot over his head.

"Hola, Hugo!" I shouted. "What are you doing riding with this bunch of criminals and child-killers? Ain't no place for a man like you!"

"These anarchists are the most honorable gringos I know, muchacho," Hugo Montez hissed back, lunging towards me. "My country, my people, have been oppressed by the parents of these children for centuries."

"Now that ain't true, Hugo." I took a step back and holstered one of my pistols as I went for my Bowie knife. I didn't want to kill Hugo Montez, but I would if there weren't no reasoning with him. "My own kid is in here and he's never done nothing. And these kids are still wearing knickers and playing with hoops and sticks! They ain't never hurt you!"

"But they will, some day." Hugo Montez lashed out at me with his machete, narrowly missing my face. I leaned back and stabbed downwards with my Bowie knife, but Hugo swiftly leapt out of the way, and then elbowed me hard in the chest. I fell backwards and the Mexican bladesman raised his machete for the kill, just as I brought up my Peacemaker to his face.

"That ain't no reason to go beating up defenseless children, Hugo, and you know it!" I shouted. "Now, amigo, tell me what the hell you're doing here holding my little boy hostage?"

Hugo stared down my Peacemaker. "I need a child," he said slowly. "The curse will haunt me unless I placate it with a child. A little ninjo, just one, and my torment will be no more."

"Son of a gun," I hissed, keeping the gun level. "What are you going on about?"

"La Llorona," Hugo Montez whispered wistfully. "She demands a child."

We would have gone on, had not another dynamite explosion rippled through St. Walpurgis Academy. Hugo and I were knocked off of our feet, and then several small voices, nearly drowned out by gunfire, caught everyone's attention.

"Please don't hurt me, sir. Oh God, please, I haven't done anything wrong. Oh God, I want my mommy, oh please…"

The Man with No Face and several of his anarchist followers, all dressed in flowing black coats and balaclavas, stood behind a row of young boys in school uniforms, neat little jackets, checkered ties, knickers and caps. I saw Charles, kneeling down and not saying anything, but holding his glasses tightly across his chest, right in front, and then I holstered my knife and pistol and held up my hands.

"No more fighting!" I yelled out. "Let's get out of here!" I slowly walked backwards, the surviving police officers following me. I reckon nobody wanted a bunch of innocent kids getting killed.

Then I spotted Isaac Eisendrath, his automatic pistol in his hands. He was preparing to fire. "I can hit them!" he whispered to himself. "Bam! Take them down! I can pull it off!"

"The hell you can," I shouted. "Put that cannon away!"

Instead, Isaac dropped to one knee and took aim. "Clam up, cowboy! You ought to trust my shooting abilities!"

"Not when there are kids on the line." I grabbed my Peacemaker by the barrel and smacked him with the handle, buffaloing the detective and knocking him out cold. Then, I gently carried him out of St. Walpurgis, the policemen following me out of the school.

I reckoned it was gonna take more than a couple of guns to free those kids.

While we were waiting for Eisendrath to wake up, I wandered around and racked my brain trying to think up who 'La Llorona' was. Then it hit me. It was some kind of Mexican legend or folktale about a weeping woman. I wasn't sure why she was crying, but I knew it had something to do with children, and violence. In my experience a lot of legends have a pretty good basis in fact, and I began to get real worried about why exactly Hugo Montez was here.

By and by, Isaac Eisendrath recovered and he was real pissed at me for slugging him earlier. He came out of the tent, his fedora at a cocky angle, and looked like he was going to pick a fight.

"You hillbilly idiot!" he shouted. "Why'd you clobber me like that?"

"You were gonna get a bunch of children killed!" I shouted back. "I wasn't gonna let you do that."

"You hit an officer of the law, cowboy! I have every right to break you in half!" I towered over Eisendrath, but he still looked like he was liable to do what he threatened.

Eldridge Drump stepped between us. "Please. This fighting only benefits the anarchists and hurts the schoolboys! You must cease your hostilities and try to save our children!"

We both stared at him and sighed.

"Fine," Eisendrath said. "Try not to get in my way while I'm doing my job, cowboy."

I frowned at him but said nothing.

"Much better!" Drump cried. "Now, while Mr. Eisendrath was unconscious I made some calls to some associates of mine in the War Department, and I believe I have stumbled upon a solution to our problem that will bring our children back!"

"What?" I asked breathlessly.

"Automatons!" Eldridge Drump answered. "Mechanical killing machines without souls! The steel warriors of the future! One is on its way right now! The iron will of the mechanical—"

"Hold on a second," I said, placing a hand on his shoulder. "You want to send some rust-buckets in to rescue the kids, after a flesh-and-blood attack failed miserably? What about just listening to their demands?"

Eldridge stared at me. "Really, Mr. Reeper. My slaughterhouses and stockyards do not deserve to be investigated! My workers are treated fine!"

"What about Franks?" I asked. "He ain't got much of a face left."

"An exception!" Drump's face was as red as the meat he sold. "The sanctity of industry will not be breached!"

"Even if it means your son's life?" It was a bad question, but I had to ask it.

Eldridge Drump's mouth made an 'O' and the color drained from his face. "Darby..." he whispered. "My dear Darby...Perhaps his life is worth more than the company..."

I was about to apologize, saying that we was all on edge and nervous, when someone shouted my name. I spun around and saw a black-cloaked anarchist rifleman standing in the ruins of the door, his rifle cocked, and a white tablecloth draped across it. "Clark Reeper!" he shouted. "Comrade Franks wants to speak with you!"

The lawmen and Eisendrath went for their weapons, but I held up my hands. "I'll go, I'll go." I walked over to the anarchist, my hands on my hips. "I'll go with you, but don't do nothing sneaky."

"Comrade Franks abhors violence," the anarchist said.

"I can tell." I nodded as we walked into St. Walpurgis Academy, staring at the corpses of the policemen, some blown to bits, littering the ground.

The anarchist led me to the main chapel, which I figured for the Man with No Face's headquarters. He knocked on the door, it opened just a crack, and a coach gun was pointed out and aimed right at us. I held my breath.

"Bakunin, Proudhon?" the person wielding the coach gun asked, like it was some kind of code.

"Kropotkin, Berkman, Goldman," my escort replied. The doors to the chapel were opened, and we were led inside. It was a real big building, with a towering triangular ceiling and a large interior filled with benches that had been mostly moved to one side. The whole thing was lit with electric lights, and my eyes flashed around and took in the scene they illuminated.

Every schoolboy in St. Walpurgis was in there, some in bedclothes and others still wearing their school uniforms. Some of the younger ones slept or rested on the bedrolls; the more boisterous ones chased each other around the chapel, weaving in and out of pillars; others sat around talking, reading, or playing a variety of board games. A small group of adults stood off to one side, and I reckoned they were the teachers. Leaning against the pillars, sitting on some of the benches, or even joining in with some of the kids' games, were the anarchist hostage-takers. My eyes scanned the room for Charles, but it was simply too crowded.

"This way," the anarchist leading me commanded. I followed him through the crowded room, squeezing out of the way of a game of tag, and came to the far corner near one of the altars. The Man with No Face was there, his face covered by his balaclava. He was crouched on the altar and talking gently to some of the schoolboys. I gasped when I saw Charles Green sitting right next to him, a thick book in his hand.

"Is Mr. Wells a...what did you call yourself?" Charles asked in his shrill voice, making my heart cringe as he absent-mindedly polished his thick spectacles.

"An anarchist," Franklin Franks answered Charles. "And no, H.G. Wells is not one of us. He is a socialist, and while I respect his ideals and his work, I do disagree with him on some points. His portrayal of us as monomaniacal bomb throwers in his short story of the Stolen Bacillus was maddening, but I did like The Time Machine very much." He showed the volume he held. "Would you like me to read it to you? I'm afraid it may be a very long night."

"Please!" they all answered in happy unison.

The anarchist leading me tapped Franks on the shoulder and he turned around and spotted me. "Oh, excuse me, boys," Franks said politely as he stood up. "Let me talk to Mr. Reeper and then I will begin."

Charles must have heard my name, because he looked up and ran towards me, nearly bowling me over when he jumped into my arms. I held him close and felt some tears in my eyes, and saw some tears in his. "I'm worried sick about you," I whispered to Charles.

"So am I!" Charles cried. "Mr. Franks is being really nice to us, but I'm still scared, and I'm afraid you or someone else will get shot!"

I looked up from Charles and saw the Man with No Face, a smile on his lips. "Your son?" he asked, nodding to Charles.

"My adopted son, yes," I answered, setting Charles down.

"A very smart boy. A good reader."

"He sure is," I agreed with Franks. "Charles, hold on a second while I talk to Franks. We'll get you and all your friends out of here safe, I promise." My eyes were still watery as he ran back to his new friends. I walked over to where the Man with No Face was waiting.

Franklin Franks sighed. "I'm very sorry about this, Mr. Reeper. I don't know if I'm doing the right thing..."

"You sure ain't," I said, a little anger in my voice. "Why the hell you doing this anyway? I figured you for a damned psychopath, but you seemed like a nice feller dealing with those kids, and you got no good reason to go storming in here and threatening these youngsters!"

"I have to wake the world up!" Franks shouted at me, raising his hands. "This is the way to tell the world what is happening in the slums of Chicago and New York, and everywhere working men are abused and beaten down!" He pointed to his masked face. "I have to live with this for my whole life! The daily pain and insults, and you should see the rest of the urban jungle! Long hours and miserable conditions, kids younger than the ones here freezing to death and being worked into a miserable stupor!" He paused for breath, massaging his face through the black cloth.

"But does that give you a warrant to go holding a bunch of innocent kids hostage?" I demanded. "The men out there don't even want to listen to your wants, they just want to shoot this place up. You already saw what the cops did when you cut them down!"

"Nobody was supposed to die here," Franks said, his voice once more emotionless. "You brought this on yourselves."

I looked right and left, making sure none of the kids were close enough to hear what I was about to say. "The bunch out there, I don't like them. They want your blood, no two ways about it, and I think they're going to call your bluff. So there's only one question left. Are you willing to kill one of these kids, Mr. Franks?" My hand fell to my pistol. "Well, are you gonna fold when they come bursting in here, or are you going to reveal a full house and make some horrified parents leave the table in tears?"

The Man with No Face stared at me with tormented eyes looking out through his balaclava. "I...don't...know," he finally said. "I know what Bakunin said, that the ends justify the means, but I don't know if I'm strong enough to put that into action."

"Man who hurts kids don't have any kind of strength," I said firmly.

Slowly, Franklin Franks nodded. The anarchist leader blinked several times. "Maybe you're right. Go outside and tell the plutocrat tools that I'll take whatever they give me. Twenty horses to get my men and myself to safety will be enough." He looked down at the floor. "I want revenge for what those money-loving capitalist swine did to me, but this just isn't the right way to get it."

I smiled and patted the Man with No Face on the shoulder. "You're a good man, Franklin Franks. We'll get through this. Sun will be coming up soon, and then this whole thing will be behind us."

"Get out." He didn't even look at me as I headed out of the chapel. I took one lingering look at Charles as the doors were slowly closed behind me.

When I got back to the police encampment, everyone seemed a mite preoccupied with the large wooden box, about twice the size of one of those newfangled horseless carriages, which had been delivered and was now being opened by crowbar-wielding cops.

Detective Eisendrath and Eldridge Drump watched it, Drump rubbing his gloved and ringed hands together with glee.

"Howdy," I said, taking their attention away from the package. "Listen here, I got some mighty good news—"

"So do we!" Eisendrath said. "Drump came through! He had this special package delivered, and you won't believe what's bundled up inside!"

"A Model Z!" Drump cried joyfully. "A brutal killing machine and the last of the 1887 Torrent Combat Automaton Line! It has cogs to prevent it from going rogue and killing its master like Model X did, and is much more heavily armed."

"Well, there's no reason to use it—"

"You won't believe the cannons this thing's packing!" Isaac Eisendrath seemed to be ignoring me. "It's got an actual cannon, an honest-to-god Howitzer located inside the chest."

"And that's not all!" Eldridge Drump chimed in. "It's got an electrified blade located on the right arm, and a powerful high-speed motorized Gatling gun on the left arm! Oh, it will be as if the wrath of God has fallen upon the anarchist scum!"

"But there ain't no reason to use it!" I shouted. "Franks is surrendering!"

Eisendrath and Drump stared at me. "Impossible," Eisendrath said.

"Incomprehensible," Drump agreed.

"Them's the facts!" I shouted. "All he wants is twenty horses so he and his boys can leave this place and go home."

"My good man," Eldridge said sternly, "you must have fallen for a clever dynamitard ruse. That faceless fiend is not going anywhere."

"Yeah," Eisendrath said as he drew a cigarette out of his jacket and stuffed it into his mouth. "This wise guy has kicked me around too much to be let off that easily. He's got to die."

The box was being opened, and I caught sight of a metal, spidery leg sticking out of it. "But the children!" I said. "What if they get hurt when you send in some metal-minded super weapon?"

"The Model Z is known for its precision," Drump said certainly. "No need to fear. Ah! It is ready!"

The box fell away as the Model Z rose up and shook itself like a dog that had just taken a bath. It looked like a big six-legged metal spider with a stomach and two arms stuck on it. I spotted the mouth of a Howitzer in the chest, and a large steel blade on one arm, while a Gatling gun was stuck on the other. Each leg curved downwards in wicked serrated points. Two light bulbs, faintly glowing red, stuck out of the top of the chest like demonic eyes. The whole contraption was covered in intricate scrollwork with little roses, stars, and eagles in silver and gold all over its steel body. Smoke poured out of several small holes on its back.

"It's beautiful!" Drump said. He walked over to it, and picked up an ornate gramophone that was lying on the floor, sliding it into a small slot in the Model Z's chest. A blast of patriotic music, the Stars and Stripes Forever, erupted from the gramophone, followed by a grand-sounding voice.

"I am the Torrent Combat Automaton Model Z! Congratulations for activating me on this auspicious day!" It had a brassy announcer's voice. The automaton moved its arms as it talked, almost like it was gesturing. "Now, please relate to me the people you want killed, and in what fashion I may destroy them, and I will do it to the utmost of my considerable abilities!" One red eye blinked on and off, like the contraption was winking.

Drump clasped his hands together and tapped his foot in glee. He bent forwards to whisper into the gramophone, but I grabbed his fur collar and hauled him backwards.

"What are you doing?" I demanded. "What about little Darby? What if he gets hurt when this automaton crashes in with all guns blazing?"

"Please, Mr. Reeper!" Drump said. "The Model Z is the most precise model of automaton on the market! There's no danger at all for little Darby!"

I guess he must have said that last word a little too close to the gramophone because the Model Z shivered and puffed out a great cloud of smoke. Then it began to speak. "Little Darby. Target's name received! Where is target currently lurking, and how best may I destroy him?"

"Don't hurt him!" Eldridge Drump yelled. "Please, he's my only son!"

"Don't. Negate. End. Little Darby will be ended!" The Model Z had started up, and there was no shutting it down. "Sun. Burning. Fire. He will be immolated!"

"No! Stop!" Drump's face had turned red and he was screaming into the gramophone. "Please, he's just a child!"

"Child. Children. Stop all the children. By killing them! All the children around Little Darby will be ended! Where are they?"

We all fell silent, not wanting to give the Model Z any more ideas. The machine stood there expectantly, slowly twisting right and left. "Since coordinates have not been specified, I will begin executions of everyone in the nearby vicinity! Prepare to be ended!" He leveled his Gatling gun at us.

"They're in the school!" Isaac Eisendrath shouted. "The kids are in the school! The big stone building right behind us! Now don't hurt us!"

"Thank you! Coordinates received. They will be ended as will anything that gets in my way!" The Model Z began to move, its pincer legs cutting into the earth as it walked towards the school. I turned in rage to Eisendrath.

"What the hell was that?" I shouted into his face. He was hunched over and looked scared.

"That thing was gonna kill us! Now it's going away!"

"Yeah, to hurt a bunch of innocent little kids!" I slugged Eisendrath again, I couldn't help it. I slugged him hard in the chest and he buckled over and gasped for breath.

"Oh dear, oh dear," Drump moaned, biting his fat hand. "My Darby!"

"We gotta shut that thing down," I said. I turned to the detective. "Come on, get everyone together and we'll go after that rust-bucket."

"Go ahead, cowboy, I ain't going after that thing. Be my guest!" Eisendrath shrank to the floor, proving himself a goddamn coward. I spat on him and then rushed off to get some firepower. I picked up a Springfield rifle and slung it over my back. I grabbed a riot gun and primed it with one hand.

Then I turned to see the Model Z blasting a hole in the wall with its main cannon and charging into St. Walpurgis Academy just as the first rays of daylight appeared.

I ran after it, easily getting close to the trundling Model Z. I drew out my riot gun, laid it down on my left arm, and fired, worked the pump, and fired again. The bullets cracked into the metal, smashing the gilding and making the automaton stop in its tracks.

"Hey metal-head!" I shouted. "Why don't ya'll go back to the junk yard?"

"An obstacle!" Model Z proclaimed. "Preparing for removal!" It swung its chest around and opened fire at me with every weapon it had. I leapt backwards, scrambling away from the pouring bullets and the cannon shot, but I was still hurled onto my back as slugs flew around me.

"Son of a gun!" I cried, getting up and running to avoid the speedily-fired bullets from the Gatling gun. The Model Z charged towards me, pointed legs sending dirt flying, and it moved mighty fast for something so large. It fired one cannon shot, sending me flying into the air. When I landed, my face was bruised, and the riot gun had fallen from my hands and was lying out of reach. The Model Z was running towards the chapel. Maybe it had heard the children's voices or something, and it seemed to know where they were.

The Model Z fired a single shot from its Howitzer, blasting into the side of the chapel. Stained glass shattered and children screamed as I jumped up and started running towards the automaton, my Springfield rifle cocked and ready. It didn't see me coming, and I jumped up onto its back and fired straight into its chest with the Springfield.

"Have some of that!" I yelled, stabbing down with the rifle's bayonet. The blade cut away gilding and made streaks in the steel, but it wasn't having any luck at shutting the automaton down. My heart sank as I realized I was going to need some heavier artillery. The Model Z swung its bladed arm around, and I ducked to avoid it, the wind whooshing over my head as the blade nearly cut through my hat brim and skull.

I jumped off just as the automaton swung its bladed arm again, this time nearly cutting off my feet, and then the arm shot out a blast of electricity at me. The lightning struck me square in the chest, sending sparks all over my body. I tried to move, to shoot, to do anything, but that bolt of lightning forced me down and was burning me up. I began to realize that I was going to die.

Then an explosion rocked the Model Z and the lightning clicked off, allowing me to fall to my knees and howl in pain. I looked up and saw Franklin Franks, another bundle of dynamite in his hands. He hurled it at the Model Z and it exploded, sending the mechanical monster rocking on its legs. Behind the Man with No Face, all the students and teachers of St. Walpurgis were running away from the smashed chapel, struggling to get away from the homicidal construct.

"Franks!" I cried. "We gotta take this thing down! It was told to kill the kids!"

"I can stop this, Comrade Reeper!" he shouted, running back to the chapel. "Keep it busy until I can get up to the steeple. This bourgeoisie beast will be destroyed!" He ran inside, leaving the Model Z and me alone.

I went for my pistols, firing at the Model Z's light bulb eyes. One exploded in a shower of glass and sparks.

It fixed its second malevolent red eye at me. "Obstacles will be removed!" it said cheerfully, firing its Gatling gun.

But this time I was ready. I ducked down behind a stone bench, letting the bullets thud uselessly into the cover, and then I popped up and fired again. The second light bulb shattered.

"Obstacles will be removed!" The Model Z said, with a little less confidence. "I will end you!"

An explosion from up above distracted all of us. The Model Z and I looked up and saw the huge chapel steeple, a giant stone spike, being dislodged by a dynamite explosion. It fell downwards, the point aimed straight at the Model Z.

The automaton looked upwards, and then played a strain of the Star-Spangled Banner before the steeple smashed down onto it, skewering the Model Z right through the middle. Its legs shook and twitched and then it lay still.

Franklin Franks came running out from the chapel. "It's down!" he said.

"You did good, Mr. Franks," I said. "That was some quick thinking."

"And thank you, Comrade Reeper," the Man with No Face congratulated me. "Your own exploits were quite heroic."

"Yeah, boys, crackerjack job!" We turned around and saw Detective Isaac Eisendrath, several police officers, and Eldridge Drudge all behind us. Eisendrath and the cops had their guns trained on Franks. "Now grab some air and give up!"

The schoolboys were nearby, and before anyone could do anything, Franklin Franks grabbed a kid from the crowd and pressed his Volcanic 10 pistol to the boy's head.

I was frozen, and for a few seconds there was no sound but panting breaths and the terrified squeals of the brown-haired schoolboy. Slowly, I recognized him as Drump's son, Darby. Eldridge Drump was shivering, wringing his hands as he saw his child with a gun to his head.

"Get back, plutocrat lap-dogs!" the Man with No Face called. "I'll kill him. I will not hesitate!"

"You don't have the guts," Eisendrath snarled, turning off the safety of his automatic. "Come on, anarchist, kill him, I dare you."

"There's no reason to do this!" I shouted, waving my hands. "Please, put your guns down!"

"Shut up, cowboy, this is my case!" Eisendrath yelled, and then turned back to Franklin Franks. "So, Franks, are you gonna do it?"

The Man with No Face was bluffing, and we all knew it. I could see sweat staining the inside of the Balaclava as Franks tried to figure out what the hell to do.

But then, Eldridge Drudge stepped in front of Isaac, shielding Franks and his son with his own obese body. "You win, Mr. Franks," he said. "God help me. I'll allow a federal inspection, and I'll let you go. Just don't hurt my Darby!"

I figured there was only so much a father could take.

"What are you doing, Drump?" Eisendrath demanded. "Let me do my job and kill this anarchist!"

"I could buy and sell you, Eisendrath. Drop the gun and let Franks go on his way, and let me get my Darby back!"

Eisendrath reluctantly holstered his automatic, and his policemen lowered their guns as well. The children ran over behind the police, and Darby leapt into his father's arms. They embraced and it was a mighty heartwarming scene.

Hugo Montez walked over to Franks and tapped him on the shoulder. "You promised me a child, gringo. For La Llorona!"

"Sorry, Comrade Montez," The Man with No Face said. "No child will be hurt today. Get out of here and get to safety."

Montez reached for his machete, but then looked at me, Franks, and all the cops, and realized that he was licked. He walked away muttering to himself angrily in Spanish.

And then Charles came out and ran straight into me, nearly knocking me over, almost like the Model Z's cannon. I hugged him tight and ruffled his hair. For a long time we didn't say anything.

Well, the police had a couple of horses and they let the Man with No Face and his comrades ride out into the country. Franklin Franks got pretty high on the country's most wanted list, and now every lawman and bounty hunter seems to be gunning for him, except for me. Hunting Franklin Franks is one job that I'm going to pass up.

Eldridge Drump allowed the federal inspectors, and they didn't like what they found. The conditions in his slaughterhouse and stockyards were a little bit worse than Hell, with unsafe machines maiming workers and disgusting stuff I don't even want to talk about going into the meat, and worse. Drump was almost forced to resign and go under, but he began a new initiative of cleaning up his company and making everything better. I figure he'll do anything, just as long as he and Darby are happily together.

As for Detective Isaac Eisendrath, well, he got one hell of a dressing down for handling the St. Walpurgis crises the way he did. He got himself kicked out of the Diamond Detective Agency, and is now looking for other employment. I hope our paths don't cross again, but I can't say they won't.

The Model Z line got retired, and now Torrent Combat Automatons is working on the Model A Mark II. It sure is taking them science fellers a long time to make an automaton that won't malfunction and attack people. I don't know if they'll ever do it, but I guess they aim to try.

Hugo Montez headed out and wasn't seen again. I found out La Llorona is some sort of ghost woman, but I'm not sure why Montez needed a child to please her. I'm still glad he didn't get one.

St. Walpurgis seemed to be a safe place, but it was still not the place for Charles Green. I thought I could part with Charles, but after him being held hostage because of what I did, I don't think we should go our separate ways just yet. I got a telegram from out west asking for my services in shutting down a sasquatch infestation of some kind, and I decided I would take Charles with me.

"Thank you Mr. Reeper!" he said cheerfully. "And you don't have to worry about me getting hurt. There's nothing you can't save me from!"

"I hope you're right, son," I said, but I didn't know if he was.

Well, that about sums up my story. I still don't like to have anything to do with politics, but I guess I got to have some beliefs. It seems to me that there's good folks on both sides, and politics ain't never worth coming to blows over. I reckon that's as good a belief as any.

The Weeping Woman

Now I'm not the kind feller who goes around looking for trouble. It just seems to find me no matter where I go. It's probably on account of my job. The name's Clark Reeper and I'm a bounty hunter, specializing in the odder jobs that are out there. Because I make a living in ending lives, I get a fair share of people trying to end mine. Still, sometimes you just can't predict who is bearing a grudge against you, and when they're going to try to even the score. I didn't figure Hugo Montez for an ornery feller, and I had no idea what kind of grief he was going to cause me.

It all started when Charles Green and I were headed west. Charles is this little feller, a ten-year-old boy with brown curly hair and spectacles thick as sarsaparilla bottles. I had saved the boy from some walking corpses a while back, and I loved him like a son. I had tried to send little Charles to a boarding school, but the place had been attacked by some anarchists and so I reckoned it would be best if he rode with me for a while.

Me and Charles were riding on a little buckboard wagon pulled by a tired old mule I had rented. I was on the lookout for a new job. Charles, his legs swinging idly off the side of the wagon, was reading a book, some scientific romance by a British gent. H.G. Wells, I think his name was.

"How's the book coming?" I asked him.

"It's good," Charles said, dog-earing the page and then closing the volume.

He looked out at our surroundings. We were driving through some West Texas prairies, miles and miles of empty scrubland. It was mighty pretty to look at, scattered red stones, dull green and brown plants, and the pale sky as far as you can see.

"This place looks really empty," Charles said.

"Well, Charles, ain't no towns out here for a while. And at the rate this mule's going, we'll both have a gray beard before we reach one." I gave the reins a slap, but the mule just gave me an annoyed look and kept on plodding.

"Mr. Reeper?" Charles asked, his voice going thin as he asked the question.

"Yeah, Charles?"

"Are you ever going to go away from me again?"

I looked away from the road and ruffled his hair through the dark felt of his little peaked cap. It was a tough question. Charles is short for his age, weak and harmless; I was a tall, lanky feller, and with my two six-guns, I was a lot more than harmless. I wanted to protect Charles, but I didn't want to smother him either. "I'm here for you now," I said. "And no matter where you go or what you do, I won't let you get hurt."

Charles looked a bit happier. "Thank you, Mr. Reeper."

"No trouble, son. None at all."

We rode on for a while in comfortable silence. Charles just stared out at the passing landscape with a content look on his amiable face. I was wondering just how long it would take to get to the next settlement when I heard some horses coming up fast from behind. I turned around, and when I saw who was riding the horses, I wondered if my promise to keep Charles safe was a lie.

The leader of the gang was Hugo Montez. Montez was a Mexican bladesman, skilled with a machete or a revolver and the only person to survive the booby traps of the famed Montezuma's Fortress. He had been fighting alongside the anarchists who held Charles and his schoolmates hostage, but he didn't seem to be the kind of feller who would get himself involved with politics. When I asked him what he was doing there, he told me that he needed a child, and then mentioned something about 'La Llorona,' which I think is some kind of Latin American legend.

I know a thing or two about legends: they usually have some basis in fact. That's what worried me, particularly when I remembered that La Llorona was some crying woman who had something to do with murdered children. The hostage situation all worked out pretty swell though. None of the school kids got hurt, the anarchists were able to flee, and Hugo Montez didn't harm a single child. But now Montez had returned. He was up to something, and it couldn't be good.

Hugo Montez was riding a black steed. He was wearing a loose leather vest, two machetes at his side. His weathered face and tired black eyes, as well as his tangled black hair, were all shaded by a wide-brimmed sombrero. Four men rode with him, harsh-looking desperados with bandoleers over their ponchos and rusty firearms dangling from their saddles.

Charles spotted them and shivered in the desert heat. I put an arm on his shoulder and held him close to me.

"Don't you worry," I said. "We'll get through this all right."

"Hola, Clark Reeper!" Montez shouted, slowing his horse to a canter as he rode close to me. I saw the twin machetes fastened to his saddle glisten in the sun. "What's a gringo like you doing out here, all alone in the Tejas desert?"

One of my hands slowly fell away from the reins, inching backwards to the Winchester Rifle I had resting in the wagon. "Just getting by, amigo. You looking for trouble?"

"Oh no! No!" Hugo Montez held out his hands and some of his companions laughed and chuckled. "Well, not unless you wish to give it to me, gringo."

"What exactly does gringo mean?" Charles asked curiously.

"Nothing good," I answered. "But it depends on who's speaking it."

"Nice boy you have there." Hugo Montez pointed to Charles. "Neat little suit. Curly hair. He would be perfect for La Llorona."

"He ain't going nowhere!" I shouted. "Now move on and leave us alone!"

Montez shook his head. "I will do anything to end this curse, Clark Reeper. I will take this child."

"Go ahead and try," I said, raising the Winchester. "You'll be dead if you make a move, Montez, and the same to any of your amigos!"

I eyeballed Montez's thugs. They all laughed, and a particularly ugly hombre rode to the other side of me. He had dark mud-colored skin and multi-colored beads in his plaited hair. He smiled at me with pointed teeth.

Hugo introduced his friend. "Tequila Tim here's got Aztec blood in him, pure Indio. They say his father trained him in the old arts of the Nagual, the Nahualli."

"What a coincidence. I was trained in the old arts of shooting fools through the head," I snickered.

Tequila Tim emitted a low growl as he leaned forward on his horse.

Montez chuckled. "You don't know what the Nahualli are. You stupid gringo."

"Yeah? And you smell bad." I chuckled at my joke, but I was the only one laughing.

Hugo Montez gripped the hilts of his machetes. "You're more worthless than General Walker."

"Walker? Name sounds familiar."

"A Texas Ranger turned mercenary. He is the reason I'm in this mess." Montez looked away from me, up into the clear blue sky. He didn't say anything for a while and then he cried out like he was in pain. "Every night I feel her close to me, her cold flesh touching my face, while her cries deafen my ears!" He clenched his hands into fists. "But enough talk, gringo. Now is time for action. Ariba!" He slashed the reins of my wagon with his twin machetes.

I quickly drew out my Winchester, pushing Charles away from Hugo Montez's flashing blades as I fired. The poor kid let out a cry of terror and struggled to the back of the wagon. I ain't no stranger when it comes to violence, but this was too close to Charles for my liking.

My first shot hit one of Montez's machetes, pinging off steel and knocking the big knife from his hand. The Mexican knife-fighter cried in pain and anger and then yelled some command in Spanish. One of his companions aimed a revolver at me, but I blasted the gunman right off of his horse. I worked the lever and spun it around, daring another Mexican to make a move.

Tequila Tim made his. He jumped off his horse, flying towards me with hands outstretched. In seconds, a change washed over him. His skin became yellowish and furry, tinged with dark spots. His eyes gleamed yellow ringed with black, and long claws sprouted from his hands. Just like Hugo Montez said, Tequila Tim was a Nagual—an Aztec Shaman who could transform into a jaguar at will. He knocked me over, forcing me to the ground and raking my face with his long claws. I yelped in pain as blood filled my eyes. My Winchester was pressed uselessly to my chest. Tequila Tim had pinned me to the ground, but I still had my six-guns tucked away. I grabbed one and fired into Tim's chest. He let out a deep growl.

"Son of a gun!" I cried, as the jaguar batted away my revolver and bloodied my hand. "Overgrown kitty!" I reached for my Bowie knife in my boot, grabbing onto the handle with the tips of my fingers. With a deadly twist, I jabbed the blade into Tequila Tim's side. The big cat roared and lithely slithered off of me.

I came to my feet, reaching for my other gun, ready to give those damn Mexicans hell. Hugo Montez had grabbed Charles and had thrown the boy over his shoulder like a bag of flour. Charles yelped and struggled as best he could, but Montez was too strong.

I drew my revolver to blast Hugo Montez's brains out when something crashed into me. I fell to the ground as Tequila Tim once more covered me in deep painful scratches, and my gun fell from my hand. I found myself staring up at Hugo Montez and Tequila Tim as he instantly changed back into a human. Montez, still carrying the struggling Charles, shook his head at me.

"Adios, gringo," was all he said before he slammed his machete handle into my head, knocking me out cold. It didn't matter that he didn't do the killing himself. Left alone in the wide desert, with no nearby civilization or water, I was dead nonetheless.

I lay there, I don't know how long, but I reckon it must have been a fair spell. The shock of some cold water being poured on my face woke me up. I felt the sand in my hair, the pounding in my head, and the aching of my body. But most of all, I felt fear for Charles.

Slowly, I opened my eyes, and spotted this elderly feller looking over me. He was dressed in a black suit and tie, had curly black hair and thick whiskers, and he was wearing a plug hat. He sniffed when he saw my eyes open.

"So you're awake then?" he asked, holding out a hand. "Please, can you stand?"

I took his hand and let him help me up. I wavered on my feet a little before standing firm. "Yeah, I reckon I'm okay," I said.

"Are you certain? Looks like you took quite a beating and your assailants left you to expire in the middle of the road. May I inquire as to who did this to you? If you are so inclined to answer, of course."

I looked down the road. There weren't no sign of Hugo Montez, and I weren't expecting none. "Damn," I whispered. "A no good snake-in-the-grass Mexican by the name of Hugo Montez. The varmint is probably over the border by now." I took another gander at my rescuer. He was walking along with a small donkey carrying his supplies next to him, and he was holding a walking stick. Something about him seemed a little bit familiar, like I had seen his picture before.

"I think I may have seen your assailants," my rescuer said, gesturing to the open road. "A bunch of Mexican riders passed me. A gang of ruffians if I ever saw one!"

"Did they have a kid with them? A little boy with glasses and a brown Norfolk suit?" I asked tensely.

The old man nodded. "That they did. Poor little chap, he was. I noticed a large bruise on his face, but he otherwise seemed unharmed."

"Ah hell," I muttered, "They're already beating up Charles even before they feed him to La Llorona!" I looked around. There was no horse for me, and the only animal around was the stranger's mule. I was going to have to walk. At least my knife and revolvers were still lying on the ground. I sheathed the blade and holstered the guns with a spin.

"I'm gonna head on down to Mexico to find them," I said. "That kid is my adopted son. He's a mighty good boy and I can't let anything happen to him."

My rescuer sighed. "I know how it feels to lose a child," he whispered. "Both of my boys died before their time: one in a pointless duel over a romance; the other drank himself into a cold grave." He brightened up. "You know, I was taking a tour of some of my old haunts around this frontier, but I would be honored if you would let me accompany you into Mexico to free your boy. I'm no ace with any weapon, but I've got a good mouth on me."

I was grateful for any help. "I'm much obliged to you sir, but this rescue is gonna take us all the way into the heart of Mexico. I wouldn't ask you to travel across the continent for a feller you just met."

"No trouble!" the old man said with a hearty laugh. "I've been considering wandering away into Mexico for some time. Leaving all of my old false friends and sniveling fans behind and ending my life somewhere beautiful and peaceful. Every man's dream."

"Well, if you feel that way." I held out my hand. "My name's Clark Reeper. I'd be glad to partner up with you. What's your handle?"

"B." he said, and then stuttering, "T-Traven. Yes, B. Traven, that is my name, and that is what you shall call me." He smiled apologetically. "Ah. I'm no good at creating an alias. No, I'll tell you the truth, for I take you for a trustworthy man." He leaned in close to me. "My name is Ambrose Bierce."

"That's a familiar name," I said, trying to place it. "You a gunslinger?"

"Heavens no! I'm an author, a journalist, a writer." He waited expectantly. "The Devil's Dictionary? An Occurrence at Owl Creek Bridge?"

"Haven't heard of them, sir, mighty sorry," I admitted.

"Typical. Perhaps I should have expected this." Ambrose started walking down the path and I followed him. "Well, let's make the best of this. There's a town a few miles down the road, and it will be simple to trade this old donkey in for some faster steeds. Then it's over the border and into Old Mexico." He paused. "Say, do you perchance know where in Mexico your boy's kidnappers have gone to?"

I shook my head sadly. "Ain't got a clue, Mr. Bierce. That's what I'm so worried about. He mentioned something about La Llorona, some ghost or legend, and he also talked about a General Walker."

"Walker?" Bierce asked. "The Texas Ranger?"

"That's him. Know anything about him?"

"Oh, he's one greedy brute! And an opium addict if I recall correctly. Willy Walker was one of the top members of the Texas Rangers before it was revealed that he had been torturing many of his prisoners to obtain confessions, and, as with most tortures, the confessions were rarely truthful."

"What's he doing in Mexico?"

"I believe he fled our country to escape the scandal and became the leader of a mercenary army serving the Mexican Haciendas, the big landlords. I hear he uses his considerable fighting talents to put down would-be insurrectionists. He's currently based in the Yucatán, I think."

"Then that's where we're headed," I said, determination in my voice. "I don't care if I have to kill a Texas Ranger, a Mexican ghost or a jaguar-man. I'm gonna get Charles back."

After purchasing a couple of sturdy horses at the nearest town, we rode across the border and into Mexico. A bucktoothed, old farmer on the border told us he had spotted Hugo Chavez and Charles, who so far hadn't been hurt. That didn't make me feel any better though.

As we followed the trail, me and Ambrose got to talking. I told Ambrose Bierce a little bit more about who I was and how I made my living. I'm not sure he believed everything I said, but he did a good job pretending. Ambrose was a real nice feller, and even though he was mighty old, he neither complained nor slowed me down. He told me about some of his stories, and I promised I would read them when this whole thing was over, and I'd share them with Charles. I also asked him about La Llorona.

"Mexican legend," he said simply. "It's about a woman, a weeping woman, crying because she killed her offspring for some reason. A local superstition, quite colorful."

"Might be more than colorful," I said. "I've got a notion that we're gonna run smack into that La Llorona woman, and only the Devil knows what's gonna come out of it."

We rode straight through the middle of Mexico, not stopping for too long except to take short naps, get some grub, and find out more information about Hugo Montez and his gang. The days passed, and the reports from helpful locals told me Montez was slowing down. By and by, we rode into a dusty cantina in Jalisco. The bartender asked my name. I told him and he said he had a message for me. He handed me a napkin with some words hastily scrawled on it.

"A little boy from El Norte told me to give this to the hombre named Clark Reeper," he said, after I introduced myself. "He was muy asutado."

I looked at the napkin, and read it to myself. "Dear Mr. Reeper, Hugo Montez is taking me east of here to someplace called the Yucatán. I also heard about General Willy Walker, and about some woman called La Llorona. He talks about Zapatistas too, but I'm not sure what those are." My heart clenched up real tight when I read the end of the little note. "I am very scared, but I am trying to be brave and help you rescue me. I love you very much. Yours truly, Charles Green."

"Ah hell," I whispered. "I'm gonna kill that goddamn Hugo Montez! I'm gonna slit his belly and pull his guts out. Kidnapping poor Charles who ain't done nothing to hurt him. Son of a gun, he hurts that boy..."

Ambrose Bierce comforted me. "There, there, old man. We'll free your boy, I'm sure of it. Whatever the La Llorona creature is, I doubt she can hold a candle to the rage of a parent protecting a beloved child."

"La Llorona?" the bartender asked. "Oh, no, my friends, you must not anger La Llorona! She is so powerful! She can kill a man with her cold breath or with her burning scream."

"You know about her?" I asked.

"Oh, sí, sí. Too much perhaps." The bartender sat down behind his bar and poured himself a beer before continuing. "There are many legends about La Llorona. Some say she is La Malinche, the Aztec maid who betrayed her country and let Cortez conquer all of Mexico. Some say she is a poor Indio woman who fell for a rich man. But all the legends have one thing in common." His dark eyes grew wide as he talked. "She had children. Little innocent children. And because the rich man she loved did not want her children and spurned her, she killed them."

"Quite the bloody tale," Ambrose Bierce said. "And I thought The Death of Halpin Frasier was bad. One of my classics, you know." He raised an eyebrow. "So, what happened, exactly?"

"One dark night she took her children to the river, and perhaps stabbed them first, or just threw them in, but she drowned them all. Then she returned to the rich man, her white nightgown stained with their blood, and begged him to take her in. But again, he spurned her, for she was poor and wretched. And then she realized what she had done. She ran back to the river, to her children, but they were all dead. In despair, La Llorona threw herself into the water and took her own life."

"And then?" I asked, a sinking feeling in my chest.

"God cursed her for murdering innocents. He forced her to walk the world, crying and searching for her children, dragging down others to a watery grave if they crossed her tear-stained path. And they say she found a new lover: El Diablo. He gave her his loyal hounds, los cadejos, as friends to accompany her in her travels."

The bartender drained his glass and set it on the table. "If you are searching for La Llorona, you had better stop."

"Not an option, barkeep," I said, coming to my feet and slapping down a five-cent piece. "I'm gonna rescue my kid before La Llorona gets him. No weeping woman is going to stop me. Come on, Ambrose, we done spent too long here."

Ambrose Bierce grabbed his hat and followed me out of the door. My duster flapped in the light wind.

We rode on, getting closer and closer to the Yucatán. The open plains gave way to dense scrubland, and then jungle. Dirt paths snaked through the green expanse, with palm trees, swinging vines, and branches going on for miles. There was nothing to break the monotony of endless trees and foliage except for the occasional rushing river and ancient Mayan ruin.

It was the perfect place to hide, with caves and underground lakes called 'cenotes' hidden in the hills and uninterrupted forests. A feller could hide an army in there. My hopes of finding Charles began to dim as I realized how impossible it would be to fully explore the jungle.

Every so often we would pass a Hacienda, one of them big ranches or plantations owned by the Mexican landlords. Ambrose and I stared at the army of peons clearing land and preparing it for farming. Overseers watched them and cracked whips when the workers weren't to their liking.

"Are they slaves?" I asked. "They sure are treated like slaves, but I thought slavery was outlawed in Mexico."

"They are free, if you can call it that," Ambrose said, leaning back in his saddle. "The landlords work their peons to the grave. They're treated worse than Russian serfs. Look over there," he said, pointing at an overseer cracking his whip on a kid that couldn't be that much older than Charles.

"Why don't we stop them? The United States, I mean. We fought a war to stop slavery, why not stop this serfdom, or whatever it is, right on our borders?"

Ambrose shook his head. "You're a better man than our politicians, Clark. The haciendas sell their crops northward, and America buys them for cheap prices. As long as it serves the interest of Wall Street, the haciendas and their system of peonage will continue unabated and untroubled. Truly, a corporation is an ingenious device for obtaining individual profit without individual responsibility."

"Ah hell," I muttered, urging my horse on.

We were about to leave, when a fat man in a cream-colored suit and a panama hat rode over to us on a large horse. When he saw we were white, he smiled and extended his hands.

"Ah! Americanos! Buenos Dias! I own this hacienda, and I would be very honored to help you with anything. Do you require room, board, women maybe?" He winked.

"We're just passing through," I explained. "Say, have you spotted a couple of gunmen riding by here, led by a feller named Hugo Montez?"

The hacienda owner let out a string of curses in Spanish. "Montez!" he cried. "That revolutionary scum, servant of Zapata. Sí, Americano, he attacked us just two days ago, taking some of my peons with him."

"He's a revolutionary?" I asked. "Doesn't seem the type."

"Oh, Montez and his machetes are the biggest allies in this part of the country of the insane Zapata!" The hacienda owner looked around as if to make sure his workers weren't eavesdropping. "You know, I even hear he has made deals with El Diablo and the spirits to help him. Wild rumors, no doubt, but still."

"They may be a little more than rumors," I said. "Did you see a little kid with him? Ten-years-old, short, with glasses?"

The hacienda owner nodded. "Sí, I could make out a child like that. I did not get too close, because Hugo Montez is muy peligroso. Do not worry about him winning, my American friends. General Walker will see him hang."

"Pray tell, where exactly is Walker located?" asked Ambrose Bierce. "Perhaps he could direct us to Montez's current lair."

"General Walker is in Fort Walker, named after himself," the landlord explained. "It is perhaps half a day's travel down the road. You will find Walker a very capable man, and he will know how to get rid of Hugo Montez."

We thanked the hacienda owner for his help and went on our way. The road continued winding right through a thick jungle. After a couple hours of hard riding, we came to a large wooden palisade that was doubtlessly Fort Walker.

It was a well-made fort, wooden spikes sticking out from the walls to prevent anyone from getting too close, and a metal gate was the only entrance. A couple of guard posts with cannons and Gatling guns peaked out to make a strong defense. There were firing slots for many soldiers to protect the perimeter.

A couple of riflemen spotted us and yelled in Spanish until we told them we didn't mean no harm and just wanted to talk to General Walker. The sentries then noticed we were Americans, and they became real friendly.

"More to join the force, eh?" one of them asked. "Very good! We'll get the gate open, and I'll fetch the General."

"Much obliged," I said, as Ambrose and I walked inside.

The fort was a busy place with soldiers walking around, loading and checking weapons, talking and smoking, and doing other soldierly things. I saw a firing squad doing their grim business, gunning down a row of prisoners without blindfolds in the far corner of the fortress. The soldiers were all sorts: some were Mexicans; others were American or European soldiers of fortune, just like General Willy Walker himself.

He met us right after we had tied up our horses, and I could see the moment I laid eyes upon him that this Texas Ranger wasn't all right in the head. He had thick black hair, and a huge mass of stubble covering his chin. He wore a fancy blue uniform with epaulettes, a sash, a mass of medals and two large revolvers in a holster at his waist. A large campaign hat with a big ostrich feather sticking out of it was perched on his head. He let out a leering grin and held out his hands.

"Ah! More recruits! Come to join the Walker Army and keep these peasant greasers in line, eh? Perfect! Come let me give you the grand tour." He spun around and started pointing out the sights of his fort. "There is the gallows where we do most of our hanging. There is the firing range where we execute prisoners by firing squad. There's the whipping post where we sometimes beat prisoners and there—"

"Sir," I interrupted, trying to be respectful. "We ain't looking for a job. We're just looking to find Hugo Montez."

"Montez." Walker gritted his teeth. "That greaser has been giving me all sorts of trouble. He's my only opposition in this Godforsaken piece of forest. I've tortured hundreds looking for him, but no one's talked yet." He turned to me. "You know something about him?"

"We are not in league with Hugo Montez," Ambrose Bierce said, holding out his hands. "Though, you do seem a little overzealous in your methods, if I do say so. What is the purpose of executing so many prisoners?"

"We gotta discipline these greasers, show them their place." Willy Walker snorted. "It's the only way. Now, what do you want with Hugo Montez?"

"He kidnapped my son," I said angrily. "Little harmless kid only ten-years-old and Hugo Montez said he was gonna give the boy to La Llorona. The poor kid ain't never hurt no one and I got to get him back safe."

Walker nodded. "Yeah, I can see how someone would have a soft spot for children. Some of my men don't want to shoot them. Those are the ones I send away." He let out a raucous laugh before abruptly ending it. "I'll give you guys a job, if you can stomach it, and then when Hugo Montez makes another move against us, we can all go kill him together and then rescue your son. Sound good?"

I turned to Ambrose. "I think we ought to take his offer," I whispered.

"Are you mad, Clark? This fellow obviously is a few bullets short of a clip if you know what I mean. He's positively deranged and I don't think it would be wise to serve under him." Ambrose pointed to Walker, and twisted his finger around to show that the general wasn't right in the head.

"I know he's no good, Ambrose, but this might be the only chance to rescue Charles. I hope Montez hasn't hurt the little guy already..." I trailed off and I guess Ambrose heard the exertion in his voice because he nodded his agreement.

"If you think it will help your son, there's no argument with which I can refute you."

I turned back to Walker. "General, sir, we'll take the job. But as soon as your scouts spot Montez, you let us know."

"Perfect!" Willy Walker smiled, his big teeth white and gleaming. "You can start by joining the firing squad. We're executing a whole convent of nuns who were aiding some of the Zapatistas. Go to the armory and grab a piece and then get shooting!" He laughed madly.

A soldier, a big American feller, ran up to Walker and tapped him on the shoulder. "Sir! Montez and the belligerents have been spotted down at the bend of the river! They're all headed straight for the fort."

"Even better!" Walker started running to the walls. "Join us on the walls, boys, we've got some greasers to massacre!"

Ambrose and I hightailed it to the armory, where a large choice of weapons was awaiting us. I picked up a Winchester lever-action repeating rifle, and Ambrose selected a Springfield. Strangely, he held the gun like he knew how to use it, something I wasn't expecting from the old author.

"I've fought before," he said when he noticed my curious stare. "The War Between The States. It still haunts my nightmares."

"My hats off to you, Ambrose," I said. "Now let's get onto the ramparts. I reckon this will be a one-sided fight, especially when we got everyone in the fort on our side." We headed out of the armory and joined the rest of the soldiers and General Willy Walker up on the wall.

Sure enough, the resistance, the Zapatistas as they were called, was visible in the underbrush. They were a motley group, with a few tough looking pistoleros wearing sombreros and bandoleers. Most of them were short Mayan fellers with antique guns if they were lucky, and machetes, pitchforks and other farming implements if they weren't. They came slinking through the jungle, and I soon spotted Hugo Montez at their head. Charles was not with him, and I felt awful. Had the poor kid already been given to La Llorona?

"Amigos!" Hugo Montez shouted at the fort. "I come to offer you your lives! Surrender now, and you will be spared! I will not chase you as you leave the country!"

"He's lost his mind," General Walker shouted to his men, some sergeants quickly translating his words into Spanish. "Look at his pathetic band of peasants and banditos. We'll blow them apart before they even reach walls!"

"That's not all I have, Señor Walker!" Montez shouted up. "I have begun to make a deal with La Llorona. And in return for a child, she has promised me the services of her loyal hounds, los cadejos!"

At the mention of La Llorona and los cadejos, some of the Mexican soldiers began to talk uneasily amongst themselves. One of them threw down his rifle and held up his hands. Without the slightest hesitation, Walker took out one of his large pistols and shot the surrendering soldier in the chest. He fell off of the wall.

"Pagan superstitions!" Walker said. "I'll have no superstitious men in my army! Now, gun them Zapatistas down!"

With those words, the Gatling guns started up and bullets began to fly down into the jungle while rifleman clattered away. Hugo Chavez just stood there, his arms outstretched. "Come La Llorona!" he called. "Loan me your hounds! Give me a taste of your power, and I will give you the child!"

A harsh wind came from the east, and the Mexican flag in the fort flapped wildly. Thunder rolled over a distant hill, and rain spattered down from the heavens. We were soaked in seconds. The rain came down in torrents and started turning the ground into a pool of mud. And out of the mud came the cadejos. They burst out from the ground like strange plants, dozens of them, as if they had been buried there centuries ago. I spun around and watched as the strange animals experimented with their first steps. They were black dogs, ferocious animals with sharp teeth, beady black eyes, and muscles rippling under their midnight fur. Each cadejo looked a little different. Some of them had hooves instead of claws, some had twisting horns growing out of their skulls, other had their legs and muzzles wrapped in chains that rattled and clanked as they moved.

The creatures began pouring up the ramparts like ravenous wolves. A few of the soldiers spun and fired at them, but the cadejos were just too fast, burying Walker's men under a dark tide of fur and teeth.

"Son of a gun!" I shouted. A cadejo broke off from the pack and came loping towards us, fangs barred. I fired with the Winchester three times, expertly working the lever. It took four slugs to the skull before the creature finally dropped. It fell to the ground, instantly decomposing and rotting away to nothing.

"It's all right!" I told Ambrose, working the lever again and aiming at another incoming cadejo. "They're just big dogs. Easy to put down."

Another advanced towards me, roaring. Out of its mouth shot a snaking steel chain, which wrapped around my arm and dragged me down. The Winchester fell from the hands as I felt my arm being torn in two by the sharp metal. Ambrose brought up his rifle and fired into the black dog's mouth. It howled in pain and fell off of the ramparts.

"Just like Chickamauga, where I served," Ambrose said, working his bolt. "My, there sure are a lot of these hounds, aren't they?"

He was right. The cadejos, though slowed by withering rifle fire, kept on coming. I fired a few more shots with my Winchester, and then went for my Colt Peacemakers, firing one in each hand. Ambrose and I slowly walked backwards, gunning down the charging cadejos with every step.

General Willy Walker still stood at the top of the gate, screaming and hollering and firing his huge revolvers every which way. "They're coming to the gate!" He shouted, sinking some shots below him. "The damn greasers will take the fort!" But his men were too busy fighting the cadejos to care.

A particularly large cadejo, a bipedal critter that was swinging its chain like a morning star, leapt down for General Walker. I squeezed both triggers at once and sent the dog toppling over the side of wall, decomposing as it fell.

"Ah, thank you, new recruit!" Walker said, laughing. "What are these stinking dog beasts?"

"Cadejos," Ambrose explained. "Though I think Bharghest, Gytrash, Black Shuck, or simply Hell Hound would be an equally accurate epithet."

"General," I said urgently. "We ain't gonna be able to hold them. And the resistance outside is breaking in." That weren't no lie. Hugo Montez's rebels were laying down dynamite

charges, preparing to blow the gate down and get inside. The soldiers and mounted guns that would have stopped them were too busy dealing with the cadejos.

"Well, we've got no choice but to blow up the fort!" The General laughed as he handed me a single stick of dynamite. "Toss this in the armory and then get the hell out of here. I'll round up whatever survivors I can find and we'll meet up outside." He went running off down the wall, kicking aside a snapping cadejo at his heels.

"I reckon we better do it," I said, staring at the dynamite. "Come on, Ambrose, let's get a move on."

We ran down from the ramparts and headed towards the armory. It was slow going with all the cadejos in the way, and I got a couple of painful bites on my arm before I could fend them off with my revolvers. We got about halfway to the armory before the gate blew up and Montez's men began their assault. They let loose a couple of volleys, forcing us to duck for cover. The Zapatistas ran through the shattered gate and joined the fight.

I scored a headshot through a Mayan's headband as Ambrose and I ducked behind the gallows. The armory was just a couple of steps away, when I heard a familiar growl behind us. It was Tequila Tim, now carrying one of them Aztec obsidian swords and dressed only in a loose loincloth and headdress.

"Get along, Ambrose," I said, bringing up both of my revolvers. "Me and the cat have some business to attend to."

"The cat?" Ambrose asked. "I'd better not ask." He headed off, carrying the stick of dynamite under his arm.

Tequila Tim leapt into the air, neatly avoiding all six of my first shots. He twisted like a cat, landing on his feet and struck out at me with his obsidian sword. I ducked it and fired at his legs, one bullet luckily grazing his foot. The Nagual struck downwards, slashing my chest and making me holler like a stuck pig. Before I fell backwards, I managed to aim and send two bullets straight in Tim's chest.

"Out of nine lives yet?" I asked, laughing.

In answer, Tequila Tim hurled his obsidian sword at my head. It scraped the top of my skull and pinned my hat to the ground. Then he was on me, his skin becoming slick fur and his hands turning into claws. I felt him digging into my flesh and cutting too deep for me to walk away. My hand slipped down to my boot, drawing out the Bowie knife I kept there. I had been saving it just for him.

I stabbed the thick blade into Tim's chest, and then kicked him with both legs to throw him off of me. The big cat went down in a heap, blood matting his pelt. In an instant he was up again, charging at me. My guns were empty and I didn't have no knife. I spun around looking for some kind of weapon, and then I spotted the gallows.

The noose was tied already and the trapdoor was set to spring. I clambered over the gallows, putting myself right below the noose, and prayed Tequila Tim was too angry and wounded to see what I was planning. Sure enough, the jaguar leapt into the air to pounce on me. Instead of landing on me, his body got stuck in the noose, the rope closing around his middle and suspending him in air. I rolled away from his slashing claws, pulled out my Bowie knife, took one more look at the thrashing cat, and planted the blade in his face. I wiped the blood off on his fur and left him swinging there, still stuck in the form of a jaguar. Blood covered my chest and the scratches the Nagual had made were mighty bad. I could feel myself swaying.

"Ambrose?" I called as I walked to the armory. "Where are you?"

There was no answer, and I knew I didn't have the strength to go on walking. I sank down to the ground just as Ambrose's dynamite went off. I could see a wall of fire coming towards me as the explosion ripped through the fort.

"Son of a gun!" I shouted. With my last ounce of strength, I threw myself on the ground and covered my head with my hands.

I woke up slowly, the light cracking in through my closed eyelids. Slowly, I opened them, and took a look around. My body felt pretty bad, but nothing I couldn't walk off after a strong drink. Old Ambrose Bierce was still in my mind. The old feller must have died when Fort Walker blew sky high. Poor guy.

I was in a tent of some sort, lying down in a cramped cot. The place was illuminated by a small lantern hanging from the top of the tent, and I could make out some packs of supplies lying under my cot. Slowly, I turned around and my mouth fell open when I saw who was there beside me.

It was Charles Green, his Norfolk jacket resting on top of him like a blanket and his glasses resting inside his peaked cap, which lay by his head. He was very still, and for a while I got real scared, until I noticed his chest rising and falling evenly. He was sound asleep.

Not wanting to wake him, I stood up to find a way out. My revolvers and Bowie knife had been removed, but there was nothing holding me down. I pulled aside the tent flap and walked outside. It was dark, the moon and stars glimmering down from above. Several other tents surrounding a campfire convinced me that I was in the Zapatista encampment. A couple of Montez's men were sleeping around the fire, and I tiptoed around them.

A bit away from the encampment, there were two voices, one of them belonging to Hugo Montez and the other to a woman, arguing about something in Spanish. I followed the voices and crouched behind a tree, getting a good view of Montez and the woman he was talking to. She was a real beauty, hair as dark as the night sky and dressed only in a loose white nightgown. I saw tears covering her face and rusty brown bloodstains on her bedclothes.

"Yo no quiero dolerlo!" Montez was shouting, angrily gesturing with one of his machetes. "El es un chico bueno!" I got the idea he was denying her something, or trying to.

The woman sadly shook her head. "Usted hizo una promisa. Neccisito al nino." Her voice was mournful and sad, but she seemed determined.

Hugo Montez raised his machete and slashed down at her, but the woman expertly bent backwards like she didn't have a spine and avoided the blade. Then she pressed her palm against his chest and held it there. Montez began coughing and gargling, like he was drowning or something, and the machete fell from his hand.

The woman held him like that for a couple of seconds and then let go. Montez doubled over, a gallon or two of water pouring out of his mouth. I couldn't believe what I was seeing. The woman was La Llorona!

"I want the child," she said, in English this time, and then strode away, her hands on her hips. I ran over and helped Hugo Montez to his feet.

"Gracias," he said before he got wind of who I was.

"Señor Reeper!" he cried. "You don't understand, you don't know what is going on here!"

"I don't speak much Spanish, amigo," I said. "But it was plain as day what was going on. That was La Llorona and you just told her off. Judging that Charles is still breathing air and not water, I reckoned you didn't want to give my boy up."

Montez nodded. "He is such a good boy, and very loyal to you. Do you know he tried to escape so many times I had to restrain him? It was one of the hardest things I have ever done. And when he saw what life is like down here in the Yucatán, he agreed with what we were doing, and even wanted to help!" Montez sighed. "La Llorona would give him a slow, painful death. I don't want that to happen. But we made a deal!"

"Can't you just tell her the deal's off?"

"No, señor. I gave her my word that I would bring her a child, and I already used her hounds to destroy Fort Walker. She would kill me if I refused."

I narrowed my eyes. "So it's you or Charles. Well, Hugo, you did try and kill me a bunch of times, and I care about Charles more than anything else in the world. I think I'm going to take him, hightail it out of here, and let her have you."

Hugo Montez sighed deeply. "You know, Clark. I can't blame you." He kneeled down on the jungle floor and set his machetes down beside him. "You may leave. Your weapons are in a basket near the tent. I'll fight her when she comes, but I don't think I will win." He looked up at me, and the scars that lined his face were pale in the moonlight. "I'll pray to the Virgin of Guadalupe, but I've committed too many sins for her to hear me."

I turned around and left him there, thanking whatever saints and gods they worship down here for helping Montez make the right decision. I ran back to the camp, ready to save Charles and get the hell out of here. The boy was still asleep, and I gently tickled his chin until he woke up.

"Clark?" he asked. "Oh Clark!" We embraced, and I picked him up and held him. "I knew you'd come!" Charles said to me.

"Yeah," I agreed. "Okay, get your jacket on, and I'll get my guns, and then we'll steal a horse and get out of here."

"Okay!" Charles raced to get dressed while I found my tools outside, just where Hugo Montez said they were. Charles met me outside, and I held his hand tightly as we snuck out to where some horses were kept.

"What happened to Hugo?" Charles asked. "Did you kill him?"

"No," I said. "He let you go."

Charles nodded. "I knew he would. He acts mean, but he's a nice guy. Like you. Did you know that his wife was killed by General Walker? He told me that when I asked him why Walker and him were fighting..." Charles trailed off. "What's going to happen to Hugo?"

I thought of him, sitting out there and waiting for death to find him. "He's given himself up to save you."

"Oh..." Charles squeezed my hand. "Oh God. He doesn't deserve to die, Mr. Reeper. I like him. Even if he does act mean, he doesn't deserve to die!"

"I'm mighty sorry, Charles, but there ain't nothing I can do. La Llorona's got to have someone to drown."

Charles thought for a little, putting his hand on his chin. "Let me talk to her. I've heard the story about why she's so sad, and why she needs to kill children. Maybe I can convince her not to."

"Hell no," I said without thinking. "I just rescued you from that ghost woman, and I ain't letting her get you again!"

"Please, Clark, I know I can help her!" Charles's eyes were big and wet behind his spectacles. "It's better than letting her just kill Hugo!"

"She's insane, Charles. She'll kill you on sight! Son of a gun, we can't save Hugo!"

Charles stopped walking. "I'm not leaving. I can't let him die like this!" There was a lot of determination in his high voice, and I was wondering if I would have to forcibly carry him out of here.

Then a messenger ran in, an old Mayan feller on a mule. He was swaying in the saddle and had a wound in his chest. "Ayuda! Ayuda!" he shouted. "Ellos veinen!"

The fellers in the camp, grizzled Zapatista veterans of the battle before, as well as some new recruits, woke up and sprang to action. Charles and I ducked behind a fallen log and watched. The man on the mule slid off, clutching his chest. It was covered in blood. Hugo Montez ran out from the forest, clutching both of his machetes, and ran over to the man.

"What's happening?" he asked.

"General Walker..." the old man wheezed. "He is coming with an army, ten times the size of what we destroyed in his fort. They are killing...all in their path." With that the old man gave out a final cough and died.

Montez shook his head and then shouted to his men. "We'll hide in the jungle! Meet them here! We will catch them by surprise and destroy them! Come on, amigos, Tierra y Libertad!"

"Tierra y Libertad!" Montez's soldiers cried holding their weapons high.

"Please, Clark," Charles whispered to me. He was so pitiful, just a little boy asking to me save someone's life. I relented. I stood up and walked over to Hugo Montez, who was staring at me with wide eyes and an open mouth.

"Charles thinks he can tell off La Llorona," I said. "Here's what's gonna happen: all three of us are going to meet her together, and I'll let Charles say his piece, then we'll leave and you'll be on your own. That's all you're gonna get, and you're lucky you're getting that. Understand?"

"Sí, sí. I could not ask for anything more." Hugo Montez nodded his head and smiled at Charles. "You have an honorable son, Señor Reeper. In the meantime what will you do about General Walker?"

"Well, I'll get Charles somewhere safe and then we'll fight him together, I reckon," I said. "Got to keep you alive for La Llorona, after all."

Hugo Montez showed me a good hiding spot for Charles, inside the hollow of a large rotting log. We put some blankets down to make Charles comfortable and I told him very clearly not to come out during the fight that was about to break out.

"Don't worry, Mr. Reeper," Charles said as he lay in the log. "I can convince La Llorona. I know just what to say to her. She'll believe me."

"Whatever you say, son," I said. "But I won't let her get you, that's for sure."

We embraced and then Hugo and me went off to find a place to hide. We climbed up a tall tree hanging over the jungle path and waited for General Walker to come marching down. We didn't have to wait long.

General Willy Walker and his gang of Mexican soldiers, foreign mercenaries and down-right mean thugs came down the road in neat columns. There was a lot of more of them this time, all armed to the teeth. He even had a big artillery piece dragged along by a couple of mules.

I drew out my revolvers and held them ready, aiming them at the middle of the column. "Not yet, Señor Reeper," Hugo Montez said. "I will strike the first blow, then the barrage will follow."

We waited for a few more tense seconds, and then Hugo Montez nodded. He leapt into the air, a machete gleaming in each hand, and landed straight in the middle of Walker's troops. He stabbed and hacked, separating limbs from bodies and tearing men apart. I opened fire with both of my Peacemakers and didn't stop until I needed to reload.

The Zapatistas in the woods came charging out, some wielding cudgels and pitchforks, while others hung back and fired. It was chaos in Walker's army as his men struggled to find cover and start shooting. I saw more men charging in to intercept Montez, and then recognized General Walker at their head. He was wearing a metal breastplate on his chest and had a large sword on his belt; in his hands, his two massive revolvers blazed away like miniature cannons.

I jumped down to get him, falling to my knees and blasting him with both pistols. Willy Walker laughed madly as the bullet pinged harmlessly off of his steel armor.

"Well, if it isn't my old soldier!" he bellowed, scratching his beard. "Looks like you chose the wrong side! Shouldn't be messing with Walker, Texas Ranger!"

He ran towards me, leapt into the air and delivered a spinning kick straight to my jaw. I went down and he pressed his big pistol to my head. "Sorry, partner," he cackled. "Just the way it's gotta be!"

Then a shot rang out and Walker's gun fell from his hands. He spun around and we both saw Ambrose Bierce standing there, a smoking rifle in his hands. "You're the reason war is so unbearable, you pugnacious cretin!" Ambrose said, working the bolt of his Springfield. "It would be my honor to kill you!"

Walker let out a roar of rage and fired faster than Ambrose could. The old writer gasped and sank down, grasping his wounded shoulder. The manic general let out another laugh and spun back to me, drawing out his sword. "No distractions this time!"

He brought the sword down, and I figured I was finished, but a machete blocked Walker's blade. It was Hugo Montez, a glaring hatred in his eyes.

"I've been waiting a long time for this, gringo general," he said, pushing Walker's sword back. "Let's go."

They clashed right in the middle of the fight, Walker's long sword wailing down, only to be blocked by Montez's shorter machetes. The Mexican and the Soldier of Fortune hacked at each other without mercy, not slowing down or stopping for a second; there was no sound except for steel on steel, and then a shout of pain as Walker's sword slashed down and cut Montez's cheek. Walker twisted down and nearly cut off the Mexican bladesman's arm, but Hugo stepped backward and sliced sideways with both of his machetes, scratching the stainless steel of Walker's breastplate.

"You killed my wife," Hugo said viciously, as the two foes circled. "You killed her in cold blood!"

"I don't doubt you," Walker answered. "I've killed so many of you greasers, men, women and kids. I can't tell you apart no more."

Montez let out a cry of rage and leapt into the air, his machete poised like a scorpion's stinger. He hacked downwards with one, found it blocked by Walker's sword, and then slashed with the other, cutting off Walker's sword hand. The American General howled in pain as blood poured out of his wrist. He fell to his knees, and Montez drew back his arm for the killing blow.

"I've killed so many gringos. I can't tell you apart no more," Montez whispered. "But this one I will remember." He drove his machete straight through General Walker's skull so that it stuck out the other side, bits of brain matter still clinging to the blade.

After that, the battle was pretty much won. The remaining mercenaries pointed at Walker's corpse and turned to run. They were only in it for the money, anyway. The Mexican soldiers were just terrified conscripts who were trying to get out alive. Soon as Walker went down, they started shouting the call to retreat and fled, leaving the victorious Zapatistas behind.

I ran over to Ambrose, who already was being attended to by a Mayan medicine man. "Thanks, buddy," I said. "You saved my life back there."

"That I did…" Bierce wheezed. "Now perhaps I have traded my own in. A fair trade, I think."

"Ah, you ain't gonna die," I said, looking at his wound. "The bullet just clipped you is all."

"Perhaps I shall live," Bierce mused. "But what of it? There's simply nothing left to do with my life."

"What about writing?" I asked. "I'm sure all this must give you a little inspiration."

"But the preconceptions about my name!" Bierce shook his head. "They'll think of Ambrose Bierce and their opinions will inevitably be biased!"

"You could use an alias," I reasoned. "B. Traven, that's what you called yourself when you met me, right? Nobody would be able to question that if it was on the cover of a book."

"Perhaps you're right," Ambrose agreed. "Yes. B. Traven. I like the sound of it."

Hugo Montez ran over to me. "Clark! Come quick! It's Charles!"

I left Ambrose lying on the ground and followed Hugo to the log where Charles had been hiding during the fight. It was empty, and there were thick pools of water on the ground. I stuck my finger into one and tasted it. Salt, like tears.

"It's her," Hugo said. "La Llorona!"

"I know, damn it!" I clenched my fist. "We gotta go rescue him. Where is she?"

"There's a clearing nearby. That's where she would speak to me." Hugo was up and running and I was following him.

The cadejos were waiting for us, dozens of them along the forest path. Not having time to fight them, I drew out my pistols and fired as I ran; Hugo Montez hurled one of his machetes, decapitating a cadejo, and kept up with me. The big black hounds couldn't stand up against us, not with the fury that was in our hearts. Every bullet I fired was a direct hit, and every slash Hugo made was a killing blow.

We made it to the clearing and stopped to stare at the sight that greeted us. There was La Llorona, her white, blood-stained nightgown dim in the forest light. Charles was standing next to her, and she had her hand on his chest. The poor kid was coughing and wheezing and didn't look like he would live for very long.

"Let him go!" I yelled, firing my remaining shots and throwing myself on top of her. It was like punching into a brick wall. I fell to the ground, La Llorona still pressing her palm to Charles's heaving little chest.

"Please!" I cried, pounding my fists against La Llorona's legs. "The boy already lost his father! He's an orphan, he ain't got nothing in this world and I ain't got nothing but him! Don't you hurt my boy! Please, ma'am, don't you hurt Charles!"

She stopped. "He's an orphan?" she asked in un-accented English. "No parents..."

Slowly, she let go of Charles's chest. The boy fell into my arms, coughing out a lake and half of cold black water. I held him close to me.

"Orphan," she said slowly. "Just like me, a mother with no children, and he's a child with no mother." She cried again, the tears running down her nightgown. "I should have killed myself before I killed my children!"

"Ma'am?" Charles asked. He looked sick, and his round face was pale and wan. He felt limp in my hands. "Ma'am, you shouldn't go around hurting people. It's not nice, and they haven't done anything to you."

"El Diablo makes me do it," La Llorona said. "He made me a ghost, a monster, something for parents to scare their children with. That is my duty."

"But you don't have to do it!" Charles replied, surprising me with his energy. "Children already have too many things trying to hurt them. In Chicago, I hear that they make a lot of the kids work in big factories, and they get cut up and hurt on the unsafe machines, and here in Mexico, Hugo Montez told me that kids get executed by the armies that are fighting all over the place, and in Russia my father used to say there were pogroms and the Cossacks would kill children, and that's why he left!" He crossed his arms. "The world doesn't need you, La Llorona. There are plenty of real boogey men and women to hurt innocent kids."

Slowly, the weeping woman nodded. "You are right. I will tell El Diablo what you have told me, and then maybe my torment will be over." She turned around, her black hair flying as she did, and then she walked off, still weeping, into the jungle.

Charles needed a couple of days of rest to recover. I was mighty proud of him for convincing La Llorona to leave us alone. I was also mighty glad that Charles hadn't been hurt too bad. I told him that he was the smartest feller I ever knew and that he would have a bright future as an author or professor. He turned red when I talked about him like that, and said I was embarrassing him, which I guess is something parents ought to do now and then.

Hugo Montez apologized so many times in English and Spanish that I had to give him a little punch on the jaw to make him stop. He and his Zapatistas were going to fall back deeper into the jungle and hook up with the main army led by Emiliano Zapata himself. Chavez didn't know if they could beat the hacienda owners, who had the money and guns, but he said they would try their damnedest. Those Zapatistas were determined to fight for more than a hundred years if needed. I told him that they would probably get their 'Tierra and Libertad' before that, but he wasn't so sure.

Ambrose Bierce decided he would stay with them. "I'm going to be writing a series of books dealing with the problems the peons and peasants of Mexico face, and possibly chronicling their revolution," he explained. "All under the name of B. Traven. I might even work Clark Reeper in there, if I get the chance."

And so Charles and me headed out and went back up north to the American side of the border. He told me that maybe La Llorona was wrong when she said he was an orphan, because he weren't; he had me to take care of him. Well, that was about the nicest thing he could say to me.

I've been getting some more telegrams from all over the country. Some whacko cult in Texas is supposedly stockpiling dangerous weapons and preparing to attack the government, a feller by the name of John Muir said he needed me to help him deal with some prehistoric creatures crawling around a cave system underneath the Valley of Yosemite in California, and there's even something about fish-people taking over a little New England town.

But maybe I'll put all of those jobs off for now now. Charles ain't an orphan any more, and I reckon I ain't all alone in the world either. I've got me a child, and I really owe it to him to keep him safe and happy. It's probably the hardest thing to do, but I think it will also be the best.

The Elephant

Now, I'm not the kind of feller who cares much about animals.
I'm not cruel by nature, and you won't catch me kicking horses
or whipping mules, but I see them critters as tools and nothing
more. Hell, this one time I used a mule with dynamite strapped
to its backs as a mobile bomb to blow my way into a demon-
infested mission down in California, but that's another story.
A man in my line of work can't afford to go carrying on about
every beast I have to put down. You see, I'm a bounty hunter,
specializing in the odder jobs out there.

I've also got to look out for more than my own well being.
I've got an adopted son, a little ten-year-old boy by the name
of Charles Green. He's a kind-hearted kid who has a different
opinion about animals. This one time he even befriended a
giant squid that was ravaging San Francisco, but again, that's
a different story. Charles and me are about as different as light
and day. I'm a gaunt, tall gentleman with a long tan duster on my
back, a weathered Stetson on my head and two six-guns at my
waist. Charles is small for his age, has a head of curly brown hair
under a peaked cap and wears a little Norfolk suit and tie, with
thick spectacles over his eyes.

Thinking differently about animals was what caused the
problem about what to do with Thomas A. Edison's elephant.
That's right, Edison's elephant. Seems the inventor had one in
New York he wanted put down, and he was willing to pay me
top dollar to do it. But Charles and I had differing opinions on
the matter.

"Elephant's just a brute," I explained. "Best to just kill the
damn thing and move on." We were on the train to New York,

zooming along at a good clip, and Edison was supposed to be waiting for us with an automobile at the station.

"Animals are a lot smarter than we think they are," Charles said, his small voice high with excitement. "I mean, dogs can feel emotions, and an elephant, a big animal, must be able to do and feel lots of stuff!"

"Have you ever seen an elephant?" I asked, sort of changing the subject. I liked Charles and it didn't appeal to me to be arguing with him.

Charles shook his head. "Never. What's one doing in New York, anyway?"

"I don't rightly know," I said, truthfully. "I reckon we'll find out soon enough."

The train rumbled to a stop past some adverts for an Aleister Crowley speaking tour, and sure enough, Thomas Alva Edison was there at the station, dressed in a black suit and coat, with a cane between his hands just like I had seen him in the photographs. He was an elderly feller with wavy white hair and a stern expression. When he noticed me, he raised his hand slightly, and Charles and I walked on over.

"Ah! Mr. Reeper! I have quite the situation for you. I am so glad that you could come on such short notice. I am afraid that the phenomenon I have unwittingly unleashed may grow to truly elephantine proportions."

"I'm here to help, Mr. Edison, sir." We shook hands, and then I introduced Charles.

Edison and Charles looked at each other before shaking hands. "Are you going to have Mr. Reeper kill an elephant?" Charles asked, a lilt of nervousness in his voice.

"I am."

"That's kind of mean. It's just an elephant. Maybe you could show it a little mercy—"

"Nature is merciless, indifferent. Electricity, boy, that's where the future is." Edison snorted as he walked away with Charles and me following. "Hmmph! Nature-lovers! Worse than Tesla and his utopian daydreams," the great inventor continued. "Practicality, boy, that's where the future is, simple practicality."

We came to a parked automobile, a massive horseless carriage with an enclosed compartment that could seat a gaggle of people. Edison sat down and motioned us to be seated. The curtains of the car closed, and Edison began fiddling with an odd looking metal apparatus in the center of the automobile.

"Here's an invention I doubt the world is ready for—a film projector built inside an automobile." Edison finished getting the machine set up and stuck in a reel of film.

"Sounds mighty entertaining. Why do you think we ain't ready for it?"

"Distraction. It could take the mind off driving, and will lead to countless accidents. But for us it is a necessity. Please, Mr. Reeper, watch the moving pictures."

He spun a crank and the projector went to work. I had been in a moving picture palace before, but that was just a dirty nickelodeon in Chicago. This was something else. The picture was projected in grainy green waves inside the dark automobile, and we watched a show as we automobubbled along.

The movie showed several men surrounding the silhouette of a great elephant. As the film continued, Edison narrated. "This is Topsy, the elephant I mean." Topsy was a real big looking critter, with tusks and flapping ears and a curling trunk. I had seen pictures of elephants before, but never moving and active like in this film. "Topsy is, or was I should say, a female elephant performer at the Luna Amusement Park on Coney Island," Mr. Edison continued.

"You killed her?" Charles asked. He squeezed my hand.

"She had to be killed, son. She became enraged, as of late and has killed three people, making her a particularly pernicious pachyderm. In order to demonstrate the dangers of the Alternate Current as opposed to my benevolent and liberating Direct Current, I proposed to have the beast electrocuted using the Alternate Current. For posterity, and advertising purposes, I captured the event on film. The public has a right to know that Alternate Current electricity is dangerous in the extreme."

The projection continued, and suddenly, the elephant sagged and collapsed. Charles gasped and I gulped. It was real queer seeing something so big and powerful one moment and lying there dead a split second later.

"This is the portion of the film that will be shown around the country. But the last segment will be deleted. You'll soon see why." Edison pointed to the projection. There was Topsy, sprawled on the ground, but then, the elephant suddenly reared up. After a few minutes, she raised her tusks and charged forward. The dead elephant had come back to life! Some men tried to restrain her, but Topsy smashed them under her feet, gored them with her tusks and tore one in half with her trunk. Then she stood up, waving her feet in the air, and sent out a blast of lightning from her tusks into an unfortunate bystander. The poor man wriggled like a hooked fish and then lay still. Charles and I looked on in amazement.

"You see," Edison explained, "Topsy's diet contained a large amount of magnesium and other metals that are excellent conductors of electricity. The beast is now completely electrified, able to harness the deadly power of Alternate Current at will, as well as use it to project kinetic force from her own body."

Topsy slammed her two feet down onto the ground. Each footfall caused a miniature explosion, and the shockwave sent the elephant zooming into the air. She was jumping so high that she was plumb flying! The projection ended seconds after Topsy jumped up.

Edison switched off the machine and turned to me. "The police have evacuated Coney Island and sealed it off, but there are still a few people inside. It would be a waste of breath for me to describe the negative publicity we'd get if Topsy is not put down post-haste."

"Negative publicity?" I asked. "I figure it could be a hell of a lot worse than that!"

"That's why you're here, Mr. Reeper. You will enter Coney Island, find the elephant, and terminate it. Proper weaponry will be provided for you, and proper payment will come at the end of the job." Edison fixed me with a steely gaze. "Can you handle this, Mr. Reeper?"

I nodded. "Mr. Edison, I reckon I can."

Edison dropped us off right in front of Coney Island. It was where New Yorkers came to relax, and it was one of the weirdest looking places I had ever seen. There were flashing lights, Ferris wheels that seemed to touch the top of the sky and roller coasters that creaked and groaned. The rides were usually all filled with excited guests and folks in colorful costumes, but today they were empty.

A group of cops in round helmets stood at the entrance, nervously looking into the amusement island and fidgeting with their rifles. One of them handed Edison a powerful rifle, which was twice as tall as little Charles. Edison handed it to me.

"An elephant gun, borrowed from President Roosevelt's former quarters. He likes it and wants it back." It was a mighty gun, with warthog ivory sights, and I could feel its raw power just by looking at it. It fired bullets that could tear a man in two, and they were perfect for taking out big game, even though the recoil could break a feller's shoulder if he weren't careful. I hefted the rifle on my back and felt its weight.

"Good luck, Mr. Reeper," Edison said, pointing at the entrance to the island. "Show that beast what for!"

I nodded and off we went. Luna Park, featuring some kind of Moon theme, was the first amusement park we visited. There were rides that looked like space-flying machines with flapping wings and such; and the ground was pocked with craters and dust so that it resembled the surface of the Moon. Charles and I wandered through an empty midway, looking at all the flashing lights and stands selling 'Chester's Moon Cheese' and other goodies.

We walked for a long time in that blinking, flashing wonderworld before saying anything. "Are you going to shoot Topsy the elephant?" Charles asked, nearly tripping over a crater.

"I reckon I am. Topsy's a dangerous critter."

"I don't know if you should. They were trying to kill her! You can't blame her for defending herself."

I put a hand on Charles's shoulder. "Look, this elephant's killed three people already, and four in the projection we just saw. That means its killed seven men. Gunfighters like Doc Holiday ain't killed that many!"

"You have, though..." Charles seemed to regret saying those words. "Mr. Reeper, I um, didn't mean to say that you were—"

"Don't fret, son. I've killed a hell of a lot of things, and I hope Jesus forgives me, but I never spilled innocent blood if I could help it or killed a feller when I oughtn't to. Still, I get what you're saying."

I stopped walking and sniffed the air. "You smell something?"

Charles sniffed, his little nose widening as he stood on his tiptoes. "Peanuts."

"Yeah, and something else." I spotted a large peanut stand—Paul's Moonuts. Munching on the bags of peanuts with her long trunk was Topsy.

She seemed even bigger in real life, a great gray giant with sorrowful black eyes, four massive legs, a pair of tusks, flopping ears like a Southern lady's fan, and a long snakelike trunk. There seemed to be something extra shiny about her, like she had been given a spit and polish, and I swore there were tiny sparks coming off her gray hide. Topsy looked mighty peaceful just sitting there, eating those peanuts, and it didn't seem like she would hurt a fly.

I kneeled down and drew out the elephant gun. "Charles," I said. "Maybe I don't want to do this, but I took the job and I gotta finish it. Go on back to the Moon Cheese stand and wait for me there. You don't have to see this."

Charles looked like he was about to raise a protest, but then he nodded, took one long look at Topsy, and ran off.

I looked through the ivory sights and got a fix on Topsy, aimed right for her big skull, and fired. The recoil sent me sprawling to the ground, nearly tearing my shoulder out. I saw the bullet fly out towards the great elephant.

Then, in the blink of an eye, a bolt of lightning flashed out of Topsy's tusks and intercepted the bullet. The piece of lead balled up and fell harmlessly into a fake crater.

"Ah, hell." I stood up and started to run, yanking a bullet out of my belt and trying to stick it into the breech-loading elephant gun while running, a mighty difficult maneuver. Topsy let out a ferocious trumpet blast from her trunk and charged after me, lightning crackling from her body. Nearby shops and stands burst into flames.

"Charles!" I shouted, as Topsy trumpeted again. "We gotta get out of here!"

I turned the corner, Topsy right behind me, and spotted Charles munching on a piece of moon cheese. He dropped the greenish cheese, wiped the crumbs from his face, and started running. Soon we were next to each other, the elephant pounding behind us. I had another bullet in the elephant gun and was ready to put Topsy down.

"Keep on running, Charles," I said, panting. "I'm gonna give this elephant something she'll wish she could forget." I spun around, worked the bolt, and fired at point blank range. The recoil sent me flying, and I knew I'd have some bad bruises the next morning.

Topsy's trunk trumpeted a pain-filled call and she tumbled to the ground. I stood up and smiled, looking at the big critter just lying there in a pile of dust with a big bloody gash in her chest. Just as I was about to inspect my kill, Topsy shook off the dust and stood back up. The gash seemed to be sewn together with flickering sparks and disappeared. I gulped.

I started running again. Apparently, the elephant gun would not be enough. I began looking for some form of cover that would hold up to an electrified raging elephant. A large tower, some kind of observatory, caught my attention. I started running for it, Charles close behind me.

"Why haven't you killed her yet?" Charles asked, panting as he ran. I could tell he couldn't go much further so I picked him up and threw him over my back.

"This animal's tougher than any bison, bear, or sasquatch, and these here bullets just don't do much damage. Come on, we're gonna hole up in that tower and think of something else."

The tower was some kind of "Aeroplane to the Moon" mechanical contraption. A maintenance ladder was the only way to the top when the contraption wasn't moving. I pushed Charles up and got the boy climbing. Then I started up myself. We made good headway, getting about halfway up the tower before Topsy charged and crashed into the base.

The tower shook violently and we held on for dear life. But then Charles lost his grip and fell off, screaming as he went. I leaned back and grabbed his hand, holding him there as Topsy continued ramming into the tower and shaking it every which way.

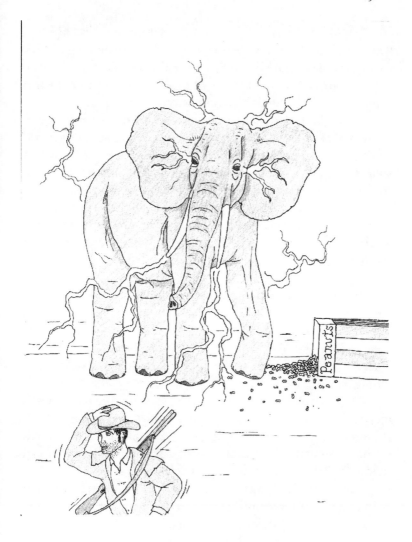

"Hold on, Charles," I shouted, struggling to lift him up, while holding the boy with one hand and the elephant gun with the other. Even though Charles was light and was probably the most important thing in the world to me, I could feel my grip slipping away. I needed the damn tower to stop shaking.

I aimed the elephant gun and fired. The shock of the recoil nearly knocked me off, but the bullet sailed out and hit its mark. There was a large plaster moon overlooking the tower, and as soon as the gun's round crashed through the supporting beam, the entire sculpture came tumbling down right on top of Topsy.

The elephant bellowed and ran off, giving me just enough time to swing the big rifle on my back and pull Charles to safety. We both quickly scampered up the rungs until we came to the top of the tower. There was a small viewing portal that gave us a view over all of Coney Island.

"Now do you believe that elephant's trouble?" I asked Charles.

"I guess so," Charles whispered, but he seemed unconvinced. "But it did seem like Topsy was defending herself against you. There must be a better way to get her under control without killing her."

"Nah," came an angry, familiar voice from behind a model moon. "Elephant ain't the problem. It's the stinking horse that's the problem!" I drew out one of my Peacemakers and aimed at the diminutive devil that walked out from behind a model moon. Well, he wasn't a devil, he was just dressed as one.

The little man in the red jumpsuit, sporting tin horns, and holding a pitchfork in one hand and a derringer in the other, was my old foe Little Napoleon. He was a midget, dwarf, or whatever you want to call it, and he had ridden with the Sideshow Gang, a group of former circus freaks who had turned to crime.

"Clark Reeper," he said, his voice squeaky and snarling. "What a pleasure! Last time we met, you had sold me to P.T. Barnum as a creature from Mars. Maybe I ought to get a little vengeance!"

"Don't you try nothing, Napoleon," I said. "I ain't gunning for you, I'm hunting elephant, so stay out of my way."

"Well, that's the thing, ain't it?" Little Napoleon walked a little closer, a grin still on his face. "You see, I know what's making Topsy so angry, and I know what led to her getting electrified. There's a whole conspiracy you don't even know about! Nobody knows about it but me!"

"You mentioned something about a horse?" Charles asked.

"Yeah, a goddamn horse by the name of Clever Hans, from Germany. After P.T. Barnum let me go, no thanks to you, I ended up here in Coney, working the stands in the Dreamland Amusement Park. That's where I met Hans. Everyone thinks I'm crazy, but I've watched that stinking pack animal, I've seen the signs, and I know what's what."

"Hold on," I said. "You say a horse is responsible? The kind of horse you ride?"

"Yeah, I said it. You think I'm nuts too, huh?" Little Napoleon shook his head grimly. "Well, tell you what, big guy, I'll show you what I mean, and in return, you give me half of Edison's reward."

I turned to Charles, who nodded. "We have to learn more about what's going on before we shoot anything," he said.

"Okay, Napoleon, I give." I holstered my pistol and so did he. Then we shook hands. Little Napoleon pointed to a rope hanging off of the end of the viewing platform. "Just shimmy down and you'll be in Dreamland. That's where I work and that's where Clever Hans is."

"Say, Little Napoleon, how come you're in that get-up as a devil?" I asked, helping Charles get on to the rope.

"Well, Clark, all of these amusement parks have a theme. Luna Park's theme is the moon, but Dreamland's a little something closer to earth."

That theme happened to be Hell. There were large wrought-iron gates, and pitchforks and fire-pits everywhere. Big sculptures of terrifying looking demon-creatures, advertised hot dogs and popcorn. We made our way through the deserted, hellish Dreamland until Little Napoleon stopped at a large building that was identified in ornate script as the 'Pandemonium Funhouse.'

"Clever Hans stayed in the stables, but he hid out here every time he could, getting everything ready. Come on in and you'll see."

I've braved scarier things than a funhouse, but I was a little shaky in my boots as we went inside. I held Charles's hand and nearly yelped when a demonic jack-in-the-box reared out from a wall as a phonograph played spooky sounds.

"Don't wet your trousers, cowboy," Little Napoleon sneered, leading us down several flights of stairs. We entered a dark chamber at the bottom. In it was a chair, a wooden table covered in mechanical gears and switches, and a chalkboard in the corner. Just as Little Napoleon had said, there was an average horse with a bridle and blinders on.

"Here he is!" Little Napoleon said. "Clever Hans. Say hello, horsey!"

Clever Hans snorted.

I looked at Little Napoleon. "You trying to bunco me?"

"No! I am not, and I'm insulted by the very idea of me betraying you!"

"Well, on account of this here horse ain't nothing more than what you'd find in any stable, I'd say you are."

"Um, Mr. Reeper?" Charles was pointing at the horse. "Clever Hans is writing something!"

I looked up and saw the horse picking up a piece of chalk with its mouth. It went over to the chalkboard and wrote out a couple of words. *I am Clever Hans.*

"That's a pretty good trick, but it don't mean nothing," I said. "You could have trained this horse!"

Don't insult me, Clever Hans wrote, *if anything, I have trained Little Napoleon to do my bidding. Look at the apparatus on the table and ask yourself if a dumb animal, or a dumber midget, could have created it?*

I turned to the contraption on the table. It looked like something Edison himself would be proud of, a difference engine mixed with a cash register and covered with light bulbs.

"What does it do?" Charles asked.

By manipulating complicated alchemical-electric fields, it allows me to control Topsy the elephant.

"Yeah, Hans was the one who was putting all of them chemicals into Topsy's food," Little Napoleon said. "He did it soon as he heard that the elephant was gonna get fried. Edison walked right into this horsey's trap!" Little Napoleon picked up the contraption, which was about as big as him, and began disassembling it.

Clever Hans stomped his foot and whinnied. He continued writing. *I built it out of spare parts recovered from the various amusement parks. You wouldn't believe the kind of things they throw away.*

"How come you're packing it up?" I asked as Little Napoleon put the whole thing into a leather messenger bag.

We need to put it at a higher point, such the top of the Dreamland Inferno Roller Coaster. This will expand Topsy's effective range to include the entire city. With an invincible, rampaging elephant at my control, I can soon become master of the city, and then through careful manipulation of port prices, the world. Clever Hans snorted and stomped his foot, dropping the chalk from his mouth.

Little Napoleon suddenly raised his derringer at Charles and me. "Don't try nothing, both of you!" he said. "Me and Clever Hans got a date with a roller coaster, and then an elephant!"

I raised my hands, not believing what was happening. "You betrayed me for a horse?"

"Yeah. Ain't that something? Hey, Hans, forget about the long face and give him the hoof!" Little Napoleon snickered and Clever Hans reared up on his hind legs. The steed gave me a horseshoed foot square in the face, and that was all I saw after that.

I woke up a while later, with Charles hovering over me. "Clark! Clark!" he seemed real upset, but after I opened my eyes and sat up he calmed down. "Oh, you're okay!" He helped me up.

"Little Napoleon and Clever Hans left just a few minutes ago," Charles said. "We can still reach them, but Little Napoleon said something about traps in the funhouse."

The stairwell we had entered was blocked by the overturned table, and the only way out was a ladder that led to the center of the Pandemonium Funhouse. I stood up and patted Charles on the head. "Traps, eh? Well, I got my irons and this elephant gun, so I figure we can get through it all right. You just stay behind me and don't touch nothing or move anywhere without me telling you, okay?"

Charles nodded, and I started up the ladder. We got into the main portion of the Funhouse, and even though I knew there weren't nothing behind all of those leering demons prancing everywhere except clockwork and springs, I still drew out one of my Peacemakers and motioned Charles behind me. I took one step, felt my leg snap a thin wire and then leapt backwards. I threw Charles and myself to the ground just as a rain of spring-loaded arrows zoomed past us.

"Maybe we ought to go a bit slower?" I suggested, but behind me I heard something creak loudly. I turned around slowly, and saw a large swinging pendulum, topped with a metal spike pointed at my heart. The spike came swinging down and I grabbed Charles, held the boy under my arm, and started running. I jumped under a blade projecting from the wall, leapt over a papier-mâché goblin that was filled with real flames, and then jumped outside through a nearby window. The pendulum smashed out behind me, nearly cutting a hole in the seat of my trousers as Charles and I plummeted downwards.

If it weren't for a large open crate of popcorn, Charles and I would probably be flattened and smashed. As it was, all we got was hot and buttery. I fell out of the popcorn barrel with a sputter and landed on the ground. The bruise where Clever Hans had bashed me was still aching, and I was getting shaky on my feet.

"Mr. Reeper!" Charles cried, pointing. "It's the Inferno!"

I turned to look, and there it was—the biggest roller coaster in the Dreamland amusement park. Like the rest of Dreamland, it was covered in red flags and flashing red and orange lights so it looked like it was on fire, and I could make out a small carriage approaching the highest hump on the roller coaster.

"That must be them," I said. I took the elephant gun from my shoulder, reloaded it, and tried to get a good shot, but they were just too far away. I just shook my head and put the big hunting rifle back on my shoulder. "We'd better get closer. I reckon we're gonna have to take a ride on the roller coaster."

A few moments later Charles and I were sitting in the front seat of a rickety wooden carriage slowly climbing up the first slope of the inferno. It had been a simple manner of sitting down and pulling the right levers on the side to make the carriage go forward. Little Napoleon and Clever Hans were right ahead and I figured I should make my presence known.

I took out both Peacemakers, stood up and fired. The bullets fell short, but they got the midget and the horse's attention. I heard a loud whinny from Clever Hans, and then Little Napoleon turned around and started firing at me with a mounted Hotchkiss machine gun. I ducked down, pulling Charles with me, and the bullets soared over our heads.

The roller coaster rumbled as Clever Hans sent his carriage rolling down the opposite side of the hump. I cursed under my breath and prepared to give chase. Soon our own carriage was speeding down the slope, the rush of wind nearly knocking me out. I had fought on horseback and on top of stagecoaches and trains, but there weren't nothing in the world like this.

The roller coaster zoomed along. Charles crouched low as I stood up and fanned off a couple of rounds at Little Napoleon, who rattled away at me with his Hotchkiss. It was hard to hit anything, on account of the roller coaster's rumbling, but I heard a yelp of pain from Little Napoleon and the Hotchkiss fell off of his carriage, clattering on the pavement below.

"You can't outrun me, you little devil!" I shouted at Little Napoleon as Charles tapped me on the shoulder. "I'm a mite busy, Charles," I said, firing off some more shots with my six-gun.

"Mr. Reeper! It's Topsy!"

That made me turn around and I was glad I did. Topsy the elephant, under the control of Clever Hans, flew through the air and landed on the wooden planks of the roller coaster. The flimsy wood strained under her weight and nearly broke, but she began to charge after us, each footfall shaking the roller coaster to its foundations; I saw her big black eyes and the shiny sparks coming off of her ivory tusks.

I heard the whinnying laugh of Clever Hans as Topsy gained on us. "Stinking steed!" I muttered. I took out my elephant gun, aiming straight between the elephant's eyes. There wouldn't be no time for the electricity to heal when the bullet was lodged right in Topsy's brain.

"No!" Charles cried. "Mr. Reeper! Clark! The elephant doesn't matter! We have to stop Little Napoleon and Clever Hans!"

"This is stopping them!" I shouted back. "Stay quiet and let me concentrate!"

"Mr. Reeper!" Charles shouted, pushing the elephant gun up. "They're controlling Topsy! All we have to do is stop them, and she stops being so mean!"

I couldn't make my shot on the elephant. I thought about that and nodded. "I reckon that's not too far from the truth." I turned around and aimed the elephant gun at the carriage in front of me. But instead of picking off the horse or the midget inside, I aimed for the place where the carriage touched the wooden rails of the Inferno Roller Coaster.

I breathed in deep, squeezed off a shot, and the recoil threw me backwards. This time it was a bit too much. I fell out of the carriage and landed right in front of the charging Topsy. I closed my eyes, hearing the creak of metal, the trumpets of the elephant, and Charles's terrified yelp. Then, I felt something thick and rough wrap around my chest. I opened one eye, and then the other. I was in Topsy's trunk. The elephant weren't moving none, just standing there on the roller coaster and letting me look into her big black eyes.

A loud screech caught my attention. I twisted around to see Clever Hans and Little Napoleon heading down a huge slope, their carriage careening to the side. The slope evened out and then went over a small hump. Their carriage zoomed over it, lifted off of the roller coaster and sailed up into the air. They got further and further away, and I saw Little Napoleon's tiny form falling from the carriage, but Clever Hans was still riding it as it vanished from view.

Charles jumped off of our own carriage, rolling on the wooden rails and bloodying his nose. He ran over to Topsy and stood his ground before the massive beast.

"Topsy," he said. "You're free. You can go home now, to Africa or the moon, or wherever. But you have to let Mr. Reeper down."

Topsy didn't move, and I was beginning to think she would toss me away, or eat me, or fry me up with her electric tusks, but she just stood still and blinked her black eyes. Charles reached into his jacket and took out a peanut. He carefully broke the shell, and held out the tiny nut to the great elephant.

Topsy unfurled her trunk to get the peanut, letting me fall roughly to the ground. Slowly, she munched on the peanut and regarded us without moving or making any noise. Then, she raised one leg and smashed it down, letting herself lift off into the sky.

"Did she take my advice?" Charles asked. "Is she going back to Africa?"

"I don't rightly know," I said. "I reckon she can go anywhere she wants."

Charles and I watched that big elephant go up and up until there weren't nothing left of her.

After we got out of the park, Thomas Edison begged to know what had happened. I told him we had shot the elephant near one of the piers and the beast's body had disappeared beneath the waves, and that made Edison real happy. He paid me in full, and then went on his way.

Well, to celebrate Topsy's death, all of the amusement parks on Coney Island opened up, not charging a cent for the entry fee. Charles and I went to every park on the island. We rode some of the roller coasters, which made poor Charles a little nauseous, and we did the pony rides, and saw the animals and played games on the midway.

Just as we were thinking about leaving, I felt a hankering for some fairy floss, or cotton candy as the kids call it, and went over to get myself a bushel. After eating my fill, I noticed that there was a small red figure stuck deep inside the cotton candy machine. I reached a hand in and pulled out Little Napoleon, still in his red devil costume and covered in sticky pink fairy floss. He must have fallen in after he toppled from the roller coaster, and knocked himself out.

Well, I don't take kindly to someone double-crossing me, so I shoved the unconscious Little Napoleon under my arm and went downtown for an audience with the English occultist Aleister Crowley, who was still in town on his lecture circuit. He was a real odd feller, wearing robes and a conical hat and a big gold medallion with a weird diamond symbol on it.

I showed him Little Napoleon and explained the situation. "This here demon just appeared right in front of me. I captured him and tied him up. How much will you pay for him?"

Crowley's eyes sparkled and I sold Little Napoleon for twenty-five dollars and thirty cents. I'm sure he'll wise up soon enough, and by then Little Napoleon will end up somewhere in England or God knows where. It will take him a hell of a long time to get back home. If we meet again, maybe I'll put a bullet in his little head, maybe not.

There weren't no sign of Clever Hans. A lot of scientists went and re-examined the reports on him, and they said they had proved he wasn't smart and it was just fancy tricks he was doing, but I know what I saw, and that horse weren't a dumb animal. Maybe there was a rocket pack on that carriage, and he's soaring up above us all and waiting for a chance to come down and take control of the world. I hope he goes to the glue factory.

Topsy hasn't been spotted either. Maybe she went down to Africa, or because she was raised in Luna Park, to the real moon, where her electrified lungs will probably allow her to survive. I don't rightly know, and I don't care to find out.

Charles and I are leaving New York and heading out west. I don't know if elephants or horses are really dumb animals, but maybe I'll try to be nicer to them from now on. I also don't know if Edison was right when he said that machines were the future and nature was all wrong. I've seen all sorts of horrors, and some of them were man-made, while some of them weren't.

Well, I got a telegram from an English spy named Sidney Reilly who needs an assistant, and a message from a Hollywood Director by the name of Cecil B. DeMille who needs a technical advisor for one of his films, and I'll probably get around to answering some of them soon.

After seeing the elephant, I don't know if there's much more that can shock me.

Big Bad Voodoo

Now I've found myself in plenty of desperate scrapes. Hell, it's probably part of my job description. I've been trapped in a town of hungry walking corpses, battled intelligent automatons and fish people, and even met a few beings from another world. You see, my name's Clark Reeper, and I'm a bounty hunter specializing in what you might call odd jobs.

I've made my share of enemies and friends, even finding and adopting an orphan child of about ten years by the name of Charles Green. I really care for Charles. He's a little feller, with curly hair, thick glasses, and he always wears a neat little Norfolk suit and peaked cap. I'm a tall, gaunt gent and I wear a crumbling Stetson, a flowing tan duster, and I carry two Colt Peacemakers on my belt. We couldn't look more different.

Hanging around with me has caused Charles all sorts of grief, and whenever he's in pain or trouble I feel like a God-awful piece of scum to have dragged such a nice kid into it. Luckily, I've always managed to keep him safe, but when I got into one of the most desperate fixes in my life, way down in New Orleans, I had my doubts that either of us was gonna survive. I had to do a whole lot of things that I ain't proud of in order to keep us safe. But I'm getting ahead of myself. Best to start at the beginning on account of I don't want to confuse nobody.

It all started when Charles and I were at a saloon in New Orleans, taking some time off after a dangerous job. We had just helped an English feller, a spy by the name of Sidney Reilly, to help save his country and maybe the whole world from an insane millionaire and his diabolical schemes. With a good amount of money in my pocket, courtesy of the Queen of England, I figured some celebrating was in order.

I ordered a big tall glass of whiskey and got a bottle of sarsaparilla for Charles. He sipped it through a straw and I sipped mine through pursed lips. Charles had an old book under his arm, something I had bought for him in New York, and he took it out and started reading. He was real smart and it did my heart good to see him reading away like a little professor in some fancy university.

"Good book?" I asked, after I had finished the whiskey.

"It's fascinating, Mr. Reeper," Charles explained. "It's all about some of the local superstitions and stuff. Did you know that African, Indian, and Catholic religions got all jumbled up, and all of these things like Santeria, and Umbanda and something called Voodoo came out of it?"

"Voodoo," I said, rolling the word around in my mouth. "I've had a few run-ins with that stuff. It's a bad business, if you don't mind me saying."

Charles closed the book. "It can't be that bad. I mean, all religions have weird stuff, but most of the people who worship them are okay. I mean, I'm a Jew, and you're not, and we get along fine."

I ruffled his hair and smiled. "That ain't what I was going on about. There's just some things man weren't meant to know, but a lot of fanatic people try anyhow."

"Like who?" Charles asked.

The saloon doors swung open. I turned around and stared at the tall figure who had wandered in. I felt my blood turn to ice and cold sweat appear on my brow, even though it was a typical hot and humid day in Louisiana. It only took me a second to recognize the man standing there in the doorway, the wind stirring his tangled black hair. He had piercing eyes under a broad-brimmed hat set low on his face, a hat with a silver pentagram on the brim. A howling wind seemed to blow through the saloon as he walked inside, his black boots leaving singe marks on the wooden floor. He carried a long barreled Colt

Buntline Special and a long-bladed knife known as an 'Arkansas Toothpick' on his back.

"Speak of the devil," he said, standing in front of me. "If it ain't Clark Reeper." His voice was low and crackling, like a burning fire.

"Brimstone Brown," I said, a hand falling to my holster. "What are you doing here? I saw you dragged down to Hell by the devil himself!"

"Old Scratch and I came to an...understanding." Brimstone Brown pushed his broad-brimmed hat up and let me stare into his eyes. They were pure red, and I don't mean just bloodshot. Each one was completely crimson, through and through. "I found out it's better to rule on Earth than serve in Hell."

I stood up. "If you want to settle a score with me, Brimstone, let's do it outside, and away from my boy here."

Charles shivered, staring up at Brimstone Brown. I reckoned the poor kid was thinking back to the last time he had a run in with Brimstone. The devil-worshipper nearly sacrificed Charles and I was lucky enough to save him. I put a hand on Charles's shoulder.

"Remember me, little boy?" Brimstone Brown leaned down, grinning at Charles. "I nearly gave your blood to the devil. He took mine instead, for better or worse."

"Yes, I remember you," Charles said, his voice a whisper. "You're a mean man."

"I've been called worse."

The owner of the establishment, an overweight man in an apron, walked out, carrying a pistol like he knew how to use it. "If you gentlemen are going to blast away at each other, I'd suggest getting out of my joint," he said, raising the gun. "I am completely within my rights to—"

Brimstone turned and snapped the fingers on his right hand, causing them to burst into bright flames. The patrons of the saloon gasped, and a few limping drunks and upright citizens hightailed it to the door. The bartender stood still, transfixed by the sight of a man with his hand wreathed in bright red flames that didn't burn his skin.

"Human laws don't concern me anymore," Brimstone whispered. "I serve a...lower power." He lashed out with his burning hand and the flames leapt off and scorched the bartender. The man roared in pain as Brimstone cooked him up like a Christmas goose right in front of us. After a few seconds, the flames vanished without leaving a single trail of smoke, and the charred corpse of the barkeep disintegrated onto the ground.

I brought up my revolvers, fired at Brimstone without warning. He turned to face me and my slugs seemed to melt before they hit his skin. The lumps of useless lead tumbled to the ground, and Brimstone grinned cruelly as he leveled his Buntline at me.

"My employment has some benefits," Brimstone said. "Goodbye Clark. I'll see you on the other side. It's not everything it's cracked up to be, but you'll get used to it."

I figured I was done for, but Charles had other ideas. The courageous boy pummeled into Brimstone's legs and knocked the demonic gunslinger to the ground. Brimstone lashed down with a gloved hand, plucking out a single hair from Charles's head, and then shoved the boy off him. I grabbed Charles's shoulder, pulling him away from Brimstone, and dashed to the door.

"You saved my life back there," I said, firing behind me as we ran. "I'm much obliged."

"You've saved me tons of times," Charles explained, sounding a little shy.

We ran out with most of the other drunks and well-dressed New Orleans saloon-goers. Suddenly, Brimstone Brown let out a low laugh. I holstered a pistol, clutched Charles's hand and turned around to see what Brimstone was so jolly about.

He stood in the middle of the deserted saloon, holding a simple burlap doll, a little poppet decorated with simple stitching and stuffed with herbs. He laughed at me, held the doll aloft and I saw a tiny thread, a strand of Charles's hair, wrapped around the doll's toe. "Clark, Clark, you fool." Brimstone shook his head as he chuckled. "If I wanted you dead, you'd be dead ten times already! I wanted a strand of your boy's hair, and by the Lord of Darkness, I got it!"

A sinking feeling came across me, and Charles looked up at me with wide eyes and quivering lips. I pointed my pistol at Brimstone but I knew that it was useless. Brimstone pulled out a small needle from his belt and jabbed it straight into the chest of his poppet. The breath left Charles in a rush and he fell to the ground.

"You satanic snake-in-the-grass!" I shouted, firing with my pistol as I picked up Charles and held him steady. Tears were in the poor kid's eyes and his normally pale face was the color of ash. Brimstone's grin never left his face. "I'll kill you!" I yelled. "I swear I will!"

"Better get help for your boy," Brimstone said, stabbing the doll once more, causing Charles to let out a strangled squeal. "You know who to run to."

Out of my rage, and idea came to me. I leveled my Peacemaker, squeezed the trigger, and shot the chain holding up a lantern right behind Brimstone. The lantern crashed down, falling right on top of a couple of whiskey bottles. It set the whole bar on fire. I picked up Charles and ran as fast as I could.

I ran a few blocks from the bar and came to a park bench, somewhere in the gothic French Quarter. New Orleans is an interesting city. It's got some of the oldest buildings in all of North America, and the Frenchman, Spaniard, Pirate, American, Indian, and African have all left their mark on the place. But I wasn't admiring the nice architecture, not with Charles in pain.

I laid him down on the bench and looked him over. There weren't a single mark on him, and I figured that Brimstone had been using some pretty bad magic on the poor kid. Charles's teeth and hands were clenched, and sweat dripped down his forehead. I wiped it off with a handkerchief and gave him a slurp of water from my canteen.

"How you doing, son?" I asked, gentle as I could.

"My book." Charles coughed and kept his eyes closed for a long time. "I left my book in the tavern."

"Don't you worry about that none," I said. "How you feeling?"

"My insides are burning up. It hurts every time I breathe." Charles smiled weakly through his tears. "I'm sorry, Clark. I shouldn't have jumped on Brimstone."

"Don't go saying that," I told him. "I'll get you well."

"Brimstone said you knew somebody who could help." Charles coughed and I noticed a thin line of blood running down his cheek. "Was he lying?"

I looked away from Charles, not wanting him to see my frowning face. "Yeah. I know someone who could heal you up, but she ain't the kind of woman a feller ought to go see if he's fixing to stay alive."

"Maybe I'll get better. You don't have to go to her," Charles whispered softly. Suddenly, he let out a scream of pain, grabbing his chest and nearly falling off the bench. Passersby stopped to look, and I held Charles close to me as his spasm passed. The poor kid was dying, and I knew it. I didn't want to do it, but I knew I'd have to swallow my pride and go crawling down to the French Quarter to ask for help. It was a matter of life and death. The only person I cared about in the world was on the line.

I stood up, carrying Charles in my arms. The boy seemed to be as light as a spider's cobweb. I steeled myself as best I could and then I went deep into New Orleans, where the buildings were as old as the surrounding swamps, and dark mysteries from far and nearby jungles lurked around every corner. I needed an audience with Marie Laveau, the Voodoo Queen.

Laveau ruled her part of the city out of a high-class manor in the French Quarter. I was a mite surprised that my feet still knew the way, going down all the right back alleys to the red and white baroque manor. I reckon I've walked that path so many times it's burned right into my mind.

I walked up the flight of stairs to the manor doors, eyeing the evil-looking gargoyles that perched on the ends of the stairwell. Choking back my fear, I knocked on the door and waited while I watched Charles's ragged breathing. I still held the boy in my arms, on account of he wasn't able to walk.

After a few seconds the door opened a crack and a muscular black man stuck a sawed-off shotgun in my face. He looked right out of the eighteenth century, with a fancy silk suit and a lacy cravat; a white with contrasted with his dark face; and an eye patch covered his right eye. I could tell he weren't happy to see me.

"Howdy, Caesar," I said nervously. "Pleasure seeing you again."

"Clark Reeper." Caesar's rumbling voice spoke my name with nothing but contempt. "Shall I kill you now, or should I let my curiosity get the better of me and kill you later?"

I choked on my answer, and then I heard a familiar and frightening voice from deep within the manor. "Why, Caesar! That's no way to treat a guest! " the voice was feminine and dainty, part Southern Belle and part Caribbean Island Girl. My knees shook just hearing it.

"It's me, ma'am, Clark Reeper," I said nervously. I thought of Charles and went on. "I've come to ask for your help."

"A plea for aid? From Clark Reeper? My goodness, Caesar, open the door and show him in!"

Caesar frowned, but withdrew the sawed-off. The manor doors were pulled back and I walked into Marie Laveau's mansion. The place was decked out with opulent furniture coated in enough red velvet to make you go blind. There were hanging tapestries depicting bizarre rituals and ancient rites, and ornate chandeliers all a-glimmer with gold and baubles. It was all illuminated by countless candles.

Marie Laveau reclined at the far-end of the room on a gilded chaise lounge. She looked just like she had when I was child, beautiful as an angel and dressed for business in a loose skirt that showed off her charms splendidly. She was mighty pretty, with light brown skin and elegantly coifed hair. She was smiling and her eyes were bright.

I set Charles down on a couch, told him not to be afraid, and stared at Marie. "Hello ma'am."

"Clark! Still polite as the last time I saw you. That was such a long time ago. I was almost worried you would forget who I am."

"No, ma'am, I remember." I took off my hat and held it in my hands. I had been taught to respect Marie Laveau like she was my mother, and those lessons were still drilled into my head. "I've come to ask for your help."

"Let me get a look at you." Marie stood up, walking around me and sniffing her nose. "You were just a boy when you left us, and now I see that you have a boy of your own."

"My name is Charles, Charles Green," Charles said between coughs.

"He's my adopted son and a no-good snake-in-the-grass fiend put a curse on him," I explained. "The kid ain't never touched a gun in his life. He don't got no relation to me, my father, or any vendetta between us and you."

"It was never a vendetta between your father and me." Marie Laveau shook her head. "It was so much more than that. And even though you did cause a great deal of pain to me and my household—" Caesar winked his single eye "—I have it in my heart to forgive you." She paused. "For a price."

"Name it."

"You do one job for me. Nothing you're not used to. I've been following your career, what I could hear of it, with great interest, and there's something I need that your skills would be perfect for."

If there was something Marie Laveau wanted me to do for her, I reckoned there weren't no good coming from it. The Voodoo Queen cared about power and nothing but. She was willing to do almost anything to get it. My father had found that out soon enough and he had almost paid the ultimate price. Still, Charles was in a lot of pain, and just looking at the boy made me ache.

I nodded my head. "Okay, but you can't hurt Charles or do nothing to hurt me or him in the long-term, and I don't want any tricks or traps or any of that. You hear me?"

"I hear you, Clark." Marie leaned forward until her dark eyes were inches away from mine. "I am very good with children. You know that." She turned away from me. "Come. We'll put your boy in one of the upper-story rooms. You can look it over if you are still paranoid, though I see no reason why you should be."

She led me upstairs, passing stony-faced servants and nervous girls, coming to a room that looked like it was stolen from the house of J.P. Morgan. I laid Charles down in the king-sized bed, taking off his hat and jacket and folding them neatly on a nearby chair. He looked very small, surrounded by all of them giant pillows and ruffled sheets, and I couldn't help ruffling his hair.

"You mind leaving us alone for a bit?" I asked Marie.

The Voodoo Queen curtsied gracefully and bowed out of the room, closing the door behind her. Despite his pain, Charles propped himself up in the bed. "Um, do you know her?" he asked.

"Yeah, but it don't mean I trust her. She'll take good care of you, though. I know that first-hand."

"What do you mean?"

I sighed. I don't like talking about my childhood, on account of there's a lot of bad things buried away, and remembering them ain't enjoyable in the least. "I was raised by her, since I was ten-years-old. See, my father and Marie were friends. Close friends."

"She is very pretty," Charles whispered, his pale face turning a little red. "But she looks too young to be your mother."

"She ain't, and her age don't got nothing to do with it. Marie Laveau was young and pretty when Napoleon was waltzing around, and she hasn't changed a bit. But she was sweet on my dad something fierce, and when I was born, she got real upset. My old man, Josiah Reeper, carried me around for a couple of years until I was ten, and then he asked Marie Laveau to raise me."

"Why'd he do that?"

"I don't rightly know. Maybe he thought it was too dangerous to have a kid like me riding with him. My Old Man was a big feller with a huge beard and a buckskin jacket and he did a lot of the kinds of things that I do, you see." I didn't think about my Old Man that much, but I always felt a little happy and a little poorly when I did.

"You take good care of me," Charles said stubbornly. Then he paused, looked at his surroundings and seemed to remember his condition. "Well, most of the time," he coughed.

"Well, whatever the reason, Marie Laveau raised me like I was her own child. She's good with kids, a lot more tender than my Old Man had ever been, and I even loved her a little."

"What happened?"

"Well, my Old Man had a falling out with her, and then she tried to kill me to get back at him. I was sixteen-years-old, and she put me in a position where I had to kill four men and gouge out Caesar's eye in order to get out alive." I sighed. "Those were the first folks I'd ever gunned down, and it changed me forever. I never really forgave her, and she never really forgave me." I stood up, putting my hat on my head. "But none of that matters. You just stay here, let her do that Voodoo that she do, and rest up."

Charles leaned back in bed, and I smiled at him. He was my son, and I wondered if my father had ever tried to fight the terror that I was feeling now. The door opened and Marie Laveau walked in. Without saying a word to me or Charles, she went to work. She whispered some words in a Caribbean language and tossed a handful of herbs across Charles's bed. She lit candles and incense and called out to something called the 'Loas' and something else called the 'Three Barons' and then Charles closed his eyes and his little chest rose and fell evenly with sleep.

"Whatever big bad voodoo got stuck on him won't do him no harm?" I asked. "He'll be okay?"

Marie nodded. "Yes. Now follow me, Clark, and we'll see some real big bad voodoo."

She led me downstairs, and then outside of the manor into the backyard. It was getting dark now and the steaming Louisiana swamp the mansion overlooked was full of shadows and darkness. I stared into the greenery and gulped, thinking about what the Voodoo Queen was going to have me do. Caesar was out there, standing next to his mistress, and so were six crouched figures that lay motionless on the ground.

"There will be a full moon tonight," Marie said grandly.

"What the hell has that got to do with anything?"

She stared at me. "It will make your task much harder. Let me tell you what it is you must do. There is a paddle steamer boat out there. It crashed in a murky area of the swamp, where a gang of outlaws now resides."

"You want me to kill a couple of outlaws?" It didn't seem like her.

"If you have to. In the crashed paddle steamer is a safe, and in the safe is an artifact that I want very much to have in my possession. You must go into the boat, find the safe, and bring me the artifact."

It didn't seem that difficult, except for one important detail. "How am I supposed to open the damn safe?"

Marie Laveau smiled at me. "You'll know the code. After all, the safe's combination was set by a man you may be familiar with: Josiah Reeper."

The mention of my Old Man made me gulp and shiver. If he didn't want Marie to get her hands on the object, maybe I didn't want her to get it either. But then I thought of Charles and steeled myself.

"What about the outlaws? Who are they?"

"A gang of Confederate holdouts, some of the most loyal sons of Dixie." Marie seemed disgusted when she talked about them. "They are called the Swamp Dogs and are led by a man named Lou Garou, a good soldier and able fighter." She stared into the greenery and shook her head. "I got into a little scrape with them during the war and put a curse on them, which is now their blessing. Yes, a full moon will make your job very dangerous indeed."

"Do I get anyone riding with me?" If it was a suicide mission and an easy way for Marie to get rid of me, then I weren't going on it.

To my surprise, Marie nodded. She snapped her fingers, and then the six forms came shambling to their feet. The smell alone told me they were long dead, and when I saw them shuffle over to me, all rotting and falling apart, I knew that these were old corpses. I had fought the walking dead before, but these corpses seemed a little more steady on their feet than the ones in Dead Man's Gulch, and they all carried firearms of some sort.

"Jacques, Luis, Benedict, Belinda." Marie named each of the corpses. "Once they were my lovers or servants, all of whom failed me in some way. Through my allegiance to Samedi and the Three Barons, I was able to utilize them even after their death. Clark, meet the zombies."

I knew that Marie Laveau was a Mambo of unfathomable power, but it always chilled me to see her in action. I stared at the zombies. "They don't say much, do they?" I asked.

"They are men and women of few words." Marie pointed to Luis's mouth, and I saw that it was sewn shut with tight thread. "But they fight well and they know the way to the paddle steamer. " She snapped her fingers and pointed to the swamp, and the zombies shuffled off.

I took one more look at Marie Laveau, tipped my hat to her, and headed off into the swamp.

Just as she said, the zombies knew the way. They ambled through the swamp moving mighty fast for dead folk. It was dark now, and when one of the zombies saw I was having trouble seeing where I was going, he broke off a branch and held it out to me, moaning.

"Thank you kindly," I said, taking the branch and wrapping some dry leafs around it. I had some matches in my belt, struck one on my boot, and lit the torch. The zombies moved slower now, staying clustered around the torch. I tried to make small talk.

"So, you lot are all former lovers of Marie? Except for you ma'am." I tipped my hat to Belinda, a withered corpse in a frayed dress.

They moaned and nodded and Belinda tried to grin as best she could with her sewn-together lips.

"Hell. I reckon my Old Man would have ended up like you if he hadn't gotten out in time." I took out one of my Colts and pulled back the hammer. "All right. Let's find that boat."

We walked on in silence, me not saying nothing and the zombies not able to. Too soon we came to a large Mississippi paddleboat beached on a strip of swampy land. I could see lights in the wheelhouse and around the passenger's quarters. I spotted a ragged Confederate battle flag hanging loosely from the mast. Men with rifles patrolled the deck.

I crouched low in the mud and stared up at the paddleboat, planning my attack. I handed my torch to one of the zombies. "Three of you take this and attack from the front. Try to find the place where they keep all the ammo. Then toss the torch inside, and hightail it out of there. You understand?"

They moaned, shuffled off, and I figured that was good enough. I crawled over to the bottom of the ship and clambered up a loose bit of rigging. I dropped silently onto the deck and looked around, and then motioned for the remaining zombie to join me. The dead feller climbed up while I pondered my next move.

The other group of zombies must have followed their orders, because we heard gunfire. Swamp Dogs ran to the other side of the boat, firing at the zombies hiding in the dense swampland. While the renegades on the deck were occupied, my dead partner and me headed for the wheelhouse. We crept low and stayed quiet, and we would have made it too, if the zombie hadn't gotten his foot caught on a protruding spike.

He didn't notice it, and when he shambled forward there was an audible tearing noise as his leg was ripped clean off. For a few seconds, there weren't no sounds except for the crickets in the swamp and the dripping water. And then the Swamp Dogs were on us.

They had a variety of guns, pistols, rifles and shotguns, and I just managed to dive behind a pile of crates before the shooting started. My zombie pal weren't so lucky. He fought back, shooting and even shambling forward and sinking his teeth into one of the Swamp Dogs, but he was still shot to pieces and beaten down.

The Swamp Dogs were a ragged group, each one wearing a torn and old Confederate uniform and a forage cap, but they were fierce fighters, and howled with bestial voices after they had taken out the zombie. I had heard the rebel yell before, but it didn't ever sound so wolfish.

While they were busy, I started running for the wheelhouse. The group of zombies with the torch must have boarded the boat and were holding their own now, because I saw Swamp Dogs running every which way and heard alarm bells clanging. I kicked open the wheelhouse door with both revolvers in my hands, firing even as the door was smashed away.

My first sweep of bullets killed two Swamp Dogs instantly. The third was a tall man with a wild, tangled beard and an animal look in his eye. He wore a cocky campaign hat and growled at me as I entered. I reckoned he was the leader. Behind him was a rusty metal box that I figured for the safe.

"Who put you up to this, tenderfoot?" he asked, his Southern accent thick as molasses. "Was it that witch? Marie Laveau?"

"That's so," I replied. "And you'll be Lou Garou, I'll wager."

He grinned and let out a low growl. "That's my name. Did Marie tell you about us?"

"Not too much." I motioned with my Peacemaker. "I just want what's in the safe. Step out of the way and I won't blast you apart."

Lou Garou took a step towards me. I kept the Colts level. "Those bullets silver, tenderfoot?" Lou asked. "I don't believe they are. Them boys you just killed didn't have the curse on them, but I do. Looks like you are plumb out of luck."

He roared, and I mean an actual animal's roar, then he began to change. Fur sprouted out of his face, his nose got long and his teeth grew into razor sharp fangs. Claws shot out from the fingers of his gloves and he fell down on all fours. Soon I found myself staring at a large, angry wolf.

"A werewolf," I muttered. "Well, I reckon every dog has his day."

Lou Garou snarled out a challenge and leapt forward, knocking me over. I had been up against his kind before, but never without preparation and never at close quarters like these. Lou's claws lashed out, scratching my face and spilling blood in my eyes. I fired with both of my revolvers, the bullets tearing chunks out of his hide, but they didn't slow him down none.

I let one of my revolvers clatter to the ground and pulled my Bowie knife out of my boot. Blindly stabbing with it, I managed to slice down on Lou Garou's toothy mouth. He howled in pain and backed off, allowing me to come to my feet. I angled the knife downward.

"It's laced with silver," I explained. "I always come prepared, fleabag."

The wolf howled and charged. I crouched low and held the knife out, but I still wasn't ready when he pounced on me. I managed to get a stab in on his chest, but he bit my shoulder something fierce and I howled in pain. Clenching my teeth, I bent down low and pushed Lou Garou away with all my might. He tumbled out of the door and skittered on the deck.

"Son of gun!" I hissed, clutching my wound. "Now I've got to grow fur every time there's a full moon."

"That's a myth, tenderfoot!" Lou Garou said, his head turning human for a few seconds. "You'll stay pale and hairless unless you get cursed by a no-good Voodoo witch!" He lunged for me, but one of his gray-clad boys bumped into him while walking backwards and firing his Winchester at my zombies.

A mighty big battle raged on that deck, with the zombies blasting away with their weapons and the Swamp Dogs shooting back, or turning into wolves and trying to pounce on the zombies. The zombie with the torch stood at the middle of the deck, struggling to open a large trap door.

"Stop him!" Lou shouted to his men. "That's the armory! This boat will blow sky high if he gets that torch in there!"

All the Swamp Dogs fired on the zombie and he dropped his torch with a moan. But the flaming stick landed on his foot just as the trap door swung open. The zombie was soon set on fire, and with flame consuming his withered body, he leapt inside the armory. The explosions started within seconds.

The paddle boat rocked under my heels, shaking violently. I ran into the wheelhouse. Finding the safe, I struggled to think of what my Old Man had picked for the code. I spun the dial almost randomly, trying to remember any important numbers. I tried his favorite caliber of bullets, but that didn't work. Then I tried how many men he had killed with his bare hands, but that didn't get nothing neither. As a last resort, I tried the year I was born. To my surprise, the safe door swung open with a rusty creak. Inside was a silken top hat on a velvet cushion. Quickly, I snatched up the hat, held it under my arm, and ran out of the wheelhouse. I barely remembered to pick up my dropped revolver as I ran.

I headed for the edge of the deck, running past Swamp Dogs, humans and wolves, as explosions rippled through the boat. Finally, I came to the edge of the deck and jumped off, landing in the mud below. On my feet in seconds, I ignored the pain in my shoulder and ran away. Just as I got into the woods, the final explosion went off, and the entire paddle steamer blew apart. Chunks of wood and wolves fell from the heavens. I slogged through the swamp and headed back to Marie Laveau's manor.

She was waiting for me a big smile on her beautiful face. "You got it?" she asked expectantly. "Did you find it?"

Wearily, I handed over the hat. "Hell of a lot of a trouble for some fancy headwear."

"Oh, Clark, it is not just any hat. This is the Crown of Samedi, the Loa of Death and Graveyards." Marie held the top hat gingerly. "You have done me a great service, Clark. I am very thankful." She pulled a silken scarf from her dress and bound my wound. She may have been a witch, but I suppose Marie was also a doctor.

"Much obliged," I said, shortly. "Did you cure Charles?"

Marie shrugged. "I did what I could. I'm sorry." That was all I needed to hear. I left her standing there, holding onto the hat that she loved so much, and I ran into the manor and up the stairs, until I came to Charles's room. I slammed open the door, running to the bed.

Charles was there, and the poor kid wasn't breathing a bit. He lay there, staring up at the canopy above his bed, still as a stone. I stood over him, called out his name, screamed out my rage. And holding up his head, I wept. But there was no bringing him back. Charles was gone.

Marie stood in the doorway. "I'm sorry, Clark. I know how hard it is to lose someone that you love."

"Go to Hell, Mambo!" I shouted, pounding my fist on the bed. "Go to Hell!"

The Voodoo Queen walked over to me. "Take a walk, Clark, it will help. Go outside and walk through the streets. There are a few saloons nearby that you might enjoy."

I stared at her in horror, but finally, I numbly nodded. I needed to squash the awful feeling in my chest and dry up the tears running down my face and the way to do that was numb everything with drink. I left Marie's manor and wandered aimlessly down the darkened New Orleans streets until I came to a saloon that was open this late. I stared at the sign on the door, and then turned away. I reckoned I just had to say goodbye to Charles.

I walked back to the manor and found the place pretty empty, but I didn't pay that no heed. I headed upstairs. I walked over to the bed and stared at Charles.

He looked so serene, so peaceful, like he was just sleeping, and I couldn't help grinning at him. I ruffled his hair and sat down in a chair next to the bed. There was nothing to do and I found myself looking at my pistols. A simple pull of the trigger and it would all be over.

"Mr. Reeper!" The voice made me freeze. It sounded like Charles. I figured I must be going crazy. "Clark!" the voice called.

"Charles, is that you?" I asked. "Are you one of them ghosts the spiritualists talk about? Or am I just going crazy?"

"I'm alive, Clark! I'm in the wardrobe!"

My heart soared. I brushed the tears from my face and ran over to the wardrobe, pulling it open and feeling happier than I ever had before. Charles stumbled out of the darkness, blinking his eyes. He took off his dusty glasses and rubbed them on his jacket, and then smiled up at me. He was a mite dusty, and he only had one shoe, but otherwise, he looked unharmed. I pulled him to me and gave him a big hug.

"Charles," I said, happy to say his name. "What in the name of God happened over here? And why are you lying on the bed, dead as a doorknob?"

Charles started talking fast. "She tricked me, Mr. Reeper, and she tricked you too! This isn't me, it's made of wax." Charles walked over to his dead body and scratched it with his fingernail. White wax peeled away under his nails. "And the Voodoo Queen, Marie, she's working with the Brimstone guy! They're together, Clark, they were all kissing and stuff!"

"Hold your horses," I said. "What happened to your sickness? Are you still retching?"

Charles shook his head. "I got better after you left, but then they came to get me, and I hid in the wardrobe and threw one of my shoes out of the window so they thought I had escaped. But we've got to get out of here, Clark. Brimstone and Marie are together! Brimstone only made me sick so you would go to Marie for help and have to do something for her!"

"Son of gun!" They had been playing the tune, and I had been dancing along to it.

We headed for the door. Charles was safe, but I would have to act fast to keep him that way. We left his room and headed to the stairwell, Charles walking kind of funny on account of his missing shoe, but it wasn't until we got down the stairwell that we stopped dead in our tracks. Brimstone Brown and Marie Laveau stood kissing at the doorway. Caesar and a few more of Marie's servants had us covered with loaded shotguns. I raised my hands, and so did Charles.

When he was done smooching, Brimstone walked over to Charles and me. "You got a smart boy, Clark, a little too clever for his own good." Brimstone frowned at Charles. "Everything was working out so well before that little whelp escaped from our clutches. You got the hat, and you were going to leave and drown your sorrow in whiskey and never come back."

"I didn't know that Voodoo folks and Devil-Worshippers were so close," I said. "And I figured that you were too ugly to ever be loved by anything except demons, Brimstone."

Brimstone Brown shook his head, shuffling his long hair. "You know nothing of demons, Clark." He turned to Marie. "My love, what shall we do with them?"

Marie put a finger to her chin. "Toss them in the dungeon. We'll feed them to the alligators in the morning before I don the Crown of Samedi."

They bound us up and dragged us away. I cursed myself for being so stupid and not putting together all the coincidences. I was mighty glad that Charles was alive, but unless I figured something out quick, the both of us weren't gonna be that way for much longer.

Under the manor, the dungeon was made up of a group of cells with low ceilings, dripping with fetid brown water. I took off my duster and covered the bench with it, set Charles on top of that, and then covered him with his little coat. I had nearly lost Charles, and I didn't want the boy catching cold in such a dank place.

We talked for a little, and it did me good just to hear his voice. Soon he grew tired and nodded off to sleep. I crouched in the stinking water and tried to find a way out, playing with the locks and such, but to no effect. Just as I was about to give up, I heard footsteps coming down the hall, and the hiss of water evaporating. I peered down the hallway and saw Brimstone Brown coming. With every footfall, the water around him turned to steam. He walked over to our cell and stared at me.

"Howdy, Reeper," he said.

"Howdy, Brimstone, you double-crossing scum ball." I tried to reach out of the jail cell and strangle him, but he was standing too far back. "What brings you down here?"

Brimstone sighed. "You ever wondered what Hell is like, Clark?"

"Not really. I'm trying my best to stay out of it."

"It's a...queer place. I saw things there that changed me forever." There was fear in his pure red eyes. "Clark, I don't want to go back there. The devil gave me a second chance if I would serve, and I had to take it, I just had to." He looked remorseful. "He made me join up with Marie, and then we fell in love."

"So, you're trying to say none of this was your fault?" I weren't gonna let Brimstone Brown off the hook that easy.

"I hurt your boy under Marie's command, but I don't know if I wanted too. I just don't know." He stared at me plaintively. "It's like that with Marie. I love her, but sometimes she does and says things that disgust me. Everything seems mixed up and out of joint."

I nodded. "It's like that with Marie Laveau. She makes you love her, and then, right when you think she's ready to be your wife, or even your mother, she turns on you. Then she animates your body, sews up your mouth, and has you do her bidding. She nearly did it with my Old Man, almost had her way with me, and now she's casting her spell on you. The only thing she wants is power."

"What? She told me I was the first!" Brimstone said angrily. "And the Dark Lord said she was trustworthy."

"Listen, Brimstone, how long do you think she's gonna keep you around after she's put on that Big Bad Voodoo Hat I gave her? And ain't your master called the Prince of Lies? He's probably got plenty of other sinners he can use as willing agents after you're gone and dead."

Brimstone's face screwed up with rage. "Marie would never do that."

I spread my arms and grinned. "Fine. You can just tell yourself that. But tomorrow morning, Marie will put on that fancy hat, get her Voodoo together and blow you apart. You'll be sent back to Hell."

My remarks seemed to have an affect on Brimstone, and I reckon he really did fear Hell more than anything else. Brimstone turned away from me, letting me look at his black cloak, and then walked off, the water steaming at his footsteps.

I slumped down in the cell and waited. After a few minutes past, I heard the hissing of steaming water again. Brimstone Brown had returned. He walked over to the jail cell and handed me both of my revolvers and my Bowie knife. I holstered the guns and put the knife in my boot.

"Much obliged, Brimstone. Maybe you ain't all bad."

The satanic gunslinger shook his head. "Tomorrow, you can try to escape. If Marie has turned against me, I'll help you. If not, you're on your own, and that means you're done for." He smiled joylessly and turned away. I watched him go, and sat down next to Charles and tried to get some sleep. If we was to survive tomorrow, I would need my rest.

The morning came too soon. Caesar unlocked the cell door, and he and some of his friends roughly dragged me and Charles outside. I quickly put on my duster, hiding the handles of my Colts and the Bowie knife from view.

Charles looked nervous at first, but when he saw the look of grim determination in my face, he must have figured that I had a plan, and he calmed down. Caesar and Marie Laveau's other servants took us to the backyard of the manor, where a large crowd was gathered.

It was the occult community of New Orleans. Spiritualists taking a break from their séances, cultists in ragged robes and wild eyes, mambos and houngans ready to see a master of Voodoo at work, and all sorts of other palm-readers, mystics and outright charlatans had assembled to see what Marie Laveau was planning.

She stood in front of the crowd on a wooden platform, and Caesar and his goons tied Charles and me up and brought us before Marie. She smiled down at me, radiant in a sparkling purple gown. The top hat, the Crown of Samedi, was in her hands. Brimstone Brown stood next to her, looking nervous.

"Sleep well, Clark?" she asked. She gestured to the river. A few cow carcasses had been tossed in the water, and a good number of alligators were swimming around and hungrily waiting for more.

"I'm fine and dandy, thank you kindly," I said pleasantly. "And how are you, ma'am?"

She smiled. "Perfect. Caesar! Tie them up and suspend them over the river. I'll cut the ropes when it's the proper time."

Brimstone was on edge. He paced around the stage, his feet leaving scorch marks on the wood, and his red eyes steaming. "Are these theatrics really necessary, Marie?" he asked angrily.

"Brimstone! Of course they are." There was cruelty in Marie's smile, and I reckoned the betrayal was soon coming.

"You should be prepared for this moment, Brimstone, and you're all dirty."

He stared at her. "W-what do you mean?"

"You're simply covered in dirt." Marie's smile never left her pretty face as she pulled a vial of clear water from the folds of her dress. "But don't worry. I can clean you off."

"You traitorous—" But that was as far as Brimstone got, because it was then that Marie made her move. She splashed the vial of water all over Brimstone Brown. Instantly, he crumpled down on his knees and roared in pain as steam pulsed off of him. "Holy water!" he cried. "You'll pay, Marie Laveau, my master will see to that!"

"Your master won't mind losing just one of his agents, and soon I'll be so powerful that the Devil Himself will take pause before angering me." Marie laughed as she motioned Caesar forward.

The crowd cheered as Caesar kicked Brimstone to the floor and tied him up. Soon he stood beside us, waiting to be fed to the alligators. I felt the ropes tighten around my sides as Marie's servants attached a long wooden pole to the rope and then lifted me up in the air over the river. They did the same to Charles and Brimstone. All of us were hung out like laundry on long extended poles overlooking the alligator-filled river. We all dangled there together, waiting to be lowered in.

"Clark?" Charles asked, in a fearful high-pitched voice. "I'm scared."

"Don't worry son, everything's under control." I reached low, bending the ropes, and managed to get down to my boots. I grabbed the Bowie knife and pulled it out, holding it with a grip of steel.

"Make your move," Brimstone whispered. The steam billowed off of him, and I figured that holy water was burning him something fierce. I started working on cutting my bonds just as the first alligators started swimming around below me. I could have tried to get myself out earlier, but I reckon alligators are easier to face than the guns of Marie's servants.

Back on the shore, the crowd was focused on Marie Laveau. She had raised the top hat over her head and mumbled words very fast in a strange language. I could hear the crowd gasp as she slowly levitated above the platform, just as the brim of the hat touched her head. I stared back at the alligators swimming around below me. If I was gonna do this, now was the time.

I cut my bonds and fell downwards, splashing in the shallow waters. A big alligator with a yawning mouth swam straight towards me, and I slashed him across the face with the knife as I splashed to the shore. The other alligators leapt on him, gobbling the big lizard up and leaving me alone. I made it to the shore.

Caesar turned his attention from Marie Laveau to me. He leveled his sawed-off shotgun and fired, sending lead splashing down in the river. I jumped back and dove under the water, the bullets spraying all around me. Then I came splashing out with my Bowie knife gripped by the blade. I threw it with all of my might, and Caesar yelled in pain as the blade sunk into his remaining eye. I pulled the blade from his eye-socket and wiped it clean on the edge of my duster.

Blind and screaming, Caesar stumbled across the raised platform, tumbling off into the river where he thrashed about and attracted every gator around. "Charles, close your eyes!" I shouted. "A boy ought not to see this!" Charles closed his eyes. Watching Caesar getting devoured by a bunch of reptiles was an ugly sight.

I grabbed the pole and started hauling it back, hoping to get Charles and Brimstone away from the gators, when the crowd let out a low sigh and I felt a cold hand on my shoulder. Slowly, I turned around and saw Marie standing there on the platform, but it weren't Marie I was looking at. Her skin was black, midnight black; pitch black, and skeletal white bones were visible through her body. Her eyes were wide black pools as if she was wearing smoked glasses, and the Crown of Samedi was on her head.

"Marie," I said. "What's with the new look?"

"The Blood of the Three Barons flows through me." Marie's voice was even, but it was as if she was shouting at a loud volume. "Samedi. Cimetíere. Le Croix. All of them are one within me. The Loa of Graveyards breathe the air that I breathe, feel the ground under my feet. They ride me."

Suddenly, an impossibly strong force knocked me to the ground. A group of snakes, each one looking like a twisting shadow, appeared out of the ground and coiled around me. I struggled against the shadows, but they held me fast. Marie Laveau walked over to me, staring down with her giant eyes, and I could sense the death radiating off of her.

"Free me, Clark!" Brimstone Brown shouted from somewhere faraway. "Free me!"

I breathed in what air I had left and went for my guns. The Colt Peacemakers were good, trusty weapons and the water of the river hadn't hurt them a bit. I closed one eye as I aimed, pointing the pistol at the ropes binding Brimstone Brown. Just as I felt the last gasp of breath leave me, I squeezed the trigger. The bullet snapped the rope holding up Brimstone and he fell down into the river, disappearing under the water. Several alligators lunged for him.

Marie retracted her snakes, and I sucked in air as the revolver fell from my hands. The Voodoo Queen walked to the edge of the platform and looked in the water. She giggled. "He's drowned," she said, turning back to me. "He's drowned!"

The water began to steam and suddenly parted. Brimstone Brown reared out of the river, holding a huge gator above his head. His dark hair streamed down his back and the water boiled around him. We watched Brimstone tear that alligator in half, letting the two chunks splash back into the river.

He jumped into the air, his red eyes blazing, and landed on the platform to stare at Marie Laveau. Someone in the crowd screamed, and then someone else, and pretty soon they were all running away. At first I thought it was because of Brimstone, but then I saw something else. A dozen or so men, all dressed in ragged Confederate uniforms and armed to the teeth ran through the crowd, howling like crazy. Lou Garou was at their head.

He leapt up to the platform and leveled his revolver at Marie. "We've come for you, witch!" he shouted. "Prepare to meet whatever drunken, stupid god had the gall to make you."

Marie regarded Lou Garou calmly. "Kill him," she said, pointing to Brimstone, "and I'll remove your curse."

Lou looked at Brimstone Brown and then back at Marie. He nodded. "I'll hold you to it, you backstabbing witch," he said. He began to transform himself. The fur returned, the wolf's maw and teeth appeared, but he stayed on his two feet, creating a weird looking wolf-man hybrid that didn't look friendly at all.

He howled a challenge to Brimstone and pounced on him. Brimstone raised both of his hands, each one bursting into pure red flame, and the wolf and the demon battled. Brimstone had the upper hand at first, scorching Lou's skin and forcing the wolf to the edge of the platform, but then the werewolf sunk his teeth into Brimstone's leg, knocking him over.

I managed to come to my feet, and saw Charles still suspended over the alligators. The beasts rose up and snapped their jaws at him. I grabbed the pole and pulled it, with all the strength I had left. Bullets whizzed by me, and I saw the other Swamp Dogs blazing away. With one hand on the pole, I drew out my revolver and shot back, hitting one of them in the forehead

and blasting another in the chest. Then, with one last shove, the pole was retracted and Charles landed on the wooden platform.

Brimstone and Lou Garou were still locked in mortal combat. Lou was nearly burned to a crisp, but Brimstone had been bitten and scratched up so bad that it looked like there wasn't a single piece of him that wasn't bleeding. Lou went to all fours, lashing out with his claws, and sent Brimstone sprawling. The swamp dog raised his claw to deliver a death blow.

"Help him, Mr. Reeper!" Charles called. Even when he was in danger, the boy still cared about others. I used my Bowie knife to cut the ropes binding the boy, and then tossed the blade to Brimstone. The satanic gunslinger reached out a hand and caught the knife, then stabbed it into Lou Garou's chest. The werewolf howled in pain, fell off of Brimstone and collapsed on the ground. Brimstone pulled the blade out and then made a large fireball appear in his hands.

"Looks like I'm gonna have to put you down, you mangy mutt," he said, and then blasted the flames onto Lou. The Confederate canine roared and howled in pain as he was roasted alive. In seconds there was nothing left but ash. Brimstone handed me the knife, muttering a thank you.

Charles stood at my side, smiling, happy to be alive. I squeezed his shoulder and smiled back, and then we remembered the one thing that didn't want to be forgotten: Marie Laveau was standing at the edge of the platform. She raised her finger like it was a loaded gun, and pointed it at Brimstone. The demon went down, shadow snakes forcing him to the ground. I went for my Colts and tried to put a slug in Marie's head, but she was faster on the draw. A shadow snake bit me in my tender shoulder, its fangs burning like acid and making me fall to the ground.

Marie stood in front of Charles, her shadow obscuring the small boy. Charles was shaking, but there were no tears in his eyes or screams in his mouth. He folded his hands and looked up at Marie Laveau, then he took off his spectacles and put them in his pocket.

"This is going to hurt me," Marie said to herself. "I normally am so good with children." She raised her finger and pointed it at Charles. Coiling and hissing, shadow snakes descended on the boy, and for a terrible second he was completely obscured by dark, writhing shapes. Then the snakes were gone, and Charles stood there, his eyes closed and his hat askew on his head.

"What?" Marie asked, seemingly to herself. "The Barons? They deserted me?"

She answered herself in a booming, unearthly voice, a man's voice, and it scared me to hear it coming out of a woman's mouth. "The Loa are not playthings," said the strange voice. "There are rules for the Barons. Death only comes to those who are ready for it. Children have nothing to fear from the Loa of Graveyards." Marie seemed to be arguing with herself.

"But this is my body! I can use you as I please!" She answered herself again.

"Impudent Mambo. You are but a vessel."

Then the snakes were gone. I came to my feet and drew out my revolvers, firing out all the remaining shots at Marie's top hat. The big black hat tumbled off of her head and turned to dirty rags on the ground, and the blackness vanished from Marie's skin. She stood on the stage, shivering and afraid, as Brimstone Brown came up behind her.

"Brimstone?" she asked. "Clark? My two best loves?"

In answer, Brimstone raised a burning hand. Marie screamed in terror. She leapt into the air, turning to ash on the wind, and was blown away down river. I watched her flutter away, and then I reached down and grabbed Charles's hand. He squeezed, and I squeezed back.

Now, I don't reckon I've seen the end of the Marie Laveau, the Voodoo Queen. She'll be back plotting a scheme that's as tricky and complicated as ever. But she'll be gone for a while, and that's fine by me. When she does come back, Brimstone Brown and I will be ready for her.

Speaking of Brimstone Brown, he offered to buy me a drink after the battle in Marie's manor, and I was willing to take him up on the offer. But he got some kind of message from his boss downstairs. Serving the devil wasn't all bad, he told me, but he always had to be on the move. The Prince of Lies was sending Brimstone into the South Seas, were some kind of creature that scared even the Devil was stirring. Brimstone and I will cross paths again, and if he's truly reformed, he may well be on my side.

Charles and I had enough of New Orleans, and left the city as soon as we could. I've tried leaving Charles at a boarding school, where I figured he would be safe, but it was attacked by anarchists; but standing by my side don't seem to be the safest place for Charles either. The thought crossed my mind about settling down, getting a little dry goods store or something, and starting over in a quiet town somewhere. Charles could go to school and be with kids his own age, and I could hang up my guns and sleep in mornings if I wanted to. It might be a pretty nice life.

But then I got a letter from this German archaeologist saying some ancient creature he brought back from the ruins in Troy had gotten loose in the Missouri prairies, and I got another telegram from a hotel in the Dakota Territory that was supposedly infested by terrifying shadow monsters. I looked at the letters, and then I figured maybe another job or two wouldn't hurt.

There was always time to get a house and settle down, but adventure was calling me and I had to answer. Charles would go with me, and whether I settled down or was on the move, he'd be by my side, and I was mighty glad to have him there.

Everything's Bigger in Texas

I've seen my fair share of odd-looking critters. I've tangled with a gigantic squid from the bottom of the ocean, an electrified elephant, a type of Mexican Hell Hound, and other creatures that are too strange to put a name to. I reckon it goes with my career choice. My name is Clark Reeper, and I am a bounty hunter. Most of the time I'm gunning for people, but I've killed a decent number of God's creatures over the years. I don't like being a poacher, but it pays the bills and if I'm hired to go after an animal, odds are it's pretty damn dangerous.

But I ain't never seen nothing like the kind of critters whisked up by Jefferson 'Soapy' Smith down in Salinerno, Texas. I had just finished taking a break after a real tough job in Alaska when Soapy Smith sends me a telegram begging for help. We had met a few times before, and were pretty good buddies. Plus, Soapy promised to pay handsomely for my services. Now, old Soapy Smith was a surefire bunco-man, a con artist of the first degree, but he knew what would happen if he tried to pull a scam off on me.

I needed the money, and not just for myself. See, I had Charles Green, my adopted ten-year-old son, to think of. Charles was small for his age, had curly brown hair, thick spectacles, and always wore a neat little brown suit and peaked cap. I'm a tall gent with a weathered Stetson on my head, a long khaki duster, and two Colt Peacemakers on my belt. We couldn't look more different. But I loved Charles like he was my own flesh and blood, and taking care of him meant earning money. And so Charles and I took a stagecoach down to Salinerno, right in the west corner of Texas, to see what sort of a mess Soapy had got himself into this time.

"Clark! You've got to save me!" Soapy cried soon as he saw me. Charles and I had just gotten off of the stagecoach, and found the town of Salinerno in an uproar. Soapy was running towards me, pounding down the dirt street with a large mob in hot pursuit. Soapy was a slight feller in a fancy hand-tailored black suit, a wide brimmed hat and a thick beard. He looked like a cat standing next to an empty fishbowl with the bones still in his teeth. His coat billowed around him as he ran. Soapy collapsed at my feet and raised his hands like he was praying to me.

"Save me!" Soapy cried. "They mean to kill me, Clark, they will bring great pain and suffering upon my completely innocent hide!"

The mob had reached us now, and they all stared as Soapy begged me for help. They were tough looking men, armed to the teeth, and I wasn't in a mood to pick a fight with them, not with a surprised Charles standing nearby.

"Ah hell, Soapy, what have you gone and done this time?" I asked, hauling the con man to his feet. "Done your famous soap swindle and not gotten out of town fast enough?"

"Nothing of the sort," Soapy said, pointing to the mob. "They truly wish to kill me for something that is not my fault!"

"The hell it ain't!" This came from a feller who appeared to be leading the mob. He was a tough-looking black man with a Winchester rifle in his hand and the golden star of a sheriff on his vest. "This town might be filled with nothing but corpses come morning, and all thanks to you and your damn snake oil!"

"I swear, Clark, I didn't mean to cause any harm—"

"Shut up." I elbowed past Soapy and walked over to the sheriff. "Howdy, mister. My name is Clark Reeper, and this is my boy, Charles Green. I'm a friend of Soapy, so you better have a damn good reason for wanting to blow him to pieces."

"Name's Moses Brown," the sheriff said, holding out his hand. "I represent the law around these parts. And Mr. Smith here may have just damned us all to death."

"What he do?"

Moses pointed to Soapy. "Ask him yourself. Even I don't quite understand it."

I turned around. "All right, Soapy, spill it. What'd you do?"

Soapy gulped. "Mama Milton's Miracle Serum. Will make the tiniest lad grow into a bare-knuckle boxer over night. A special profusion of the highest quality ingredients, including herbal secrets from the Orient, creates an elixir that will cause unrivaled growth in practically anything." Soapy's eyes were downcast, and his voice was afraid and soft, not big and boisterous as it usually was when he was trying to sell something.

"Is that true?" Charles asked. The kid was polite as pie and very nice, but he could be a little naïve. "Maybe I could use some to get a little bigger."

"Nah, it ain't true," I told Charles. "Just a bunch of snake oil. Probably a mix of petrol, alcohol and whatever else Soapy could get his hands on." I turned to the bunco-man. "Well, Soapy, what happened? Did some of these folks get sick off your elixir?"

"It ain't that," Moses explained. "The stuff works fine. It works a little too well, actually."

"What do you mean?" Charles asked. "Did it turn somebody into a giant?"

"It works fine," Moses continued. "Just not on people."

"It's not my fault!" Soapy turned to me, begging again. "As I was riding into town, a crate of Mama Milton's fell off of my mule and landed in the dirt! It spilled everywhere! But it wasn't my fault! I had it lashed down good and proper!"

I sighed. "Well, Soapy, I guess it ain't your fault then, on account of it was just an accident. I figure these people don't have much of a right to kill you."

"The hell we don't!" Moses stepped close to me, holding his rifle tightly. "Listen, Reeper, I ain't got no quarrel with you or your boy. But if you stand in the way of the law, I'll be glad to decorate the streets of Salinerno with your brains."

I let one of my hands fall to the Colts at my waist. "You're welcome to try, Mr. Brown, and I reckon you may even succeed.

But if things are as bad as you say, you don't have the time or the bullets to waste on Soapy or me."

Moses Brown looked at me for a long time. "You throwing your lot in with us, stranger?"

"I believe I am," I said, nodding.

The Sheriff of Salinerno let his rifle point to the ground. "Well, maybe you're all right then. But first, I want you to know just what we're dealing with. I'll get a horse from the stables, and you and your boy can ride out with Soapy and myself. You can get an eyeful of what that bastard has done."

"What do you mean?" I asked, already walking to the stables.

"Well, Mr. Reeper, let me just say that you will soon find that everything is bigger in Texas."

I wanted to know a bit more than that, but I didn't figure pressing the sheriff was a good idea, so I kept my mouth shut and my eyes open.

We rode out of Salinerno, with the hot desert sun beating down on us. Charles was sitting in front of me on one horse, Moses Brown riding another, and Soapy and a few other men from the town kept up the rear. The ground was typical Texas prairie and desert, open and barren except for a thin covering of tall grass and weeds. A couple of twisted rock formations were the only landscape worth mentioning as we rode down to the creek.

"So, Moses, tell me," I said as we rode along. I was trying to break the silence more than anything else. "How does a colored man get to be the sheriff of a Texas town that belonged body and soul to the Confederate States of America? If you don't mind me asking, that is."

Moses grinned. "Well, Mr. Reeper, as a matter of fact I do mind, because I don't like it one bit. I was a Buffalo Soldier, fighting with the cavalry. We were sent here to take out a bunch of Confederate guerillas who didn't realize the war was over. You may have heard of their leader—Elihu Wren."

Even though the war was long over, that name sent a shiver down my spine. "Wren, huh? Weren't he the one who rode with Bloody Bill Anderson and William Quantrill?"

"The one and the same. Bastard ran all the way over here and was terrorizing the country. We never got him or his band, but the powers in Washington decided that the town of Salinerno needed some authority here to keep an eye on Wren and make sure he didn't try anything. As a freedman, they figured I would be as loyal as a housebroken dog to the emancipators."

"Did they figure right?"

Moses stared at me. "What do you think? Half the time here I spend worrying that Elihu Wren and his boys will come and blow me apart, the other half fearing the Salinerno townsfolk might just beat them to it. But I think I've done a decent job. I've killed enough outlaws to earn the townsfolk's respect."

"Hey, boy," called one of the Salinerno men. "Creek's down that way. You can see the tracks and everything!"

Moses sighed. "Well, most of their respect," he muttered, and then urged his horse down to the creek bed. We all followed, and then dismounted to get a better look at things. Sure enough, there was a whole mess of footprints all over the sandy creek bed, but I was at a loss as to what had made them. They were round indents, like a fat spear had been stuck into the dirt.

"Some kind of cow?" I wondered aloud. "Nah, that don't make no sense."

"Think smaller," Moses said. "Or, they were smaller, at least. Soapy's stinking snake oil has changed that considerably."

"Hey, boy! We got a live one down here!" the call came from further down the creek, and Moses Brown quickly ran over, his Winchester sliding into his hands. Charles, Soapy, and I followed. As we turned the corner of the creek, something big, black, and glistening came creeping out from behind a large boulder.

"Son of a gun!" I whispered as I saw the beast. It had a tough-looking segmented body, two large pincers, and a massive stinger held aloft over its back.

"A scorpion!" Charles whistled in amazement. "A giant scorpion!" It was as big as an ox and its stinger was as tall as a man.

Moses looked the creature over, and then pointed to a crushed crate resting in the middle of the creek. "The snake oil," he said.

"It just fell in there!" Soapy cried. "I didn't mean any harm! I had no idea it would make insects swell to tremendous sizes!"

"Well, maybe you should have experimented with the stuff a mite before you started flooding everything with it!" Moses cried angrily. "I still think we ought to string you up. It would give the town some justice, even if we're all killed the next day!"

"I meant no harm!" Soapy cried, falling to his knees.

"Uh, guys?" Charles was tugging on my arm. "The scorpion. It's coming this way."

Sure enough, the big bug crawled across the creek, its stinger poised. Moses Brown brought up his Winchester and drew a Schofield pistol out of his belt with a free hand, aiming them at the giant scorpion.

"Put your gun down, boy," ordered a grizzled bearded man from the town. He approached the scorpion with open arms. "Don't you know nothing? Most critters won't harm you unless you harm—"

In a flash, the scorpion's stinger lashed out like a whip, striking the poor man's chest and knocking him to the ground. He let out a terrible shriek. I held Charles close to me and covered his eyes as the scorpion's pincers and strong jaws tore the man apart.

"Kill it!" Moses shouted, as he unloaded both of his weapons. I took out a Peacemaker and blasted away, while Soapy pulled a long barreled Colt Navy from his black coat and fired as well. Our bullets tore into the scorpion, and it let out a high-pitched wail as the shots bore through its chitin. The giant insect abandoned its prey and charged after us. Its stinger struck at Moses Brown.

Moses stepped backward, avoided the sting and then leaned forward and fired the last two shots of his Schofield right into the scorpion's jaws. The insect let out another shriek and then collapsed, falling to the dirt. Its ichor drained away in the creek water.

We all stared in silence at the great insect. "Well," I said, pointing to the mangled body. "I reckon we know what its favorite meal is. We ought to get back to town, get everyone out."

"But it's nearly nightfall!" Soapy protested. "That's when the insects are most active, right around dusk. The crepuscular creatures will attack us as we attempt to flee."

"The lying bastard is right," agreed Moses, as he calmly reloaded his pistol. "We'll go back to Salinerno, but not to run."

I gulped. Fighting a pitched battle in a city was always dangerous, but I could handle any fight against pistol-packing outlaws. Problem was, I didn't have much experience in pest control, especially not a bug problem this big.

We got back to Salinerno right as the sun was going down. Lanterns and torches were lit, and the citizens were going about their evening business as we rode in. Moses fired his rifle into the air, and soon a large crowd had gathered in front of us. Salinerno wasn't a big-sized town, but it had its fair share of people. Men, women, and even little kids gathered in front of Moses Brown to hear what he had to say.

"All right, everybody, listen up," Moses proclaimed, holding his rifle across his chest. "Now I don't care much for you, and you sure as hell don't like me, but if we don't work together, we're all going to be bug chow. First of all, the rumors are true. Scorpions, and God knows what other critters, have gobbled down Soapy Smith's growth serum, making them giant-sized. These bugs are hungry and their preferred meal seems to be us. That means that they'll be coming here." The crowd gasped. Moses pointed to the western side of the town, facing the creek bed, where Soapy had spilled his serum. "They'll probably be coming from that direction, can't say for sure. I know a lot of you are veterans, and others have experience hunting, or maybe killing Indians, outlaws and Mexicans. As long as we stick to our guns, we should be able to make it through the night."

In a sense of disbelief, we went about fortifying the town as best as we could. A couple of wagons and barrels were used as barricades, and we smashed open windows so riflemen could get clean shots off.

While everyone was busy working, I walked over to Soapy. He was sitting on the ground, his hat in his hands, looking very nervous. I guess he figured the people might decide to string him up at any second. I put a hand on his shoulder and hauled him to his feet.

"Howdy, Soapy," I said. "We ought to have a talk."

"Of course," Soapy answered. "What can I do for you?"

"You know any way of reversing what you did to all of them insects?"

Soapy Smith seemed dismayed. "Well, hmmm. That is the question, now, isn't it?"

"Well?"

"I've got some of the serum with me. I may be able to create an antidote, just by switching chemicals around. But I'm not promising anything."

"I'm not asking you to," I said, patting him on the shoulder. "All right, get inside the bank or somewhere fortified and work there. If you can reverse the gigantism, you may get out of this okay."

Soapy nodded and hurried to the bank.

Charles walked over to me, holding a small armadillo in his hands. "Mr. Reeper!" Charles cried, holding the little panzerschwein as a mother would her babe. "Look at what I found." He let the armadillo onto the ground where it curled up in a ball and rolled around him. "I'm naming him Winston."

"That's nice, son," I said, not paying much attention. "You and that armadillo best get yourselves tucked away in one of the buildings. Stay low during the fight, and don't you go running outside for nothing."

Charles understood the seriousness in my voice. "Okay, Mr. Reeper. Please don't get hurt."

I grinned at him. "I won't. Gonna take more than a bunch of oversized bugs to squash Clark Reeper. Get yourself to safety now, okay?"

"Okay." Charles and I embraced and then he headed off. I looked over at the barricades and saw the men and a few women of Salinerno loading their guns and preparing for war. The women and kids laid out fresh weapons and ammo, and the men held their guns close. The sun was nearing the edge of the ground and the air was thick with the tension of the coming fight. A loud buzzing sound, like a thousand Gatling guns blazing away at once, cut through the silence, and then the big bugs were upon us.

"Incoming!" someone shouted, pointing upwards. "They're flying in!"

I ran to Moses Brown, and found him looking skyward. "Holy Hell," he whispered. "I think they're mosquitoes."

He weren't lying. A whole swarm of mosquitoes, each one about the size of a large dog or a small horse, hovered above us and slowly began to descend on the town. They all had glassy wings, thin legs, and a long proboscis that looked like a spear point.

"Start shooting!" Moses shouted, firing upwards with his Winchester. He worked the lever on that gun mighty fast, and soon his shots split several flying insects in twain.

The buzzing bloodsuckers swarmed down on us, and I drew both of my revolvers and fired away. Torn apart by the bullets, the mosquitoes' body parts splattered on the ground. One mega mosquito sunk his long proboscises in a man, stabbing through his overalls and sucking his blood. The poor feller screamed and cried, and his face turned a ghastly white as he was quickly drained. Moses struck the mosquito with his rifle butt, and then fired several shots into the

squirming insect. He helped the stunned, bleeding man off of the ground and carried him to safety.

Meanwhile, a couple of mosquitoes charged after me. I started shooting at them, my first bullet shattering the shell of a mosquito's skull, and my second shot tearing off a couple of legs. The third mosquito flew up on me and stabbed my arm. My pistol fell from my limp hand. I hollered like a stuck pig as I felt my insides getting sucked away. Quickly, I went for my Bowie knife, pulled the weapon out of my boot heel and hacked off the proboscis. The mosquito screamed as it pulled away, and then I buried the blade in its chest.

I bandaged up my wound as best I could, and then retrieved my Peacemaker from the ground. The mosquitoes had been thinned out, and now their carcasses littered the town. Soon a ragged cheer went up as the last insect was slain.

"Think we made it all right?" I asked Moses. He looked over the barricade, and looked back with grim eyes.

"You spoke too soon, Clark Reeper. Much too soon." He pointed over the barricades. "Scorpions coming in for their evening meal, and that's just the start."

The townsfolk ran over to the barricades and started plinking away with everything they had. Scorpions, some as big as dogs, others larger than a stagecoach, were scuttling our way. Swarms of horse-sized ants advanced as well, spraying formic acid from their rear ends and chomping their mandibles. And right in the middle of the pack, came a giant, hairy black shape that I soon realized was a tarantula.

"Son of a gun!" I exclaimed. "We ain't got enough bullets for all of that!"

Moses must have been thinking the same thing. He tossed a hatchet to me and picked up a stout pickaxe handle for himself.

The insects hit the barrier with the force of a locomotive, and the townsfolk fell backwards, still firing. Many bugs shrieked squeals of pain that sounded almost like birdsong just before dropping dead. But more followed them, crawling over the shells of their dead companions and entering the fray. Soon the fight was close up, with pitchforks and cudgels going against mandibles and stingers.

I fanned out my revolver, slaughtering a group of charging ants. Then, I drew out my second pistol as a scorpion crawled towards me. I fired everything I had, but the scorpion kept coming, so I holstered the gun and went for the hatchet. I charged the bug, dodging a stab from its stinger and then slamming the hatchet down on its face. A spurt of ichor stained my khaki jacket, as the scorpion convulsed and died.

"Oh Jesus, get it off of me!" someone in front of me screamed, rolling on the ground and tearing at his skin. I saw that a dozen or so hairs, each one about the size of a stiletto blade, was sticking out of his chest in large clumps. I ran over to the poor feller and tore open his shirt, only to see his skin turning purple as the thick black hairs dug deeper into his flesh.

"What did that to you?" I cried.

"The spider!" the man screamed, still shaking from his pain. "Please, mister, end it!"

Just as the skin of the poor man's face turned purple with poison, I quickly reloaded my revolvers, and dispatched him with a shot to the skull. I turned and looked at the tarantula. The massive spider was rubbing its two front legs together, sending out waves of razor sharp poisoned hairs into the city.

"Hey, all legs and no brains!" I shouted. I ran over to the giant spider. "You looking for something to snack on?!"

It lunged at me, and I rolled low to avoid a wave of tarantula hair, and then I hurled the hatchet at its eight-eyed face. The big arachnid reared backwards, the hatchet wedged between its eyes. That instant, it shot out a clump of sticky white web from its bottom. The sticky webbing grabbed me like a noose, holding me down as the tarantula slowly advanced. I fired, but the spider weren't fazed at all.

I thought I was about finished, when suddenly a shrill voice came screaming from behind the spider. "Hey, get away from Clark!" It was Charles. The boy had his pet armadillo perched on his shoulder and a blazing torch in his hand. He hurled the torch at the spider, setting the hairs on fire. The great beast fell back, thrashing and writhing, its hairs burning up on top of it as a stinky smoke filled the air.

Using my Bowie knife, I succeeded in cutting myself loose and coming to my feet. I walked over to Charles and put a hand on his shoulder. "You saved my life, son," I said. "Thanks."

"You're welcome, Mr. Reeper," Charles said. He watched the spider burn. I knew he didn't like to watch a critter suffering, so I put a couple more bullets right in its head. The tarantula finally stopped shaking and lay down to die.

"Good to see you made it through." Moses Brown walked over through the carnage of dead bugs and people, holding a bloody pickaxe handle in one hand and a machete in the other. "Lots of folk didn't."

I nodded. "We can't hold out much longer, and that's a fact. We need something besides guns and blunt objects to stop the bugs."

Moses looked at the corpse of the tarantula. "Fire seems to give them pause." He turned to a weary rifleman. "Get me all the bottles of alcohol from the saloon and plenty of rags!" he shouted. "And maybe some other rags too—for our noses. It's gonna raise a hell of a stink."

Quickly, every bottle of flammable alcohol was taken from the saloon. Rags were stuffed inside the bottles, matches lit, and soon we had a large amount of lethal whiskey bombs. I picked up one of the firebombs and hurled it into the midst of the insects. It exploded, showering the giant bugs with fire. Even the giant scorpions steered clear of the flame. Soon most of the insects were either blazing away or creeping out of town.

The smell reminded me of overcooked skunk mixed with the contents of New York's sewers, but we all wrapped rags around our mouths and noses and managed. As the sun came up, there was nothing left to do but bury the dead, clean up all the squashed bugs, and wonder what to do next.

The cemetery lay out back. We spent a long time digging graves, and Moses Brown grumbled and gritted his teeth after the dead were laid to rest. Finally, he stood up and stuck a crude wooden cross in the last grave. Charles stood in the background respectfully, and I urged him to go off and play with his new armadillo as Moses Brown walked over to talk.

"I was supposed to protect this town," Moses said, clenching his teeth. "Now about half of the men are dead and buried, and the other half might be joining them shortly."

"How do you figure?" I asked. "We burned all them bugs."

"Not really, not enough." Moses walked over to the destroyed barricades and pointed off in the direction of the hills. "They're all hiding up there. Maybe some of them burrowed straight into the hillside. Come nightfall they'll all come swarming out and finish us off."

That was a pretty cruel thing to say, but I reckoned it was absolutely true. "There must be something we can do. Run, maybe?"

Moses shook his head. "Where to? Nothing but desert all around. The Confederate guerillas and outlaws would finish us off before the bugs could catch up with us."

"Clark! I've done it!" Soapy Smith shouted as he ran down the street. "I really did it!" He puffed, out of breath.

"Done what?" Moses asked.

"I've reversed the effects of Mama Milton's Miracle Serum!" Soapy held out his hands. "And for the small price of ten dollars a bottle, I would be glad to provide you with a large supply of the shrinking agent—"

I pointed my Peacemaker at Soapy's chest, and Moses' Schofield was soon there keeping my gun company.

"Or, I'm sure I could arrange a discount?"

Our hammers clicked backwards.

"All right, for free then. But just this once!"

"Sure, Soapy." We all started walking back to town, and I noticed even the dour Moses Brown had a little spring in his step. "Problem is, how do we get the shrinking juice to the insects?"

"That's a real problem," I said.

"Well, just leave it out, and I'm sure they will drink it up." Soapy chuckled as the problem dawned on us. I figured we might be able to lead a giant scorpion to the juice, but we sure as hell couldn't make it drink. "Or perhaps if we dispersed it into the air, maybe using explosives, the blasted bugs would breathe it in and then shrink back to their normal size."

"But we don't have any explosives," Moses said sadly. "Goddamn. We ain't gonna make it, bug juice or no bug juice."

"Now hold on," I told Moses. "We ain't got no dynamite or nothing, but I think I know someone who does."

It only took Moses Brown a second or two to realize who I was talking about. "No way in hell. They'd just as soon shoot me as look at me. Then they'd string up my corpse! I ain't going to Elihu Wren for help!"

"It's not like we got a goddamn choice!" I shot back. "Face it, Moses, the bugs are going to chew us up unless we get the shrinking serum evaporated into the air. And ex-Confederate outlaws like Wren have got to have plenty of dynamite lying around."

Moses Brown tore at his clothes, pulling off his coat, and then his vest and shirt. He turned around and I stared at the numerous lashes in his back. Thick marks stood out, red and raw-looking.

"I belonged to the Wren family, Mr. Reeper. I didn't get these for behaving myself. You can't imagine the horrors that were visited on me, before, during, and even after the war by men like Elihu Wren. I'm not about to go crawling back to beg him for help."

"He whipped you?" said a small voice. It was Charles. The boy was standing at my side, holding his pet armadillo in his hands.

"Well, it wasn't Elihu, but his old man's overseers. My family and I belonged to his father's farm in Missouri. Soon as the war came we all headed north. Most of us made it." There was nothing but hatred in Moses' voice. "When I heard the Wren boy had joined the Bushwhackers, well, I signed up as soon as I could to go after him."

"Oh," Charles said nervously. "M-maybe he feels bad about it. Could be he might apologize to you."

"Not likely," Moses muttered.

"But Mr. Brown, if Elihu Wren doesn't help us, we won't survive. And the bugs will eat him too! Maybe if you explained that, and did it very nicely, he'd give us the dynamite," Charles added, sounding very logical. "Then, after the bugs were gone, you could all go back to killing each other!" Charles's voice was thin and it wavered, but he made his point better than I ever could have.

Moses stared at my boy and slowly grinned. "Smart kid, Mr. Reeper," he said, ruffling Charles's curly hair. "He sees things the way they are." He sighed and turned to me. "Well, I suppose it couldn't hurt to try, considering we're all dead anyway. But how are we going to get over there? Wren is holed up in the mountains out of the town, and the bugs are infesting the hills. No horse could be fast enough, or tough enough, to get through."

I looked at Winston, Charles's pet armadillo, and rapped a knuckle against his hard armored skin. "Shame horses didn't have tough skin like this here armadillo," I said.

"But what if the armadillo was a little bigger?" Charles asked. A crazy idea popped into my head.

Soapy Smith reappeared, rolling a barrel of what had to be his shrinking elixir. I looked up and waved to him. "Hey, Soapy! Got any more of Mama Milton's Growth Serum?"

A couple of hours later, Sheriff Moses Brown and I rode out of Salinerno on a buckboard wagon pulled by a giant armadillo. Winston proved a pretty good horse, and after offering him a couple carrots to fill him up after his growth spurt, and a few cracks of the whip over his head, he charged forward at a great speed.

Moses held the reins, urging the great armadillo on, and I rode shotgun. Our cargo was the large barrel full of the shrinking serum, as well as a few rifles, shotguns, and almost all of the ammo Salinerno had left. We drove fast towards the hills, the wagon rocking as Winston hauled us along.

"Yeee-haaa!" I shouted, waving my hat in the air as the wagon went over a large bump. "If I'd of known armadillos made such good steeds, I would have hooked my wagon behind one a long time ago!"

"Yeah, but this smooth sailing ain't going to last forever," muttered the sheriff of Salinerno.

Just as he spoke, a swarm of giant mosquitoes fluttered out of the hills. I picked up the shotgun and fired at the nearest bug, shattering its body in a blast of lead. The insect's bits splattered over us as we drove by. Moses cracked his whip over the armadillo's back and Winston sped himself up. We reached the top of the hill just as I fired off my second barrel. This one managed to splatter two mosquitoes. I tossed the shotgun down and picked up another one.

"How we doing, Moses?" I asked, firing off both barrels at once. The mosquitoes made another pass and came swooping down towards the front of the wagon. Winston slashed at them with his claws and even caught one in his mouth. The flying blood suckers struck out with their sharp legs and snouts, and managed to take away some of our blood.

I winced in pain as the mosquito sucked a little blood out of my shoulder before I blew it out of the sky.

"Almost there!" Moses shouted back. "Then the damn Confederates can kill us instead of the bugs!"

We came to the mountains, where large reddish brown rocks made the perfect hideout for any band of guerillas. We rode into a narrow canyon until it dead-ended, blocked by red rocks on all angles. The swarm of angry mosquitoes came straight for us. Their shadows seemed to block out everything else as they zoomed down and their buzzing was deafening.

Just when we were about to become bug food, dozens of rifles and pistols cracked. Mosquitoes fell from the sky and splattered all over the rocks. Soon there wasn't a single one left up there.

I turned to Moses and saw that he had his hands raised. I looked up and saw why. A small army of men in ragged Confederate uniforms and other clothes of a vaguely gray color were perched up in the rocks, aiming down all manner of wicked-looking weaponry at us.

"Well, master," Moses whispered to himself. "Your faithful slave has returned."

The Confederate Holdouts blindfolded us and then took us and our wagon up into their base of operations. When we opened our eyes, we saw a lot of guns pointing straight at us. Moses Brown didn't look at them, but at the tall man with shoulder-length brown hair, a bearded face, a Confederate cavalry hat, and a saber at his waist who was staring back at him. He had eyes like a hungry wolf and scars to match.

"Moses Brown," the bushwhacker said, smiling. "How nice of you to join your old owner."

"Elihu," Moses said, hatred in his voice. "Still trying to make your damn pappy proud?"

Elihu Wren walked over to us, looking us over. The guerilla camp was a busy place, weapons, ammunition, and even explosives all neatly stacked and ready to be used. Wren looked at me for a while before speaking.

"Clark Reeper!" he said, pleased to have recognized me. "Your reputation precedes you. Heard you gunned down Lou Garou and the Swamp Dogs in Louisiana. That true?"

I nodded. "Yeah. They were just a bunch of outlaws."

"They were my comrades in arms!" Elihu shouted, raising a gloved fist and nearly hitting me in the face. "We fought together for Jefferson Davis, Dixie, and Southern Rights! Hurrah!"

"War's over, Wren," I said calmly.

"Well, you could have fooled me!" Elihu Wren pointed to Moses Brown. "This no-good Darkie has been dogging me like I was a run-away slave and he was a slave-catcher. No chance for peace with scum like him around."

Moses stared at the rocky ground and said nothing.

"My boys ain't tired of fighting, not by a long shot, they ain't!" Elihu chuckled. "And now you two fall right into my lap."

"We're looking for help," I blurted out. "The giant bugs, the mosquitoes, and ants, and scorpions, you must have seen them. We need your help."

"Maybe that's not my problem," Elihu Wren answered, stroking his thick beard.

"Well, once Salinerno is gobbled down, the bugs will come for you and it will be your damn problem!" I nearly shouted. "The war is over and done with! Can't the both of you idiots see that and stop fighting!"

"No chance in hell," Moses Brown said defiantly.

"Likewise," Wren agreed.

"Reeper, you just don't get it." Moses glowered at me. "I still carry the wounds from the Wren Family's overseer. They burn me every time I put on a shirt on. My family worked for his for generations, and it took most of us dying before we got out of bondage. That's enough to make a man a little angry."

Elihu stared at Moses. "You think you deserve revenge?"

"I think I'm entitled to my fair share."

The bushwhacker cavalryman spat in Moses Brown's face. "Not a week after you coloreds cleared out, a band of Kansas jayhawkers hit the farm. Killed my ma, my pa, my little brothers and sisters. I was the only one to survive. Been fighting back ever since." He furrowed his brow as his hand fell to the handle of his cavalry sword. "Maybe I ought to get some vengeance right now."

"Shut up!" I shouted. I came to my feet, ignoring all of the guns pointed at me, and walked over to Elihu Wren. "You're both fools if you think those monstrous bugs give a crap about your skin color or what side you fought on! All they care is that you're food to them, and that they can eat you! Now, either you two put aside your differences or we all die. Make your choice."

Wren and Brown stared at each other for a long time.

"What you got that makes the bugs go away?" Elihu Wren asked. "And why do you need my help?"

"The feller who is responsible for making the bugs get giant has a way to shrink them down back to normal," I explained, pointing to the barrels of Soapy's shrinking serum. "But we need your explosives to put the juice into the air. The bugs will breathe it in and get nice and small."

Eilhu reached into his cavalry coat and pulled out a single red stick of dynamite. "We got enough explosives. I suppose we can spare a few."

"Much obliged," I said, grinning. "And don't you worry. After this is over you two can kill each other all you want."

I must have convinced them, on account of everyone settled down and started working together. It took a little while to get the shrinking juice set up. We took the barrel of it up to the highest peak on the mountainous terrain, and then stuck a whole bunch of dynamite sticks under it. A long fuse was lit, and then we watched it slowly worm its way down the wire until it reached the barrel. There was a powerful blast and the whole thing went up in smoke, the clouds of it drifting across the sky.

"Is that the end of that?" Elihu asked, sounding skeptical.

I shrugged. "I don't rightly know. Maybe it will take some time for the bugs to breathe it in and shrink down." I turned to Moses. "Check on Winston. See if he did any shrinking."

We all went back and saw Winston, tied up to a hitching post in the guerillas' camp. He was still the same freakishly oversized armadillo. I ran my hand down his rough armored sides and shook my head. "Must take a little time then."

"Or maybe it's not working at all," Moses Brown said fearfully.

Moses said what all of us were thinking. What if Soapy Smith had screwed up and the bugs were gonna stay giant? That did not bode well for our survival.

"Hey, get a look at this!" Someone, a lookout or sentry, shouted. He was standing on a precipice overlooking the plains and Salinerno. We ran over and looked down, and the sight filled us with fear.

The bugs were on the move. Maybe the insects caught wind of what was in the air, or maybe they were just hungry, but they were headed to eat the survivors of Salinerno. The big bugs swarmed down on the town. Hundreds of ants and scorpions trundled along, and even a couple of humongous hairy tarantulas charged on Salinerno.

"They'll wipe the city out," Moses whispered. He turned to Elihu Wren and the Confederate holdouts. "I'm going to go back there and fight. We're doomed, but maybe we can hold them off for a little. Prolong death."

Elihu nodded. "I ain't gonna stop you."

Moses gulped. "And Elihu?"

"Yeah?"

"I must say, I didn't know what had happened to the Wrens in Missouri. I am sorry. Despite the whippings, and all the other daily evils, they didn't deserve what happened to them."

Eilhu Wren grinned at Moses Brown. "Well you know what? I must say I am sorry for what happened to your family. They were hard-workers, and if they weren't loyal, I can understand why." He held out his hand. "Well, Moses, what do you say we all ride down and go stomp some bugs?"

A wide smile appeared on Moses' face and he pumped Eilhu's hand. "That sounds like a mighty fine proposition."

We charged down on the insects like the wrath of Almighty God. All of the Confederate holdouts came, some of them shouting out the rebel yell as they urged their horses onward. The galloping steeds thundered out of the mountain and towards the flank of the insect horde.

Moses and I rode in the wagon pulled by Winston. We hollered just like the cavalrymen. As we crested the first hill and spotted the bugs, our charge almost came to a muddled stop. There were a hell of a lot of bugs. Swarms of them, at least a thousand ants were there, as well as larger beasts. And they were all so big. We seemed to ride into their shadows as we closed in.

"Give them some dynamite, boys!" Elihu Wren shouted. "That'll cut them down to size!"

Every rider produced a red stick of dynamite. I pulled two from my boot and tossed one to Moses. We all lit them. The slow hiss of a dozen or so lit fuses filled the prairie.

"Let them have it!" Elihu shouted, and we hurled the dynamite sticks forward. The explosives landed in the insect swarm. There was a deafening blast. Big red clouds of fire and death tore through the insects, splattering ants and scorpions.

"Now! Charge!" The bushwhacker leader galloped ahead, his cavalry saber in one hand and his revolver blazing away in the other. We followed, firing away with everything we had as we crashed into the ranks of the insects. Southern steel hacked through chitin, separating insect limbs from bodies. Revolvers and light carbine rifles fired at the bugs at close range, gunning the beasts down.

I stood up in the back of the wagon, firing with both of my pistols. I shot off the tail of a scorpion and the deadly stinger plunged down into the body of the beast. It squealed and died as I pumped it full of bullets. Moses Brown held the reins in one hand and fired his Winchester with the other. An ant smashed its head through the bottom of the wagon, but Moses rammed the butt of the Winchester against it and crushed its thick skull. Even Winston the armadillo hacked at the insects with his claws, chewing them apart with his sharp teeth.

Then a low hissing sound came that drowned out all the other sounds of battle. "Ah hell," Moses Brown said, pointing his finger to the edge of the battle. "Looks like insects ain't the only things that are bigger in Texas."

A rattlesnake that had to be the size of a large Union Pacific train slithered down from the hills. It lashed out with venom-dripping fangs, devouring giant insects and horsemen alike.

I jumped off the wagon, reloading my six-guns as I ran towards the snake. "Damn snake-in-the-grass," I muttered. "Maybe you ought to pick on someone your own size!" I fired at the rattler, my first shot taking out one of its eyes and my second shot chipping one of its teeth. The rattler's tail sound like an avalanche, and then the massive reptile slithered towards me.

I still had one stick of dynamite left. I pulled it out, lit the fuse, and then tossed the explosive into the snake's open mouth. The explosion blew the snake apart and covered the hillside in gore.

Back at the battle, the insects were winning; there were just too many of the creatures. The Confederate bushwhackers ran out of bullets, and fought with cavalry sabers against mandibles and pincers. I found myself stabbing incoming ants with my Bowie knife. A scorpion got me from behind, grabbed me in his pincers and squeezed the life out of me. I tried to lash out at him, but the bug held me too tightly. The scorpion raised his stinger for a killing blow. But his stinger fell a few inches short. The pincers slipped away, and I stepped back as the scorpion seemed to get smaller and smaller.

And then I saw that it was on account of the scorpion was shrinking!

The other bugs were doing the same. In a few seconds, they were the size of dogs, then no bigger than lizards, and then they were just about as small as they had always been. The Confederate holdouts let out a few war whoops of victory as their opponents shrank away. Some of the gleeful soldiers lashed out with their boots to stomp the now tiny insects into oblivion.

I walked back to Moses Brown. The wagon had stopped moving, the armadillo pulling it now no bigger than, well, a normal armadillo. Moses was laughing, overjoyed.

"I can't believe it, Clark!" he said. "By God, we won!"

And he was absolutely correct.

That night, Charles and I stayed for a little victory party in Salinerno. The townsfolk and the guerillas seemed to accept each other, and were getting along just fine. Even Moses Brown and Elihu Wren seemed more inclined to share a drink than to try to take each other's scalps. Next morning, Charles and I headed out of there on the stagecoach.

Soapy Smith was in the stagecoach with us. He was talking about settling down sometime, creating some sort of an organization of people like him, confidence men and bunco salesmen. I guess he'd call them the Soap Mob or something. Well, I wished him the best of luck, and told him that he ought to keep his nose clean and not ask for me to bail him out all the time.

Charles decided to take Winston the armadillo along, and I decided to let him. The little feller had been a great help to us, and I think we owed him something. The armadillo mostly got his own food and behaved himself fine. I also swiped a little bit of Mama Milton's Serum from Soapy. Maybe someday I would have need of a giant armadillo. It was best to be prepared.

Well, I've been getting a bunch more telegrams from all kinds of folks. Some Parisians sent me a note about a 'phantom' terrorizing their city. I got a note from some Belgian fellers needing me to look up some sort of flying monster that was terrorizing the Congo.

I don't know if I'll take any of these international jobs, but I reckon they pay well, and maybe I do need a little break from America. After seeing some of the wildlife in Texas, I'm willing to give anything a try. I suspect it can't be much tougher, and it certainly can't be any bigger.

The Troublesome Courtship of Jennifer Chaos

Now I don't know too much about women folk. It's not that I don't like women, quite the contrary. But I just don't run into them much in my line of work. You see, my name is Clark Reeper, and I'm a bounty hunter, which has always been a man's profession. Sure, I've seen girls waltzing around town, dressed in them big flowing dresses, and I've spent many a night ogling the girls in the saloon with their tight outfits and feathery hats. Truth is, I ain't never really talked to one for an extended period of time, and, if I ever did, I'm quite sure I wouldn't know what to say.

It's not like I don't think about it. A feller does get mighty lonely out in the prairies. But I've more important things than calico on my mind. You see, I've got me an adopted son to look after, a little ten-year-old boy by the name of Charles Green. He's a great kid, small for his age, with curly brown hair, thick spectacles; and he always wears a neat little Norfolk suit and a peaked cap. A boy that age should be with his mother, but Charles's ma was dead and buried. I wasn't really thinking too hard about getting him another one.

I'm also not the kind of man ladies fall head-over-heels for. I'm a tall, gaunt, feller, and I wear a long khaki duster, and a crumbling Stetson. Two Colt Peacemakers are never far from my hands. Maybe if I washed my face once in a while and had a big bath with fancy French soaps and enough cologne to drown a rat in, I wouldn't look and smell too bad. But trying to look pretty would slow me down, and in my career, it would also make me a laughing stock.

Come to think of it, there is one lady who would accept me, bad smells and all. Just thinking of her makes me feel a bit light on my feet and wrong in my head. Her name is Jennifer Plesance, but on account of her manner and actions, everyone calls her Jennifer Chaos. Now, Jenny Chaos ain't exactly the kind of girl you'd bring home to your folks. She's wild as a mustang and ornery as a mountain lion, but out there in the lawless west, she sure is something special.

I hadn't seen Jennifer in a while, so it was a surprise when she bumped into me on the road to Red Creek, Wyoming. I was on the trail of a wanted outlaw and self-styled preacher name of Revered Wiley Drake. Rumor was him and his 'Flock' was holed up in Red Creek, so I went there to see for myself. Turns out I got a hell of a lot more than I bargained for.

Charles and I rode into Red Creek on an old buckboard wagon I had picked up for a decent price down in Cheyenne. As usual, Charles was reading, and I was focusing on keeping the wagon on the road. The landscape was your typical wide open desert interrupted by tall rocks, sparse vegetation, and little else. Riding with us was Winston, Charles's pet armadillo. The little panzerschwien had saved our lives back in Texas, so I figured the least we could do was carry the critter around with us.

"Good book?" I asked Charles, giving our mule a warning swipe with the whip.

Charles nodded, not looking up. "It's okay. It's a gushy romance, and I don't know if I like it or not, even if it is a classic."

We rode on in silence for a little more, and then Charles closed his book and looked at me. "Um, Mr. Reeper?"

"Yeah, Charles?"

"Do you ever feel a need, for a girl? Or a woman or anything?"

I smiled at Charles. "Sure, son. But the bounty hunter's lot is a lonely one, and there ain't nothing for it. Besides, what sort of woman would like me?"

"Well, a lot of them would!" Charles explained. "You're very kind, and brave, and you've saved me so many times, and you always do the right thing."

"Yeah, maybe." We were passing around a couple of rocks, big old boulders that overlooked the trail. I slowed down the wagon a little. "But I don't know if I could find someone right for me, you know? What if something happened to her? Or me? Bounty hunter's life is a dangerous one. There ain't no contesting that."

Just as I had spoke, a gunshot rang out, and several men appeared from behind the rocks. They all had red bandannas covering their faces and they were holding various kinds of firearms, training the weapons on Charles and me.

"Reach for the sky, you miserable greenhorns!" shouted one of the bandits.

"Road agents!" I cursed, raising my hands. There were six of them bandits and they had the drop on me. Now, I had the means to make sure they would never bother anyone again except for their fellow souls in Hell. But with little Charles sitting next to me, I really didn't want to risk taking them all out at the same time.

I put my hands up, and so did Charles. The road agents moved forward. "I ain't got but a little cash on me," I said. "You boys are wasting your time."

"That's all right," laughed a big feller with a silver hatband. "We'll take what we can get." He held out his hand. I reached into my pocket, pulled out a roll of bills, and dropped them into his hand. "Thank you kindly," the robber said. He turned to Charles. "Now the boy. What you got in your pockets, little whelp?"

Charles was sitting next to me, very still and quiet. He reached into his pocket and pulled out a few coins. The road agent roughly took them from the boy, and then pointed to a golden watch Charles had dangling from a chain on his small suit.

"How about the watch, boy?" the Road Agent asked. "That looks like it cost you a pretty penny."

"Please, sir," Charles whispered. "My father gave that to me. Please."

"Leave the watch, you damn scoundrel," I told the road agent. "You got your payday, now move along."

The big outlaw stuck his pistol close to my face, nearly putting the barrel up my nostril. "You ain't in any position to be giving orders, greenhorn," he said maliciously. "But you know, I admire your spunk. So, I'll kill you and your brat, just like me and the boys always do, and then, after you're both dead, I'll take his watch. Then you won't mind none. Sound good?"

"You son of a—"

But my words were cut off as a gunshot rang out through the air. All of us stopped what we were doing and looked around. Charles was shaking, but unharmed. I swung back to the thug sticking his six-gun in my face, and noticed that he was okay too. Then we all heard a thud as one of the bandits slowly toppled over backwards and hit the ground, with a large bullet hole square in his skull.

"What the hell was that?" the road agent said, pulling me off of the wagon and pressing the gun to my face. Charles yelped and ran into his legs, knocking him over. Then another shot rang out, and another outlaw fell backwards, dead before he hit the ground.

I drew one of my Colts, and pointed it at the varmint who had been holding me hostage. We both pointed our irons at each other. His men were frozen, too scared of the sniper, and what I might do to their boss.

"Find the sniper!" the boss shouted to his men. "Kill him!"

"He's on top of the rock!" one of the outlaws shouted. A road agent raised his shotgun to his shoulder, but then a brown blur charged out from behind the rock, slamming its head into the robber's knee, and knocking him to the floor. It was a brown, shaggy goat.

I stared at the goat and shook my head. "Ah hell," I whispered. "Jennifer, what are you doing out here?"

The sniper walked to the end of the rock and jumped down on my wagon. She was holding a smoking breech-loading Snider rifle in her gloved hands, and had a wide grin on her face.

"Clark! You lazy scumbag!" Jennifer Chaos yelled, smacking aside a road agent with the butt of her gun and then blasting him in the face. "You gonna thank me for saving your miserable behind or do I got to take out my knife and cut the gratitude out of your mangy hide?"

"Much obliged, ma'am," I said thankfully. The bandit pointed his pistol at me and then, stared at Jennifer Chaos's smoking Snider. Jennifer was dressed like a man, with worn trousers, a shirt and vest. She carried a revolver and a hunting knife at her waist. Covering her head was a small bowler hat with a couple of feathers in it. She looked like she had taken a bath in Missouri mud. In short, she was a sight for sore eyes.

"Y-you?" stammered the bandit, not quite believing his eyes. "You wiped out my band?"

"Sure did. And what a miserable bunch of ugly goat-faced bastards they were!"

"But you're just a lady," the outlaw whispered. "I could be courting you..."

Jennifer laughed. She hopped down off of my wagon, walked over to the road agent, and threw her rifle to the ground. "Listen you dirt-licking son of a monkey," she crooned. "You court me, you court chaos itself!" She slugged him, knocking the pistol from his hands, and then drew her hunting knife, stabbing it straight through his throat. The road agent coughed and gurgled for a little and then fell silent.

Jennifer Chaos whistled, and the little brown goat ran over to her side. "Why Erasmus!" she said, petting the animal, "you done got a little bit of blood on your horns. Let me wipe them off for you." She drew a handkerchief from her pocket and cleaned the horns.

"Beehhh," answered the goat, gently chewing some of Jennifer's shirt.

She picked him up and scratched his ears. Then she gave Charles a beautiful smile. "Why hello, little fellow!" she said, ruffling the stunned Charles's hair. "Clark, you opium-sucking crap-head, I had know idea you had gone and made yourself an offspring!"

"H-he's not mine," I stammered. "Charles is my, um, my adopted son." For some reason, whenever I was around Jennifer Chaos, I tended to get a little weak in my knees, and didn't quite know what words to say and such. Maybe she cast some kind of spell or curse, but whenever she was around, I felt dopey and bashful.

"What an adorable child," Jennifer said, turning to Charles. She held out her hand. "Hello there, young man. My name is Jennifer, but you may call me Jenny."

"Hello, Jenny," Charles said politely. "Thank you for saving us."

"No trouble at all. Clark here is a bad shot, and a real waste of breath in any fight. I don't know how he's been surviving without me these past years. Probably got a whole mess of angels, I reckon, watching out for him." Then, Jennifer turned to me. "Well, Clark, what do you say you let me and my goat on that wagon and we ride into town? It's the least you could do after I saved your worthless life."

"Sure," I said. "Be glad to have you."

Jennifer Chaos and I sat in the front of the wagon, Charles between us. Winston the armadillo and Erasmus the goat were chasing each other around in the back.

I whipped the mule, and we set off towards Red Creek.

"So, um, Jennifer." I was trying to make conversation, and not producing anything of the sort. "What, uh, what exactly you doing in these parts?"

"Well, Clark, I reckon it's the same sort of thing you're doing." Jenny pulled a cigarette out of my belt, and lit it with one of my matches. "This is terrible tobacco, Clark. You should treat yourself a little better. Or maybe not. How did you let those two-bit thugs get the drop on you back there?"

"I'm sure Mr. Reeper had a plan to save us," Charles said apologetically. "He's saved my life tons of times."

"Probably endangered it plenty times too," Jenny muttered. "Clark, you ought to get this nice boy to a good home, instead of dragging him all over creation with you. Frontier ain't no place for a child."

"Clark does a fine job!" Charles said defensively. "In fact, the only thing he really needs to do in order to make my life completely normal is to find me a mother." Charles stared at me, and then stared at Jennifer Chaos.

I grinned weakly. I guess Charles had taken a liking to Jennifer Chaos, and wanted me to do the same.

"Yeah, I'm sure he does himself right proud. Until he up and leaves without warning." Jennifer turned to me. "Why'd you do it, Clark? Leave me all alone in some hotel in El Paso? We had a nice thing together, until you went and spoiled it."

"Ah hell," I muttered. "I don't want to talk it about it, Jenny, I really don't." I tried to change the subject. "So, can you give me a better answer about what you're doing?"

Jennifer pulled a folded wanted poster from her inside her vest. She unfurled the poster and I saw a crude drawing of an angry-looking feller with a black, broad-brimmed hat, a long black coat and a preacher's white collar. He had a curling scar on his cheek and a murderous look in his eyes.

"Reverend Wiley Drake," I said. I looked up at Jennifer. "You taken up bounty hunting?"

"Sure am." She grinned. "Jesus, Clark, if a regular idiot like you can do it, it can't be too difficult. Beats the hell out of shooting at Indians and sleeping on the ground." She squeezed my shoulder. "Say, Clark, what do you say we double-team this poor bastard and split the reward money?"

"That would be great!" Charles exclaimed. "I'm sure Mr. Reeper would love to work with you. Right, Mr. Reeper?"

"Uh, sure, son. It would be to my liking," I muttered, not feeling anything of the sort. With Jenny around, making my head light and my limbs leaden, even any easy job could turn into something else entirely.

"Sounds good!" Jennifer slapped my back. "All right, let's get us some rooms in the hotel and see if we can't find ourselves the preaching knot-head."

Red Creek was a typical small settlement, a couple of rows of shops and houses, a two-story hotel, and more saloons than was necessary. It seemed like a normal town, with a lot of the townsfolk going about their daily business, but there was something a mite strange about it.

First of all, there was a lot of crosses around. They were hanging in front of doors, propped up against the sides of stores, and it seemed like you was always staring straight at a crucifix. Another thing was the way people walked, and they all seemed to be watching us kind of funny, like they was wondering what sort of a threat we could be.

"Nice town," Jennifer said. "About as cold as a preacher's backside. Well, there's the hotel and the livery. Let's stash this sorry mule before it drops dead and get us some rooms."

We got a stall for the mule and then walked into the hotel. Jennifer was holding her goat; Charles had his armadillo in his hands. The two animals seemed to be getting along okay, though I reckoned they enjoyed a good tussle with each other.

I walked over to the man at the desk, and then I realized I didn't know how many rooms to get. Should I get a room for myself and Charles? And then have Jennifer sleep in the one next door? Or maybe I ought to put me and Jenny in the same room, and get Charles his own, so he wouldn't be in the way in case anything happened. And should I be paying for both of them, on account I was the man and that was a man's duty, or maybe Jennifer should pay for her own?

"What'll it be?" the feller at the desk asked.

"Uh, two rooms," I said. "One for the boy, and one for me and the lady—"

"And one for me and my goat." Jennifer interrupted me. She pushed me out of the way, paid for her own room, gave me a smirk, and walked upstairs.

"Uh, just one room," I said, quickly paying for it, and then taking the key and walking upstairs with Charles at my side, feeling like an idiot.

After we had gotten situated, we met in the dirt street outside of the hotel to divine our next course of action. Jenny wanted to start shooting at random people until the preacher gave himself up, but I figured we should be a little more subtle. Something weren't right about Red Creek, and I wanted to figure out what it was.

We decided to head down to one of the saloons. Jennifer needed her daily shot of whiskey, and I wanted to wet my own whistle before looking around. We headed down the street to the nearest bar, but then something happened that changed our whole plan. It made me realize how little I knew about the Revered Wiley Drake.

"Excuse me, Mr. Reeper, why is that man dragging a coffin?" Charles asked, pointing at an odd man in the middle of the street.

Sure enough, there was a feller walking along the middle of the dirt street, and dragging behind him, tied to a couple of ropes, was an old, splintery coffin. The man just wore black, a big black cloak, black hat, and he had cold dark eyes that made you shiver when you looked into them. Soon as he realized I was looking him over, he turned around and fixed me with his steely gaze.

"Howdy," I said, tipping my hat. "Nice day, ain't it?"

He didn't say anything, and continued dragging his coffin.

Jenny Chaos stared at him. "Hey, why you dragging that pine box with you? Got your dead grandma in there or something?"

The stranger stared at her, but still did not say anything.

"Oh, Christ, won't you say a single damn thing? Stupid mute!" Jennifer walked over to him. "Come on, you idiot, show me what's in the coffin."

The stranger finally said something. "I'll show you these, ma'am." He opened his cloak, revealing a couple of pearl-handled revolvers. The white of the handles gleamed against his black shirt and pants.

"Ah, you think a couple of fancified six-guns will scare me? I'm Jennifer Chaos! Now, open up the box. What you got in there?"

"There is a body. Of sorts." The stranger pulled the coffin close to him. "My name is Cole Corbucci, and I've come to bury a corpse. You don't need to know any more, ma'am."

"Why here?" I asked. "Couldn't you have dug a hole and plopped that stiff down anywhere?"

Cole Corbucci shook his head. "It must be here."

"Why's that?" Jennifer was a curious one, and didn't want to let this matter rest.

"Can't tell you." Cole roughly shouldered past her, and continued walking down the street. He would have kept walking too, had not a gunshot echoed through the city. Cole stopped walking. The citizens of Red Creek started screaming and running out of the way, women tripping on their aprons, folks pulling kids in doors, and even stout, strong men closing windows and shouting in terror. I drew one of my one revolvers and held Charles close to me.

Down the street came a couple of men on horseback. One of them carried a big crucifix made up of two sticks nailed together. Their leader wore a preacher's collar and had a big scar on his cheek. It was Revered Wiley Drake, and he stared down at Cole Corbucci with a look that was anything but friendly.

Cole returned the hostile gaze. "Good afternoon, Drake," Cole said evenly. "Enjoying this spell of good weather?"

Wiley Drake grinned. "Well, if it ain't Cole Corbucci! I didn't think you would have the guts to come and face me here. Smart thinking to bring your own coffin with you. Hell, why don't you open it up? When we blast you to kingdom come, you'll fall right into it!" The Reverend had a deep, rumbling voice. "It'd be the Good Lord's Mercy."

"I'm not going to keel over for you," Cole said defiantly. His hand fell to the revolver at his side.

"I never asked you to."

Me and Jenny also reached for our guns. If Corbucci and Drake got into a shooting war, we might be able to help the black-clad gunslinger take out the rogue preacher, and collect the bounty.

Drake whistled and then several more horsemen approached from behind, all of them armed to the teeth. Some of the stores and shops opened, and even more gunmen walked out. They were gruff looking badmen and outlaws, dusty, unshaven, and cold-eyed. A small army, around a hundred or so men, stood out there in the streets of Red Creek, each one of them spoiling for a fight.

We stared at the huge gang the Reverend had put together. One thing was for certain: Jenny, Cole, and I couldn't kill them all no matter how handy we was with a gun. There were just too many of them, and we were surrounded.

"My Flock is rather large." Drake lit a fat cigar and jammed it in his mouth. "What can I say? The Good Lord provides."

"The Reverend says we'll get salvation if we do what he says!" said a bucktoothed outlaw next to the Reverend. "And he tells us to do fun stuff too!"

Drake smiled, then, lightning fast, drew a revolver and blasted a hole straight through the outlaw's head. The bucktoothed man toppled off of his horse without having time to scream.

"Nobody interrupts me when I'm preaching!" Drake fired his pistol into the air. "Nobody! Now the Good Lord is speaking through me as his vessel, and he's telling you this, Cole Corbucci: There's a special place in Hell waiting for you."

"Yeah." Corbucci walked backwards to the coffin. "I'll keep it real nice for you, Drake."

Cole reached to open the coffin, but then one of Drake's Flock jumped off of his horse like he was spring-loaded, drew a pale white club of some sort, and smacked Corbucci upside the head. The gunslinger gasped and fell to the ground.

"Thanks, Ringo," said the Reverend, tossing a cigarette to the man who had knocked Cole out. Ringo was a weird-looking one, wearing a wide-collared shirt and dingy trousers, his hair scraggly and black. He was lean, hungry looking, and pale as a corpse at a funeral. After a while I realized that the club he was holding was a human leg bone.

Ringo bowed low. "Always a pleasure to do the Lord's work, Reverend."

Wiley Drake was about to turn his horse around, when he noticed me, Jennifer Chaos, and Charles. A grin formed on his scarred face. "Why, Clark Reeper, is that you? And Jennifer Plesance with him?"

"Yes, sir." I answered without thinking.

Drake doffed his hat. "It is an honor, Mr. Reeper, and Ms. Plesance. I take it you're here to join my Flock. Well, the shepherd is always willing to accept new sheep into the fold."

I was about to correct him, when Jennifer Chaos interrupted him. "Yes, sir. That's why we're here."

"Good. Welcome to salvation. I know the two of you by reputation alone, and it will be an honor to have you amongst the Saved. Please, there is a dance tonight at the saloon and variety theatre in the middle of town. I would be delighted if you two would join us."

"We'll be there," Jennifer Chaos said quickly.

Wiley Drake smiled, and then urged his horse on. His outlaw army left with him, some of them taking up places around the town. The citizens of Red Creek warily came out of their hiding places and resumed their business.

"Why'd you agree with him?" I demanded as we walked into the saloon. "Jesus, I don't want to go to any goddamn dance!"

"Better make sure you don't use the Lord's Name in vain," Jennifer said. "It's not like I had a choice! Did you see how many henchmen Drake has? It's like every scumbag and chigger-infested loser with a gun from here to the Mississippi is in town!"

We quickly got two whiskeys and a sarsaparilla for Charles, and then sat down. Charles hadn't said anything for a while and I noticed he was trembling slightly.

I put a hand on his shoulder. "Something the matter, son?" I asked gently.

"Oh, it's just that the preacher guy seemed very mean, and I was wondering, what if he finds out that I'm..." Charles gulped. "What if he finds out that I'm Jewish?"

"Ah, don't sweat it, Charles," Jenny said, grinning as she downed her drink. "If that ugly preaching bastard pisses you off, I'll preach him a sermon he won't forget, and then slit his belly from navel to nose!" Jennifer Chaos laughed. "Tell you the truth, the only thing I'm worried about is this dance thing. I ain't too sure on my feet, least not unless I'm kicking the teeth out of some fool."

"Well," I said, before I knew what I was saying, "maybe you can dance with me?"

"Why, Clark, you retarded son of a gopher, how positively gentlemanly of you!" Jennifer grinned. "I'm looking forward to it."

I gulped and smiled. For some reason, I weren't.

I spent the rest of the day getting ready. I couldn't rightly say why, but I wanted to look all clean and dandy for the dance. I went into the general store and bought myself a slick blue suit with a bolo tie. Then I got me a shave, and even had them trim some of the hair coming out of my ears. Finally, I took a fancy bath, and I rubbed myself up with some fancy soap with French names that I couldn't pronounce for the life of me.

I also bought a Fauntleroy costume for Charles. It was this blue lacy thing with a big yellow lacy collar and a fluffy white shirt. To top it off, there was this round cap that looked like a schoolmarm's bonnet.

His eyes widened as soon as he saw it. "I am not wearing that, Mr. Reeper," he said, shaking his little head. "I am not going to wear that!"

"Ah come on, Charles," I said. "We're gonna walk into that there dance hall together, and I want every little detail to be nice as a pie."

"Why?" Charles asked.

"Well, I don't rightly know. I mean, Jenny's gonna be there and—"

Charles smiled. "You want her to be impressed?"

I nodded guiltily. "Yeah. I'm not a mushy feller, but she was looking so pretty today when she cut up that road agent through the throat..."

"Well, just be yourself, Mr. Reeper. I'm sure she'll like you. I mean, I like you."

I patted Charles on the head. "I know that, son. But Jennifer's a lady. They got a whole different way of thinking than us men folk do. And I hear this here Fauntleroy costume is the hottest thing in big eastern cities and all over Europe. Please, son, will you give it a try?"

Charles looked again at the costume and then back at me. "Well, okay. But just for tonight." Charles took the outfit from my hands and walked into the changing room. When he came out, he was all laced up and looked more like some sort of clown with a big piece of blue cow's dung on his head. He groaned, but I told him he looked right handsome. Then, I straightened my bolo tie, and we walked down to the dancehall. The sun was just setting as I got there, and the shadows were being beaten back by a whole mess of lanterns that illuminated the dusky town.

The place had just opened up. This was gonna be a real fancy dance. There was a big bowl of punch; an honest-to-god glass chandelier hanging down from the ceiling; a band with a couple of banjos, a cello, trumpets; and a whole mess of guests. The guests were folks from Red Creek. They all seemed a little nervous but it didn't take long before they got to dancing and merry-making. A whole bunch of the Preacher's Flock was there as well, and they seemed to be drinking heavily and enjoying the night.

Charles and me walked in and sat down. Charles's Fauntleroy costume must have been itching him something fierce, and the poor kid scratched it a lot. I felt kinda bad for putting him into it. My own clothes were also a bit stiff. It felt like I couldn't bend my knees unless I put a little effort into it. But I figured all our suffering would be worth it soon as Jennifer Chaos walked in through the doors.

But when she did, it wasn't at all what I was expecting. I figured she'd be in some big hoop skirt and have bows in her hair, but instead, Jennifer Chaos was wearing the same clothes she always wore. Hell, she still had the road's dust on her pretty face. Jennifer strode over and looked at me. Following her inside was Erasmus the goat, a satin bowtie wrapped about his neck.

"Jesus Christ, Clark! Why are you in that ridiculous get-up?" As I tried to figure out an answer, she turned to Charles. "And what exactly are you supposed to be? Some sort of monkey?"

"It's the latest fashion, Jenny," Charles piped in. "Mr. Reeper said I should wear it."

"Any man dresses his boy up in that costume ought to be shot, hung, and shot again." Jenny stared at me. "What was the big idea, dressing up like this? You two look as stupid as you can be before they lock you up in the asylum."

"Well, Jenny, I figured, uh, for this dance, we ought to, um, look our best, um, on account of—" I gulped.

Jennifer Chaos smiled. "You trying to impress me, Clark? Is that it? Well, maybe you shouldn't have left me back in El Paso."

"Ah, Jenny," I said. "I didn't really want to, but I didn't know how things were going, and I didn't trust myself to keep you safe."

Jenny touched the revolver at her side. "You think I need safekeeping? I got no need of a bodyguard, Clark."

I was about to say more, but then the music started up. The band began to play, and couples started wheeling around the dance floor. Jennifer Chaos looked at the dancers and then at me. "Well, Clark, you lazy scumbag, are you going to ask me to dance, or I am gonna have to cut an invitation out of you?"

"Ma'am, I would be honored if you would accompany me in this waltz." I bowed low and offered my arm. She took it, and we walked out onto the dance floor. I held her the way the other men were holding their women, and tried to make my stiff feet do the right steps, but nothing much came of it, except I felt my heart skipping every other beat.

"So, I been doing some snooping around, while you were playing dress-up." Jenny got close to my face and whispered into my ear. "Seems the Reverend Wiley Drake has taken over the whole city with the aid of his Flock. Townsfolk are pretty much held hostage. Drake doesn't exactly have his act together either. He's been reading the bad bits out of the Bible, and causing all manner of havoc for those who don't think like him."

I looked up on the stage near the band, and saw the Reverend standing there, tapping his foot in time with the beat.

"Most of the Flock are just your basic western scum," Jennifer explained. "But that Ringo character is something else. He's dangerous, Clark, no two ways about it. And something ain't right about him, if you get my drift."

I nodded. The thug called Ringo, with his emaciated features and bone club, was certainly a queer one. I was thinking up a mess of theories to explain what he was, but none made much sense.

"What about Corbucci?" I asked. "What's his feud with Drake? And what's in his coffin?"

Jennifer Chaos shuddered. "Vengeance, I do believe. Drake murdered Cole Corbucci's wife a while back. I don't know what he's been lugging around in that coffin, but when he's ready, I'll wager there's gonna be a reckoning."

The band finished playing, and the dancing couples came to a stop. Jenny and I applauded as the players took their bows. Wiley Drake applauded as well, and marched to the front of the stage. He continued clapping long after the crowd's applause had died off. Then, he pointed to the edge of the stage, and doffed his hat like was introducing the next act, but instead a group of men, women and children chained at the neck walked in. They were in a pitiable state, their clothes little more than rags. They were thin and scared. Cole Corbucci was among them, chained to the rest and stuck right in the middle. Drake regarded them like a hungry wolf as he reached into his cloak.

"What fun!" he cried. "What joy! All thanks to me, my Flock, and the Will of the Almighty. Providence rewards loyalty, as do I. So, those that follow the shepherd, get to dance. Those who stray from the fold,"—he stared at chained prisoners—"receive the Lord's Wrath. These people have sinned. Adultery. Homosexuality. Questioning the power of God made manifest through me!"

As he spoke, Jenny's grip on my arm grew tight with rage. I looked at her face, and I saw one of her hands fall to her revolver. My own guns were back at the hotel, and I cursed the goddamn stupid mindset that had made me dress up like some high-faluting toff and leave my Colts at home.

Drake drew his hand from his cloak. He unfurled a rawhide whip with a flourish as his Flock began to cheer and yelp. "Now I shall put the fear of God into these unchaste creatures."

He raised the whip, grinning wildly as it cracked in the air. With the lantern light in his wide eyes, and a sick smile on his face, Reverend Wiley Drake looked like a demon out of Hell. The whip cracked downwards, about to slice through the clothes and skin of the prisoners, when a gunshot rang out through the dancehall. Ladies in their hoopskirts screamed, gentlemen covered their eyes, and Jenny holstered her revolver. The whip had been severed, cut in half by Jennifer Chaos's bullet.

"You fiend!" Drake shouted. He turned to run, almost tripping over the prisoner's chains as he ran. "Interrupting the Lord's work. Men—destroy her!"

The citizens of Red Creek hightailed it out of there real fast as the Flock closed in around Jenny and me. Charles tried to run to my side, but he tripped over his Fauntleroy costume, and one of Drake's thugs grabbed him and held a knife to his throat.

"Ah hell, Jenny," I whispered as the Flock surrounded us. "What we gonna do?"

"It's a dance," she said, raising her fists like an expert pugilist. "Let's dance!"

Jenny threw her body into the attacking gunmen. She lashed out with her legs, then struck right and left with her fists. She tore through them like a hurricane, knocking out teeth and sending Drake's lackeys flying. I started using my mitts as well, socking a thug in the stomach and then pushing him out of the way.

"You like that?" Jennifer asked, kneeing an attacker hard in the crotch. "I'll break the lot of you! You court me, you court chaos, you hear?" She head-butted another outlaw, giving him a kick in the face as he went down. "You want the fear of God? I'll put it in you, I swear I will!"

I wasn't having too good a time of it. I slugged some of the toughs, but I took a hit to the face, and then a chair crashed against my back. Managing to stay upright became a full-time endeavor as I struggled over to Charles.

Charles bit into his captor's hand and then squirmed out of the way. The big-nosed bastard tried to stab the boy in the back, but Erasmus the goat leapt into action and knocked the thug out of the way. Charles ran into my arms, and I tried my best to shield him from the blows.

"Jenny!" I shouted. "We gotta leave!"

"Not without those prisoners, we ain't!" Jennifer pointed to Cole Corbucci and the other chained prisoners. "We free them, then we run for it!"

"I'll go look for a key!" Charles shouted. He took off his Fauntleroy hat and hurled the lacy bonnet at an attacker's face. The boy's lacy cap stuck in the man's mouth, and while he was trying to spit it out, I gave him a solid hook to the jaw.

"Erasmus will take you." Jenny whistled. At her command, Erasmus came charging in through the crowd, butting aside anyone in his way. Charles leapt out of my arms and landed on the goat's back, riding the brown blur all the way to the stage.

Meanwhile, the dancehall brawl continued. I gave as good as I got, but Jenny was a veritable engine of destruction. She smashed a whiskey bottle in a thug's face, cracked a chair leg across a feller's back, and kicked a pistol out of another gunman's hands.

Charles found the keys in the corner of the stage where Reverend Wiley Drake had dropped them in his haste to flee. Charles unlocked the latch and freed the prisoners. Some jumped into the fray, punching and kicking like madmen, while others headed for the door. Cole Corbucci fought like a hornet. He picked up an entire table and hurled it into a group of charging outlaws.

"Time to leave, Jennifer!" I shouted. I ran over to the stage, kicking and clawing my way to the top, and Jenny joined me. We looked down at the large number of bloodthirsty criminals, and then up at the large chandelier.

"It's almost like they're asking for it," Jenny said. She drew her pistol, fired a single shot, and sent the chandelier crashing downwards. Cole Corbucci pulled himself onto the stage seconds before the chandelier's impact.

"Thank you kindly," Cole shouted. "We'd best be leaving now. There's an entrance in the back."

"Thank God, I can finally get myself out of this suit." I touched the fabric of my clothes. "Lord knows why I wanted to wear this." Charles looked at his Fauntleroy costume and nodded.

We ran through the back of the theater, exiting into the street. The Flock was up and about, riding down the avenues and patrolling the streets. Some of them were shooting out windows or firing into the air, and I felt that every shot fired was a six-gun aimed at us.

"Sure are a lot of the bastards," Jennifer whispered as we crept towards the hotel.

"Yeah," I agreed. "We ought to get our guns and gear, hightail it out of here, and then come back with the Federal Marshals. Or maybe the United States Army."

"Not an option," she muttered coldly, hastily reloading her revolver as we ducked behind a house. "Jenny Chaos don't run."

Cole coughed. "We don't need to. All we have to do is find my coffin and let me do the rest. Their numbers won't count with what I've got."

"What is it?" Charles asked curiously. We had almost made it to the hotel. Jenny had to grab Erasmus before he bounded ahead into the view of some outlaws.

"It's a surprise." Cole shrugged. "Problem is, I don't know where the coffin is."

"It's in the graveyard," Jenny explained. "I saw some of the Flock dragging it there. But Ringo is there guarding it, along with a whole mess of his friends."

At the hotel, Charles and I quickly ran into our rooms to change. Charles tore the Fauntleroy costume in his haste to get out of it. I can't say I blamed him. I got into my normal trousers, shirt and duster, and it felt good to feel my Colt Peacemakers at my waist once more. Charles put his Norfolk suit back on.

"You like Jenny, don't you?" he said abruptly as he put on his little cap.

I gulped. "Well, maybe I do. A mite, or so. She's a fine lady, I suppose."

Charles smiled. "I think she's very nice. Maybe you should tell her how you feel?"

I shook my head. "Nah. I don't think I could muster up the courage. Being in a gunfight is one thing, describing your heart's inner workings to a lady like Jennifer is another."

"She'd be happy, Clark, I know she would." Charles polished his glasses as I slid my Bowie knife into my boot. "We'd better go downstairs now." Winston the armadillo leapt into Charles's arms as he headed down.

We walked down to the lobby of the hotel. Jenny had loaned one of her extra revolvers to Cole, and she had her Snider rifle in her hands. They waited for us on the street.

"So now we go to the graveyard," Cole said thoughtfully. "There's something about finishing this all in the town's final resting place. Good place to end it all."

I walked over to Jennifer Chaos. "Um, Jenny?" I asked.

"Yeah?" She turned to face me and then I was looking into her big old eyes and my heart was pounding like a hundred drums and I plumb forgot what I was gonna say.

"Uh...I just wanted to, um, to thank you. For helping Charles and me."

She laughed. "Come on, Clark. You know I'm getting half of the bounty for this bastard. Now, let's go to the graveyard, and lay a couple more bodies to rest."

We walked down the streets of Red Creek with our heads held high. A couple of the Flock got in our way, but none of them had any skill with a six-gun. Jennifer Chaos, Cole, and I blasted them apart before they knew what was happening. The townsfolk of Red Creek stayed in hiding, but I could swear I saw them silently cheering us on from behind closed doors and windowpanes.

The graveyard was in the far corner of the town, planted on a small hill. A little field of crosses and monuments, stone, metal, or simple wood, stretched out in front of us from behind a wrought-iron gate. About ten members of the Flock sat in a semi-circle around Cole's coffin, now lying on the ground.

Ringo stood on top of the coffin, waving his bone club like an orchestra conductor's baton. All of the outlaws was singing away, and Ringo was directing them.

"Shall we gather at the river, the beautiful, beautiful river!" the outlaws howled. "Gather with the saints at the river, that flows by the throne of God!"

I have seen a great many sights during my career, but none stranger than a pack of hymn-singing outlaws in a graveyard.

"I reckon they got some nice harmony," I said to Jennifer.

She was already looking down the barrel of her Snider Rifle at Ringo. "Maybe they do. But we're gonna have them doing an entirely different form of singing. Ready, Cole?"

He nodded, his Colt already in his hand. I drew both of my Peacemakers into my hands with practiced spins. Charles and Winston drew back to the bottom of the hill. I didn't want the poor kid getting hurt on account of me, especially not with someone as odd and dangerous as Ringo around.

"Shall we gather at the river! The beautiful, beautiful river!" the hymn ended and then the Flock hollered and applauded as Ringo took a long bow, his stringy black hair nearly falling off of the top of his head.

"Now!" Jennifer Chaos cried. She fired, her shot taking Ringo right between the eyes. He toppled over backwards, landing in the graveyard dirt. Cole fanned his revolver, sending out six shots lickety-split, and killing six members of the Flock before they knew what was happening. I jumped over the fence, my revolvers blazing away. The remaining outlaws managed to get a few shots off before they went down.

"That weren't too hard!" Jenny said, slamming another round into her Snider. "Hell, Ringo was a bit of a push over. I feel a bit let down by that—"

A human leg bone sailed through the air, smacking into Jenny's head. She fell over, her rifle falling from her hands. When I saw her fall, it felt like me or Charles was getting hit too. It was the same kind of awful, cold feeling in my gut.

"Jennifer!" I ran to her side. She was all right, just a little knocked about. But Ringo jumped out from behind a gravestone and was advancing on us. He carried a long skinning knife in his hands.

I pointed my revolver at him. Something weren't right about Ringo. He had been shot straight in the head, and yet here he was, walking around like he had just emerged from a good night's sleep. The bullet hole was right there in his forehead, bleeding lightly over his face.

Ringo walked to one of the dead bodies lying on the ground. With a grunt, he hacked down and cut off the man's right arm, and then with another little yelp, he pulled his own right arm off and let it fall to the ground. Then he jammed the new arm into his socket, flexed it experimentally, and then made a muscle.

"Wooo-weeee!" Ringo shouted. "This feller was strong!"

It was then I realized just what exactly Ringo was, and I didn't like it one bit. He was a Fossor—one of those pagans employed by the early Roman Christians to dig up the catacombs. Because handling bodies was seen as unholy, the sort of people who were employed for the job weren't exactly the most ethical. A Magus who was around dead bodies all the time soon got ideas, and so the Fossor were created. They were creatures of dark magic, old as can be and hard to kill. No wonder Jenny's headshot hadn't done jack against him.

"Ah hell," I whispered. "Now Ringo, why don't you walk away? I know what you are, and I reckon you know what I am."

Ringo laughed. "Do you? Well then, let's all call each other by our real names. Mine is Remus. And you? You're my new set of legs."

He ran at me like a charging beast, moving on his hands and legs and loping forward. I fired my revolvers, and Cole blasted away as well, but the bullets didn't do nothing but tear into his flesh without slowing him down. He came closer and closer, howling as he went.

Quickly, I holstered one of my revolvers and drew my Bowie knife from my boot. I held the shining blade in front of me like I was some kind of swordfighter, and stabbed it into Remus's chest. But the blade sank through his skin, passed straight through him, and my arm stuck out the other side. Ringo looked down at my arm and laughed, and as I struggled to get it out I realized I was stuck.

Slowly, Ringo pushed himself forward, his bleeding body inching over my arm. He opened his mouth wide, and I saw rows of sharp teeth inside the Fossor's mouth. I closed my eyes, trying to get my arm free while feeling his hot breath on my face. But just as I figured him about to sink his teeth into my face, something whacked into him and knocked him off my arm.

I opened my eyes, and I saw Jennifer Chaos, fully recovered and holding a gravedigger's shovel in her hands, standing over the fallen Fossor.

"What in tarnation is the undead body-stealing bastard doing beating the crap out of you, Clark, you sorry idiot scumbag?"

"Uh, thanks," I said quietly. "Now let's put this freakish Fossor six-feet under. Any open graves or coffins nearby?"

Cole Corbucci ran to his coffin. He cracked it open, but his back was turned so that I couldn't make out what he had taken out of that pine box. He ran back holding the coffin, just as Ringo was getting up. Cole put the open coffin right behind the Fossor. Ringo stood up, and began to walk towards us.

"Now, give him everything we got!" I shouted. We all opened fire, Jenny with her Snider rifle, and me and Cole with our revolvers. The bullets pounded into Ringo, knocking him backwards and into the coffin. As soon as he touched the pine box, I slammed the coffin lid shut, sitting on top of it to stop Ringo from busting out. Cole picked up a shovel handle and stuck it in the coffin's handles, blocking any escape.

Then we shoved the box towards the nearest open grave. It landed six feet under with a clatter. After that, all we had to do was get some shovels and cover it with dirt. It took a little while, but soon Ringo was totally buried. With every bunch of dirt that landed on him, the Fossor screamed. I could swear he was talking to me, promising revenge on the ones I loved, but I figured it was just my imagination.

After Ringo was buried and the danger was passed, Charles, Winston, and Erasmus joined us in the graveyard. As soon as he saw that I was all right, Charles ran into my arms and we held each close. Jenny stared at us and smiled a little.

"Mr. Reeper! Jenny! The Flock is coming! All of them!" Charles pointed to the edge of the graveyard. Sure enough, a small army of men and horses was marching towards us, all armed to the teeth. Jenny, Cole, and me together didn't have enough rounds to kill them all. The night was over, the sun was just rising, and the Flock was coming in with the dawn.

"Don't worry, child," Cole said, walking back to where his coffin had previously been standing. He bent down, his black cloak blocking what lay on the ground. "I've got something they won't expect. Their numbers ain't worth a damn."

And when he turned around, Cole Corbucci was holding a large Maxim machine gun in his arms, round, gray and with a circular barrel that looked like an angry eye.

"Ain't that something!" Jenny said, letting out a whoop of joy. "Well, what are you waiting for, Cole, let's waste them!"

Cole nodded. He walked over to the wrought iron gate of the cemetery and set the Maxim gun down, using the fence posts as a kind of bipod for his weapon. He had a big string of ammo, and he carefully jammed it into place. Just as the Flock got close to the graveyard, they broke into a charge, hollering out a terrifying battle cry.

Cole turned around to Jenny and me. "Don't shoot these men. This is my revenge, and no one can take it from me."

He turned back to the charging outlaws, and opened fire. The rapid-firing Maxim gun shot out lead at an incredible speed. I've seen machine guns in action before, and there is something inhuman about the way the bullets tear through people so quickly.

The Flock wasn't expecting it, and charged right into the blazing Maxim. Dozens of them went down in seconds, pumped full of lead and torn asunder by the stream of bullets. Men and horses were blown away, some tried to run and got blasted in the back; others bravely charged forward only to be gunned down anyway. Cole worked the Maxim gun like some kind of demon, firing out long bursts and moving the gun back and forth constantly to fill the streets of Red Creek with gunfire.

It went on for minutes, hours, I don't rightly know how long. I grabbed Charles and held him close, and then, like I couldn't control it, my arm went around Jenny's shoulder and I pulled her close as well. We huddled together as the Maxim gun blazed away.

Finally, the gun stopped firing. The street was covered with corpses. If a feller was keen to, he could have walked from one side of the town to the other, only stepping on dead and dying men.

Cole stood up and let the Maxim fall to the ground. "That's all of them," he whispered. "All except the preacher."

"Son of a gun," I whispered. "You must have killed one hundred men or more, Cole!"

"So, maybe I did." Cole talked without a bit of emotion. "I think they deserved it, particularly when you consider what they did to me."

"And what was that?" I couldn't help asking.

"My wife. Our wedding day. Shot down in her prime." Cole jabbed a thumb back to the graveyard. "She's in there, somewhere, dead and buried. Yeah, they deserved it, and this was as good a place as any to end it."

He had had done all that to avenge his wife. He must have loved her something fierce, the kind of way I loved Charles, but no one else. Then I realized my arm was still wrapped around Jennifer Chaos's arms. Hastily, I removed my hand and let it fall to my side.

Jenny stared at me and shook her head, and as we stared at each other, Charles tugged at my sleeve.

"Mr. Reeper!" he whispered. "You should tell her!"

I looked up at Jenny. "Yeah, I ought to."

"Tell me what, Clark? That you're a sorrier shot than a man with no arms aiming a gun with his mouth?" Jenny asked.

I gulped. "Nah, it ain't that. Jenny, I been thinking about me and you, and I realized, well, you're one hell of a woman."

"I could have told you that, Clark." Jenny shook her head. "You left me all those years in that El Paso hotel room. Did you have a different opinion of me then, Clark Reeper?"

"I'm not sure why I left you like that." I looked at my feet. "I reckon it's because of, um, well, it's sort of like with Cole."

"What do you mean?"

"Like, with his wife. I didn't want to love you, not if you were gonna get hurt. I couldn't ever live with that. I weren't ever really close to anyone. Never knew my ma, and my Old Man was a gruff, old codger who was just too tough to care much about. After the woman who raised me changed her mind and tried to kill me, well, I didn't know what to think."

"But you love me," Charles pointed out.

"Yeah, but I wasn't sure I wanted to at first. But once I was in charge of taking care of you, well, you were such a nice little feller that I figured you for my son. If I only done one thing right in my life, Charles, it was adopting you."

The boy smiled at me. Winston the armadillo perched on his shoulder and seemed to be clapping his little claws together.

There was a bit of silence after I had spoken, and I couldn't stand it. I turned to Jenny Chaos. "Well?" I asked. "I've gone and confessed my love to you. What do you say about riding with me for a while?"

Jenny was about to answer, when Cole Corbucci let out a gasp and pointed at the town. A lone figure walked down the street, all dressed in black. We could just make out the white of a preacher's collar at his neck.

"There he is." Cole dropped the Maxim gun and his hand fell to his revolver. "If you would excuse me for just a moment."

Cole Corbucci marched down the hillside and into the streets of Red Creek. Wiley Drake and him squared off, staring each other down for a long while. Drake had two shotguns stuck in his belt, and his hands fell to them as he saw Cole. We could hear them talking as they prepared to fight.

"Reverend," Cole said, bowing his head slightly. "I'm going to kill you. You got no Flock to hide behind now."

"I don't fear death!" Wiley cried, but I could see he was shaking slightly. "I will live forever in Heaven!"

"Sure you will." Cole pointed to the shotguns at Wiley's waist. "What are those?"

Wiley Drake pointed to the first one. "This one is Abel, and the other is Cain. They are the shepherd's keeper."

"Well then," Cole said evenly, "let's see how well they work."

There was tense silence for a few seconds afterwards, and then both men went for their guns. Cole fired first, his bullet taking Wiley high in the chest. But the Reverend did not go down. He drew one of his shotguns and opened fire with both barrels. The shot tore into Cole's gun hand, and the black clad gunslinger dropped his pistol.

"I've beaten you," Wiley whispered. "The lord protects."

Cole reached out with his left arm and pulled the second shotgun from Wiley Drake's belt. He pointed the double-barreled weapon straight at the Reverend's surprised face.

"Yeah," Cole said. "He sure does." He pulled the trigger twice, tearing off the Reverend Wiley Drake's face, and dropping him instantly. Then, Cole collapsed into the dust himself.

The townspeople of Red Creek came out of their houses as if a big storm had just passed. They saw the large number of corpses sitting in the street, and a cheer rose from up and down the town. Some of the citizens ran to help Cole, giving him a drink of whiskey for the pain and bandaging his arm, while others piled up the corpses into wagons. They would be buried in a pit outside the town.

That night the good people of Red Creek threw a party in Cole Corbucci's honor. Jenny Chaos, Charles and I attended. Cole was lying back on a sun chair, his gun hand bandaged up and hanging loosely at his side.

"That don't look too good," I said, pointing to the injury.

Cole stared at it. "Yeah. I may never kill another man again, not as long as I live. Drake's shotgun tore out most of my fingers, and a lot of meat as well. But you know what? I don't mind much. I've done enough killing for a lifetime."

Jenny and I agreed. "What do you aim to do now?" Jenny asked.

"Settle down here, I suspect." Cole moved aside his black cloak, and I saw a silver star glittering on his breast. "With the Flock gone, these folks need a sheriff, and I'm willing to take the job. I don't know if I'll be much good. Maybe I can learn to shoot left-handed, and until then, hire a bunch of deputies. But one thing is for sure—the law has returned to Red Creek."

Charles picked up Winston the armadillo and held him out. "Um, Mr. Corbucci?"

"Yeah?"

"This armadillo, he's very smart and helpful, and he helps me pick up things sometimes, sort of like a helper. Maybe he could help you, because your hand is hurt." Charles set Winston down in Cole's lap. The armadillo and the gunslinger stared at each other, and then Cole smiled and scratched the armadillo's chin.

"Thanks, kid. I'll take good care of him."

I put my arm on Charles's shoulder. He liked Winston the armadillo a lot, but I figure that sometimes a feller ought to let go of what he loved. But just as that thought was in my mind, Jenny Chaos tapped me on the shoulder. I turned over and stared up at her, and I felt my heart pounding away again.

"Hey, Jennifer," I said.

She held out a bouquet of flowers. "Um, Clark?" she said. "We got to talk about something."

I took the flowers and sniffed them. "Sure, Jenny."

"Well, Clark, you know how you've changed since El Paso?" Jennifer Chaos asked. "Well, I have too. We were really just kids back then, and I wasn't sure what I wanted. I'm still not too sure, but I think I ought to tell you something. It might take you a while to get it through that thick skull of yours."

"Sure. What has changed about you?" I had a sinking feeling in my chest, not as bad as when Charles or Jenny was in danger, but still a pain in my gut.

"Clark, I don't like men." Jenny gulped. "I prefer the company of women. You understand?" She smiled weakly. "And that's just the way it is."

"You sure?"

"Yeah."

"Honest injun and all? You ain't pulling my leg?" I asked plaintively.

Jennifer Chaos shook her head. "Doesn't mean we can't be friends. I am sorry, Clark, I truly am. But I'll tell you this, if I did prefer men folk, you'd be the one I'd want up there on the altar with me."

I turned red. I couldn't help it. "Thanks, Jenny."

Jennifer Chaos grinned. "Much obliged. Well, I've got Drake's body loaded up on the wagon. What do you say we ride to Cheyenne in the morning and turn him in before his carcass starts stinking?"

"Sounds like a plan."

Well, I reckon I still don't know too much about women. I wasn't that upset about Jennifer Chaos, but I still felt right poorly for a while. Jennifer Chaos and I are still good pals, and we split the bounty for Wiley Drake right down the middle. It was a substantial sum. After that, Jenny headed west and I headed east. She gave me a little kiss as we parted ways and I must have turned redder than the sun when I got it. Charles and I are looking for other jobs now, and maybe someday I'll find some woman who likes me for the dusty son of a gun that I am. But I ain't gonna hold my breath. I reckon I'm a decent enough father for Charles, and he can get by with just me for some time.

I got a telegram from a Tong leader in the New York City known as Mock Duck who's pestering me about taking out something called a Shaolin Monk that's been running around in the desert. Also there's a bounty on a feller called the Six-Gun Guru, and I may have to go and bring him in. One thing's for sure, though. I'll never meet a girl like Jenny Chaos.

Lines in Praise of Clark Reeper by William McGonagall

Note to the Reader: Now I ain't the kind who goes in much for poetry, or has much truck with the written word. It's partially on account of my career. My name is Clark Reeper and I am a bounty hunter. I've always existed in the physical world, and poetry just never really sparked my interest, except for maybe a couple of Walt Whitman's bits. My adopted son Charles Green, a very well-read little feller, knows a lot more than me about these kinds of things, and it was on account of him that we went to Boston for a large Literary Convention of the world's best authors and poets; and some other authors and poets who weren't that good, and weren't even invited, but came anyways.

One uninvited guest (who came anyhow) was a Scotsman by the name of William Topaz McGonagall. He was an odd gent, with longish hair, a three-piece suit, and a half-crazed expression in his eye. He had heard I was attending the conference and desperately wanted to meet me. I had no idea why. But when we finally met, his face lit up.

"Clark Reeper himself!" he said excitedly. "Oh what an honor! I have been following your adventures in Scotland for some time! You are almost like the heroic knights errant of old!"

"Well, I don't know if I got any shining armor," I told him. "But I'm pleased to meet you."

"Oh, please, I simply must show you this poem I've created in your honor!" He reached into his coat and came out with a sheet of paper covered in scratchy writing. "Please take it," he gushed. "It is simply magnificent, and enshrines you forever as an immortal hero!"

I got the poem, we read it a few times, and then Charles and me exchanged a glance. This poem wasn't exactly what I had in mind for something based on my life. But I suppose McGonagall did his best writing it, so here it is.

Lines in Praise of Clark Reeper
By William Topaz McGonagall — Scottish Master of Verse and Candidate for Poet Laureate of Her Majesty's Empire

Oh Clark Reeper, you two-gunned rogue,
Never was your American tongue filled with Scottish brogue.
But still you are a hero of the chivalric sort,
If there is villainy afoot, your pistols are quick to retort.
Foul outlaws and highwaymen
You shoot them and shoot them again.
How many cruel gunmen have you slain?
If you tried to count them all, it would be in vain!
When a bad guy is coming, you don't take any guff,
It's blam blam (no scones and jam) and they fall dead in the dust.

But sometimes there are hideous monsters and beasts,
Who would chew you up or claw you at least,
Or maybe use you as a beastly feast,
These creatures of flashing fangs and biting teeth!

And there are strange creatures that lurk in the dark,
Ghouls and goblins that would give me a start!
Werewolves, witches, and even vampires,
You see them all and then open fire.
Oh Clark Reeper, your story so bold,
Such a pity that one day you will be old.
And turn to dust and slowly die,
But luckily you are immortalized,
By such a skillful poet as I.

Yes, for never a better poet will you see,
Than William T. McGonagall, from the banks of Dundee.
Lines in praise of you I will sing,
And sing them as well as I sing anything.
By powerful wit, by lightning quill,
You'll read me again and again until you get your fill!
And I am modest too, I must confess,
I've spent too long talking about myself and must digress.

So back to that heroic bounty hunter named Clark Reeper,
When demons and foes are about, he is not a sleeper.
He cuts them down with his bowie knife,
And hacking and stabbing he takes their life.
Or maybe not their life, if they are undead,
But a walking corpse he'll still shoot in the head.
Clark Reeper, you give those fiends a sound drubbing!
And what of the dear child you are constantly hugging?

Yes, I speak of young Charles Green,
The greatest companion the world has ever seen
Loyal as a dog, he stands near Clark's side,
Whether the two be outside or inside.
Though Charles is wise beyond his years,
Never has he swallowed a glass of beer.

But now I return to my praise of dear Clark,
On the Wildest Plains of the West, he has made his mark.
The great Clark Reeper, bounty hunter master,
He fights with great skill, and tries to stop disaster.
Evil tycoons think they can buy him,
They should have known not to despise him.
Clark Reeper with your lead-blasting Colts,
All the other gunslingers are straw-headed louts!

So, Clark Reeper, humbly accept my praise,
And know that I've been working on it for many, many days,

And read it to yourself before you go to bed at night,
And think, "William McGonagall is very, very right!"

Well, that's the poem. I thought it was pretty good, except for the bit where he went off and talked about himself for a while. I also didn't like how he called Charles a dog. Like I said, I ain't the best judge of poetry, and I was thankful that anybody wrote a poem about me.

Charles and I thanked William McGonagall and then went off to the main convention and had a good time. Charles was real polite about it, and McGonagall was just basking in his praise. Later, I asked Charles if he thought McGonagall deserved any of them nice things he had said about the poem, and Charles said he did deserve them. He said that even if William Topaz McGonagall wasn't that good, at least he was trying. And even if his poem is the worst one ever, it's good that McGonagall is doing what he wants and not listening to anything but his own heart.

I reckoned Charles was right.

Twilight Cowboy

Now I reckon I've been just about everywhere, and I ain't no stranger to odd sights. I've traveled all across these United States, spent time in Canada and Mexico, and even been off the continent a few times. I suppose it goes with my career choice. My name is Clark Reeper, I'm a bounty hunter, and I don't really got much control over exactly where I go, and that's not including what I gotta do when I get there.

Not much has slowed me down over the years, and even in the queerest place I can always come to my senses and figure out what's going on. I'm a tall gent with a long khaki duster, a crumbling Stetson hat, and there's always two Colt Peacemakers not far from my hands. I got a face liked tanned rawhide, but I'm a little less tough. I traveled alone for a while, and then I found myself in charge of a little boy of about ten years of age by the name of Charles Green. He's a real nice little feller with curly brown hair, and thick spectacles. He always wears a neat, Norfolk suit and peaked cap.

I love Charles like he was my own flesh and blood. He's kind and polite, and probably deserves a better father than me. It was sort of on account of him that I ended up going to the one place I ain't never even considered setting foot in.

It all started when I got this letter from a feller name of Doc Torrent. I had done some work for the Doc in the past, hunting down a rogue automaton for him, and I had come into contact, and sometimes conflict, with several of his creations throughout the years. Anyway, Doc Torrent asked me to join him at a Worldwide Technology Summit in New York City. He wasn't showing off another automaton or anything, oh no. What Torrent had this time was a lot more special.

"I have discovered through countless experiments," said a letter which I read aloud to Charles, "a machine which, when activated, will allow the user to travel through time at will."

I put the letter down and shook my head. "That Doc feller must be crazier than a bucket of rattlesnakes. Some kind of machine that can travel in time! Ridiculous."

Charles's eyes widened. "A time machine!" he cried. He turned to a small backpack I had purchased for him where he carried most of his clothes and things, and he pulled out a dusty book. "Just like in the story!"

He handed me the tattered little volume and I looked it over. It was *The Time Machine* by H.G. Wells, and it showed a feller riding some sort of odd-looking bicycle through a tunnel with glowing, multicolored walls. "Son, that there book is fiction and nothing but. I don't think traveling around in time is possible!"

"But what if it is?" Charles's voice was almost pleading and I really felt for the little guy. "We should go find out. I'd really like to."

I read the rest of the letter, and I found out that Doc Torrent really did want me to go along with him. He was pleased with the way I had dealt with his creations in the past, and he wanted me along as a sort of security. I was thinking about declining, but then I saw how much Charles wanted to go.

"Well, all right," I said. "But don't go expecting us to be hobnobbing with the Egyptians and knights and things. It all sounds like a load of snake oil to me."

"Okay, Mr. Reeper. Thank you." Just seeing that gratitude in my boy's freckled face made me feel like there was a warm glow inside me, so next morning we got on the first train back east and hightailed it to New York in time for that science meeting.

The convention was held in a fancy convention center; a large hall packed with different booths, each one extolling a crazy new invention. Edison and Tesla had booths right next to each other, **and they** were sending sparks and lightning bolts across the room. Red, white and blue bunting was everywhere, and a big brass sculpture of the American Eagle hovered over the room.

Charles and I headed to the corner of the hall where Doc Torrent had his booth. It was a small attraction, just a couple of chairs seated around a large stage. Resting on the stage was a large item covered in a cloth. Doc Torrent was calling into the crowd with a speaking trumpet.

"Come forth and witness the miracle!" he shouted, his voice squeaking a little as it got louder. "See the power of Kronos held in the hands of man! The temporal seas have been calmed at last! And the ship that will ride them will be the 'chronomobile!'" Torrent was a spindly man dressed in a white lab coat, vest and a bowtie. He had an explosion of white hair on his head and thick square glasses on his nose. He looked a little bit like a steer after getting tangled in barbed wire.

"Howdy, Doc," I said, announcing myself.

"Ah, Clark! So glad you could make it!" Torrent didn't lower his speaking trumpet, and the blast of sound nearly knocked my hat off. I reached out and gently pushed the speaking trumpet down. Torrent was brilliant, but he had a tendency to forget simple things like that. "Who is this?" the Doc asked, pointing to Charles.

"This here's my boy, Charles Green. Soon as he heard you were making some sort of time machine, he couldn't wait to come."

"Hello, Dr. Torrent, sir." Charles stared at the cloth-covered object, about as big as a stagecoach. "Did you really make a time machine?"

"I did indeed, my lad. And I would be honored if you and your father would accompany me on its maiden voyage! Chrononauts, bold and brave, we shall be!"

Charles smiled. "Thank you very much, Dr. Torrent. Um, do you know where we're going?"

"I mind not at all, my dear child! And as for our destination, it is decided." Doc Torrent wandered backwards to the stage. "The past has its temptations. I would like to meet my predecessors: Da Vinci, Archimedes, Merlin. But I think the first place we will go will be the future!"

"The future?" Charles asked. "You know what's going to happen there, I mean, then?"

Torrent nodded. "Well, extrapolating today's attitudes and technologies, I can make some accurate predictions. The future will be a time of great scientific advancement. Men of my caliber will be heroes instead of pariahs, getting vast amounts of money and countless lady friends! It will be a wonderland utopia of moving sidewalks, hovering cars, and all people will be connected with an amazingly large series of pneumatic tubes for the purpose of instantly sending and receiving messages. Yes, it will truly be a golden age!" His face sparkled and his wild eyes lit up.

"When exactly are we going?" I asked.

"Far into the future. The year 1970." Doc Torrent winked at me. "Trust me, Mr. Reeper, you will never forget this voyage."

He went back to his megaphone, shouting into the crowd. "Come one, come all, bear witness to my amazing intelligence!"

While he was gathering a good crowd of onlookers, I went over to Charles. "So, the future?" I asked. "You sure you want to go?"

"I don't know. 1970 is pretty far away. Who knows what will be there? It could be something awful." But then Charles straightened his little tie. "Well, that's all right. You'll be with me, so I'll be safe. Okay, let's go forward in time."

By now Torrent had a good crowd, some of them sitting in the seats, others standing around. The Doc began to address them as he paced the stage. "For centuries, man has longed to travel the centuries! For eons, he has wanted to go backwards or forward through the eons! Well, now I have done the impossible! I have made a time machine! Behold, the chronomobile!"

With that, Doc Torrent pulled the sheet off of his creation. It was the strangest looking vehicle I ever saw. It was a bit like a stagecoach, but open-topped and with big glassless windows in the side. Clocks, levers, cogs and dials covered everything, and all open space was gilded and inlaid with jewels. The chronomobile stood on four wheels, and had four seats inside.

"Not only can this machine ply the seas of infinity, but it can also zoom through the longest distances! Yes, time and space have been conquered by me!" Doc Torrent chuckled, and his spectacles seemed to slip off of his nose a little. "They all laughed at me, but I've proved them wrong! All of them!"

"Why don't you prove it, you old coot!" a heckler in the audience called.

"Oh, I shall. I shall." Torrent walked onto the stage over to his machine. "Clark, Charles, would you please take your seats and strap yourselves in? I wouldn't want you falling out and ending up lost in the Devonian Period as a tasty snack for a trilobite."

I walked up, and even though I didn't expect the contraption to work, I still felt a mite nervous. I sat Charles down next to me, made sure he was strapped in snugly, and then did the same to myself. He reached out and we grasped each other's hands.

"Now, I will sit in the controller's seat." Torrent plopped himself down and strapped himself in as he yanked some of the levers. "The controls are very simple. A dial of the years, months, weeks, days, hours, and seconds is right in front of me! I will set them for this day and time, 1970."

The crowd gasped. Maybe some of them believed what Torrent was selling them.

Torrent seemed to love the attention. "Now, to you it will only seem as if I am gone for a few seconds, for I will set the time machine to return to this day and hour, but a few moments after we disembark. But for me and my friends here, we will be in the future for much longer." Torrent finished adjusting all the dials and clocks. "Now, let us begin our journey into time itself."

I was considering backing out on the whole thing, but now it was too late. Doc Torrent reached forward and punched down on a big red button in the middle of the chronomobile.

"Well, Doc, I guess you'll have to go back to the lab," I said. "Don't look like nothing's happening." I pointed outside. The crowd, the hall, and everything was still there, just like it was before Torrent pressed the button.

"Ye have little faith! Well, Clark, give it...time!" Doc Torrent cracked his fingers and leaned back. "The temporal fields are rapidly moving. Our voyage has begun."

I was about to get out of my seat and walk out, but then I looked outside. The people were gone, and most had moved a lot faster than anyone could run. The booths were gone and the scientists with them, and then the lights in the hall went out. I blinked, and the sun outside had descended, and then rose up again. More people filed in, then left just as fast, and then the sun rose and fell again. Before my eyes, time was speeding up until it became a blur of colors.

"Son of a gun," I whispered. "It's really working."

Doc Torrent smiled. "I know! As the temporal fields continue to shift, the faster we will travel." As he spoke, the transition from day to night grew shorter and shorter, until it was like I was blinking as fast as I could, and then they both blurred together into one dim mass.

"Wow," Charles whispered.

The hall around us changed, become old, overgrown, and then collapsed all together. The rubble vanished, a construction crew appeared, and a building began to grow right where we were sitting.

"When we reach 1970, won't we be stuck inside the walls of this building?" I asked Torrent. The prospect of being turned into wallpaper made me sick to my stomach.

"Not to worry. A quick spatial adjustment, and we'll be okay." Torrent pressed down on one of the levers. The chronomobile lurched forward, left the building and rested on the sidewalk. Other buildings, dozens of skyscrapers, were appearing all around us. I had thought New York was massive in my time, but it seemed like it hadn't even begun to grow.

The passage of time began to slow down, and the people outside became visible. I saw people walking around with dusters and fedoras, and ladies in what looked a little like their underwear. Snow came down, and was gone in a few seconds before coming again. The time continued to pass, and then things slowed down even more.

"We're in the year!" Torrent announced. "1970, the distant future! Just a couple more seconds…"

Sure enough, in just a couple more seconds, the machine came to a stop. Our journey hadn't taken but a couple of minutes, and we were now about seven or more decades into the future. Slowly, Charles and I undid our straps as Torrent pulled some more levers.

"Let us go forth!" Torrent said. He stepped outside of the chronomobile, and then Charles and I followed. We held hands, for my comfort as much as his. Things were sure different in the year 1970.

The skyscrapers loomed tall, so that we couldn't see anything else. Sidewalks and streets stretched out every which way, which wasn't too odd for New York, but now the streets were filled with the funniest looking automobiles, and not a single horse-drawn carriage. The city was full with litter, boarded-up buildings, and graffiti, again, not too different from the New York that I knew. It was midday, and the streets and sidewalks weren't too crowded, but the people wore the strangest clothes.

Men wore long hair, for example, sort of like Wild Bill Hickok, but unkempt and greasy. Some folks wore vests and beads so they looked like Native Americans. Other folks wore these suits without vests, and some didn't even wear ties. Now I've seen people dressing pretty oddly, but I ain't seen nothing like this. People stared at us as we walked by, pointing and talking amongst themselves. I tipped my hat to them, not knowing what else to do.

"Hmm, we appear to be nowhere near the flying cars or the moving sidewalk," lamented Torrent. "Perhaps people use personal flying machines instead of flying cars. Maybe that's it." The Doc scratched his chin. "If I could just find some friendly locals to talk with, I'm sure everything could be figured out."

Then a couple of youths came walking down the sidewalk, laughing and talking with each other. Some of them were colored, and others were white and they all had on matching vests and jeans, decorated with an insignia of an Indian chief in a war bonnet. As soon as they saw the Doc, Charles, and me they started laughing and talking about us.

"Ah, looks like a far-future version of Lord Baden Powell's Boy Scouts. I'm sure they'll be able to help us," the Doc said, waving to them.

"I don't rightly know if you should, Doc—" I started to say, but Torrent had already stepped forward.

"Excuse me? Eager lads, I could use a hand."

The youths walked over, surrounding us and the machine. "A hand?" A dark-skinned teenager said, laughing to himself. "Man, can you dig this honky sucker? Asking us for a handout when he just parked the hippest little set of wheels right here on the sidewalk?" His friends all laughed.

"My name is Doc Torrent, and I would be most grateful if you could direct me to the nearest moving sidewalk. Perhaps one that circles all the wonders of the city, such as the miracle garden and the pneumatic tubes?"

"Man, oh man, what have you been smoking?" the dark-skinned youth asked. "I've got to get me some of that weed, or whatever it is."

"Are you accusing me of being an opium fiend?" Torrent said, gulping. "Rest assured, I am not!"

"Sure, you ain't, sure." The youth leaned forward, putting his hand on Torrent's shoulder. "Now, any money you didn't spend on smack or whatever, why don't you hand it over to me and my buds?"

"What?" Torrent stepped backwards, obviously flustered. I didn't like the look of them far-future boy scouts, and I stepped in front of Charles.

"What kind of scouts are you?" I asked.

"Not scouts, brother. We're the South Side Savages." The leader pointed to the Indian Chief insignia. "Toughest gang in the city. Don't nobody mess with us." His friends nodded. "Come on, my boppers. Show them some steel."

Instantly, the other South Side Savages produced weapons, chains, clasp knives, and bricks they picked up from the street. Now I knew they were looking for trouble. I stepped forward.

"You kids best step back, or I'll be forced hurt you."

"What are you gonna do, cowboy-hat wearing fool?" one of the Savages asked, brandishing a switchblade.

I drew my revolvers out and fired off a single shot, shattering the knife.

"Whoa. Savages out!" The leader turned to run and his lackeys followed him. Soon we were alone again. Doc Torrent watched them go in disbelief.

"There must be some mistake," he whispered to himself. "The utopia is nowhere to be found! I know, I'll stash the machine in some back alley and then we'll look around some more. We'll find out the true glorious future, I know we will."

"Uh, Doc, maybe there ain't no glorious future," I said. "Maybe things are just as screwed up as they've always been."

"I will not accept that!" Doc Torrent began pushing the chronomobile. "Here, help me store our means of transport in the alley. I can engage an invisibility field to hide it from passerby."

Well, since Torrent was our only ticket out of there, I figured I would help him now, and then he'd come to his senses later. Charles and I helped Torrent hide the time machine, and then the Doc pulled a few levers and it turned see-through-like. If a feller was looking for it, they'd find it, but anyone else would just see a trick of the light. We all memorized the address of the alley, so we could find the chronomobile again. After that, we picked a random direction and started walking, trying to find Torrent's hovering cars and moving sidewalks.

What we found instead was more graffiti, garbage littering the streets, and even a fair number of homeless people. More of those kids wearing the same colors, gangs I figured them for, were walking the streets and I kept Charles close to me and let one hand fall to my gun.

Torrent became more and more upset as the city got worse and worse. We passed vacant buildings, some of them damaged by fires and just as crowded and uncared for as the tenements of our time. Cops were still there, not hesitating to use force when they had to, and there were plenty of liquor stores, saloons, and places I would never want Charles to go into until he was a good deal older.

"Maybe something awful happened to America," Charles said, seeing how miserable Doc Torrent was looking. "Maybe a bad guy took over the country?"

"Yes. That may be it! Let me just ask a nearby citizen." Torrent approached a long-haired young man sitting on a street corner holding a clipboard. "Excuse me, sir?"

The young feller turned around and looked us over. "Groovy threads, man," he said. "Say, would you mind signing this petition to get US troops out of Vietnam?"

"Vietnam?" I asked. "That some crazy name for the Philippines?"

"You know, man, Vietnam, Indochina! Where you been, dude?" He gestured around the street. "Listen man, Tricky Dick's taking over the country. Even killing kids at Kent State. Can you dig that?"

"Tricky Dick?" Torrent asked. "Is he the dictator who has driven our country into its present pitiable state?"

"What have you been smoking, man?" the young feller asked. "You talk all trippy and stuff."

"For the last time, I am no opium fiend!" Torrent turned away from him. "Goodbye, sir. I wish you luck in your war against this Dick character."

We walked on, and Torrent began to slowly break down as the day passed. The sun began to go down, and the shadows grew long as more people filled the street. We had been walking for hours, and not one hovering car or moving sidewalk had we seen. The only automobiles were packed into the street, honking away at each other; and the sidewalks were full of vagrants and crowds.

Finally, when we were walking through a particularly dismal part of town, poor Doc Torrent just sank down to his knees. "No!" he cried in despair. "This was supposed to be a golden age!" He ran away from me, and before I could stop him, clambered into a dumpster. "Leave me alone, Clark, I'll hide in this futuristic mini-hotel until I can get my thoughts together."

"Doc, maybe we should go back to our time," I suggested, "on account of there ain't nothing here you like."

"No, just leave me alone!" Torrent was crying like a little boy who had lost a favorite toy, and I felt right sorry for him.

"C'mon, Charles," I said. "Let's explore the city a bit more."

"What about Dr. Torrent?" Charles asked. "Is he okay?"

"The Doc's fine. Just needs some time alone."

We walked along the streets for a while, and then it began to get cold. It rained a little, and while the water dripped off of my hat and coat, poor Charles shivered from the night air. We got a bit hungry too. I was gonna buy something from a Viennese sausage stand, but then I realized that my money was no good here, not in a future where new cash notes had been issued.

"Ah, hell," I muttered. "I don't want to rob nothing, but I figure we might have to."

Charles gulped. "I'm not that hungry," he said, but I could tell he was just saying that.

Just as I was wondering how exactly I should get some cash, a man and woman approached me. Both of them were dressed oddly, in brightly colored jumpsuit-type things covered with embroidered flowers and other designs.

"Hey, cowboy." The woman's voice was low and seductive.

"Um, howdy, ma'am," I said, not knowing exactly what to do.

"Party tonight, at the Factory." She reached into her shirt and pulled out a paper flyer. It had some crazy designs on it, things like political cartoons but more bizarre. I could make out some instructions and street names. The place was nearby.

"Are you inviting me, ma'am?" I asked.

"Thank you," Charles said, a little nervously. "That's very nice of you."

"But you don't even know me," I pointed out. "What sort of a party is this? A sewing circle, or some sort of square dancing?"

The man and the woman both grinned at each other. "We dig your costume, man. It's far out." The feller patted my shoulder. "And the party, well, it will just be a damn good time. Come tonight, whenever you want."

The two of them wandered off. I didn't really want to go to a place where I didn't know no one, but I figured it couldn't be too bad, even if the couple did dress a little weird. And there'd probably be food and warmth there.

I looked the flier over one more time, and then followed the instructions until we came to East 47th Street. The Factory didn't look like any textile mill or steel plant I've ever seen, but maybe it was just a nickname. Charles and I exchanged a glance, and then we walked in through the double doors.

It was like we had walked into another world. I had been in plenty of saloons and gambling dens, but they weren't nothing like this. The place was packed with people, some of them standing up on stages and doing the strangest things with their bodies. I had to cover Charles's eyes a couple of time to keep him from looking on account of their indecency, something I've never had to do before. A thick cloud of smoke hung over the place, and it took me a while to get my bearings. Everything was silver and see-through, walls, floor and even furniture. I wondered if Doc Torrent would like it here.

A band was playing away, with electrified guitars, a big drum set, and not a single banjo. A movie was projecting itself onto a wall, showing people doing bizarre things and all the smoke, music, and the strangely costumed people seemed to go into a blur.

"Wow," Charles whispered. "What do they make at this Factory?"

"I don't rightly know." I spotted a large table filled with cold cuts and appetizers. Holding Charles's hand, we walked over there and then proceeded to chow down. I was wondering if the food would taste as queer as the party looked, sounded and smelled, but it was actually pretty tasty.

As I was eating my fill, someone tapped me on the shoulder. I stood up and turned around, finding myself face to face with a balding feller dressed in a sheepskin leather jacket and colorful, floral shirt. He had on wide smoked glasses and a cigarette in his mouth.

"Now, I got a bet," he said, his voice deep and scratchy. "I think you're just some crazy cat who likes to play dress up. But Norman and Tom back there, well, they think you're a flaming gay." He jabbed a thumb behind him at two other men, one wearing a neat white suit, and one with short, curly hair. "Abbie should be here soon, and I can't wait to see what he thinks, but I gotta know now. So, what is it?"

I shrugged. "Well, I ain't exactly that happy right now, so I couldn't really be gay, and I ain't no kind of cat neither. My name's Clark, Clark Reeper. What's your handle?"

"Just call me...Raoul." The bald feller gestured to his two friends. "I like your style, man. C'mon and sit with us for a little. Your little friend can come too."

Charles and I exchanged a glance and then we walked over to sit with Raoul and his friends. They talked about all sorts of things. That Vietnam place got mentioned a few more times, and I decided it must be near Siam or so. They mentioned Russia, and that Tricky Dick guy. Turns out he was the President and his name was Richard Nixon. He didn't sound too nice at all.

"Hey, Clark, you ever smoked grass?" Raoul asked, offering me a cigarette.

"Never saw much point in it." I took the cigarette, wondering if it was just tobacco or some odd far-future substance. I took a whiff, and then everything seemed to get a lot happier. I puffed a few more times before I realized it was hashish of some sort. By then it was too late, and everything started to get more colorful and blurry.

"Fellers," I said. "I reckon I can see the music." I brushed my hands around like an idiot. Poor Charles was still sitting next to me, and he looked very worriedly at me, but I was too inebriated to pay him much mind.

Then, a guy with dark curly hair and a collared shirt decorated like an American flag ran over to us. "Man, can you believe who Andy's letting into this place?" he asked, sounding outraged. "Nappy Little! He's gonna arrive here any second!"

"Who's he?" I mumbled. The name sounded a little familiar.

"Jesus, Clark, you don't know anything. Nappy Little owns Waterloo Industries, one of the biggest companies in the country. He runs drug smuggling operations, Wall Street stock portfolios, and he's best friends with the President." Raoul took the joint away from me and gave it a puff. "You're a real lightweight, Clark. I thought someone who dresses like you would be doing this all the time."

"What?" I asked.

"Nappy Little?" Charles mused thoughtfully. "Mr. Reeper, it's Little Napoleon!" he exclaimed. "He must have got to the future somehow. Maybe in another time machine. Mr. Reeper, we'd better leave before he comes!"

"Who?" I asked. For some reason I found that really funny and I started laughing. Poor Charles had realized the truth, but I was too messed up to listen to him. Little Napoleon was a midget, a performer who later became a member of the notorious Sideshow Gang. He and I had had a few run-ins over the years, and they always ended with me dressing him up as some creature and selling him to a collector. If I had been a little less filled with hashish smoke, I could have gotten out of there before he came in. But I was giggling like a jackass, and I didn't even hear Nappy Little's giant-sized long automobile pull up outside the factory.

As soon as he walked inside, the music stopped. The chattering guests fell silent, and even the smoke seemed to clear out of the way. The doors swung open, and in walked Nappy Little, or as I knew him, Little Napoleon.

He was short, about a head smaller than Charles, and he was dressed in a slick black suit and bolo tie. His hair was pulled back and tied in a pony tail, and his face seemed a little pale. But the size and angry expression cut through even my drugged stupor.

"Little Napoleon!" I blurted out. "How in hell did you end up in the future?"

Nappy Little turned to face me, his mouth opening. "Never mind that," he said in a shrill and squeaky voice. "How did you get here?"

"Don't tell him, Clark!" Charles cried, but I didn't listen.

"Time machine. You know Doc Torrent? He done whisked himself up a time machine, and brought us all forward. What about yourself?"

"A time machine?" Nappy Little stroked his chin. "An ice cave was what brought me here. After you trussed me up and sold me to Aleister Crowley as a demon, I went to England, escaped, and hid in an ice cave. I was frozen solid, until a stray ray of sunlight melted me about ten years ago. I've been working hard, Clark, and I've made some powerful friends. The only thing I really wanted was to get even with you."

"Huh, well I'll just go on back to our time and leave you here, you stupid little midget!" I convulsed in laughter.

"I have powerful friends, Clark. I'm going to speak with them, now." Little Napoleon turned on his heel and marched right out of the Factory. As soon as he left, the band started up again, and the crowd resumed chattering.

"Whoa, man, you really told him off. Groovy!" Raoul patted my back.

But Charles was agitated. "Why'd you tell him about the time machine? What if he gets a hold of it? He could go back in time and mess up everything!"

"Chill, little dude," Raoul said, pushing a joint towards Charles.

Charles pushed the smoking cigar away, and then began to haul me out of the room. He splashed my face with some water from the food table, and then managed to drag me to the door.

"Come on, Clark!" he cried. "We have to get out of here and find Doc Torrent and go back to our time before something awful happens!"

The drugs had mostly passed over me, but I was still a bit woozy. The water helped a lot, and my senses slowly returned to me. "What do you figure could happen? Little Napoleon can't have that many tough friends."

"Wrong again, Clark Reeper." The voice came from down the street. It was night time now, and the street outside the Factory was illuminated by a couple of streetlights. I looked down the rain slicked pavement and saw a number of stretched-out automobiles blocking the path, and a small army of men in dark suits pointing automatic pistols at me and Charles.

Nappy Little stood in front of the motorcade with a tall man in a dark suit. The man had a protruding, upturned nose, a big forehead, and graying black hair. "This here's my best buddy, Clark—President Richard M. Nixon."

I went for my guns, but Nixon's damn Secret Service thugs were quicker. One of them stepped forward and gave me a left hook to the jaw that left me reeling, while another one grabbed Charles and pulled the yelping boy away from me.

Nixon reached into his jacket and pulled out a revolver. "Beautiful weapon, isn't it?" he said, his voice a low rumble. "I've always admired the cowboys. Rugged, independent individuals. It would be great to have one of them as president. There's a young actor named Ronald who played a cowboy in the movies, and he might even end up in the Oval Office."

"Tell your man to let go of my boy, you long-nosed tricky bastard," I said. The drugs were out of my system now, and I had eyes only for Charles. The poor kid was squirming, but the Secret Service man held him fast.

"I don't think so." Nixon aimed the revolver at Charles and pulled back the hammer. Charles stopped squirming, and took slow, shallow breaths. I could hear my own heartbeat, booming inside of me like thunder. "You think I care about the life of one child? Please. Airplanes use napalm to burn Vietnamese kids alive everyday, all so I don't appear soft on communism. Now, let's talk about the time machine."

"Don't tell him!" Charles cried, but Nixon smacked the barrel of his pistol against Charles's head. I gulped and felt sick to my stomach. I saw Little Napoleon shudder at the way Nixon was hurting poor Charles.

"Tell me the location, and I'll let your boy live. Now talk." Nixon didn't have an ounce of mercy in his voice. I wondered what kind of a country would elect a feller like that as president.

I didn't want to talk, but he had Charles, and I would rather watch the entire world burn than let that boy come to harm. I told him the address where Doc Torrent had stashed the chronomobile.

Nixon nodded and his bodyguard let Charles go. "Goodbye, cowboy," Nixon said, opening the door to his automobile. "I won't see you again, but you'll be seeing plenty of me."

The motorcade drove off, leaving Charles and me standing in the street. I watched them go and shrugged. "Well, what can they do with that machine anyway? Go back and bother the dinosaurs?"

"They can change the past!" Charles shouted. "Clark, we have to stop them! They could make things all weird and horrible! Everyone is in danger unless we stop them!"

It made sense. If they went back in time and told Caesar not to go to the Senate on the Ides of March, or if they told

Robert E. Lee not to attack at Gettysburg, history might get all messed up.

Charles and I ran after them, but we didn't get too far.

See, President Nixon, Little Napoleon and all his men had found the chronomobile, just where I told them it was. It might have taken them a little while to figure out how to pilot the damn thing, but Doc Torrent made the controls pretty simple. And while we were running after them, Nixon and Little Napoleon went into the chronomobile and headed back in time.

How do I know what they was doing? Why, because the effects hit us like a sledgehammer. In a single second, everything around us changed. It was like the ground was a carpet, getting all raveled up, and then flopping out all differently. Charles and I were both knocked back on the ground, and when we woke up the next morning, we found that we were lying in the middle of a totally different street.

It was daylight now, the early dawn, and for a few seconds, I figured I was dreaming. The crumbling New York with its broken down buildings, homeless people and crime was gone. What replaced it was a wonderland of even streets and avenues, lined with multicolored trees, and neatly built, uniform, geometric buildings.

I came to my feet, and I was wondering if an automobile wasn't gonna come and run me down, but then I looked up and saw that the cars were all flying in the sky, hovering just like Doc Torrent had said. Charles woke up, and he looked at the flying cars and then he pointed at the sidewalk. It was moving, carrying the pedestrians from one spot to another.

The people were all wearing the same gray jumpsuit uniforms, and all of them, men and women, had bald shaved heads. Every so often, an automaton constable of some kind, a bulky, black armored machine carrying a large stubby rifle, would walk by, shoving folk out of its way.

Charles and I wandered through the orderly streets for a while without saying anything. Then, someone came running towards us, his white lab coat flying about him. It was Doc

Torrent, and though he looked just as confused as we were, he was smiling.

"Clark! Charles! The hover cars! The utopia! I've found it!" He ran around us in a circle, skipping with glee. "Yesterday, I was sitting in the garbage, thinking, and I realized that maybe it's unfair to think that the future is going to be any better than the present, but then I woke up today and everything had changed! And now the utopia is all around us!"

"Um, Doc?" I gulped, not really wanting to spoil his fun. "This stuff, well, it ain't exactly supposed to be here."

"What ever do you mean?"

"It was the President, and Little Napoleon." Charles and I slowly explained what was going on, how Nixon had took the chronomobile back in time and changed things all around.

Doc Torrent's face fell. "Oh." He tottered a little, and I wondered if he was going to faint. "Well, we'd better, um, oh, we should uh..."

"We have to stop him!" Charles said, and I nodded.

"We got means of tracking Nixon down, Doc?" I asked.

It seemed like as long as Torrent had a purpose, he could handle himself. "Yes," he said, after much thought. "We need certain chemical elements, minerals and such, and I can create a temporal-spatial field that will surround us and follow the signal of the chronomobile. We will go directly to the first time and area they traveled to."

"All right, but we gotta find ourselves a museum of some sort that has those ingredients." I looked at the passerby, who all looked alike, and picked one at random. "Excuse me, sir, me and my friends are looking for a museum, something with minerals and chemicals in it?"

"May Nixon bless and keep you," the feller said. I stared at his eyes, and then I realized that it was none other than Raoul from the party at the Factory. He looked like he had been smoking too many joints. "There is the Center of the Great Nixon in the middle of the city. It houses all of his achievements, and some mineral specimens too."

"Thank you," I said. "I reckon that's our best bet for taking Nixon down."

"Don't thank me," Raoul said, still sounding drugged. "Thank Nixon. Wait." He stopped. "Did you say 'take Nixon down'?"

"Yeah," I agreed. "What of it?"

"Security! Subversive Thought! Security!" Raoul cried, waving his hands and crying.

People started screaming and running away from us. Some of the hover cars landed on the ground, their passengers fleeing. Four of those constable automatons walked over to us, gripping their rifles with steel fingers.

"What's the problem?" one of them said in a mechanical voice.

"T-they said, t-they said..." Raoul could barely contain his fear. "They said they wanted to 'take Nixon down!'"

The automaton nodded. "You have been exposed to subversive thought. You will be terminated."

"Okay." Raoul smiled, and then the automaton blew the poor guy's head off, the rifle acting like it was some kind of cannon. I didn't want to stay to find out any more about this nightmare future. I drew my revolvers and fired at the automatons. One of them went down with a shower of sparks. The others began to return fire, but they were pretty bad shots.

We ran into one of the hover cars and all jumped in. The controls were a simple stick and pedal, and Doc Torrent soon figured out how to fly one. We soared into the air, only to find a couple of black, hovering steel automobiles loaded with automatons was chasing after us.

"Any luck at finding the Center of Great Nixon, Doc?" I asked. I leaned out of the window as we zoomed through the sky, and threw some lead at the automatons chasing us.

"It shouldn't be that hard to find," Charles said. He pointed out the window, and I saw a building that I knew was the Center of Great Nixon, partly on account of it was in the middle of the town and took up most of the space in the city, and partly because the building looked exactly like Richard Nixon's face.

We flew towards it, and the Doc drove the car in right through the roof of the building, crashing through Nixon's leering eye. Mortar and plaster showered downwards as we landed in the middle of the Center of Great Nixon.

The place was more like a shrine than a museum, all filled with images of Richard Nixon's glory, from all throughout time. There was a piece of stone taken from a cave, covered with ancient paintings on it, that showed a big-nosed man who had to be Nixon gunning down numerous spear-wielding figures, and then Nixon standing in a circle of worshippers. There was a marble bust of Nixon's head, as old as the Caesars, standing in front of a Roman Mosaic showing Nixon standing before a cheering crowd in a coliseum, a smoking revolver in his hands. An old medieval tapestry showed Richard Nixon sitting in the cupola of some kind of armored vehicle, gunning down hundreds of knights and foot soldiers with machine guns and cannon. Leonardo Da Vinci's *Mona Lisa* was there, but it showed Mona tied up to a chair, being smooched by Richard Nixon. The famous picture of George Washington crossing the Delaware was there, as well, but it was a bit different. The boat was sunk and Washington and all his friends were floundering in the icy water, while Nixon stood on top of a half-submerged submarine, grinning at his handiwork.

There was a photograph from the Civil War, showing Nixon standing in front of a tree, the forms of both Jefferson Davis and Abraham Lincoln dangling from nooses in the branches. Another photograph showed a number of men, a thin feller with a tiny moustache in a military uniform, a fat bald guy, another fat feller in wheelchair, and a stocky man with a thick dark moustache all bowing before Nixon. *Yalta, 1945*, the caption read.

"Son of a gun," I whispered. "He's gone and changed everything."

Doc Torrent nodded gravely. "With the chronomobile at his disposable, any man could become a god. Avoiding old age and death, carrying weapons back and forth through time and space. He must seem to everyone like some kind of immortal god-king."

"But how come we haven't changed?" Charles asked curiously.

"Well, perhaps we are already loose in the chronological sea, and the changes do not affect us. In fact, when we follow Nixon, it won't be to any of these places, but to the very first time he chose to travel to, thus changing all of history once more!"

Just then, I had to stop the Doc's pontificating because the automatons had arrived, crashing their hover cars through the building and firing at everything with their automatic rifles.

I held them off while Charles and Torrent ran to the opposite end of the great hall where a large glass container held a variety of rocks and vials of strange chemicals. I fanned out my six-guns at the automatons, blowing several to smithereens. The constable contraptions were bad shots and went down easy, but there were a lot of them, and more and more kept landing in the Center.

Finally, Doc Torrent came scampering back, Charles close behind him. Both of them were carrying a variety of odd-looking rocks and chemical samples. As I continued to hold the automatons off, Torrent mixed the vials, ground up the stones on the floor, and generally made a mess of things.

After what seemed like a couple of centuries, he had his concoction ready. I holstered my Peacemakers, and we all held hands.

"All right," Doc Torrent said, holding a steaming vial of something I didn't want to know about in his hands. "Either we'll appear a few seconds after that ingrate president does, or our very atoms will be scattered across existence and eternity." He grinned. "Here goes nothing."

He dropped the vial on the ground, into the circle of dust and goop he had made around us. The bullets were still whizzing about, and President Nixon's sneering visage was still looking down on me from a dozen different depictions from across time. But then everything began to change, all the world getting rolled up and spilled out again. It felt like someone was dousing my innards in whiskey and giving each one a good caning.

Slowly, things started to get back to normal. We were standing in a forest somewhere. It was dark, with stars and the moon peeking down on us. A cobblestone road ran through the woods, a few feet from where we were standing.

"Where are we?" I asked. "Back east somewheres?"

"Not just where, but when," Doc Torrent reminded me.

"Someone's coming!" Charles whispered, and we all fell silent. The sound of horseshoes on cobblestones rang out through the night as a lone rider came galloping down the path. He was dressed in an old-fashioned coat and had a tricorne hat on his head.

"The Redcoats are coming!" he shouted. "The regulars are out!"

"Who the hell is that?" I asked.

Charles's eyes lit up. "That's Paul Revere! My father made me memorize the poem: 'listen my children and you shall here, of the midnight ride of Paul Revere.'" Charles shook his head. "I didn't like that poem that much, but that's Paul Revere."

"And there's that criminal politician, and his diminutive partner in crime!" Torrent pointed across the road. There was Richard Nixon and Little Napoleon. Nixon was holding a branch back, and I figured that as soon as Revere rode past, Nixon would let that branch go and it would knock the rider right off of his horse.

Without thinking about the consequences I drew both of my revolvers and fired at Nixon. He leapt backwards, letting the branch go and ducking behind a tree trunk. A second later, he and Little Napoleon opened fire with automatics. I aimed my pistols at some low hanging branches and fired off a couple of shots, sending a large hunk of wood clattering down on Nixon and Napoleon.

The two of them were surprised and stunned, and they turned away and ran into the woods. I ran across the cobblestones to get them, but then stopped. Paul Revere was sitting on his horse, motionless, right next to me. I reckon all of those gunshots must have scared him something fierce.

"What in God's name?" he asked.

"Uh, nothing much. Just ride on. Redcoats are coming, remember?"

He cantered on past me, breaking into a gallop as he went on further down the road. With Paul Revere safe on his way, Charles and Doc Torrent came out of the trees and crossed the road. We followed Nixon and Little Napoleon through the woods, ducking back behind trees when they tried to shoot at us.

They came to the chronomobile, parked in the shade of a bunch of trees, and the two of them jumped into the vehicle and began to turn it on.

"Stop the pair of thieves!" Doc Torrent shouted, jumping onto the machine and aiming a punch at Nixon.

"I am not a crook!" Nixon shouted, accidentally twisting a dial as he tried to slug Doc Torrent back.

"The hell you ain't!" I shouted. Charles and I jumped into the chronomobile, throwing our bodies against Nixon and Little Napoleon. The midget was biting into my leg, I was punching the President in the face, and Charles was grabbing his right hand, when somebody hit the red button in the center of the chronomobile and it went off again. We continued battling as the chronomobile took off, rocketing through time and space.

It reached its destination, which happened to be several feet above the ground. The time machine fell through the air and crashed on the ground, sending us all sprawling every which way. Unfortunately, Nixon and Little Napoleon came to their feet first. They both pointed their guns at me, and there was no way around them.

"Drop your irons, Clark," Little Napoleon said. "It's over."

Reluctantly, I drew out both of my revolvers and let them fall to the ground. We were in another forest, but this was a jungle teeming with strange-looking plants, buzzing insects of impossible size, and it was humid enough to make a man of the plains like me sweat.

"We must be in the primordial world," Doc Torrent whispered. "The dawn of time itself!"

"Shut up, science-man," Nixon said, his voice a low growl. "Christ, you're worse than Kissinger." He looked around, as if somebody might be watching. "Well, we have a dumb cowboy, a mad scientist, and a little boy." Nixon cocked his automatic. "I'm killing the little tramp first."

"No!" Little Napoleon and I shouted at the same time. I stared at him in surprise. "It's not right, Richard. Let's just leave them here or something. We don't have to kill them." Little Napoleon was sweating and shaking, and it weren't from the heat.

"No. They'll follow us somehow. What's wrong with killing them anyway?" Nixon asked.

"Well, Clark Reeper has done awful things to me. But he's always left me alive at the end of the day." Little Napoleon pointed his pistol at Nixon. "I want to return the favor."

Nixon fired his gun, shooting Little Napoleon in the arm. The dwarf dropped his gun and grunted in pain.

"Fine," Nixon said. "I'll kill all of you. No problem." He pointed his weapon at Little Napoleon. "Starting with you."

Just then, a loud growl resounded through the jungle. Slowly, Nixon turned around. A humongous reptilian beast was standing in front of him, its mouth open and drooling.

"Well, I screwed it all up real good, didn't I?" Nixon muttered. Those were the last words he ever said. The beast reached down and gobbled him up in a single bite, crunching hard on the President's bones.

As soon as he was gone, Little Napoleon, Charles, Doc Torrent and I hightailed it to the chronomobile. Torrent was already playing with the dials, getting everything set right.

Soon, the machine was moving through time and space again. I turned to Little Napoleon. "Thank you kindly," I said.

He shrugged. "Yeah, sure. You would've done the same."

"What about the President?" Charles asked. "Won't the people in 1970 notice that the President disappeared?"

Little Napoleon shrugged. "Not really. The people in power will probably clone him, and then kick him out of power by creating some kind of scandal. Then the vice president will pardon him, and everyone will forget about it and move on."

"Is everyone all right with returning to the present?" Doc Torrent asked.

We all nodded. "I think I'm done with time traveling for a while," I said.

Charles nodded. "I think so too. Would like to come with us, Mr. Napoleon?"

Little Napoleon nodded. "Yeah, I guess so. It was groovy in the 60's, but I miss top hats and penny farthings. And this stinking pony tail is getting on my nerves."

A few seconds later, we reappeared on the stage back at the convention. We had been gone for a good long time, but for the people in the hall, we had only vanished for a second or two, and then reappeared a moment later.

Slowly, we all exited the chronomobile. The crowd stared up at us, waiting for something to happen, all holding their breath. Doc Torrent looked at the crowd with glassy eyes.

"Did it work?" a heckler called.

Torrent looked at the eager faces of the crowd, and then turned to the chronomobile, and finally looked at Charles, and Little Napoleon and me. Slowly, he shook his head.

"It...it was a failure."

The crowd gasped, not believing it after all the selling Doc Torrent had done. I couldn't quite believe it myself.

"Yes, a failure," the Doc continued. "All it does is make a midget with a pony tail materialize. I'm sorry for wasting everyone's time." He gulped and then sat down on the stage. The crowd waited for him to say something more, and when he didn't, they all ambled off to see other exhibits, grumbling and chuckling.

"Why'd you go and say that?" I asked Doc Torrent.

"Because maybe time travel isn't something man is supposed to be able to do." Torrent sounded like he couldn't believe the words he was saying. "After seeing how...normal the future was, and the terrible damage that one man wreaked upon the timeline, I just don't think it's a good idea. I'll destroy the chronomobile tomorrow, and then move on to better things."

I patted the Doc on the back. "That's probably best for everyone," I said and I reckoned that was true.

Well, Little Napoleon left New York early the next morning after getting his wound patched up. He was heading out west. He said that if we bumped into each other again, he didn't know if it would be as friends or enemies. I didn't rightly know myself. Little Napoleon said going into the future had given him some ideas. He was gonna try to sell a certain type of pants, bell-bottom jeans, he called them, and see if they'd catch on. I wished him luck.

Doc Torrent was upset about trashing the chronomobile, but he was already thinking of other inventions. A shrink ray seemed to be what really interested him, and he was back to his normal exuberant self when we left.

Charles and I also headed out west. I got a bunch more letters and telegrams asking for my services, and I aim to answer them. I guess the future ain't that much different but I didn't really fancy being a cowboy in the twilight of this country's history. No, sir, the present suits me just fine, and with Charles by my side, I don't see it ever going sour.

The Riders of the Black Goat

Now I've seen my fair share of odd mounts. I've ridden on the animated corpse of a deceased steed, taken a ride on a hovering disc from another planet, even been pulled in a wagon by a giant-sized armadillo. I suppose it comes with the job. You see, my name is Clark Reeper, and I am a bounty hunter specializing in some of the odder jobs that are out there. Sometimes that involves the queerest critters a feller ever laid his eyes on. Galumphing about on all these strange animals sometimes gets to my head, and I figure I've seen everything there is to see, but then something comes around and knocks that notion plumb out of my head.

That's probably a good thing, because ever since my adventure involving that undead horse, I've been looking out for a little ten-year-old boy named Charles Green. He's a real nice little feller, small for his age, with slightly curled brown hair under a peaked cap, big spectacles over his eyes, and he always wears a neat little Norfolk suit. I'm a tall gent with a long, flowing duster, a crumbling Stetson on my head, and two Colt Peacemakers never far from my hands. I reckon Charles is the closest thing I got to a son, and I love him like he's my own flesh and blood.

Over the years, we've been in a great deal of desperate situations, two of which involved a satanic gunslinger name of Brimstone Brown. We were old foes, going back to a big battle at Niagara Falls or thereabouts. After I found myself taking care of Charles, the two of us met again during a range war in California. Brown managed to nearly open a portal to Hell itself, almost sacrificing poor Charles in the process. It's a long story, but I stopped that bastard, and his plan backfired when Satan took Brimstone Brown down for an extended visit.

The next time we met was in New Orleans. Brimstone had returned to earth, this time as a servant of the Prince of Darkness and was packing a whole arsenal of demonic powers. But his time in Hell had changed him for the better, and he was reluctant to do his duty for his hellish masters. Brown ended up saving my life, and the two of us parted as friends.

Then, just after a job with one of them Chinese Tong Gangs, I got a letter from Brimstone. He was holed up in some little backwater town in Missouri by the name of Buckton, and he was begging for my help.

Charles and I looked at the letter over breakfast at our hotel in Dodge City. I held up the tattered yellowed paper and read it aloud. "To my friend and companion, Clark Reeper. Dear Clark, it is with a sense of dread that I write to you, for I fear that I am not long for this world." I raised an eyebrow. People did all sorts of crazy things when the Grim Reaper was staring them in the face, and I figured that Brimstone talking all-fancy had something to do with that. I continued reading. "But it is not for me that I ask for aid. It is for a young woman named Mabel Princely, who has stolen away my heart as much as the devil has taken my soul."

"He fell in love?" Charles asked, not believing it any more than I did.

"Well, I guess there is someone for everyone, even Brimstone Brown." I shrugged and went back to the letter. "Mabel Princely is the schoolmarm sent by the Freedmen's Bureau to Buckton, but the town's allegiances still lie with the fallen Confederacy. Recently, some of the leading citizens of the town have acquired new allegiances, the details of which are all too familiar to me. I would defend Ms. Princely myself, if not for a severe weakening of my constitution. When we last met, you told me that I ain't all bad. I saved your life, and now I am asking you to save someone else's. Please, Clark, prove to me that I am not all bad. Yours in Blood, Brimstone Brown."

I set the letter down and looked at Charles. "Can you imagine that damned demon-lover pleading for my help?" I asked. "Just don't seem natural."

Charles shook his head. "He's changed, Mr. Reeper, or else he wouldn't have helped us escape from New Orleans. I think we should go to Buckton and help him, just to return the favor."

"But what if it's a trap of some kind? Brimstone's full of guile, and all this talk about falling in love ain't like him."

"But, Mr. Reeper, I think everybody could fall in love. I mean, even you liked Jennifer Chaos, and you've acted differently around her. And Brimstone did save our lives. We should go and help him."

There weren't no arguing with that. I smiled at Charles and stood up. "Well, all right, son. We'll be on the first train to Missouri." It left that evening, and the two of us headed out for Kansas City, and then hitched a ride on a stagecoach heading for Buckton.

I never really liked stagecoach rides, on account of you feel all cooped up and the coach is always rocking around and making your innards bounce every which way in your body. This coach was no different, but at least it weren't crowded. The only person riding besides Charles and me was a big-bellied man with a large yellow beard dressed in a bulging shirt and a bearskin vest. He had two long barreled Colt Navy revolvers at his belt. In his hand, he held a bag of raw mushrooms, which he was loudly munching on.

I decided to say hello.

"Howdy, stranger," I said, holding out my hand. "Name's Clark Reeper. You heading to Buckton?"

"Ja, I am." The man had a thick Germanic accent, and I quickly realized he was a squarehead. "My name is Gustav Olafson. Who is the little boy sitting with you?"

"Pleased to meet you, sir," Charles said. He was always polite as pie. "My name is Charles Green."

"So," I asked the Swede. "You know anything much about this Buckton place?"

"I have never been there before. I figure it is a lot like the climate in this country, very sticky and hot. I prefer the cold of my native Sweden." He grinned and stroked his beard. "I am going to Buckton looking for a man. You see, I am a bounty hunter."

I chuckled a little at that, I couldn't help it. Who ever heard of a Swede bounty hunter? They were more suited to farming, raising cattle, or other peaceful pursuits.

"A bounty hunter?" I asked. "Really?"

"Ja," Gustav grinned. "Is it not an exciting job?"

"Sure is," I agreed. We talked a little bit more about this and that as the stagecoach drove on. He offered me some mushrooms, but I declined. I looked out the window from time to time and saw the Missouri countryside. It was mostly thickly forested, with some clearings and fields of chaparral, perfect for farming. In time, the stagecoach rolled into Buckton, and then we all disembarked.

Buckton was a small town, just a couple rows of shops and houses, all evenly spaced apart. It didn't look particularly poor or rich, but there was a sense of tension about the place, like as soon as you weren't looking everyone would pull out pistols and start blasting away at each other. Even the children, chasing each other about and playing, stared at Charles and me with wide unfriendly eyes.

Charles smiled at them politely as we went on our way. The letter said Brimstone's best girl was a schoolmarm, so we headed down to the schoolhouse. It was a newly built building, still with its first coat of paint, and it looked like a well-equipped center of learning. We walked through the single door into the one room, and lying there on a small cot in the corner was Brimstone Brown.

The satanic gunslinger looked like he had gotten himself chewed up and spit out. His skin was chalk pale, his long black hair was falling out, and several long scars stretched across his face and arms. Instead of wearing his normal black duster or broad brimmed hat with a silver pentagram in the brim, he was dressed in naught but bedclothes.

"Clark?" he asked. "That you?"

I walked over to him and smiled weakly. "It is, Brimstone. I got your telegram and hightailed it over here. How you holding up?"

Brimstone coughed. "Not very well, I think. The Lord of Hell doesn't like it when his agents desert him. The fires that I used to wield at will now burn me from the inside." He sat up in bed and shook his head. "I don't know if I can...keep on going."

"Ah, don't you go saying that, Brimstone! You're one tough bastard, you know that. You'll pull through."

"I don't know. But you ought to meet Ms. Princely. Mabel has been so kind to me." At that, a young woman walked out of the backroom, carrying a wet rag. She gently rubbed Brimstone's brow. She was a pretty little thing, petite and dressed in calico. There was a turquoise broach at her throat, and she had dark hair in a neat bun. Soon as she saw Charles and me she curtsied and held out her hand.

"It's Clark Reeper," Brimstone explained. "He's come to help us."

"Oh, that's wonderful!" Mabel Princely replied, seeming very relieved. "Brimstone told me that you could save the schoolhouse, and perhaps my life. He spoke admirably of your skill with a six-gun."

"Well, I ain't too shabby with one," I said, taking out one of my revolvers and giving it a spin.

"He didn't mention that you have a child, and such a handsome one at that." Ms. Princely shook Charles's hand, and my boy seemed a little tongue-tied. Mabel was real pretty, and I reckon my whole day would be spent staring at her if she was my schoolmarm.

"That's Charles Green, my boy," I said.

"I'll do whatever I can to help you," Charles blurted out, and then his face turned red and he stepped back. Ms. Princely smiled at him.

"Well, Charles, if you ever need any books of any kind, just let me know, and I will be happy to provide them."

I pulled up a small desk and sat down, Charles taking the desk next to me. "So, what exactly is the danger that's made you all scared?" I asked.

Mabel shook her head and shivered. "It seems as if the town does not wish me to do my job. All I want to do is teach the children, and yet I have faced much hostility."

"What sort of hostility?" Charles asked.

"What sort of children?" I asked, getting an idea of what was going on.

"Well, all children. The sons of the shopkeepers and farmers." She gulped. "White or colored. The Freedmen's Bureau thinks education is important for the south, and I am here to educate."

"But the locals don't take to kindly to anyone educating colored folk," I said. I stood up. "They probably put on bed sheets and start raising all kinds of hell. No offense, Brimstone."

"None taken," he said. "Those Klan bastards have given us death threats and even tried to attack some of the students. I've done my best to fight back, but because of my sickness, I won't be able to defend Mabel much longer."

"Don't say that, Bartholomew," Mabel said, stroking Brimstone's hair.

"Bartholomew?" I asked. "Is that your real name, Brimstone?"

The demon-worshipping desperado nodded.

I grinned, but then remembered the serious nature of our situation. I helped Charles out of his desk and turned to the door. "Well, Brimstone, Mabel, I'd like to help you, I surely would, but I reckon one man with two Colts ain't gonna do squat against the Invisible Empire. Them Kluxers will tear me apart, and they might even hurt Charles. I ain't gonna risk it."

"But, Mr. Reeper," Mabel cried. "Please, you can't just leave us here! They'll kill me, they'll kill the colored children! You mustn't leave!"

"Sorry, miss." I headed to the door. "My advice is to get yourself out of the country."

Charles wouldn't budge. He grabbed my arm, squared his shoulder, and held his ground. "We can't leave them, Mr. Reeper," he said. "We have to help."

I looked down at Charles. The poor naïve kid must have really thought we could win. He didn't know what I knew. I had been down south before, having spent my childhood in New Orleans. I had seen the way white folk treated coloreds, and what happened if they thought one was getting uppity. I didn't like it one bit, but I knew there weren't nothing for it but to run.

Then, just as I was about to head out, the door slammed open and several men stepped inside. They wore normal clothes, but a variety of burlap bags with eyeholes cut into them covered up their heads. The bags were decorated with facial features, moustaches and eyeglasses and such. All of them were armed, and they moved with the purposefulness of men who knew they were in the right.

"Sorry, fellers," I said. "This ain't a costume party. Maybe you should try next door." There weren't an ounce of humor in my voice.

"We don't got an argument with you, stranger. Step aside." One of the Kluxers strode forward. He seemed to be the leader. He was a broad-shouldered man in a dark suit, and his mask was decorated with thick eyebrows. He had a booming voice, with the strong accent of an aristocratic southerner.

"Please, Clark, let me deal with this." Mabel pushed past me, squaring her shoulders. She was about a head shorter than the big Kluxer, and I felt mighty sorry for her. "What do you want?"

"We're giving you an ultimatum," the Kluxer said. "Tonight this school house will burn. If you don't clear out by then, you'll burn with it."

"You can't do that!" Mabel said, her voice defiant. "You can't just terrorize all of Buckton without consequences!"

"We got the power behind us," the Kluxer said, and I could tell he was grinning under his mask. "We can and we will. We're all chivalrous men, Ms. Princely, and we don't want to hurt a lady—"

"That's a damned lie!" Mabel shouted, surprising all of us. "You go after little children and old women! You're a pack of filthy cowards playing dress up!"

The Kluxer slapped her, knocking her down with his swipe. Brimstone Brown rose shakily from his cot, and then fell back with a gasp of pain. I couldn't stand someone striking a lady like that, and I stepped between them and drew my revolvers.

"How dare you call me a coward!" the Kluxer cried. "I was at Antietam, I was at Sharpsburg!"

"You ought to have died there," I said. I jabbed my pistol into his face and let him stare down the barrel for a little while. All of his men fixed their weapons on me, but they weren't brave enough to shoot. "Now get out and go to Hell. No offense, Brimstone."

"None taken," he wheezed, pulling himself back into his cot.

"You're making a big mistake, stranger," the Head Kluxer said. "You'll swing like a darkie for this, and your boy will swing with you."

"Maybe I ought to make some more holes in your bag." I clicked down the hammer on my revolver. "Course, I like to look a man in the face when I blow his head off. Take off your mask."

His eyes narrowed from behind the eye slits. Slowly, he reached up and pulled off the burlap sack. He did indeed have thick eyebrows, nestled in a severe face under pale white hair. Ms. Princely gasped.

"Leonidas Bishop! Well, I would never have expected—"

"That an upright southern gentleman, the mayor of Buckton, would defend his city's honor?" Leonidas Bishop's red face grew more crimson. "Well, Ms. Princely, I can see that you won't be persuaded. The next time you see me, you'll be dangling from a rope."

"You come riding down here on your big white horses, you might find a lot of you not riding back out," I said, keeping my revolver cocked and ready.

"Who said anything about horses? We've got better steeds." Bishop turned away, heading for the exit. The rest of his thugs filed out after him, not bothering to close the door.

I holstered my guns and sighed. My temper had got the better of me, and now there was no way we could just walk out of town. I slumped down in a desk and shook my head.

"You did the right thing, Mr. Reeper," Charles said. "Thank you."

"Much obliged, but now I have to battle an entire town all on my lonesome." I shook my head. "I've always tried to steer clear of situations like this, especially with you by my side, but now there ain't nothing for it."

"Well, I am grateful that you're staying," Ms. Princely smiled warmly. "If I remember from Bartholomew's stories, you've fought your way out of worse situations than this one."

"Maybe." I looked at the floor. "What exactly did Leonidas Bishop mean when he said he weren't gonna be riding horses? What other kind of critter is he gonna be riding?"

Brimstone gulped and sat up in his cot. "The Black Goats." He clasped his hands. "Bishop has made some powerful friends lately, and in return, the Black Goats serve him."

I raised an eyebrow. "He's gonna ride in on a goat? Seems mighty stupid. Maybe Charles could ride a goat, but a grown man would fall right off."

"These aren't your normal barnyard animals." Brimstone grabbed on to one of the desks and pulled himself up. He wavered and nearly toppled over, but he finally managed to stand. "The Black Goat is the mount of the devil himself and the Goat Riders have immense power, including invulnerability to many mortal weapons and they have the ability of flight. They terrorized the Low Countries of Flanders in the Sixteenth Century, before the priesthood succeeded in banishing them."

"Great," I muttered. "Super-powered flying horned goats carrying a whole town of folks wishing me dead. I figure things just can't get much better." I was a mite ornery at myself for getting angry, and at Brimstone for asking me to come to Buckton. I was even a mite angry at Charles for being so naïve about things.

"You won't stand alone, Clark," Brimstone turned to Mabel. "Please, dear. Get my weapons and give them to me. I will fight."

"But you can barely stand, Bartholomew!" Mabel embraced him. "You're not strong enough!"

"I'm strong enough to fire a six-gun," Brimstone retorted. "Now fetch my clothes and weapons before I collapse again."

Mabel hastened to retrieve the guns.

Somehow I still didn't feel confident. "We ain't gonna last a goddamn minute against the whole Klan," I said darkly. "Especially when they're mounted on those magic goats. Not with one man, and not with one damned invalid. No offense, Brimstone."

"Sure, Clark," Brimstone said. "You know, I am sorry about this."

"No need to be," I muttered. "It ain't no one's fault except the bastards in burlap. Still, I'd wish you'd given me more information in the letter. Maybe there's still some way we can get Charles out."

"I can fight!" Charles said. "Give me a pistol! I could hold one with two hands, and aim it, and kill some of those...those..." He struggled to find the right word. "Those bastards!"

I nearly laughed seeing that little boy all worked up like that. "Sorry, son. You'd most likely blow your own arm off. Besides, I ain't turning you into a killer like me, no matter what. No, we'll need someone else to help us."

As if on cue, the door to the schoolhouse swung open and in stepped Gustav Olafson. He carried the bag of mushrooms in his hands, and there was some kind of rifle stock peeking up over his back. He grinned at me through his sandy beard.

"Hello!" Gustav slapped his belly. "Have no fear, Gustav Olafson is here! I will help you, very much."

"Much obliged for the offer," I said, "but maybe you could use your...um...talents, somewhere else."

Gustav's grin never wavered. "Please, give me a chance! I am toughest fighter in all Sweden!" He stuck out his large belly. "They say there is troll blood in my family!"

"Well, that's great, but we don't need your help." I was trying to be as polite as I could. "I have a feeling you'll be more a hindrance than a help in this case, you silly squarehead."

"Now, Mr. Reeper, only God can make judgments, and Lord knows we need all the help we can get." Ms. Princely stepped forward and smiled at Gustav. "Mr. Olafson, we would be glad to have you along."

"Yippee! I say 'yippee' like the cowboys say!" Gustav chuckled and slapped his belly again, and it made Charles giggle. It was a mighty funny sight, but I wasn't in the mood for any sort of laughter.

"Why do you want to help us?" I asked. "The kindness of your heart ain't no reason to go up against an entire city full of gun-packing Goat Riders."

"Leonidas Bishop have, how you say, big money on his top. I mean his head." Gustav pulled a wanted poster from his bearskin vest and unrolled it. The poster showed a crude picture of the mayor of Buckton, bushy eyebrows and white hair unmistakable. "Your government has offered big dollars for his top!"

I reckoned these must be desperate times in Washington if the politicians were employing folks like this jovial Swede. I didn't like fighting alongside him, figuring an unschooled squarehead like him would just as likely shoot himself in the foot then shoot the Kluxers. Still, I couldn't argue with Mabel that even a shaky gun on our side was a good thing.

"Well, all right, Gustav, you can stay. But you stay near the window and don't go shooting off your piece unless you're certain it ain't gonna hit one of us, okay?"

"Oh, ja, I am very careful." Gustav chomped down on another mushroom. "Care for a mushroom?"

"Nah. What about that rifle you got on your back? That a Winchester or a Springfield?"

Gustav reached up and grabbed what I thought was the rifle stock, but when he pulled it over his shoulder, I realized that it was the handle of a large battleaxe. It was a real nice weapon, a shiny blade covered with odd runes, a handle inlaid with gold and silver, and an edge that looked like it could split a hair without much trouble.

"It is Skullsplitter!" Gustav said. "This weapon was in my family for generations. I will split many skulls with this."

"Well, a wood chipper is all well and good, but we need some firepower." I pointed to his revolvers. "You know how to use them irons?"

The Swede expertly drew out one of his Colt Navies and spun it around his fingers. "Like skiing down a gentle slope!" he said gleefully.

I couldn't help grinning back, just because he was so damn exuberant. "All right," I said, turning to everyone in the room. "Ms. Princely, you mind taking my boy into the back room and keeping him safe during the fight?"

"It would be a pleasure," Mabel said. She beckoned Charles and he followed her, casting a lingering glance at me. Poor kid, wondering if I was going to survive or not. I couldn't fail him.

"All right, now the two of you listen good." I turned to Brimstone Brown and Gustav Olafson. "Night will fall soon, and then those Kluxer bastards are gonna come round this here schoolhouse like a noose around a hanged man's throat. We'll fortify it the best we can, and I hope to God that we'll be ready for them."

Nightfall came all too soon. Right after the sun crept over the horizon and the shadows of Buckton started to get all long and shifty, the Ku Klux Klan made their move. They came walking down the deserted road to the schoolhouse, maybe a few dozen of them. It was definitely all the men in town.

They wore a wide variety of crazy costumes. Some of them covered their heads with the burlap bags stitched with facial features, while others had hoods and masks taken from various shades of cloth. Most of them carried torches, guns, or both. At the head of the group was the broad-shouldered form of Leonidas Bishop, carrying a Confederate battle flag. The Stars and Bars flapped eerily in the torchlight as the whole lot of them stood silently in front of the schoolhouse.

With the blazing torches behind him, Leonidas Bishop stepped up and cleared his throat.

"Tonight," he shouted. "This schoolhouse, this symbol of the degradation of the white man before his black servants, will burn!"

All of his men let out a raucous cheer that had a bit of the old rebel yell somewhere in it and fired their weapons into the air.

"I've already delivered my ultimatum," Bishop continued. "There will be no mercy given." He paused and stroked his chin under the mask. "But I'll make an offer all the same. Come out now, the Yankee schoolmarm, the invalid, the gunslinger, and the gunslinger's brat, and we'll blow you all away quickly and painlessly. Stay, and you'll be swinging from the limb of a tree."

I decided I wouldn't take him up on the offer. Instead, I hurled a desk through one of the schoolhouse's front-facing glass windows. The windowpane shattered into a hundred pieces as the desk fell through, and then I leaned in and let those masked thugs have it. Both of my revolvers blazed away, and a few of the Klansmen in the front of the crowd went down before they knew what had hit them.

The other Kluxers lowered their weapons and returned fire, but I had already ducked back behind the window. Bullets thudded into the wall; I could feel many of them whizzing past my head and ruffling the tip of my hat, but none even grazed me. I looked at the closed door to the backroom and thought of Charles and Mabel. I reckoned the poor kid and the schoolmarm must be scared out of their wits by all the lead messengers flying around.

Brimstone Brown leaned against an overturned desk for support, and used his leg to ease open the door a crack. Even as the Kluxers outside tried to jam new rounds into their weapons, Brimstone hit them with his Colt Buntline Special. The long barreled weapon proved its worth, a single precision bullet cutting through several Kluxers before a feller's forehead finally stopped it. Brown cracked off three quick shots, and then nimbly rolled out of the way.

"That will give them something to think on!" I shouted over the gunfire. "Maybe they'll convince themselves to take up a new hobby!"

"Don't count on it!" Brimstone shouted back. "They're just getting started." As much as I didn't like it, Brimstone was dead right. The Kluxers started hurling their torches, trying to smoke us out or burn us alive. Some of the torches landed on the roof and rolled off, others smashed into the schoolroom and started setting desks alight. Gustav and Brimstone hurled some of the torches back, while I tried to smother the flames with my duster.

"This schoolhouse ain't gonna last much longer!" I shouted, just as another desk went up in flames. The room was now full of smoke, and I had to crouch low to breathe. "We'd best be hightailing it out of here!"

"But the Kluxers will blow us to pieces," Brimstone pointed out. "If we so much as stick a toe outside, it will be blown to smithereens in seconds."

"I have an idea." Gustav took the bag of mushroom from his vest.

"Not now, Gustav! I do not want a goddamn mushroom!"

The Swede shook his head. He dug through the bag and pulled out one mushroom lurking somewhere in the bottom. It was a real ugly fungus, reddish brown with bright green spots dappled all over it, and it seemed to pulsate a little when you moved your eyes away from it.

"When I eat this mushroom, I will go, how you say in English?" Gustav stroked his beard for a while, oblivious to all them bullets flying back and forth like they was no more than wasps at a picnic. "Oh, I remember—berserk. The Berserkergang, it is called in the old sagas."

"Now ain't a good time to lose your wits," I said.

Gustav shook his head. "No. Now, wits are the last things I need. Please, stand clear and get the schoolteacher and the little boy out while I am busy." And with that, he tilted his head back and tossed the mushroom in between his chompers. One bite, then two, and the fungus was gone. Soon as the lump of it disappeared down Gustav's throat, the big Swede began to change.

Gustav headed for the door, his pistols coming to his hands like they was meant to be there. He kicked down the door and came out firing, each shot sliding in right between some Kluxer's wide eyes. Twelve shots blasted out of his revolvers, and twelve Klansmen went down.

"Kill the squarehead!" Leonidas Bishop shouted, and a dozen rifles and pistols were leveled at Gustav. For a few seconds, I thought that poor damn Swede was gonna be blown to Kingdom Come, but then the Berserkergang truly took hold.

Letting his empty revolvers fall to the ground, Gustav pulled that big old battleaxe off of his back. He leapt into the mob of Kluxers like some kind of whirlwind, hacking across with his axe in a lethal spiral. Heads flew off of shoulders, limbs flew from bodies, and thick streams of red blood spurted in the streets. Bullets flew around him, but Gustav Olafson danced between them without seeming to care. His axe came crushing down on a Kluxer's head, living up to its name as it split the poor feller's skull clean in two.

I was watching the whole thing with my mouth open, and then I realized just what this diversion was for. I ran to the backroom. "Charles! Ms. Princely! We're heading out now!"

Charles opened the door for Mabel, and then they both stared at the burnt and bullet-ridden insides of the schoolhouse. "My God," Mabel whispered. "We can't just abandon this place..."

"We leave or get ourselves fried," I said.

Brimstone Brown nodded. "Come on, Mabel. When this is all over, there will be time to rebuild."

She took one more sad look at her ruined classroom, and then closed her eyes and steeled herself. "All right. Let's go." We all ran to the door, running outside and making for the brush outside of town. Gustav was still going at it, but his blows seemed a little slower, and the effects of that mushroom seemed to be wearing off.

A couple of Kluxers got in our way, but I brought up my Peacemakers and gunned them down without much trouble. Behind us, the flames really were roasting the schoolhouse, and I knew the wooden structure wouldn't last long.

"Where exactly are we going?" I asked as we ran.

"The colored shantytown, just outside of Buckton," Brimstone said. "They'll harbor us."

Suddenly, a flash of lighting cut through the darkness, even though there wasn't a cloud in the sky. We all turned around and saw Leonidas Bishop standing in front of the burning schoolhouse, his arms spread out like he was worshipping it.

"I shall walk in the valley of the shadow of death, and I shall fear no evil, but thou art with me, and thine evil knoweth no bounds!" he shouted in a resonant chant. "Thy pitchfork and thy saber, they comfort me."

"We have to leave now," Brimstone said. "He's summoning the Black Goats."

"But Gustav..." Charles pointed at the Swede. He was running out of steam, and he was probably counting on us to get him out of there.

I didn't care that much for the squarehead, but he was risking his life for ours, and I had to return the favor, just like Charles said. "We can't leave him," I said. I ran towards the melee, shooting off my pistols as I ran. That took some of the heat off of Gustav, and he turned to me.

"Get your guns and let's go, Gustav!" I shouted.

He nodded, holstered his axe and ducked down to pick up his pistols as I covered him with my own gunfire.

Meanwhile, Leonidas was just putting the finishing touches on his speech. "Thou preparest a table for me, from the flesh of my enemies. Thou annointest my head with their blood. My mouth runneth over. Surely, fire and death shall follow me all the years of my life. And I shall dwell in the palace of the Dark Lord forever!" As soon as he finished his prayer, lightning struck again, and then the goats arrived.

They came down from the heavens above, running through the air like an earthly goat would lope across a field. Each was as big as a buffalo, covered in thick black wool and adorned with a silver saddle and bridle. Their horns were big curling weapons covered with silver spikes. They had hellish old red eyes and snorted steam out of their nostrils. There were dozens of them, one for every Kluxer.

Leonidas Bishop hopped up on one, grasping the reins with one hand and raising his rifle with the other. The other Kluxers mounted up as well, and they stood in front of us. I lowered my pistols and fired away, but the bullets didn't seem to do much good. They'd fly towards the goat and rider, but bounced off those critters when they hit; some of them even rebounded back and nearly hit me. I had shot off a whole revolver before I realized my bullets weren't having any effect.

"Ah, hell," I muttered. "No offense, Brimstone."

"None taken," Brimstone said. "I don't think we can outrun the Black Goats, but we have to try. Come on." He turned to go, heading into the forests surrounding Buckton. The poor guy was sick, and nearly tottered over as he started running. Quickly, we all followed him.

We ran through the underbrush, the sound of pounding hooves behind us getting closer and closer. The damn Goat Riders were closing in, and there weren't a damn thing I could do about it. I turned around and saw them coming up behind us. The big Black Goats seemed to hover just above the ground, their hooves never really connecting with the dirt.

Some of the Kluxers started shooting at us, but them goats must have been bucking them around something fierce, because all the shots went wild. Still, I figured it was a matter of time before one of us got shot. Something had to be done.

I looked at Brimstone running in front of me, and noticed a lariat tied to his belt. I got an idea: it was desperate as all hell, but worth a shot.

"Brimstone!" I said. "Quick, help me with your lasso. You take one end, and I'll take the other."

He stared at me like I had started speaking another language, but then he grinned as he understood my scheme. Brimstone took the rope from his belt, handed me one end while he took the other; then each of us ran to opposite ends of the forested road and tied them to a tree. We pulled the lariat taut, keeping it low enough so that the Goat Riders couldn't see it, but high enough so that their mounts couldn't just step over it.

The Black Goats and the Kluxers charged full speed down the pathway, not noticing the rope. There was a mighty twang as the satanic hooves got caught up in the rope, and all of them big demon goats crashed down on each other like donkeys who had been drinking whiskey instead of water. The second row of mounted Klansmen was going too fast to stop, and they crashed into their fallen friends.

While the Kluxers regrouped, we had just enough time for the head start we desperately needed. Brimstone and I followed the rest of our group, running down the overgrown trail until we left Buckton behind.

We didn't say a word to each other until we reached the shantytown. It was a small settlement. Most of the houses looked like they had been built just a few years ago. A small crowd gathered in the streets, and I noticed some of them were holding hunting rifles and fowling pieces.

Mabel Princely smiled weakly. "Hello," she said, her voice sounding a little strangled. "I'm afraid that some rather bad things have happened lately."

An elderly black feller with a thick gray beard and a shabby vest and jacket, doubtlessly a former slave, didn't look surprised. "What sort of trouble, Ms. Princely? Damn ofays going on a spree?"

The schoolmarm nodded. "They burned down the schoolhouse, Joshua. I'm sorry."

The colored folk hung their heads. I reckoned they liked getting their learning, seeing as they weren't allowed any before the war's end.

"They coming this way?" Joshua asked.

Again, Mabel nodded. "And they're riding the Black Goats."

This time some of the colored folk cried out in fear. They knew what would happen when the Kluxers would ride their Black Goats and they knew that the Kluxers were out for blood tonight. If they succeeded, Charles, Gustav, Brimstone, Mabel, and me wouldn't be swinging alone, but the thought of company at the end of a rope didn't cheer me none.

"Oh, Jesus," the old feller whispered. "No time for running when they're riding those things. Nothing to do but go and hide."

"What about fighting them?' I said. "I can see some of you boys got irons on you. Why don't you use them?"

"Clark, you damn fool," Brimstone said angrily, leaning on Mabel for support. "Bullets don't hurt the Black Goat Riders. They are impervious to steel and fire, the two qualities of any firearm."

"Son of a gun," I muttered. Brimstone was right. Every gun in the Federal Army wouldn't put so much as dent in them horned terrors. We'd have to think of something else.

"Wait," Charles said. We stared at him and he shivered nervously under our gazes. "I have an idea."

"What is it, son?" I asked gently. Charles was a real smart little feller, but he was nervous by nature and always afraid of doing wrong.

"Well, do you remember in that Mission in California, when Brimstone was trying to kill me?"

"I've done a lot of...things I'm not proud of, dear," Brimstone whispered. Mabel stared at Brimstone. He looked at the ground. "I'm working for forgiveness, but as you can see, it's slow in coming and hurts like the devil."

"Well, it's not anything about that," Charles stuttered. "It was just, well, when all of those demons and things were attacking Clark, they couldn't get at him. He was holding something, some beads I think, that saved him!"

"Prayer beads, old Padre gave them to me," I mused. "Those beads were blessed by a holy man, and the demons couldn't touch me." I understood what Charles was saying. "If we could get a holy man to bless something maybe we'd be protected from the Goat Riders and maybe we could use it as a weapon. It would be like buckshot going through a blanket. Good thinking, boy." I ruffled Charles's hair and he smiled at me.

"Joshua, you're a holy man!" Mabel said. "I've seen you marry people, and lead services on Sunday, and you read from the Bible all the time!"

The old Negro shook his head. "Ah no, Ms. Princely. They were not real marriages, just jumping the broom back during plantation days. I ain't never been to no Bible College, and I don't have a minister's collar or nothing."

"That shouldn't matter," Charles said. "I mean, just as long as the people around think you're holy, then, I guess you are holy."

"I think Charles has something there," I agreed. "Besides, it's the only chance we got."

Joshua nodded slowly. He turned to a watering trough next to one of the houses and walked over to it. He knelt down and dipped two weathered fingers in it. "Oh, Lord, bless this water, and put our hopes and dreams into it. And when we dump it on those ofay bastards with the sacks on their heads, make it burn them something awful."

"Amen," we chimed in.

After that, it was just a matter of getting ready. We lifted up a trough of water with some ropes and placed it on the roof of one of the huts. Soon as the goat riders rode past, it could be tilted over and drench the lot of them. Old Joshua blessed a few more troughs, and we did what we could to get them set up.

As we were putting the finishing touches on the trap, I walked over to Gustav. He sat on the ground with his arms crossed over his large chest. The Swede hadn't said a word since he went berserk.

"Howdy," I said, sitting next to him. "I gotta hand it to you, Gustav, those were some fancy moves you pulled off back there. I never thought of your people as the killing type."

"You should read the old tales, the sagas and epics." Gustav wasn't looking at me as he talked. "They tell of such violent acts, impossible things. Heads torn from bodies with bare hands. Throats ripped out with barred teeth." He shook his head. "I always thought they were...how you say? Tall tales."

"But back there in Buckton, that was real as could be!" I pointed out.

"Clark Reeper, that was the first time the Berserkergang has ever had a hold on me." Gustav stood up. "I did not like it. The fury I felt towards my fellow man was just too much."

I could understand what he was talking about. He had killed more men than Billy the Kid and Wild Bill Hickok combined, all in the space of a few moments. The poor feller must be feeling something awful in his gut.

"Well, I don't know if I gave off that appearance, but I like squareheads more when they're peaceful." I patted his shoulder. "Come on, Gustav, let's go help them set up the holy water. No need for you to go Berserkergang again, not if this works."

If it didn't work, he wouldn't have a chance before the Klan got to us, but that was best left unspoken. We helped the colored folk put the last touches on another water trough, and then the sound of pounding hooves came from down the road.

I turned to the entrance of the shantytown, and there was Leonidas Bishop and his army of Goat Riders.

Leonidas Bishop slowed his Black Goat to a canter, and the other Kluxers followed him. He had stuck the Confederate battle flag in his saddle, and the Stars and Bars fluttered lightly beside him as he stood in front of us.

"Hiding with the darkies," he said, clucking his tongue. "I knew you Yankees are as bad as they are."

"Got to hell!" I shouted, and then turned to Brimstone. "No offense—"

"Don't worry about it, Clark," Brimstone interrupted me. "He's well on his way to Satan's doorstep."

"What are you talking about?" Bishop asked. "All your kind are the same. Freedom, equality, all that crap! No respect for tradition! No respect for the hundreds that died so that our values could stand strong!" He narrowed his eyes behind the hood. "You want equality? You're all gonna swing from the same branch."

Then, he let out a rebel yell and gave his Black Goat some spur. The beast bellowed out a roar of anger and charged into the shantytown, followed by all the rest of Bishop's men.

I fired my gun into the air, the signal the boys on top of the huts had been waiting for. They upended the watering troughs, splashing down gallons of blessed water on top of the Kluxers.

At first, the only thing that happened was that they got drenched and angry, but then a few thin plumes of smoke drifted up from the Kluxer's bodies, followed by billowing clouds of steam that rolled off of them. They screamed and yelled in agony, falling off their goats and rolling on the ground. The Black Goats didn't take to the water either. They stomped and roared, knocked off their riders and rolled around in the dirt, trying to get the steaming holy water off.

I grinned wildly as I leveled my pistols at them. Just as I was about to fire, Brimstone put a hand on my shoulder to stop me. "They're impervious to steel and fire, remember? Nobody needs to get killed by a ricocheting bullet right now."

I holstered the guns, and then balled my hands up into fists. "They impervious to getting slugged? I hope not." I ran down towards them, giving the first Kluxer I came across a good kick to the jaw. He bucked over backwards and I stomped on his chest a few times before moving on to the next one. The freedmen also got some vengeance, using heavy wooden cudgels to bash in the Klansmen's skulls.

Some of the Kluxers tried to fight back, but there was nothing for it. The suckers were getting fried alive by the holy water, and I could lay into them with everything I had. That is, until Leonidas Bishop got wise.

He stood, didn't curl around or scream like his men, even though it looked like he had two geysers in his armpits and another one where his face ought to be. Instead, he calmly walked over to a lit torch someone had dropped, and tossed it into a nearby empty hut. The wooden house went up quickly, and soon a blazing fire was burning away.

Leonidas Bishop stood in front of the burning hut, his arms outstretched. The steam stopped coming off of him in big torrents, and then stopped altogether. He turned back to me, and I saw that the steam had fused the burlap sack to his face, so that I could make out his skull from under it.

"Dry yourselves, friends!" He shouted. "Come, mounts, dry off the stink!"

The Kluxers and Black Goats hastened to obey. I tried stopping them, lashing out with my fists and feet. I'm a fair brawler, but there were just too many of them and they rushed past me. All of them stood in front of the burning hut, warming themselves on the fire. Soon the holy water dried off and they all stood shivering and burning for vengeance in the moonlight.

Leonidas Bishop turned around, and snapped his finger. One of the Black Goats trotted to his side, and he mounted it. He turned the goat's curling horns to face me, and then charged.

I tried to run, but the beast was just a mite too fast for me. The horns crashed into my back with the force of a locomotive and sent me sprawling. I flew through the air and thudded on the ground, struggling to pick myself up and turn around. Instinctively, I drew one of my pistols and fired a shot at Leonidas, but the bullet bounced off the goat and flew away.

"Foolish wretch," Leonidas said, shaking his masked and bloody head. Like it or not, that burlap bag was his new face. "You pathetic Yankee swine."

"Ain't no Yankee," I wheezed. "I fought for your side too. I was there at Antietam, you know, at Sharpsburg. And us Rebels were as brave as hell."

"That's a lie!" Leonidas bellowed. "You're nothing but a northern skunk!"

"It's true enough!" I said. "I was a young man and it was my first job." I didn't mention that I had switched sides later on. "But now look at you, charging schoolmarms and kids instead of cannons. You're a dirty, rotten coward!"

"I'll kill you!" Leonidas shouted. He urged his goat forward, making it rear up and kick with its great hooves. It crashed into my chin and knocked my head backwards. I didn't see much more after that.

When I came to, it was morning, and we had lost. I was tied up real tight, thick ropes around my arms and legs preventing me from so much as scratching an itch on my behind. There was some kind of painful lump where my head had been, but that weren't my concern at the moment. We were laid out in the center of Buckton, a town square with a big tree in the middle of it.

I looked around me and saw that I wasn't the only one hogtied. Ms. Mabel Princely was there too, and so was Gustav and Joshua. I turned to my right and saw Charles lying next to me, a purple bruise on his forehead.

"Charles?" I asked, fear creeping into me. "Charles? You okay?"

Slowly, my boy sat up and looked at the ropes. "What's going on?" he asked.

"Justice, boy, that's what going on," Leonidas Bishop said, standing there in front of me. "And the whole town's come out to watch it." The burlap bag was still fused to his skin, but he didn't seem to mind. He gestured at a large crowd gathered in the streets of Buckton. Leonidas prodded me to my feet with a rifle. Another Kluxer forced Charles upright, and they walked us to the tree.

I looked around for Brimstone, and then spotted him. Coated in sweat, he was lying in a heap on the ground, shivering slightly despite the heat. I reckon that the damn sickness was getting the best of him. He was so weak Bishop's boys hadn't even bothered tying him up.

Leonidas picked up a rope and chillingly tied it into a noose, and he repeated the process to make another. Two Kluxers came forward, one bearing a footstool and the other carrying a large barrel. They sat them down in front of Charles and me.

"All right, cowboy, here's how it's going to play out today," Leonidas said. "Your boy is going to get up on that barrel, I'll put this noose round his neck, and then I kick the barrel from under him. After that, we get some coughing and thrashing. When he's done, it's your turn."

I stared at him, feeling nothing but emptiness in my stomach. There were only a few times when Charles was in this much danger, and both of those times still gave me nightmares. But this time, there didn't seem to be a thing I could do to save my boy.

Charles didn't cry or beg at all. He struggled as best he could, but Leonidas overwhelmed the poor kid. He put him on the barrel and then wrapped the noose around his neck. I tried as hard as I could to burst my own bonds, but a bunch of Kluxers restrained me. I bit one in the arm and got a fist in the face.

"And now, little Yankee boy, it's time for you to swing." Leonidas said, gleefully kicking out the barrel from under Charles's feet. For an awful second, Charles dangled in midair. Then a gunshot rang out. Charles fell to the ground, startled and scared, but unharmed. The bullet had severed the rope.

"What the Hell?" Leonidas Bishop shouted in rage.

"Exactly." Brimstone Brown stood upright and held his smoking Colt Buntline Special. "The fire's gone, Leonidas and all that's left is ice. I've beat the Devil, and now I aim to beat you." He charged, and even though a dozen Kluxers tried to stop him, he lashed out with his fists and beat them down. When he reached Leonidas, he pointed his pistol at him.

"I'm impervious to bullets, remember?" Bishop laughed. "Fire away, Brimstone! It will bounce right off."

"That's what I'm counting on." Brimstone jabbed his revolver's long barrel into Bishop's mouth, piercing the burlap and shoving it far down his throat. Leonidas gagged, and Brimstone fired three shots down into Leonidas Bishop's body. Just like Bishop had promised, they bounced right off, hit the other end of his belly and bounced off of that, ricocheting around in there and turning his insides into soup. Even after every one of Leonidas Bishop's innards had been blown to bits, the bullets continued to whiz around inside of him. He fell down to his knees and then crumpled to the ground stone dead.

Brimstone Brown turned to the nearest Kluxer and pointed his pistol into that feller's mouth. "Give me your knife," he commanded.

The terrified Kluxer handed over a thin blade, and Brimstone Brown used it to cut me free. He tossed me the knife so I could quickly freed Charles and the rest of the prisoners. A whole mess of coloreds from the shantytown were also freed, massaging their arms and breathing sighs of relief.

The Klansman with Brimstone's pistol in his mouth mumbled something.

"What's that?" Brimstone asked. "Wondering about your fate? Well, let me tell you." He stepped backwards and picked up the noose that would have finished Charles and held it up. "It would be a shame to let all this rope go to waste." He looked at the rest of the Kluxers as some of the coloreds surrounded them and held them fast. Brimstone turned to the townspeople of Buckton. "And all of you upright citizens of Buckton, don't you fret. You'll have your lynching."

Well, I didn't stick around for Brimstone's justice. There was no doubt in my mind that all them Ku Klux Klansmen deserved exactly what happened to them. Just the same, seeing anyone strung up just ain't my idea of a good time. Charles and I went down to the ruins of the schoolhouse where we found Mabel Princely and Gustav Olafson.

"Well, ma'am, me and Charles are fixing to head out soon as the next stagecoach rolls by," I explained. "Came to say goodbye."

"We're going to miss you two very much," she said. She shook my hand, and leaned down to give Charles a little kiss on the cheek; his face turned redder than a cherry.

We talked for a little. Mabel was going to stay in Buckton and rebuild, hopefully making some kind of change. Gustav was thinking of joining her, maybe even taking the position of sheriff. I wished them both the best.

I caught Brimstone Brown coming back from the square. He was mighty pleased with himself. He had been playing possum for a while, but he weren't lying about the Devil leaving him. I guess Satan recognized some good in Brimstone and decided to let him be. "What are your planes?" I asked. "Thinking of settling down?"

"I might stay here for a little, but I'm not good enough, not just yet," he said. "There's still a lot I got to repent for, and the best place to do that is on the open road. But I'll stay here for a bit before leaving."

I guess him and me are two of a kind, in a way. We both ain't partial to settling down, even if we ought to, and we both got someone we love depending on us.

Speaking of Charles, he was a mite shook up by the whole thing and he asked me if the Ku Klux Klan was powerful in other places.

"Sure is," I said, seeing no point in lying to him. "A lot of southerners who don't think they lost the war belong to it."

"Oh," Charles said. "But we can beat them. If we all work together, and protect those innocent people, like you and Brimstone and Gustav did, right?"

"I reckon so, Charles," I agreed, but I wasn't so sure. Them prejudices were rooted deep, and it would be a long time before they went away.

But that didn't concern us now. I got a telegram about some Australian Bush Rangers harrying a stagecoach route, and another one about some sort of masked vigilante called 'The Rawhide Avenger' who was tearing up the West. Both sound like tough jobs, but at least I won't have to fight any Riders of the Black Goat. I am mighty glad of that.

The Fountain

Sitting in the Hanged Man's Roadhouse, Clark Reeper stared across the old oak card table at his adopted son Charles Green. The bounty hunter wore a wide grin on his tanned and weathered face. Clark was a tall fellow dressed in a flowing khaki duster. A worn Stetson topped his head and two Colt Peacemakers were holstered at his belt. It was obvious that he had seen more than his fair share of blistering gunfights, bloody saloon brawls, and the darker sides of human nature. Still, a pleasant, fatherly glow emanated from him.

He stared across the table at Charles Green, who stared at a small tumbler of amber gold whiskey sitting in front of him. Charles Green's size, stature, and mannerisms contrasted greatly with the steely-eyed Clark Reeper. Charles was around ten years old, with dark brown curly hair, a freckled face and two brown eyes shining under thick spectacles. The boy was dressed in a neat Norfolk suit and tie, and his eyes sparkled as he stared at the tumbler.

The Hanged Man's Roadhouse was a bustling place, a popular Arkansas junction in Little Rock not far from the Mississippi River. A piano tinkled away in the corner, numerous card and drinking games were progressing, and conversation was loud, vulgar, and passionate. "Mr. Reeper?" Charles asked. Charles had to shout a little to be heard above the hubbub.

"What is it, son?" Clark asked. "Whiskey a bit too much for you?" Charles had asked to taste some whiskey, hearing of how wonderful it was. Clark decided that a little tumbler of the stuff couldn't hurt, so he purchased Charles the tiny glass. Charles stared at it with wide eyes, not even touching the dirty cup.

"Could I just have a sip, maybe?"

Clark nodded. "Charles, ain't no law that says you gotta drink all of it. Just take a sip to get the taste, and I'll polish off the rest."

Slowly, Charles raised the tumbler to his lips. He took a single sip, grimaced, then spat it out and shook his head with disgust.

Clark chuckled and took the glass, downing the remainder of the whiskey. He cleaned some of the liquid off of Charles's shirtfront with a napkin. "Don't you fret son, at your age I was spitting out the stuff too."

"Okay," Charles said, smiling a little. "That tasted really bad. Can I have a sarsaparilla please? To wash it down?"

"Of course you can." Clark stood up and patted Charles on the shoulder. "I do reckon that sarsaparilla goes down a little easier than Arkansas whiskey. That stuff was probably brewed in a pig's feeding trough."

Clark headed to the bar. While making his way through the crowd of saloon regulars and out-of-towners savoring the local liquors, a stoop-shouldered man with a dirty bowler hat and a ragged beard approached him. The man tottered on his feet, steadied himself on a chair, and then reached out a claw-like hand from inside his torn and patched jacket.

"Excuse me, sir, what are you aiming to do?" Clark asked, crossing his arms.

"Clark Reeper?" the man said, shouting out the name like it was a choice piece of profanity. "Is that you? You mangy jackass! I'm Stan Stellwater, and you done killed my brother!" The man pulled a rusty six-shooter out of his jacket and pointed it a few inches past Clark's shoulder, aiming squarely at Charles. "I'll kill the lot of you!"

Clark saw what was going to happen. He didn't have time to go for his revolvers, and he knew that if he didn't do anything, Charles would be shot and perhaps killed. Clark stepped in front of the drunk, and took the first bullet in his chest.

Silence fell in the bar as the gunshot rang out, and Charles screamed in horror as he saw Clark fall backwards to the table. Stan let out a drunken cry of victory and squeezed the trigger again and again. The bullets plunged into Clark Reeper's already bloody stomach. Five more shots were planted in the bounty hunter's chest before Stan was wrestled to the ground and disarmed. Clark slid down from the table and stared at the ceiling.

Charles ran to Clark's side, tears fogging up the boy's glasses. Clark was his protector, his father, and his best friend and companion. He stared at the six bullet holes in Clark's chest and couldn't stop sobbing.

"Clark!" Charles cried tearfully. "Oh, God, Clark!"

"Ah, hell..." Clark whispered, coughing up a mouthful of blood. "He drilled me damn good...didn't he? I can feel all that lead...inside of me. Ah hell..." He stared at Charles. "I ain't gonna die though...on account of this ain't my time. No, sir...I gotta look after you. I can't let you...be alone."

Charles gulped back his tears. "I'll get a doctor, maybe he can—"

"Nah..." Clark shook his head weakly. "Doc would have to be some kind of miracle worker...to patch me up. No, I can't hold on...much longer. You gotta go find a different sort of miracle...to bring me back. Reach into my jacket...I got a piece of paper you ought to read."

Slowly, Charles slipped his little hand into Clark's duster. Nestled in a pocket near his shoulder was a bloodstained note, with the name 'Josey Rep' scrawled on it in Clark's hand.

"Josey Rep? Who is he?" Charles asked.

"My Old Man...we didn't come down here on a job. Old Josiah Reeper works as a security feller for a big old Mississippi riverboat. I was hoping to find him and introduce him to you. He'd like you..." Clark trailed off.

"Clark! Mr. Reeper!"

Clark managed to shake off death for a moment more. "You find him...ask around, find him. And keep my corpse...don't let them put it in the ground. And you tell Old Man Reeper...it ain't my time, and he's got to take me to the Fountain so that I can get all healed and such... You can do it, Charles, you're a good boy... You're a good kid and I love you something fierce..." Clark shut his mouth and stared upwards.

Charles cried and thumped his little fist on Charles's chest, just as the harried doctor arrived. Some of the saloon patrons led Charles away and set him in a corner, away from the doctor hovering over Clark Reeper's body. But Charles knew it would do no good. The spark had gone out of Clark's eye, and the body lying there on the saloon's dirty floor was nothing but a corpse.

Little Rock had a small sheriff's residence—a simple one-room building with a jail cell and office. Stan Stellwater sat inside the cell, lying on the ground and rubbing his aching head. The sheriff, a distinguished Southern gentleman with a waxed white moustache, stared at his prisoner from outside the bars.

"Gunned down a fellow in cold blood in the Hanged Man Roadhouse, did you?" the sheriff asked. "And right in front of his little boy. Goddamn disgraceful."

Stellwater grinned, answering in his raspy drunk's voice. "Sure was, sheriff, sir. But I'm gonna get richer than JP Morgan because of it, and you're gonna get dead."

"You got a bunch of friends riding to your rescue? I doubt it. The only thing you've got to look forward to is a hanging next morning."

"Whatever you say, sheriff sir, whatever you say." Someone knocked loudly on the door. The sheriff walked over to answer it.

Two men stood in the doorway, each dressed in an identical black suit and waistcoat, black tie, black top hat and dark smoked glasses. They had pale skin and gloved hands. The sheriff immediately thought they were undertakers.

"Who the hell are you?" the sheriff asked.

"Is Stellwater inside?" one of them asked, his voice calm and even.

"Who wants to know?"

Both of the Undertakers reached into their jackets. The sheriff went for his gun, but the two men were faster. They both drew out long barreled pepperbox pistols and fired in unison, two shots into the sheriff's chest. His stomach exploded outward as he toppled backward. One of the Undertakers bent low. "Is Stellwater inside?" he demanded, his voice still even.

"You...bastards..." the sheriff wheezed.

"He's here," shouted the second Undertaker, pointing at Stellwater, who was gleefully watching from his cell. The first Undertaker nodded and then raised his boot over the sheriff's face. He brought it down with a thud; no expression crossed the Undertaker's face at the crunching bone under his foot.

"Mr. Brinks, you may enter," the Undertakers called. Into the sheriff's office waddled a man swaddled in his own fat. He was enormous, with a massive gut barely held in by a tailored diamond waistcoat protruding from his chest. His flabby arms swayed with lengths of fat, his pudgy face was decorated with a large upturned moustache, and a gold rimmed monocle. A cane, gripped in white-gloved and diamond-ringed hands, clicked on the wooden floor as he walked up to examine Stellwater.

"Good show," he said, staring at the sheriff. "You boys in black never fail to impress me."

"You uphold your part of the bargain and we uphold ours," the Undertakers said in unison.

"And rest assured, I shall. Now, let's have a word with Stellwater." The fat man walked over to the bars, grasping them with one of his white-gloved hands. Stan stared at the sparkling diamond rings.

"I did my job good, Mr. Brinks, I did it real good!" Stellwater cried.

"Did you?" Brinks slowly shook his head. "Somehow I think not. Do you know who I am, you filthy drunk?"

"Oh, I sure do, sir. You're Tantalus Brinks, one of the richest men in the country. You're as rich as J.P. Morgan and Andrew Carnegie put together! And you promised me a fortune if I killed Clark Reeper, so I gone and done it!"

"Wounded severely," commented Tantalus Brinks, tapping his cane on the floor. "My orders were to wound him severely, so that he would have no choice but to try and find the Fountain. But you killed him. If a man's dead and buried, he won't be leading me anywhere."

Stellwater stammered. "Uh...I didn't mean nothing, sir...I just got a little excited...You know how it is when you get the liquor inside of you!"

"Ah yes. We must all be forgiven for our little eccentricities." Tantalus Brinks idly twisted the diamond ring on his right hand. He popped the diamond off, revealing a sharp needle projecting from the gold band.

Stellwater's eyes flashed round the cell, realizing that he was trapped.

Tantalus leaned forward, pushing his fat arm through the cell bars and gently tapped Stellwater with the tip of his needled ring. Stellwater's mouth opened and closed like a hot iron had been shoved down his throat.

"Wait!" Stellwater cried. "I left his boy alive! He was talking to his boy as he was lying on the floor all shot up!"

Tantalus Brinks nodded. "Yes, Charles Green," Brinks muttered, clapping his hands. "He is an intelligent boy, and I'm sure he could guide us to the Fountain just as well as Clark would. I believe our plans can continue with minimal setbacks."

Stellwater shivered, rocked back and forth on his legs and drooled thick green streams of saliva.

Tantalus eyed the dying drunk. "Venom of the Colombian Basilisk Spider. Creates simply the most agonizing death known to man."

Stellwater collapsed to the ground, convulsing. He tried to scream, but only green bile poured out from his mouth. Tantalus Brinks stared at him and rubbed his hands. He turned to the two Undertakers.

"Please, leave me. I wish to be alone."

The two Undertakers exchanged a glance, and then left Tantalus to his strange joys.

Charles Green sat on a chair at the Hanged Man Roadhouse, now empty except for the bartender sweeping up. Clark Reeper's lifeless body lay on the table. Charles was staring at the note Clark had given him, tracing his fingers over the name. The boy's eyes were red and puffy beneath their glasses.

The bartender walked over to Charles. "Sorry about what happened, kid. Must be tough on you."

Charles nodded absently. "Yes, sir," he muttered.

"Look, I don't want to be bothering a mourner none, but that body is gonna start smelling soon, and it will stink up the whole place. You ought to put him in the ground."

"No." Charles stood up and looked Clark's body over. "He told me not to do that."

The bartender shrugged. "Okay. Tell you what, I'll pay you a good three nickels for him, then I'll get him stuffed and mounted right there over the piano. Sound good?"

Charles wasn't listening. He stared at Clark's body, thinking of their last moments together. He hadn't been able to drink the whiskey, and Clark had said it was okay because Charles was just a boy. Charles's hands balled into fists. He could not be just a boy any more.

Slowly, reverently, he removed the cartridge belt from around Clark's waist. He nearly dropped the heavy belt with its two Colt Peacemakers, but then wrapped it around his own tiny waist. He pulled the belt through its buckle and tightened. Now he wore Clark's revolvers on his waist.

Charles looked up at the bartender. "If I could have a wagon, and a mule to pull it, just to get Clark down to the piers. There's this man I'm supposed to meet, a security fellow for one of the riverboats. Could you do that?"

The bartender grinned at the nervous boy. "Well, I got an old wagon and a mangy mule somewhere in the back. I'll be glad to give a nice youngster like you a lift."

They got Clark's body into the wagon. It was hard work, and Charles continuously apologized to Clark and the bartender for his clumsiness. After that, it was just a short walk to the pier. It was in the early morning and the first riverboats were just coming in to unload cargo and passengers. The bartender left Charles at the pier standing next to the cart containing Clark's corpse.

Charles nervously tried to get the attention of the stevedores and sailors working on the docks. "Excuse me, um, sir, excuse me?" he was generally ignored. "Has anyone seen, um, a man named Josey Rep? Anybody?"

One grizzled sailor, an old river rat with round cap and a corncob pipe, stopped and stared at Charles. "Josey Rep?" he asked. "Is that what you said, boy?"

"Yes, I'm looking for him. Do you know where he is?"

"Josey runs security on the *Planter King*. Rundown little ship. Should be coming in today." As soon as he saw Charles's smile, the sailor shook his head. "My advice is not to go looking for him. Josey Rep is a right ornery bastard. He'll probably toss you overboard, maybe take those irons off of you first."

"I could stop him, you know," Charles said, grabbing the handle of one of the revolvers. But he sounded unsure, even to himself.

Charles waited at the dock with Clark's pale and bloody corpse. Every time another boat came in, Charles would run down to find out its name. He waited for most of the morning, and then bought some stale buns from a rickety stall for breakfast. As he finished eating, the *Planter King* came steaming up to the pier.

It was a rundown boat. The wheelhouse seemed to be caving in, and one of the smokestacks was bent in half. The paint was chipping on the deck, and only a few weary passengers disembarked, smelling of fish and whiskey.

As fuel and cargo were loaded, Charles saw his chance. He pushed the cart containing Clark's blanket-covered corpse behind some barrels and then headed onto the boat.

A lanky Negro with a pierced ear leered at Charles as he approached. "What business you got here?" he demanded.

"Excuse me, sir, I am looking for Josey Rep." Charles pushed up his glasses and tried his best to be polite. "I really must see him urgently."

"What the hell is your goddamn rush, you little snot!?"

Charles spun around and found himself facing a graying mountain of a man, with a barrel chest, an old fringed buckskin jacket, a plug hat, and a tomahawk thrust through his belt. "I ought to toss you overboard," the man thundered.

"Sir, I'm sorry, I'm just looking for Josey Rep," Charles stammered, stepping backwards.

"I'm Josey Rep, and I don't want to be bothered. Especially not by some well-dressed little piss like you!" His burning dark eyes, enshrouded by a curtain of thick gray hair, glowered at Charles.

"But Josey Rep isn't your name," Charles said quickly. "It's Josiah Reeper."

The man drew his tomahawk. "Who told you that?" he asked.

Charles tried to explain. He couldn't stop staring at the tomahawk. It was covered with intricate woodcarvings and inlaid stones, and the obsidian axe looked sharp enough to split hairs and hard enough to break skulls.

"I should just kill you now," Josiah said.

"Please, sir, don't. I really don't mean any harm." Charles grabbed one of Clark's revolvers. He gingerly pulled out one pistol and, holding it with both hands, he aimed it at Josiah Reeper. Clark's ancient father smiled.

"Got some spunk in you, I see. And that's a pretty big cannon to be carried around by such a little man." Josiah slipped the tomahawk back into his belt. "Where'd you hear my name spoken?"

"Clark Reeper," Charles said. "My name is Charles Green, and I'm Clark's adopted son."

"Hmm." Josiah scratched his beard. "Clarky. That obnoxious little cretin. I loved him. How's he getting by?"

Charles gulped. "Well, not too good." He led Josiah off the barge and took him down to the docks. They walked to the cart, and Charles pulled back the dirty blanket covering Clark's body. Josiah Reeper stared at his son dispassionately.

"Jesus, Clarky. Got yourself into a staring contest with a Gatling gun." He counted the bullet holes. "Six. Should know better than to let some bastard unload all six chambers of a revolver into you. Damned idiot."

Charles stared at Josiah in surprise. "But...it's your son..." Charles pointed at Clark, dumbfounded. "He's dead, Mr. Reeper, Clark is dead!"

"So he is." Josiah pulled the blanket back over Clark. "What do you want me to do about it?"

"Well, um..." Charles stammered, trying to remember Clark's instructions. "The Fountain. Before he died, Clark gave me your name and told me to find you, and told me to tell you to take him to—"

"To the Fountain. Yeah, I get it." Josiah stroked his unkempt beard. "Well, you snotty-faced brat, let me tell you something. I'm done with the adventuring life. I like riding around on the *Planter King*, I love sleeping in a warm bed and I like fighting only drunks, I'm not going to go all the way to Florida to look for some stinking spring to give my dumb son a second chance."

"Oh..." Charles gulped, clasping his hands. "Please, sir, you must help Clark! He's saved my life so many times and been nice to me, and he's like my own father. So you have to save him now. You must! Please?"

"Hmmm." Josiah leaned down until he was eye-to-eye with the small Charles. "Listen Charles, I gotta tell you a little something about my son—about his mother."

"Who?" Charles asked. Clark Reeper had rarely talked about his past.

"Saloon bartender name of Lulu somewhere in Texas. What I can say? I was lonely. She was there, and so we made Clark. Fever took her a week after she gave birth. The boy has been nothing but grief, even after I gave him up to be raised by that mystic strumpet Marie Laveau. So I'll take my leave of you and Clark, and I hope you bury him somewhere pretty."

Charles tried to protest, but Josiah Reeper shoved him aside with one hand and walked back to his boat. Charles was about to run after him, when he stopped in his tracks. An odd feeling crept over him, like he was being watched.

Tantalus Brinks lowered the telescope from his eye and replaced it with his gold-rimmed monocle. The tycoon and his henchmen stood on the shore watching the events on the dock unfold. Brinks massaged the fat rolls on his wrist as he stood near several wagons, which were painted black, towed by teams of black horses, and crewed by a detachment of two score and ten of the enigmatic Undertakers.

"There's Charles Green," said Tantalus pointing to the small boy. "But who is the bearded rogue he's talking with?"

One of the Undertakers stepped forward. "Josiah Reeper. Father of Clark Reeper. We have a large file on him."

"You have a large file on everyone, don't you?" added Tantalus Brinks, grinning and making the fat on his face ripple. He stroked his elegantly trimmed moustache. "This man must be the guide to the Fountain that Charles is seeking. That means that Josiah Reeper knows where the Fountain is, and if we have him, we can know as well. And all that makes Charles Green—"

"Expendable. Your orders?"

"Get me Reeper. Kill the boy." Tantalus tapped his cane on the ground, signaling the Undertakers to move. They swept forward like wolves in fine evening dress, their black cloaks rustling as they ran down to the docks.

Charles Green watched Josiah Reeper leave, panicking as his failure consumed him. A bullet slammed into the dock in front of the boy, causing a small explosion that knocked the boy backwards. Charles pulled himself up from the ground, dizzy as smoke danced around him. Blood trickled from his nose.

A dozen or so men, all dressed in black clothes and wearing black smoked glasses, stood in front of him. All of them held sleek silver pepperbox pistols. Charles instantly remembered who they were from the time he and Clark had met the Undertakers in Roswell, New Mexico.

"Oh, no," Charles whispered. "Not now." They leveled their weapons at Charles. Before they could fire, the youngster was already up and running, bullets flying around him. Charles slipped on the dock and hurt his nose again, soaking his shirtfront in blood.

He was helped to his feet by strong hands. Charles looked up and saw the massive form of Josiah Reeper. "Running from some black-clad bastards when you got a perfectly good pair of pistols on you?" Josiah shook his head. "What has Clark been teaching you?"

Charles stuttered, unable to get a word out.

Josiah put a finger to Charles's lips. "Stay here. I'll deal with them." Most of the dockworkers were running for cover while Josiah approached the Undertakers.

"Pepperbox pistols?" Josiah asked, pulling his tomahawk from his belt. "I thought those went out of style right after the powdered wig."

"We are not to hurt you," one of the Undertakers said in a grim monotone. "You are to come with us. We will kill the boy."

Josiah nodded. "Figured that's the way things stand. Well, best to get this over with." He ducked low and ran towards the nearest Undertaker, swinging the tomahawk round with one hand. The obsidian blade hacked through the Undertaker's pale neck, sending the severed head hurtling through the air.

Josiah turned to the next Undertaker and planted the tomahawk between his eyes, crushing the bridge of the smoked glasses. The eyepiece fell from the dying man's face, revealing eyes that were crimson and segmented. Josiah widened his own eyes before spinning around and hacking his tomahawk into the remaining Undertaker's forehead.

Charles ran to Josiah's side, looking away from the corpses. "Mr. Reeper! There's more of them!" He pointed up to the docks where Undertakers were rushing to battle. Many of them carried stubby handheld Gatling guns, and they were cranking the handles. "I'll get Clark's body and get it into your boat!" Charles called, running for the cart with the corpse.

Josiah tried to say something, but the Undertakers had started firing. The old mountain man leapt for cover behind some stacked barrels, wincing as bullets churned the air around him. Josiah Reeper's keen eyes searched the barrels, and came across one labeled 'Jack Tar's First Rate Tar and Grease.' He pulled a hand-rolled cigarette from his belt, and drew a match, lighting it on the heel of his boot. He stabbed his tomahawk through the top of the barrel, using the hatchet to winch it free and then he splashed all of the tar and grease out onto the dock. Josiah lit his cigarette, took a puff and then tossed the match into the tar. The flammable black goop blazed away, creating a barrier of flame and smoke between them and the Undertakers.

Charles was running back to the *Planter King*, struggling to push the heavier cart and its gruesome load. Josiah Reeper helped, and the two quickly moved the cart onto the ramshackle steamer.

"Josey!" a short man with a peaked cap and a red face stood on the deck of the *Planter King*. "What is the meaning of this?"

"Trouble, captain. I need to take control of the boat for a little."

"What?" fumed the little captain at the much larger Josiah Reeper. "Take control?"

"Yeah. Over you go." Without another word, Josiah Reeper picked up the captain and tossed him overboard. He then turned to the rest of the crew. "All right, you lazy bums! Let's get a move-on! The captain can catch up with us later! Right now I got places to be!"

The stunned crew hurried to their appointed tasks, and soon the *Planter King* was steaming speedily out of the Little Rock harbor. Josiah Reeper sighed and scratched his back. "I'm too old for this," he muttered. "Maybe I do need a trip to the Fountain." The large mountain man tossed Charles a dirty rag. "Clean up your nose. You look ridiculous."

"Oh, thank you, sir." Charles said, wiping away the blood. "Thank you very much, for saving me, I mean."

"I didn't want to." Josiah shook his head. "Those bastards in black were going kill you and you against them wouldn't be anything close to a fair fight. I couldn't just leave you there. And since I'm going there anyway, I guess you can come to the Fountain and get Clark back."

"Thank you!" Charles hugged Josiah, but Clark's father pulled him off and tossed him backwards. "Oh, I'm sorry, sir. I didn't mean to. I'm sorry."

Josiah snorted. "Maybe I can toughen you up. Clark ever wallop you?"

"No, sir. He was very kind, and even if I did something stupid, he would never hurt me." Charles gulped. "You're a lot like him, you know."

"Is that so?" Josiah shrugged. "I never spent much time with Clarky. I sometimes wanted to wallop him, but again, he was a lot smaller than me and it didn't seem fair somehow. How am I like him?"

"You talk like him, and you light matches on your boot heel like him."

"I suppose I keep the same kind of company, too. If we're gonna go to the Fountain, we'll need to see Johnny Rabbit."

"Johnny Rabbit?"

"Old Colored Seminole." Josiah gripped his tomahawk. "He gave me this." Josiah pulled open his fringe jacket, revealing a terrible curved scar on his chest. "And that."

Charles grimaced, but soon the boy's face was filled with a smile.

The *Planter King* continued puffing down the Mississippi, heading south to Florida. Behind it, hidden by the mists of the river, floated a swarm of balloons, painted black and crewed by men in black clothes.

The *Planter King* proved its worth, traveling at great speed down the river. Even after night fell, the ramshackle boat steamed on. Josiah Reeper watched the muddy Mississippi water drift by, knowing that soon he would be in contact with a man he had not seen for many years. He was stuck in the same sort of deadly game that he had often played in before.

The aging mountain man leaned against the railing, while Charles Green snoozed silently on a rough wooden bench behind him, next to the cart containing Clark Reeper's corpse. "You're getting old," Josiah told himself. "Best to get the tools out."

Josiah walked to his cramped quarters. He cracked open a wooden chest next to his dingy cot and took out his large Walker Colt, holstering it with a long forgotten spin. Next, he drew out the great nine-barreled nock gun, a naval weapon that would have broken a weaker man's back when it fired. Josiah set the gun on his back, pulling the strap around his shoulder. He stroked his gray beard thoughtfully wondering about the odd path that fate had set him on once more.

Josiah walked back out to the deck, and stared at Charles. The boy was sleeping on the uncomfortable wooden bench.

"Hell," Josiah muttered. "Just don't seem right somehow." With one hand, he picked up Charles, carried the boy to his room and then rudely dumped him onto his cot.

Charles drowsily awoke, and stared up at Josiah Reeper.

"Thank you, sir," he whispered.

"No trouble, really," Josiah said. "I've hefted sacks of cotton that weighed more than you." He sat down on the edge of the cot. "I gotta tell you, son. I've been thinking. We're going up against some pretty tough customers, if those black-clad folk are any indicator. I'm not the man I was, and I ain't guaranteeing a victory."

"We have to try," Charles said. "We have to save Clark. When my father died, Clark took me in, and ever since then he's given up his entire life to take care of me. Maybe he learned that from you. In any case, now it's my turn. I have to bring him back."

Josiah nodded. "We'll do our darnedest." They both fell silent.

"Um, sir?" Charles stammered. "If you don't mind me asking, why did you stop adventuring?"

"Hard to say." Josiah stroked his beard, twisting the curly hair with his fingers. "Marie Laveau and me had a falling out. She tried to kill Clark, but ended up just turning my boy into a killer." Josiah snorted. "I sent him there because I didn't want him to end up like me. I figured Marie would make him cultured, gentle and refined. Nothing of the sort happened. After Clark was striking out on his own, fighting on both sides of the Civil War before his eighteenth birthday, I figured I had failed."

"That's not true!" Charles exclaimed. "Clark was never a killer! He fought and killed men if he had to, but he was never a murderer! And he was very kind to people that deserved it. I think you did a good job raising him. And Clark raised me, and I'm not a killer."

"Those ain't squirt guns on your belt," Josiah said, pointing to the Colt Peacemakers. "A feller never knows if he's a killer until the time comes. The time's gonna come soon for you, boy. Deal with it however you can." Josiah stood up. "Stay here and blow snot bubbles or something. I'm going to the deck. We got a big day tomorrow. Johnny Rabbit's not gonna be happy to see us."

Josiah Reeper left Charles staring at the rocking ceiling of the old steamer boat. He walked outside, and watched the Mississippi float by.

"Wake the hell up, boy. We've arrived." Josiah's harsh voice startled Charles into wakefulness. Charles sat up in the cot and rubbed his eyes. He hopped off the bed and followed Josiah to the deck. The old mountain man passed Charles a chicken leg and a canteen of water, which Charles happily gobbled down.

They walked up to the deck, where Clark's corpse lay on the wagon, covered with a cloth and undisturbed. Josiah Reeper sniffed his son's body. "Goddamn," he muttered. "My boy's smelling something awful. Good thing we came so soon, before he really started to stink."

"Um, Mr. Reeper? Charles asked. "Will Clark be rotted and gross after the Fountain brings him back to life?"

Josiah shook his head. "To tell you the truth, I don't know if it works on corpses."

"What?" Charles couldn't believe his ears. "B-but Clark said—"

"If you're wounded it'll patch you up, and if you drink enough of it, you'll get so you can't die. But I don't know about folks that are already dead." Josiah Reeper shrugged. "Maybe Johnny Rabbit will know."

The *Planter King* was anchored in the midst of a great swamp. Dense trees and green waterways filled with weeds and swamp grass spiraled out in every direction. A small island of solid ground lay next to the steamboat, an abandoned old shantytown of wooden huts surrounded by a crumbling stockade.

"Welcome to Freeman's Town." Josiah pointed to the overgrown village. He raised his voice so that everyone on the boat could hear him. "All right, we're at the place! Now let me, the boy, and the body disembark, and then the rest of you best be on your way. I got no payment for you, but if any of you want to quarrel, I'd be happy to cleave your skull or shoot you full of lead!"

No sailor made a move against them as Josiah Reeper and Charles Green carried the corpse of Clark Reeper off of the boat and entered Freeman's Town. Charles felt his heart beating with every step he took in the swamplands. The sound of trickling water, buzzing insects, and splashing animals seemed overwhelming. Part of Charles wanted to stay on board the boat, but he looked at the cloth covering Clark's body and his mind was resolved. He would follow Josiah to the end, wherever that was.

They stashed Clark's body in a beached canoe, and then the two of them walked into the city. Josiah was alert and tense. They walked into the town square. "Johnny?" Josiah shouted, his words echoing through Freeman's Town. "Show your mangy hide!"

Two twin shark tooth-tipped arrows hurtled down from the sky. Josiah drew his tomahawk and raised it, grinning as the arrows bounced off of the tomahawk's obsidian blade and fell to the ground.

"Only one thing harder than volcanic rock!" a brassy voice sounded from the roof of a nearby hut. "And that's your rock hard skull!" A tall, muscular black man leapt down from the roof's hut where he had been hiding and approached Charles and Josiah. He was wearing a colorful crocodile-skin vest, and torn homespun trousers. Shining rings, bracelets, and necklaces gleamed on his dark skin. A pair of white egret feathers was pinned in his long unkempt hair.

In his hands, Johnny Rabbit carried two short recurve wooden bows; two quivers full of shark tooth-tipped arrows rested on his shoulders. On his upper arms, he wore a pair of bracers with fishhooks dangling from them. Charles reasoned that by extending his arms and slipping the bowstrings through the fishhooks, Johnny Rabbit could fire both bows in tandem, a deadly skill.

"Josiah, how nice of you to drop by!" Johnny Rabbit approached, slinging his bows behind his back as he walked.

He had an untraceable accent, African, Native American, and English all at once. "Enjoying Freeman's Town?"

"I could get used to it here, you seminal Seminole," Josiah said. "But as you must know, I'm not here to chat. I need your help."

"You always do." Johnny Rabbit let his hands fall to his belt, where he carried a large number of knives and machetes. "And like a fool, more often than not, I help you. Why do I do that, Josiah?"

"Because I saved your miserable life. I could have killed you. Colonel Thomas Jesup wouldn't have thrown me out of the army and made me an outlaw if I did."

Johnny Rabbit grinned. "True. But you didn't kill me, despite your commander's orders. Why was that?"

"Because it weren't fair." Josiah grunted. "Goddamn General Andrew Jackson and all his like coming down on all the Seminoles and their escaped slave allies, just because they wanted to be free. Jackson wanted money and support from the slave owners and Indian haters. You ask me, we had no business in Florida."

"True, but then again, you have no business in this continent, or in Africa for that matter. Ah well, there is no stopping the white man, not when he becomes stupid enough to put his greed ahead of his own life." Johnny Rabbit turned to Charles. "And who is this?"

"Uh, Charles Green, sir." Charles held out his hands, and Johnny Rabbit shook it tentatively. "Um, I'm, uh, well, I guess I'm the adopted grandson of Josiah Reeper. My adopted father, Clark Reeper, is a very nice man and I'm sure he'll like you, and he feels sorry for the Seminoles and everything, and well—"

"Is your father lying in the canoe, covered by that cloth?" Johnny Rabbit asked.

"Yes, sir." Charles's couldn't help but sound a little guilty.

"Well, I believe I know why you came to me." Johnny Rabbit crossed his arms. "You're looking for the Fountain."

"Yes, I am. Before Clark died, he told me to find it," Charles said, staring at his shoes. "Mr. Rabbit, I'm not quite sure what the Fountain even is, but if Clark wanted me to find it, than I think I should try. Clark was very smart, and he always knew what he was talking about."

"He obviously did, else he wouldn't know about the Fountain." Josiah sat down on the grassy town square. "Get comfortable, boy. The story is long and Johnny Rabbit's a crappy storyteller."

"Say what you want to, Josiah. I'll be enjoying the company of beautiful women while you rot in your grave." Johnny Rabbit grinned. "You see, Charles Green, mankind's only got one big enemy on this world, and that's Death. So of course, there's been all sorts of legends and stories about immortality. You ever heard of the Fountain of Youth, child?"

Charles nodded. "I read about it once in a story, by Nathaniel Hawthorne. But it's not real, is it?"

"Oh, it's real," Josiah said. "Johnny Rabbit is living proof of that."

"Funny story. Even though I look good, I'm old. I was born in Africa, shipped here in chains, escaped, and found friends in the swamp. The Seminoles took me in, along with hundreds of other escaped slaves. We lived together in harmony. At least, until the white men came and turned the swamps red. This was my city, a town for free men." He looked at the decaying buildings with pride before continuing. "The tribe had legends about a people called the Beemeenee, a people who lived below the Seminole but north of the Arawak, and who never grew old because of a magical fountain in the center of their village."

"Did you find it?" Charles asked.

"I didn't mean to. I was fleeing from a battle with Jackson's troops, mortally wounded with a musket ball in the chest. As I stumbled through the jungle, I fell in a pool of water. When I woke up, the wound was gone."

"The Fountain," Charles whispered.

"Yeah. I liked it, and I came back there time and time again. I lived far past my age, I fought in three wars against the white men, and lost them all. I fought in the Civil War, the Indian Wars back east, and I even went back to Africa a few years ago and fought there. And every wound dealt to me has no effect."

"This lucky bastard can't die." Josiah laughed. He drew his tomahawk from his belt and slammed it into Johnny Rabbit's chest. The Negro Seminole doubled over, but soon pulled out the tomahawk and handed it back to Josiah. The wound healed instantly, and not a drop of blood poured out of the gaping gash.

"Not...funny," he wheezed.

Charles's eyes widened. Clark Reeper had been right! If Johnny Rabbit could take them to the Fountain, the waters would bring Clark back to life, and it would be as if that terrible day in the Little Rock saloon never happened. Charles clasped his hands and gulped.

"Mr. Rabbit?" he asked, his voice light as a feather and very nervous. "Would you please take Clark Reeper to the Fountain and heal him?"

Johnny Rabbit touched his vanishing wound. "Of that, I am not so sure. You see, Charles Green, living forever has taught me that death is oftentimes not an undesirable thing. Perhaps your father's life is meant to be finished, and perhaps he needs time to rest."

"No." Charles had never said anything more firmly. "No, Clark did not deserve what happened! He was shot in cold blood, and only died to save me! Please, Mr. Rabbit, I'm not ready to just forget him right now! This wasn't his time, Mr. Rabbit, and I'm sure of that." He crossed his arms and felt his face burn.

Johnny Rabbit stared at Charles for a long time. Finally, he nodded, very slowly. "If you are certain, then there is no arguing with you." He crossed his arms. "I do not know if I can help you. The Fountain's waters may not affect those already dead. Still, we will go to the Beemeenee's Land and we will bathe your father in the Fountain."

"Good show! Precisely what I will demand of you." The voice, mellow and throaty, came from behind one of the huts. An enormously fat man in a suit and waistcoat, top hat and monocle waddled out, his cane tapping on the ground. Two Undertakers flanked him, aiming their pepperbox pistols at Charles, Johnny Rabbit, and Josiah.

"So you're the man pulling the strings of all them funerary-looking bastards, I figure," Josiah said, drawing his Walker Colt. "You sure picked an idiotic place to make your appearance." He leveled the revolver at the fat man.

"Oh, you can put your gun down, Mr. Reeper! My name is Tantalus Brinks, yes, *the* Tantalus Brinks, and I've been tracking you for quite a ways."

"Pleasure to meet you," Josiah said coldly. "Any last words?"

"Look up." Tantalus urged, pointing his cane at the sky.

Josiah, Charles, and Johnny Rabbit all stared upwards. Dozens of black hot air balloons hung heavy in the sky, all of them crawling with Undertakers, aiming small cannons and rockets down towards the earth.

A grin split Tantalus Brinks' fat face. "Now," he muttered, "let's get better acquainted."

"First of all, I am the one responsible for Clark Reeper's death. I knew he knew how to find the Fountain. I wanted him wounded so that I could follow him to the source. Events don't always go completely as planned. But they do have a way of working out."

Charles stared at Tantalus Brinks. "You?" he demanded. "You sent that man to kill Clark?" He clenched his fists. "You... um...you bastard! You goddamn dirty bastard!" It was the harshest word he could think of.

"Such a foul tongue!" chuckled Tantalus, wagging his finger at Charles. "Tut-tut, my boy. That simply won't do. Since I now have Mr. Rabbit, there's no longer a need for you and your mountain man guardian to stay alive. You are expendable." He pursed his fat lips. "So sorry, but that is the way business is run."

"What makes you think I'll go along with you?" Johnny Rabbit snarled. "I can't die, so don't bother threatening me with death."

"True, but you can feel pain, and I am an expert in the exquisite art of torture. As are my fellows." Tantalus gestured to the Undertakers by his side. "Perhaps you'd care to hear who they are? They are a rather taciturn bunch, are they not?"

"Mighty kind of you," Josiah said. "Enlighten me."

"They are the descendants of an ancient order devoted to collecting, cataloguing, and understanding all the technology and knowledge that humanity has gathered from extraterrestrial sources. They have been connected to many groups—the Knights Templar, the Rosicrucians, the Illuminati, and many more. History has known them as the Silent Orchestra."

"Very theatrical," observed Josiah Reeper, spitting on the ground. "But I got them making some noises back on the docks."

"True. They are, to their deepest regret, still mortal. You see, their research and experimentation with advanced alien technology has forever altered their physical make-up. They have become addicted to the otherworldly chemicals and substances. And soon, since they were thwarted by Clark Reeper at Roswell, New Mexico, they will die. Unless of course, they get the waters of the Fountain."

"That's why they want the Fountain," Johnny Rabbit said. "Why do you want it?"

"Hmm. Good question." Tantalus Brinks stroked his moustache. "The answer is simple, Mr. Rabbit. I am greedy beyond belief. I make no pretense of social justice, as some of my fellows do. I care not for any liberal or progressive desire to help others. I exist purely for the betterment and benefit of myself. And what would be better than immortality? To that end, I will do anything." He tossed his walking stick into the air and caught it with both hands. "Including beating a helpless child to death."

Tantalus lunged with his walking stick, catching Charles unaware and striking the boy across the chest. Charles gasped in pain, but he rolled with the blow and fell to the ground. Then he came to his feet.

"I'm not letting you kill me," Charles said, hissing in pain. "Even without Clark around, I can defend myself!"

Charles hurled himself onto Tantalus Brinks with the ferocity of a wildcat. Charles kicked, punched, scratched and bit, toppling the great tycoon over and surprising the two Undertakers.

Johnny Rabbit and Josiah Reeper exchanged a glance. "I'm getting too old for this," Josiah muttered, drawing his pistol and firing at one of the Undertakers.

The black-suited man's smoked glasses were shattered by the bullet, and he tottered on his feet for a few minutes before collapsing. Johnny Rabbit hurled one of his throwing knives at the surviving Undertaker, and the blade stuck deep into his chest.

The two men ran in separate directions as the circling hot air balloons let out blasts of withering fire. The wooden structures of Freeman's Town were blown apart as cannonball and rocket fire poured down.

Josiah Reeper and Johnny Rabbit were too fast, taking cover and avoiding the explosions. As soon as the last gun fell silent, they struck. Josiah Reeper holstered his Walker Colt and drew his massive nock gun. He ran directly under the carriage of a low-flying balloon and aimed upward, firing a single shot that shredded the two Undertakers riding inside. He spun round and fired again, this time the bullet tore a hole in the gasbag of an aerostat, and it slowly sank into the swamps, where the snapping jaws of alligators swiftly finished off its black-suited crew.

Johnny Rabbit drew out both of his bows, notched an arrow to each one, and using his unique bracers, fired two shark tooth-tipped arrows into two separate balloons. Two Undertakers fell from their carriages, one splashing into the water, and the other splattering on the grassy ground below. He aimed two more arrows and let them fly. The razor-sharp arrows sliced through the ropes that connected the undercarriage to the aerostat. The unfortunate Undertakers plummeted into the swamp water.

Tantalus Brinks was stunned by Charles's onslaught. He quickly recovered his wits and struck out with one of his massive arms, the sheer bulk of the limb knocking Charles backward. Tantalus pulled the diamond off of his ring, revealing the poison-coated needle.

"Come here, wretched boy!" Tantalus cried. "I'll stick you good, I will!" Charles avoided the blow and turned to run. Tantalus Brinks reared up, chasing after him. Only then did Charles remember the two pistols at his waist.

Gulping down his fear, Charles drew out one of Clark's Peacemakers. He held the revolver with both hands and aimed it at Tantalus Brinks. "Stop!" he cried. "Leave us alone, or I'll shoot!"

"Stinking whelp!" Tantalus shouted, charging the boy, his needle-topped ring held like a knight's lance.

Charles froze. He looked at his revolver, and then looked at Tantalus. He gulped again, and found he could not bring himself to pull the trigger.

Just as Tantalus Brinks closed in on Charles, Josiah Reeper appeared, swinging the butt of his nock gun at Brinks. He knocked the tycoon backwards. Tantalus sprawled in the muddy dirt, and Josiah gave him a cruel kick to the side before slamming the butt of the gun into Tantalus's heaving chest.

"Your gasbags aren't staying in the air very well!" Josiah laughed. He lowered the nock gun at Tantalus. "You're gonna need the Fountain's life-giving waters pretty darn bad in a couple of seconds. Too bad they won't do you any good, not with half of your damn head blown clean off."

Charles turned away, not wanting to see Tantalus's gory end. He noticed a hot air balloon swinging in over Josiah Reeper, its cannons loaded and aimed at the aging mountain man.

"Josiah!" Charles cried. "Look out!"

Josiah looked up, cursed and threw himself backwards seconds before a whistling cannonball plunged into the ground and showered him with dirt. Josiah Reeper lay on the ground, grunting in pain. "Goddamn...goddamn!" he wheezed, trying to pull himself up. "My back ain't doing its stinking job!"

Charles Green ran to help Josiah, ignoring the cannonballs and screaming rockets exploding around them. Charles summoned up every ounce of strength in his small body and managed to help Josiah to his feet. Tantalus Brinks lay on the ground, recovering from the beating Josiah had given him.

Johnny Rabbit rolled out from behind a burning hut and shot out a flurry of deadly arrows up at the Undertakers. Their bodies fell from the sky as the arrows hit their targets. Josiah grabbed Charles's hand and led him away from Freeman's Town with Johnny following. The three ran down to the edge of the island, where three canoes were waiting for them, one of them loaded with Clark's covered corpse.

"Getting old, Josiah," Johnny Rabbit said. "Wasn't for Charles, you'd have caught a cannonball."

"Wasn't for that whelp, I wouldn't even be here," Josiah grumbled. "Let's just get the hell out of this dump." He tossed Charles into one of the canoes and pushed it into the water before hopping in himself. Johnny Rabbit lashed the back of Clark's canoe to his own, and then shoved them both off. Johnny Rabbit and Josiah both drew out their paddles and sent the canoes zooming off into the weedy, dark water.

The Silent Orchestra aerostats followed them, floating low. They sent out salvos of cannon and rocket, which splashed into the water and drenched Josiah, Johnny Rabbit, and Charles. Josiah spun around and aimed his nock gun. He fired the remaining three barrels. Though the recoil nearly overturned the canoe, the shots crashed into the undercarriages of the hot air balloons, slaughtering the Undertakers within.

"This way!" Johnny Rabbit cried, sending his canoe into a thick growth of cattails below some mangrove trees. Josiah followed him. The dense underbrush camouflaged them. Though the hot air balloons fired and thundered away, no projectiles hit them. In time, the fusillade fell silent. The Undertakers had lost their prey. When it was clear, Johnny Rabbit paddled ahead, and Josiah followed. Finally, the Seminole laid his paddle and leaned back.

He turned to Charles. "You brought them here," he said simply.

"I'm sorry," Charles stared at his hands. "I didn't mean to. I'm very sorry." He was still holding Clark's revolver, and Charles holstered the weapon with a sigh. "I could have killed him!" Charles stuttered, crying. "I'm not strong enough..."

"Nah. I'm the weak one." Josiah Reeper shook his head. "I was just lying on the ground like a feeble old man."

They paddled onward, silently.

"Hell and Damnation." Tantalus Brinks wiped the blood and sweat from his face with a silken handkerchief. "To think that I was fought off by such base individuals." He sat in the undercarriage of one of the Silent Orchestra's black painted hot air balloons, accompanied by three motionless Undertakers. The effects of the Undertaker's addictions were becoming palpable, and the three normally silent and motionless gunmen shivered and shook.

"How many men have you left?" Tantalus asked. "The showdown in Roswell, the debacle on the docks, the slaughter wreaked upon you on that fetid island—it must have drained your secret brotherhood."

"Twenty men left," one of the Undertakers whispered, sounding ashamed. "That's all."

"Ah." Tantalus Brinks shook his head. "I suppose you need the Fountain of Youth now more than ever, and in quantity enough to save your entire queer race. And yet, I notice that it was your negligence that allowed Charles Green, Josiah Reeper, and that damned colored savage to sneak away."

"No." The Undertaker reached into his coat and drew out a compass; the needle twisting and pointing somewhere down the river. "We managed to put a tracking apparatus into one of the canoes. We can follow them."

"Excellent!" Tantalus Brinks laughed. "They'll lead us right to the Fountain, and then after a quick exchange of gunfire, the life-giving waters will be ours alone." Tantalus pointed his walking stick forward. "Well then, onward!"

The hot air balloons soared down the swampy waterways, following the compass's point, Tantalus Brinks could swear that the Undertaker next to him, for only a few seconds, had a smug smile on his pale face.

Charles Green began to lose track of time. They paddled seemingly at random through the swamp, oftentimes going in circles or simply reversing their direction and heading the other way. Only Johnny Rabbit seemed to know the rhyme and reason of their journey. Charles did not talk to the ancient Seminole, grateful for Johnny Rabbit's help.

Josiah Reeper grumbled and swore as he paddled, his arm still sore from the battle at Freeman's Town.

"We're almost there," Johnny Rabbit announced, surprising everyone with his suddenness. He pointed to a mossy tunnel of branches, moss, reeds and river grass. "Just through there, in fact. But first I must pay my respects to the guardian." He turned to Charles and Josiah. "Cover your noses." Charles squeezed his nostrils closed with two fingers.

Arching himself over the water, Johnny Rabbit muttered some strange chant. The water began to churn, frothing white with motion. A hand rose from the maelstrom, furry with green moss, wrapped round with vines, and with claws like branches. The rest of the creature soon emerged, a hulking giant twice the size of Josiah assembled from leafs, branches, and clumps of moss, with two shining orange specks for eyes.

"The Stink Ape," Johnny Rabbit whispered. "Ancient guardian of this place. He knows me." The Seminole held out his hand, and the green giant stared at it before nodding and sinking back into the water. Soon he had vanished into the churning swamp.

"We may go," Johnny announced.

They dipped their paddles into the water and passed through the green tunnel. On the other side, they saw an ancient pool formed by stone walls built on a mossy island, water bubbling up from some depthless spring in the pool's bottom. Ruined stone statues, their features distorted by age and the elements, stood as silent sentinels at the four corners of the Fountain.

Charles, Josiah, and Johnny Rabbit pushed their canoes up on the shores and walked over to the Fountain. They stared into the glistening water, which gleamed like molten gold in the faded sunlight of the swamp.

Charles stared. "Wow," he whispered. Then he turned back to the canoe containing Clark's body. "Let's see if it will help Clark."

"Yeah. That's why we're here, isn't it?" Josiah said, staring at the water. He knelt down and splashed his hand through it. Together, the two of them walked back to the canoes. Charles pulled off the cloth, and Josiah and Johnny Rabbit hefted up Clark's body, now in the early stages of decay.

"Make sure no bits of him fall off," Josiah muttered as he carried the body back to the Fountain. They gently laid Clark Reeper down in the shallow waters and stood back. Nothing happened.

"What's going on?" Charles asked. "Is he going to be okay?"

"I don't know, kid," Josiah muttered. "Nothing for it but to wait."

Before Johnny Rabbit could answer, an explosion ripped through the swamp. The Stink Ape appeared in the water, bellowing with rage as a large group of Undertakers fired on it with their silver pepperbox pistols. The leafy creature fell upon the Undertakers, tearing them apart with its botanical ferocity. It slaughtered several Undertakers, but the salvos of explosive pepperbox rounds proved too much. The Stink Ape fell backwards into the swamp water, dissolving into clumps of grass and leafs.

"Bastards!" Johnny Rabbit shouted. He drew out his bows and fired several arrows, each shaft striking home. Josiah Reeper pulled out his nock gun and fired all nine barrels of the weapon. But the Undertakers had learned from their mistakes. Though a few went down, the rest took cover and avoided the shots.

Tantalus Brinks and his Undertaker followers splashed through the water in a charging horde. Johnny Rabbit drew his knife and stabbed at Tantalus's fat belly, but the obese tycoon leapt backwards and then jabbed his fist into Johnny Rabbit's chest. The Seminole shrieked in pain and fell backwards, rolling on the ground as he screamed. In jubilation, Tantalus held up his hand, the poison-coated needle mounted on his ring glistening.

"That should busy him for a spell!" Tantalus laughed, kicking the fallen and writhing Seminole. "Colombian Basilisk Spider. I hear it's the most painful venom in the entire world."

Charles Green ran to Johnny Rabbit's side, clutching the injured Seminole and trying to stop his poison-induced spasms. Johnny Rabbit vomited pale green goop on the stone floor, and then lay still.

"Johnny?" Charles asked. "No. That's impossible. You told me you were immortal!"

"Evidently he was mistaken." Tantalus Brinks laughed. "That's the savage's way, you know? Always believing that they are something they're not."

Josiah Reeper let out a roar of rage and leapt into battle with his tomahawk and revolver. He fired all six shots of the great pistol, and six Undertakers were torn apart by the large slugs. Josiah hefted his tomahawk with both hands, gutting one of the black-clothed men before decapitating another. But his blows were leaden and slow, and there were more Undertakers than he could possibly kill.

"You goddamn funerary fools!" Josiah moaned, swinging at another one and scoring a killing blow. He gasped in air and clutched his chest. "Goddamn. I'm getting too old for this!"

"Well, you picked a fine place for it." Tantalus stepped behind Josiah, moving nimbly behind the aging mountain man and striking his back with the cane. Josiah spun around, his tomahawk gripped in one hand, but Tantalus stepped back and avoided the blow. He bashed Josiah again, and then ducked back behind the guns of the Undertakers.

"Kill him," Tantalus commanded. The Undertakers leveled their weapons at the gasping form of Josiah Reeper and opened fire. Explosive rounds and rapid-fired Gatling gun bullets tore through Josiah's body. Though his blood stained the grass and his bones were crunched and shattered, he stood standing and took every shot, before slowly toppling backwards.

Tantalus Brinks and the surviving six Undertakers stood before Charles Green, their weapons lowered. Charles looked at the fallen forms of Josiah and Johnny Rabbit.

"Well, whelp, now what are you going to do?" Tantalus asked calmly. "Still wearing those six-guns, I see. Are those pistols just for show?"

"You bastard," Charles said, his voice a low whisper. "You greedy, fat, ugly bastard!"

"Oh, I'm fat, I'm ugly, I'm a hideous parody of what mankind should be," Tantalus said with a sarcastic laugh. "None of that changes the fact that we have you dead to rights. All of those years traveling with a master gunman have truly taught you nothing, have they?"

Like he had seen Clark do a thousand times before, Charles drew out one of the Colt Peacemakers. His hands moved at a blur, and before Tantalus or any of the Undertakers could stop him, Charles had the weapon up and ready. He pointed it right at Tantalus's face and clutched the weapon with both of his small hands.

"I didn't know I could do that," Charles whispered.

Tantalus gulped. His bravado left him as soon as the gun was pointed in his direction. "Perhaps we can reach an agreement?" Tantalus asked. "Split the proceeds of this water and gain immense wealth together?"

"I don't think so," Charles said. He pulled back the hammer with both of his thumbs. "No, I could never do anything like that." Charles stared at Tantalus's piggy eyes and thought about a bullet splattering his brains out on the stone walls of the Fountain. But the idea was repellant to Charles. He knew he couldn't take a life, not willingly, and even though he had every reason in the world to destroy Tantalus Brinks, the revolver wavered, and Charles felt sweat seeping into his palms.

"You can't do it, can you, boy?" Tantalus laughed as he realized Charles's predicament. "It's nothing to be ashamed of. You simply don't have the will to end a life. Well, I suppose that means there's nothing to stop me from ending yours."

"Now that ain't exactly the case," said a tired, but familiar voice.

Tantalus's eyes went up from Charles and looked behind him as his mouth fell open in surprise. Charles spun around to see what Tantalus Brinks was staring at. There stood Clark Reeper, his clothes and skin soaked from the Fountain's waters, his brown hair wet and hanging near his eyes, his crumbling Stetson draining water. "I reckon I owe you a killing, whoever the hell you are."

"C-Clark Reeper!" Tantalus Brinks cried in shock. Clark's skin was still stretched and corpse pale; bits of his flesh still appeared to be rotting, but with every second life seeped back into him. The six bullets in his chest popped out and disappeared into the Fountain's waters. He was every inch alive.

"Charles, it's mighty good to see you," Clark said, ruffling the boy's hair. "Much obliged to you for holding onto my pistols. I think I'll take them back now."

Quickly grabbing the gun, Clark fanned out six shots. The Undertakers behind Tantalus Brinks didn't have time to scream or gasp or fire their own weapons before Clark had shot every one of them right between the eyes. Tantalus Brinks let out a gasp and charged Clark Reeper, his cane held in one hand and the poison-coated needle in his ring held low. He swung the cane at Clark, who nimbly dodged the blow. With a wide smile, Clark punched Tantalus directly in the face.

The tycoon let out a shriek of pain as he fell backward, and then Clark threw his whole body into the tycoon and sent him splashing into the Fountain. Tantalus Brinks sunk, thrashing and shouting as his bulk dragged him to the bottom.

Clark watched him sink and then turned to Charles. Tears sprung to their eyes. "You did okay without me?" Clark asked.

"I did all right," Charles said. "But I'm glad to have you back."

The two of them embraced.

Johnny Rabbit's ragged laughter distracted them both. The Seminole came to his feet and shook hands with Clark Reeper. "Good shooting, cowboy," he said. "I would have helped you, but that poison was wreaking havoc on my stomach."

The reunion was interrupted by a loud infantile wailing that resounded through the swamp clearing. In the waters of the Fountain floated a small infant, wrapped in Tantalus Brinks's now incredibly oversized clothes. Charles reached into the water and pulled out the baby.

"It's Tantalus," Charles exclaimed. The baby stopped crying and stared up at them with wide eyes. "He looks kind of cute as a baby." Charles paused. "Does the Fountain work that way?"

Johnny Rabbit took baby Tantalus and held the infant to his chest. "No one knows how it works. Maybe it has a will of its own. But I'll take care of Tantalus. Make sure he gets raised right." He looked up at Clark. "I'm thankful you came when you did, Clark. But I think you may have come a bit too late." He stepped aside, and let Clark stare at Josiah Reeper's corpse.

"Ah hell," Clark muttered. "My Old Man done died for me. Well, I figure I can set it right." Clark used his Stetson to scoop up some water from the Fountain and splashed it into Josiah's face.

"Father?" Clark asked. The corpse shivered as the water ran in drips down the weathered skin.

Slowly, one of Josiah's eyes cracked open. "What?" Josiah asked, his voice angry. He talked without moving his lips. "Clarky? Trying to resurrect me? No, son. I'm ready to go. Dry my face off and bury me right here."

Clark Reeper kneeled down next to his father. "Are you sure? I ain't gonna just let my own father die."

"You'd better. It's damn peaceful where I was. And your mother was there." Josiah Reeper breathed out slowly and lay still. They buried him near the Fountain, and took the canoes out of the swamp.

Clark Reeper and Charles Green were together again, and things were as they should be.

The Gunslinger's Ball

Now, I've come across all manner of odd and dangerous people in my line of work. Some of them have been right friendly. We've gotten off well from the start and are fast friends still. Others were my sworn foes at one point; but circumstances forced us to be allies, and then each of us realized the other weren't all that bad. And some of the folks I've mingled with are bad as bad can be; the only thing that could settle our differences would be a couple ounces of lead right between their miserable eyes. I suppose it's all in the job description. You see, my name is Clark Reeper, and I am a bounty hunter specializing in the odder jobs out there.

During my travels all over this old continent, I've met almost every kind of psychopath desperado, noble hero, thieving rogue, and loyal companion. I even met my adopted son on the road, a youngster by the name of Charles Green who I love more than my own life. Charles is a nice little feller, about ten-years-old and small for his age. He has slightly curly brown hair, brown eyes blinking behind thick spectacles, and he always wears a neat little Norfolk jacket and peaked cap. He's a great kid. He even saved my mangy hide by dragging me through the Florida swamps to reach the Fountain of Youth after a pistol-packing drunk filled me with bullets in an Arkansas saloon.

I look a bit different. I'm a tall gent, and I always wear a long khaki duster, and a crumbling Stetson. Two Colt Peacemakers ain't never far from my hands. I don't know what exactly threw Charles and me together, but I don't care much.

I love Charles something fierce, probably on account of he's the only family I ever really had. My Old Man, God rest his awful soul, was a distant feller and never took much notice of me. He let one of his ex-girlfriends raise me. She was the self-declared Voodoo Queen of New Orleans and went by the name of Marie Laveau. She was beautiful, and I loved her as much as he did. Problem was, she was pure evil.

She and my Old Man had a falling out, and she figured that killing me would be a good way to get back at him, so she hired some thugs to bushwhack me. To get out with breath still in my body, I had to kill four men and gouge out another man's eye. We've been foes ever since. A little while back, she nearly fed Charles and me to a bunch of alligators. We escaped, but so did she, and I've been wary of her ever since.

I reckoned she wouldn't just forget about me, but I never imagined how she might go about getting her vengeance. It would all take place in the boomtown of Deadwood, South Dakota, and almost every outlaw, lawman, and desperado out there would be along for the ride.

It all started when I was in Yankton, resting up after I had hunted down the resurrected and very angry serial killer H.H. Holmes. Charles and I were just heading out of the hotel lobby when a telegram boy walked in and called out my name. I introduced myself and he handed me a large brown envelope.

"Well, ain't this something," I whispered, looking at the large invitation that slid out of the envelope. The top bit was covered in crests and coats of arms, all featuring a shining gem. Below that, written in fancy calligraphy, was a letter.

"Who is it from, Mr. Reeper?" Charles asked.

My eyes went to the bottom of the letter. "Feller named Al Swearengen. Says he runs the Gem Variety Theatre and Saloon down in Deadwood." I looked up and read the body of the letter. "Dear Mr. Clark Reeper," it began. "Your reputation as a noted mankiller and crack shot with any weapon precedes you across the nation. I must say that I greatly admire your skill with a six-gun, particularly since I have great trouble getting bullets to go where I want them. I am currently assembling a large number of noted shootists, desperadoes, and gunmen, at my joint, the

Gem Variety Theatre and Saloon. This event will be known as the Gunslinger's Ball."

"A ball?" Charles asked, his eyes widening. "You mean like, with dancing and all that stuff?"

"I figure they'll be doing a lot more than dancing." I went back to the letter. "The ball will be a purely social function, with no violence intended. The best men in the west will be there to chat, swap stories, sample the best whiskey in the territory, and for posterity, be photographed and catalogued. I hope to make this an annual event, and your appearance would certainly go a long way to enhancing its reputation. If you do come, and I sincerely hope that you do, be aware that while firearms are not prohibited, since many of my guests refuse to part with their guns for a long period of time, your irons must be holstered at all times. Your Loyal Servant, Al Swearengen, Owner and Manager of the Gem Variety Theatre and Saloon.'"

I folded the invitation and tucked it into my jacket. "I don't rightly know if I should make an appearance," I said. "I guess I'll have a lot of friends there, but there will be a decent number of enemies too."

"But Mr. Swearengen did say that there'd be no violence allowed," Charles pointed out. "I'd kind of like to go. It sounds like a great way to meet people, and maybe see some of your friends you haven't seen for a while. Like Jennifer Chaos."

"Jennifer Chaos," I whispered, going a little bit wobbly in the knees soon as I heard her name. Jennifer Plesance was her real name, but everyone called her Jennifer Chaos for obvious reasons. I had loved her something fierce but it turned out she didn't like men at all. I couldn't blame her for that. Still, I had my hopes. And if she was gonna be there, I wanted to be there as well.

"She was really nice to me, and I'd like to see her again," Charles explained. "And she'll have her pet goat. And maybe Winston the armadillo will be there!" Charles really wanted to see his old pet. "Mr. Reeper, I really think we should go."

"I believe you're right," I said. "Stage leaves in a couple of hours, and I think we should be able to get seats." We packed up and headed out, not knowing what we was riding into.

We took the afternoon stagecoach out of Yankton, heading for Deadwood. The journey took much of the day, and we went past some open forest, down some winding hills, and past some of them newly erected telegraph poles. I was wondering who was gonna be at the Gunslinger's Ball, what I was gonna say to them, and what I was gonna say to Jennifer Chaos to make her change her mind about men in general and me in particular. Charles had one of his dime novels and read it during the bumpy ride, losing his place a few times but always finding it again. I looked at the cover and spotted the fighting outlaw Jesse James riding out of a town with a pretty girl joining him on his horse.

I grinned. "I reckon he'll be there."

"Jesse James?" Charles asked. "Really?"

I nodded. "Invitation said everyone with a reputation has been invited, and if I know the James Gang, they're mighty partial to their good reputation."

"Wow," Charles whispered, sinking back into his dime novel. I looked at the cover again, and wondered what would happen if anyone tried to take my life and turn it into a bunch of boy's adventure stories. I shook the thought out of my head just as the coach pulled up in the middle of Deadwood.

It was a good-sized boomtown, several rows of shops, businesses, hotels, cabins and tents on each side of a muddy street. It was full of townsfolk going about their business, walking out to the mines with their tools or coming back with pocketfuls of money in search of faro and poker games and whiskey. I had been there a few times. The last had ended with a bit of violence in the Celestial section that I wish I could forget about. Still, I felt pretty excited when I got out of the coach and helped Charles onto the muddy streets of Deadwood.

The coach ride had taken most of the day, and the shadows had grown long by the time we got there. The nightlife had started up with torch-bearing folk lighting up the whole town, and saloons doing a very brisk business. Everyone seemed to be on the same path as me and Charles, heading to the Gem.

The Gem Variety Theatre and Saloon was a large two-story building right in the center of town. Charles and I walked across the muddy thoroughfare wondering who was waiting for us inside.

We didn't have to wait long. "Clark Reeper!" came a familiar raspy voice. "It's been a while!"

I turned around and saw Bartholomew 'Brimstone' Brown, a former satanic gunslinger who had fallen for a pretty schoolmarm and gotten reformed. He was a gaunt feller with a head of coarse dark hair and a ragged black coat. Next to Brimstone was the blonde, bearded and heavyset Gustav Olafson, a Swede bounty hunter and berserker.

"Speak of the devil!" I said, slapping Brimstone on the shoulder. "It's good to see you. How's Mable doing?"

"She's fine." Brimstone grinned. "I could barely drag myself away once I got the letter."

"She henpecks him!" Gustav said with a hefty chortle. "Oh, ja, always nagging! Drives him mad."

Brimstone sighed and looked at his black boots. "We'd better get in, or we'll miss the festivities."

I nodded and together we all walked into the Gem Variety Theatre and Saloon. As soon as I walked in through the swinging doors, I was amazed at how many folks had filled up the place. Every table was full of hard-looking men with guns on their hips, making merry and chatting amiably. A couple of saloon girls were dancing around on the bar, kicking up their feet and shaking their short feathered dresses. A full band was playing away to accompany them with a piano, banjo and everything.

But what really got my attention were all the guests. The invitation hadn't lied none. Every feller who was skilled with a six-gun and had a fighting spirit was there. Sitting near the door was John Henry Holiday also called 'Doc.' He was wearing smoked glasses above his moustache and was putting his dentistry skills to good use by examining the teeth of none other than the famed lawman Wyatt Earp. The two of them must have traveled all the way from Tombstone to come here. Next to them, in the middle of a fierce poker game, was the British special agent and my former employer Vivian Bolt. He nodded at me and waved with his cigar before brushing away some dust from his bright purple suit and getting back to the game. Playing with Bolt were two men, one with a horribly scarred face. The other feller's name escapes me, though I think he was a cowpuncher and he hailed from Virginia.

Sitting at the bar, his face obscured by a balaclava, was the disfigured dynamitard Franklin Franks. The noted anarchist, who I had run into during the St. Walpurgis School hostage crisis, was talking politics with his pal Hugo Montez, a Mexican desperado with a liking for machetes. Also sipping his drink was Bat Masterson, a dapper feller with a bowler hat and a slick brown suit. The German master-sniper Werner Von Humboldt sat next to him, stroking his moustache. Standing on the bar, next to a bottle as big as he was, was Little Napoleon, a midget who I had fought and bested three times in the recent past. We avoided each other's eyes.

Billy the Kid was dancing a little jig near the piano. He was a young guy, but they say he killed one man for every year he'd been alive. A wild-eyed, red-bearded gunslinger wearing a rabbit-skin vest I recognized as Sam of Yosemite was dancing with him, occasionally firing one of his pistols off into the air. The James boys sat next to the piano, clapping their hands in time as Hopalong Cassidy sang along. Somewhere near the corner Wild Bill Hickok and Buffalo Bill Cody were comparing the notches on their pistol handles. Known con-man Jefferson 'Soapy' Smith seemed to be trying to sell Jose Chavez Y Chavez something, and was well on his way towards getting a good beating from him.

Two Indians were there too, passing around a peace pipe. One was the Oxford-educated Running Dog, while the other was the backwards Heyoka Red Turtle. Because of their tomahawks and bows, everyone seemed to be giving them a wide berth. The Katar Kid, an actual Indian from India, was sitting with them. Renowned hunter Trapper Jack was showing off some of his sasquatch pelts to a tall, masked gunslinger and his Indian assistant. Clay Allison, who would always let his victims eat a last meal before he killed them so they wouldn't go to Hell on an empty stomach was there as well. The murderous J. J. Webb, Sheriff Moses Brown, the colored sheriff of Salinerno, and Confederate holdout Elihu Wren were all well known to me. I'm sure there was a lot more famous and infamous personages I'd only heard of but never had the pleasure of sharing a drink with.

I walked into the saloon grinning like an idiot and shaking hands with everyone who came near.

"Howdy, Wild Bill. Not dead yet, I see."

"Why Hopalong, you have quite a nice singing voice."

"Elihu, Moses, you fellers killed each other yet? Ah hell, I didn't mean nothing by that!"

I greeted everyone in turn. The hotel's proprietor Al Swearengen was certainly right about the Gunslinger's Ball being enjoyable. When gunslingers weren't trying to kill you, they could be right decent company.

"Winston!" Charles shouted with joy. An armadillo came bouncing into the boy's arms, licking his face with his little pink tongue. I grinned at Charles as Cole Corbucci, the black-clad current owner of Winston and sheriff of Red Creek, Wyoming, walked over.

"That armadillo has been a great help to me, and I believe I am ready to return him to you," he said. A sawed-off shotgun blast had ruined his gun hand a while back, and Charles had been nice enough to give him Winston as a kind of armadillo assistant. Charles was overjoyed to get his pet back.

Just then, I noticed a small, brown goat rubbing up against my side. I patted the furry critter on its horned head, knowing exactly who owned the animal.

"Hey there, Erasmus," I said. "Where's your owner got to?"

"Here I am, Clark, you mangy, scum-sucking hardhead!" I looked up and spotted Jennifer Chaos, dirty and beautiful as ever, carrying a hunting knife and revolver, and dressed in her dusty vest, men's trousers, and feathered bowler hat.

I gulped. "Well, Jennifer, it's good to see you." I mumbled and found myself getting bashful. "Say, you know that thing you told me back in Red Creek? Well, do you think you could ever find it in your heart to love a man like me?"

Jennifer Chaos shook her head. "Oh, Clark. You sorry fool. Look, I want you to meet someone. Lula! Come on over here, darling." Another woman walked over, a slim blonde girl dressed in a beautiful crimson dress.

"Hey, Jenny," Lula said, wrapping her arms around Jennifer's neck. "This that Clark fellow you mentioned?"

"Sure is. Clark, this here is Lula Labelle, and she's my glory and sunshine."

"Well," I whispered. "Nice to meet you, and good seeing you too, Jenny." I felt a little faint, and I decided that some strong drink might be in order. "I'm gonna head on over to the bar. You mind watching, Charles while I'm getting some whiskey?"

"Not at all," Jennifer said, grinning as Charles scratched Erasmus behind his furry ears. "Charles is a nice little fellow and quite a gentlemen."

"Uh, um, thank you, ma'am," Charles stammered.

I left them chatting and headed over to the bar. I ordered a single shot and sat down, looking at the amber liquid nestled inside the shot glass. A meaty hand was clapped on my back, and I spun around to see Al Swearengen smiling at me. He was a stocky man with slick black hair and a thick black moustache, wearing an old pinstriped suit. He looked tough enough to run a place like the Gem, and smart enough to make it a success.

"Clark Reeper, glad you could make it!" His voice had a thick rasp to it. "I've been looking forward to meeting you for a long time."

"Is that so?" I asked, slowly draining my shot glass. The liquor calmed me down a bit, and I felt a mite better. "Didn't know I had much of a reputation."

"You're mistaken, sir! Folks round the world know the name of Clark Reeper."

Al patted me on the shoulder. "I can't even count how many men you've killed, and you probably can't keep count either. And of course, anytime something out of the ordinary happens, there you are, right in the middle of it."

"Much obliged for the compliment," I said. "I never really pondered my lot in life that much."

"Not a compliment, my friend, an impartial observation." He tilted his head and let me look into his big black eyes. "Problem is, now you gotta uphold your reputation."

Almost as soon as he said the words, a bearded, grizzled-looking feller ran into the Gem hollering his head off. "Indians!" he cried. "Attacking the telegraph poles and trying to block up the road! Goddamn dirt worshippers trying to cut us off from the world!"

"What the hell are you talking about?" Al asked, coming to his feet. The piano and banjos ceased their music-making, and every gunslinger in the joint got quiet and listened.

"Bunch of savages came round the mountain, started dynamiting the road and blowing down telegraph poles!"

Around two dozen pistols were drawn with practiced spins, my own among them, with another couple dozen guns waiting to be hauled out.

Al Swearengen looked at his guests. "Well, those heathen dirt worshipping Indians sure picked the wrong town to screw with!" He chuckled. "Who wants to ride out there and paint the Black Hills red with savage blood?"

Every gunslinger worth his salt raised his voice to volunteer. I looked at Red Turtle and Running Dog, who were both Lakota, and would probably be the best authority on any subject dealing with Indians.

"This makes little sense," Running Dog mentioned, his accent clipped and with a bit of Oxford English thrown in. "The only tribes in this area are friendly with the United States, or are far away on reservations, and would never launch an outright attack on a telegraph line."

"That's the way we do things," Red Turtle said, but I knew he was a Heyoka and spoke everything all backwards, so that he really meant the opposite of what he said.

"Well, them are certainly Indians attacking!" The miner looked to Swearengen. "What should we do, Mr. Swearengen?"

"Just what I said we should do. Ride out and blow them apart." He pointed to me. "Clark, you're in charge. Pick some people and go see what's going on."

I gulped, but then stood up and nodded. "Okay, Mr. Swearengen, I'll see what's what." I turned to face the crowd. All of them was standing in readiness, and I was certain that each one could hold more than hold his own in any gunfight. I pointed to Red Turtle for his knowledge of Lakota customs, Elihu Wren for his skill as a cavalrymen, Wild Bill because of his knowledge of the area, and Jennifer Chaos, for no reason I could really think of.

The other gunslingers grumbled and groaned, but then Al rolled another barrel of his finest spirits and started pouring the stuff out on the house. Everyone cheered up. Me and my handpicked posse headed for the door, mounted up on five waiting horses, and rode out into the gold-drenched hills that surrounded Deadwood.

"You really think it's the savages?" Wild Bill asked, as we pounded up a hillside, heading for the telegraph pole.

"It ain't gonna be no one else," shouted Elihu Wren as he skillfully jumped his horse over a miner's wagon that was in his way. "Down in Texas, only thing worse than us was the damned Comanche and the Apache."

"But this isn't Lakota territory," Red Turtle explained angrily. "Apache and Comanche are here. And Lakota are not forced onto reservations that are not far away from Deadwood."

"What's his problem?" Jennifer Chaos asked. "Sucked too much on a peace pipe?'

"Nah. He just talks all backwards on account of he's one of them Lakota Sacred Clowns. Whatever he says, just remember it's all backwards. Mighty confusing, but you don't get used to it." I coughed. "Excuse me. You do get used to it."

The telegraph line was a little ways up the hill, and we all dismounted and went forward on foot. It was a mountainous, rocky area, but very fertile and filled with small trees and tall grasses.

Steep mountains overshadowed the trail into the city. I narrowed my eyes, and spotted a large group of men in war bonnets planting something near one of the jagged slopes.

"Indians!" Elihu said, drawing out one of his Confederate cavalry pistols. Jennifer Chaos put her rifle to her shoulder and knelt down.

"I got a bead on them!" she whispered. "Give the word, Clark, and I'll take them down."

I held up my head. "Not yet. Red Turtle, why don't you go in and talk with them. If they're really your people, maybe you can talk some sense into them."

Red Turtle walked up the mountainside, his arms outstretched. He said something in Lakota and then jumped backwards as the men with the war bonnets turned around and opened fire with rifle and pistol.

"Son of a gun!" I cursed, drawing both of my Colts and running up the hill. I fired as I ran, and one of the Indian fellers went down with several slugs in the chest. But when I got a closer look, I saw he weren't no Red Man at all. He was pure white man, even wore normal trousers and a shirt, and the only bit of Indian clothing on him was that crudely made war bonnet, which didn't even have all the feathers in the right places.

Red Turtle turned on the false Indians, decapitating one with an artfully thrown tomahawk. Elihu Wren drew his cavalry saber and ran one through, while Wild Bill Hickok drew his revolvers fast as lightning and plugged two of them. Jennifer Chaos scored a headshot with her rifle. And that was the last sham Red Men around.

We looked at the bodies. "I was wrong," Red Turtle said. "They're not white men."

"Ain't that just a kick in the pants?" Wild Bill muttered, stroking his moustache. "There's something fishy about this whole Gunslinger's Ball, and this is getting too strange for words."

"How do you figure?" I asked.

"It's simple, really. What happens when you put all of these gunslingers, mankillers, outlaws, and bounty hunters, together in one room? Well, pretty soon they'll get to arguing about one little thing, and then pistols will be drawn, shots fired, and before you know it, every one of them is dead or shot so full of bullets that the only thing they'll be doing for the rest of their days is bleeding."

It made sense. Gunfighters were never the most cool-headed people, and if a lot of them were together, violent occurrences couldn't help but happen.

"But this little fandango will be over soon," Jennifer Chaos pointed out. "Maybe by early morning tomorrow. Then we can go home safe."

"You're moving a little fast there." The words came from one of the corpses. All of us aimed our weapons, cocking back the hammers on the pistols, working bolts, balancing tomahawks and whatever else we needed to do to prepare to fire. The corpse stood up, wiped some of the blood off of his shirtfront and stared at me.

"Reeper, and his cross-dressing strumpet!" He was thin and lanky, with a head of scraggly black hair and a pale, sallow face. One of his arms seemed too big for him, and he pulled a human leg bone out from his jacket and held it with his smaller hand. I knew this bastard.

"Remus, alias Ringo. A Fossor. From the old days." I kept my pistols leveled, even though I knew they wouldn't do a lick of good.

"What in the Sam Hill is that?" Wild Bill asked.

"One of the old pagan magicians," I explained. "The Romans used them to dig out the catacombs for the bodies. Ringo got to liking those bodies, and he's been stealing body parts and staying alive ever since. But last time I saw you, Ringo, you was six feet under with six feet of dirt on top of you."

"Yeah." Ringo narrowed his eyes. "I didn't care much for that. Got mighty boring. But by and by, someone came and dug me up, and now here I am in front of you."

"Well, I had enough of all this bull's crap!" Wild Bill shouted. He fired both of his pistols, and Elihu Wren joined in. The shells cut through Ringo and blew little bits of him off, but he stood stock still and took it. Red Turtle hurled his tomahawk, hacking off one of Ringo's hands, but Ringo grabbed his severed hand and stuck it back on his stump. With a little twist, he fitted it back on. I knew Ringo was getting angry when he made a fist.

"We ought to bury him again," Jennifer Chaos said. "That will take care of him."

"You ain't gonna bury me!" Ringo laughed and stepped backwards, gesturing with his leg bone. "I'm gonna be burying you." With that he jumped into the air and flipped backwards, landing on a rocky ledge high above us. I spotted a dynamite detonator right in front of him with strings running far into the mountainside.

"Ah hell," I muttered. "Run!"

I didn't have to tell anyone twice. We ran down the mountainside just as Ringo pressed down on the detonator, sending off a large explosion through the rock. A landslide came after us, boulders large and small rolling down the hill. We all jumped on our horses and hightailed it out of there right before the landslide crashed down and covered the trail.

Now we were all trapped in Deadwood, and many of Wild Bill's dire predictions were about to come true. Another question was nagging at my mind. Someone had dug up Ringo and sent him back here with men, guns, and dynamite. Whoever that someone was, I was sure this weren't gonna be the last we heard of him.

By the time we got back to camp, everyone in Deadwood had heard the news. Al Swearengen was waiting for us at the door to the Gem Variety Theatre and Saloon, his arms crossed, looking mighty sore.

"Heard you ran into some trouble, and now the whole camp is cut off from the outside. That true?" Swearengen asked, pulling open the door and letting us in.

"It's true," I told him. "Weren't no Indians that done it, though. Bunch of white folk, one of them an old acquaintance of mine, dynamited the ridge and dumped a landslide across the road. There any other way out of camp?"

"Yeah, just one, but it's a difficult journey that no one should take without adequate supplies. One thing's for sure: No one's getting out for a while." Swearengen opened the door and let us in. "And as you'll soon find out, tensions have already begun to rise."

As soon as I walked in, my ears were assaulted with a large number of yells, shrieks, insults and caterwauls. Billy the Kid pointed a pair of revolvers at Jesse James, who waved a smashed bottle and hollered abuse at him. Bat Masterson and the Katar Kid squared off for fisticuffs, while Chavez y Chavez and Hugo Montez harangued each other in Spanish.

Charles Green sat in the middle of the whole mess, begging everyone to stop fighting. He could barely be heard over the insults and shouts of outrage, and many of them were too foul for a boy of Charles's years to listen to. I drew one of my revolvers and pointed it at the ceiling. After a few seconds, the hubbub did not die down, and so I fired off a single shot.

That quieted everyone down. They all looked my way, some of the gunslingers pulling out their weapons and training them on me. "My good sir," Doc Holiday announced. "Why have you interrupted our discussions?"

"Because they're damn stupid, considering the timing," I explained. "Look, whoever paid those men to take down the telegraph and block the road wanted us to all be at each others' throats like this, so they can save a fortune on bullets."

"That man insulted my mama!" Billy the Kid shouted. "I'll beat him bloody! And I'll beat you bloody too, lest you shut the hell up and move aside!"

"Calm down!" I told him forcibly. "A gunfight breaking out right here ain't gonna serve no one's interest but the ones who done dynamited the mountainside and trapped us here!"

"Mr. Reeper is right," Charles said. "We should work together and try to find out what's going on. Please, stop fighting."

Charles's words seemed to finally diffuse the situation. I reckon even the most vicious outlaw didn't feel like picking a fight with a little boy like Charles. Guns were holstered and apologies coaxed from leaden lips. I sat down at the bar, right between Brimstone Brown and Little Napoleon.

"Clark, who do you think is behind this?" Brimstone asked.

"I can only speculate, but whoever they are, they had awful good timing. And they'd have to know we was all here."

Little Napoleon pulled himself up on the bar and dangled his legs off the side. "Yeah. To pull this off, someone would need advanced knowledge over everything that was going on in the camp." He turned to us and raised his eyebrow. "You boys thinking what I'm thinking?"

"Swearengen," I muttered. I turned and saw the saloon owner walk by us, his thumbs hooked in his overalls. He slid behind the bar and pulled out a bottle of whiskey.

"Can I offer you boys something to drink?" he asked.

"I'd much prefer some answers," Brimstone said, drawing out his long barreled Colt Buntline Special.

"Same here." I drew one of my own revolvers.

Al held up his hands. "All right, you got me. I must admit this whole event was a bit of a charade, and it falls apart on any amount of closer inspection. But it more than served its purpose."

"And what was that purpose?" I demanded.

"To have you here, of course." Swearengen grinned at me. "I think it's time the real operator of events was revealed."

"You'd better bring him out, or I'll blow your head off." I cocked my pistol.

"Him? Why, Clark, I had no idea your opinions of the fairer sex were so low." Soon as he let on that it was a woman who had set me up, I got a sinking feeling in my chest as I realized who he must be referring to. Al Swearengen whistled, and then pointed behind me at the stairwell to the second story of the Gem.

I turned just in time to see the door to Swearengen's office creak open. Out of it stepped a beautiful mulatto woman wearing an elegant lace and ribbon ballroom gown. She walked down the stairwell slow, showing off every gorgeous bit of her, and making all the gunfighters below hold their breath. But I was breathing heavy, on account of I knew who she was.

"Marie Laveau!" I cursed. "You traitorous witch!"

"Clark Reeper." Marie smiled as laughter rippled through her body. "I had expected better manners from you." She walked down to the floor, and gunslingers parted to let her through. Marie Laveau walked over to me and put her hand on my chest. "I've been waiting so long to see you again."

"I got no love for you, ma'am." I pointed my pistol at her. "I'll kill you, and you'll have deserved worse."

"Don't be doing anything stupid, Mr. Reeper." Swearengen's gravelly voice came from behind. I turned around and saw him covering me with a sawed-off shotgun from behind the bar. He held the shotgun with one hand and poured himself a drink with the other. "And don't go thinking me and Ms. Laveau didn't have this whole thing planned out."

I looked up. Two of Marie's creatures appeared on the second floor, covering everyone in the room with rifles. They were zombies, two rotting corpses animated with voodoo magic; their mouths sewn shut and repeating rifles placed in their hands. They slowly walked down the steps and stood next to their mistress.

"Mr. Reeper!" Charles cried. He tried to run to me, but Jennifer Chaos reached down and held him back. I didn't want that nice boy getting hurt because of me, and I was grateful to Jenny.

"What do you say we go somewhere more private and chat things over?" Marie insisted. "And put that thing away before you hurt someone." She pointed to my revolver.

Regretfully, I holstered it.

"Now, Marie, about the money." Al downed his cup of whiskey and then walked out from behind the bar, still holding his shotgun. "I didn't help you capture the great Clark Reeper out of the goodness of my heart. Or out of my love for you, I might add."

"Of course." Marie reached into her dress and withdrew a roll of bills. She handed them to Swearengen, and he hastily counted them.

He stared up at her with angry eyes.

"This isn't the amount that we agreed upon."

She shrugged. "Sorry, Al. That's all I could afford. After this..." She stared at me. "This brat forced me out of my home, I've been on the run and unable to get a substantial income. This will have to do."

"The hell it will! Now cough up the bucks!" Swearengen swung his shotgun to face her. The crowd of gunslinger gasped, Billy the Kid covered his eyes, Little Napoleon shook his fist, and I began to wonder if maybe I would get out of this okay after all. I should have known better than to hope, especially when Marie Laveau was involved.

She smiled at him. "You don't know who you're dealing with." The door to the Gem was kicked open, and Ringo the Fossor stood in the entrance. He hurled his bone club at Al Swearengen, knocking the saloon owner to the floor. The shotgun clattered from his hands. Ringo and the two zombies covered me with their weapons so I was in no mood to dive for the weapon.

"Clark, you're coming with me. And Charles—take him too."

"The boy stays!" I shouted at Marie. "I'll come, but you ain't hurting Charles none. He ain't got a cruel or contrary bone in his body and he's done you no harm."

Marie shrugged again, and one of her zombie servants pointed his gun at Charles, causing everyone to gasp, including me. "Fine," she said, as if she didn't care one way or the other. "I'll gun him down right here."

Slowly, the boy ran to my side and we quickly embraced. I put a hand on his shoulder and started walking to the door. Al Swearengen wheezed and coughed on the floor, but no one paid him much heed.

Ringo held the door open while we walked through, and he leered at Charles in a way that gave me an urge to shoot him right there; and I would have if I didn't already have a bunch of guns aimed at me. An ornate carriage, more like a hearse than anything else, was parked in front of the Gem, with a zombie coachman and two black plume-covered horses. Ringo rode shotgun while Marie, her zombie guards, Charles and me squeezed inside.

The zombie coachman gave a flick of his whip, and the horses clattered down the streets and out of the town.

Marie Laveau produced a fan from somewhere and started waving it lazily at her face. I looked at her angrily, saying nothing. Charles looked at both of us and clasped his hands together. I put my hand around and pulled him close, hoping that I could somehow protect him.

"You recognize my retainers, Clark?" Marie Laveau asked politely, pointing to the two zombies with her fan.

I looked them over. One of them was missing a lower jaw, and the other had a bit of his stomach torn away. "No," I said. "Can't say I do."

"Mad Dog Manning, Southern Nevada. Uriah Barker, a little north of Nacogdoches." The men she named were outlaws I had gunned down a long time ago, just two thugs on wanted posters. I had killed them, gotten paid, and really hadn't thought much about them since. But now, looking at their animated bodies, I suddenly remembered.

"Son of a gun!" I whispered. "It is them! How did you—"

"I've been very busy, Clark," Marie Laveau said with a smile and a swish of her fan. "I've been traveling all over the country, adding to my collection. At first it was a just a preoccupation, but a little while ago, I received some news that transformed it into an obsession."

"What news?" I demanded.

The Voodoo Queen let her fan drop. "Josiah Reeper. The only man I ever truly loved. The only man who spurned me. He is dead now, because of you."

"That's not true!" Charles shouted, surprising everyone with his outburst. "I was there, and Mr. Reeper didn't hurt his father at all! In fact, Josiah wanted to die and to be buried, and he turned down Clark's offer to pour some of the water from the Fountain of Youth on him! Please, don't blame Clark for that!"

Charles gulped after he had spoken, and for a while there weren't no sound but the stagecoach rumbling onwards. We had left Deadwood a while back, and were now heading through the town's only exit. I looked out the window and saw a large number of figures blocking the road, a small army in fact.

"You like Clark, don't you?" Marie asked Charles.

Slowly, my boy nodded. Marie reached out and grabbed his chin, forcing his bespectacled eyes to stare into hers.

"You think he's a hero, isn't that correct?" she asked.

"Yes, ma'am. Clark is a hero. He's saved my life many times, and he always does the right thing. Even though my father died, he's taken very good care of me and I do love him, ma'am, I do."

I couldn't help smiling but Marie Laveau was less pleased. She reached out with her perfectly manicured nails, and slowly, painfully, clawed his cheek until there was a bead of blood. Before I knew what was going on, I had drawn my pistol and jabbed it into Marie's face. "You leave Charles out of this," I said.

Marie shook her head. "He's a bigger a part of you than anything." The two zombies pointed their guns at Charles, and slowly, I let my revolver drop and then holstered it.

The stagecoach rolled to a stop. The zombie coachman and Ringo pulled open the door.

Marie got out first, and offered me her hand. "Please, Clark, come take a look at the company I've assembled."

I got out, and after helping Charles down, I took a gander at the crowd Marie had in front of me. I hadn't realized there were so many. There was Cactus Jack Oprey, the stagecoach robber I had shot in the back down in Arizona. There was Sullivan O'Daniels, a New York mob boss I had stabbed to death in a bar somewhere. There was Roberto Rodriguez, a desperado my horse had trampled to death a little west of Juarez. They were all here, every man I had ever killed, in every possible state of decay.

"Son of a gun." I didn't know what else to say. "Son of a gun. How many are there?"

"I lost count, as I'm sure you did." Marie Laveau pointed to all of the corpses, each one resurrected, patched up, and armed. Memories came flashing to me as I looked them all over. I never kept track of how many men I killed, never carving notches on my gun barrel or nothing, partly because it made me feel a mite guilty. Maybe some of these men didn't deserve what I done to them. And looking at them all, standing there and staring back at me, well, it made me feel mighty poorly.

"You see, Charles," Marie said. "Your hero isn't very heroic. Look at all the people he's gunned down, many in cold blood. He's a killer, your precious father is."

Charles stared at all the zombies, his eyes wide and his mouth open. "Is that true?" he asked me. "You really killed all of these men? All of them? And some in cold blood?"

I didn't want to tell Charles the truth, but lying to him would be worse. "I am a bounty hunter, Charles. I make my money off of death and bullets. You've seen me take lives before. But I don't kill if I don't got a cause too. Most of these dead folk are criminals."

"But there's so many of them, Clark," Charles whispered. I put my hand on his shoulder. Charles shrugged off my hand.

That felt like a Bowie knife twisting in my gut.

"And of course, Clark, don't forget your latest victim." Marie stood next to me as the crowd of zombies parted to let a single dead feller walk through. I recognized him instantly as my own father. My Old Man still had the bullet holes that had done him in. But I have to say, though he was corpse pale and molding, he didn't look too bad.

I ran over to him and we embraced. Maybe there was still a little of my father in that body. I pulled out my Bowie knife and cut the thread tying his lips together so he could talk, but he only made piteous moans. Wherever my Old Man was, it weren't in that rotting, walking cadaver.

I turned back to Marie Laveau and Charles. The little feller was staring at the ground, not knowing what to think of me. Marie had a wide grin on her face. She put a hand on Charles's shoulder, and he didn't react.

"Charles, what do you say we leave Clark Reeper right here with all of these dead ones, and then we ride off together? They can get their justice, and Clark can get his comeuppance."

"They'll kill him!" Charles cried.

"But he killed them, remember?" Marie Laveau kneeled down and pointed to all of the zombies. "Maybe some of them could have reformed. Maybe they weren't that bad at all, and Clark just wanted the money. He was always very greedy. You're a good boy Charles, and it's clear that you deserve better than to be raised by a murdering gunslinger like Clark Reeper."

"Don't you go poisoning my boy's mind, you dirty witch!" I shouted angrily. I drew my revolver and pointed it at her. I even managed to get a shot off before Ringo knocked the pistol from my hand with his thrown leg bone.

"Look at him, always resorting to violence without thinking." Marie walked over to me and shook her head. "He might have shot you by accident."

"Clark would never do that!" Charles exclaimed. "He loves me, I know that for sure."

"But he loves killing more. You can't trust a man like that. You've been hurt so many times by his actions." Marie turned back to Charles. "For all of my faults, I am not a simple person. I do what needs to be done in the best way I can. But Clark has only bloodlust. Let's leave him here, Charles. We can return to New Orleans and I'll raise you well. You'll go to school and have friends your own age and be very safe. You'd like a life like that, wouldn't you?"

"Well...yes." Charles reluctantly agreed.

"Then come with me. Forget about Clark Reeper, that vulgar, rotten man."

I looked at Charles. Marie Laveau was spinning lies, but like all the best fabrications, there was a hint of truth in them. Charles had been hurt so many times, and even though I could have settled down if I wanted to, I kept on with my dangerous job, always dragging poor Charles along for the ride. Sooner or later, something terrible would happen to one of us, and there'd be no Fountain of Youth to make everything better.

"Maybe you ought to go, son," I told Charles. I gulped back tears. "It's like I told you when we met back in Dead Man's Gulch. I ain't cut out to be a father. You go on with Marie, she'll raise you right, better than I could, just to spite my soul."

Charles turned to Marie and looked back at me. He took off his glasses and wiped his eyes and then set the glasses back on. Then he walked over to me.

"I'm staying with you," he told me. "I don't care if it's dangerous or if you're violent, and I don't think you are. I want to be with you."

A smile appeared on my face. "Glad to have you with me, Charles."

"What?" Marie Laveau couldn't believe Charles's decision. "You goddamn little brat! How dare you spurn me! I'll see you die! I promise I will!" She stepped back and held out her hands. Ringo whistled appreciatively and stepped back with her. "Gentlemen!" Marie addressed the zombies. "Ready your weapons!"

All of them readied their guns. Rusty old six-guns, fancy revolvers, newfangled automatic pistols, rifles, shotguns, sawed-offs, hand-cannons, carbines, muzzle loaders, double-barreled shotguns, bows and arrows, throwing knives, derringers, cane guns, coach guns, spreader guns, paradox guns, riot guns, long guns, elephant guns, and express rifles. All were drawn out and aimed at me and Charles.

I still had one of my revolvers, but there was no way in hell I was gonna take down all of them zombies. I crouched low and covered Charles with my body. Even though I'd be blown to bits, maybe Charles would survive.

"You make a run for it after I get shot to hell," I told him. "Wait until they stop shooting and then run. Zombies are slow to reload, and you can probably find a good hiding spot somewhere in the hills."

"I don't want to leave you."

"Ain't got no choice in the matter. You run and get to safety."

"Take aim!" The sound of a dozen bolts and hammer clicking back, along with arrows being strung and stranger firearms being prepared, made me hold Charles even tighter.

"And Charles?"

"Yes, Mr. Reeper?"

"I'm much obliged to you, for everything."

"Me too, Mr. Reeper."

"Fire!" Gunshots sounded from every which way. The air grew stale with the smell of gunpowder, and I could feel bullets whistling around Charles and me. But not one slug touched us. Slowly, and still keeping Charles covered, I opened my eyes and took a look around.

A large buckboard wagon with steel plates welded crudely onto the sides had driven straight in the army of zombies. I don't know why I hadn't heard it. I figure I was a mite preoccupied.

It was a good-sized wagon, and about half of the gunslingers from the Gunslinger's Ball were riding in it and firing away with everything they got.

"Clark! Get your stinking hide in the wagon!" Jennifer Chaos shouted to me. "We'll cover you!"

Jesse James, Trapper Jack and the Virginian hopped off the wagon and blasted some nearby zombies, while Jennifer Chaos, Moses Brown, Cole Corbucci and Clay Allison kept up a constant fire. Al Swearengen was at the reins and he leveled his sawed-off shotgun at Marie Laveau and Ringo.

Charles and I started running. I picked up my fallen Colt and fanned it with the other hand, sending out six-shots than blew a walking corpse over on his back. Charles struggled to keep up with me, and I had to slow down a little, but the gunslingers in the wagon kept up a good amount of covering fire and not one of the zombies got a chance to plug us.

Finally, we made it to the wagon. I picked up Charles and handed him to Jennifer Chaos, who set him down in the back behind some metal plates where none of the zombie's shots could hit him. I was mighty thankful to all of them.

"Al, you backstabbing bastard!" shrieked Marie, her face a mask of rage. When she got angry, every year she had been alive was visible on her face, a sea of wrinkles that turned her from a pretty woman to a withered crone.

Al Swearengen chuckled. "You don't know who you're dealing with." He fired his sawed-off, but Ringo jumped into the air and caught the shell instead of Marie. The Fossor went down with a grunt of pain.

"Give me Clark and his brat!" Marie snarled. "I'll kill you and everyone in Deadwood if you don't hand them over!"

"There's a special place in Hell waiting for you, you corpse-loving freakish hag-creature!" Jennifer shouted back as she blasted an incoming zombie in the face.

Hugo Montez and the Katar Kid jumped off of the wagon and ran into the battle, Montez beheaded several zombies with his machetes while the Katar Kid disemboweled one with a quick stab from his wrist-mounted swords.

Al pulled on the reins, turning the wagon around. The gunfighters who had jumped out headed back towards the wagon, hopping inside as the large vehicle started rolling away. The zombies fired after us, but the armored plates absorbed most of the shots. Maria Laveau hissed out curses in languages none of us had ever heard before and then the Voodoo Queen nodded to Ringo and pointed.

Just as Al Swearengen started on the road back to Deadwood, we looked back to see Ringo running after us. Ringo slammed his legs into the ground, and I heard bones snap as he drove himself onward. If you're a Fossor and you can just slap on a new pair of legs when your old ones get broken, I reckon it don't matter what you do to them.

Ringo was moving fast, and as soon as he got close enough, he jumped into the air and landed right in the center of the wagon. Everyone leveled their weapons at him.

"Fill him full of lead!" Clay Allison shouted, and every gunman in the wagon fired away. Bullets tore through Ringo but he just stood there and took it. His skin and muscle was blown away, his skull and bones were laid bare, and soon there weren't nothimg more than a fleshy skeleton standing in the middle of the rolling wagon.

"I like your gun hand," Ringo grunted to Jesse James. "Figure I'll take it from you. And I'm taking that feller's face, cause I like his moustache." He gave Jennifer a toothy smile. "I'm gonna take some of your lady bits. Ain't never had those before."

Ringo was a twisted and evil creature, but I couldn't think of any good way to get rid of him. Bullets didn't faze him none, and there was no way we could bury him or trap him somewhere.

Ringo reached down to his own leg and snapped off the bone. "Well, maybe after the bludgeoning no one's going to be that handsome, but I'll do what I can."

He leapt towards Jennifer Chaos, knocking her backwards with a swing from his bone-club. She drew her hunting knife and slashed his chest, but Ringo didn't seem to notice and struck her again.

"No! Jenny!" Charles ran forward from his hiding space and pushed Ringo with all of his might. They were near the edge of the wagon and Charles must have summoned up all of his strength, because the two of them pitched over the side.

Charles grabbed on to the edge of the wagon and Ringo grabbed onto the back of Charles's Norfolk jacket and held fast. I ran over to the edge and tried to force Ringo off, but the Fossor held on. He reached a skeletal hand up and grabbed Charles's throat.

"Clark!" Jesse James ran to my side. "I think I got something you should feed to this skeletal bastard. May do him good." Jesse pulled a candy red stick of dynamite from his jacket. "I always carry some around in case I need to blow a safe."

"Much obliged." I took the dynamite, pulled out a match, and lit it on my boot heel. I lit the fuse, held the dynamite stick behind my back and drew the Bowie knife from my boot heel. Then I knelt down.

"Listen, Ringo," I said, holding up the knife. "I've killed a hell of a lot of men, and I'm about to kill you unless you let go of my boy. What do you say?"

"I'm a Fossor, remember?" Ringo laughed. "You ain't got nothing could hurt me!"

"This might." I took out the dynamite stick and shoved it into Ringo's open mouth. The Fossor had both of his hands full hanging on to Charles's jacket and trying to strangle my boy, so he had no way to get the dynamite out. Then, I raised my Bowie knife and hacked off the arm that was strangling Charles and then the one holding onto Charles's jacket.

The severed arms fell onto the dusty road, and with a swift kick to his chin the rest of Ringo joined them. Ringo mumbled and spat, trying to cough the dynamite out, but it wasn't doing no good. I scooped up Charles and held him close just as the fuse burned down and the dynamite went off. The explosion echoed around the mountains like thunder. Ringo was blown to pieces and scattered to the winds, but I didn't pay much attention to anything except for Charles.

Soon, we got back to Deadwood and everyone in town wanted news of what Marie was fixing to do next. A large crowd of shabby miners and thin-skinned townsfolk gathered in the street outside the Gem.

Al Swearengen stood up on a crate.

"Okay, now I'm an intelligent man," he began carefully. "I know which way the wind is blowing, and I know when to get out of the way. And I'm not gonna lie. We're up against an awful lot here. But this time, I ain't running." The crowd fell silent. I reckon in a town as lawless as Deadwood, a saloon owner's words carried a good deal of weight.

"Mr. Swearengen!" called out a portly feller in a black-checkered suit, raising his hand. "Reporter for the Black Hills Pioneer! Is it true an army of the undead is about to descend upon us?"

"In so many words—yes." Al cleared his throat. "Look, I've got nothing but hate for this Voodoo witch and her corpses. She betrayed me, and that makes us foes for life. Plus, she wants Clark Reeper dead. Clark's my friend, and friends stand by their own. So, people of Deadwood, I'm asking you to help save the camp and your lives. Get your guns, put up some defenses, and we can hold out."

The crowd of miners looked like they didn't quite believe what Swearengen was saying. They mumbled to each other and some of them started to leave.

Seeing that he was losing his audience, Al got desperate. "My friends, if we survive this, the Gem Saloon and Variety Theatre will sell all booze half-off!"

More mumbles.

"Fine." Swearengen muttered a curse under his breath. "Absolutely free! For a full week!"

The miners let out a cheer, throwing hats and shooting guns off into the air. They went to prepare the camp's defenses as Swearengen turned to the gunslingers. Each was a force in their own right, but I didn't know if all of them put together could hold out against Marie Laveau's Voodoo army.

"You folks with me?" Al asked.

"I got no love for Clark," Little Napoleon said. "But if he's dead, there'll be no one for me to think about whenever I'm on the toilet. I say we fight."

"Jolly good!" Vivian Bolt agreed. "I'm sure that morbid mob can easily be dismissed. Let us proceed to the outskirts, where we can meet those blighters when they come." He raised his cane and led the lot of them down the street.

Swearengen watched the gunslingers go, and then headed to his saloon. I figured him for one who likes to lead from the rear.

I looked at Charles. He was shaking slightly, still recovering from our narrow escape, and also his realization about what I was. I could tell that was chewing him up inside. I sat down on a barrel and looked him over.

"Charles?"

"Yes, Mr. Reeper?"

"Something on your mind, son? About all them folks I killed, I wager."

Charles nodded. "I've been thinking about it. I really don't know, I mean, I guess it was either you or them a lot of the time, and maybe they were bad people, but killing is wrong and you've done it so many times."

"That's so." I looked at the ground. "You forgive me?"

Charles gulped. "Mr. Reeper—Clark—I want you to promise me something, and then I'll forgive everything." He took his peaked cap off and held it in his hands. "Promise me that after this day you will never take the life of another human being ever again. Can you do that?"

I thought about it. If I couldn't kill any more that meant my bounty hunting days were over. No way I could live the life that I've been living without shedding blood by the gallon. Then again, I did have enough cash stored away. I could take Charles somewhere nice, Frisco maybe. I could get a little store or a business. I could take my guns off and live a decent life, not worrying about violence or danger of any kind. Of course, it would be mighty boring, but I think I had enough excitement for all of my days. And even without taking lives, there were still other adventures a man could seek.

"Sure, Charles. I promise, on the souls of all those I've killed, and on my Old Man's soul, and my own soul, for whatever that's worth. As long as I live, I won't kill nobody—well, after we get out of here alive."

Charles grinned and he hugged me. "Thank you, Clark! Marie Laveau was completely wrong. You're not violent at all."

I wasn't so sure, but I hugged Charles just the same and stood up. "All right then. The oath is taken. Son, I want you to stay in the saloon with Swearengen and Winston the armadillo while I head down to the edge of town and fight the zombies. I got one last chance to kill folks, and I need to take it."

"Okay. Please, be careful, though."

"I will." I pulled out my revolvers and looked them over. I did love those six-guns, but I loved Charles more. I started walking away from the saloon. I took a few steps and then turned back. "And Charles?"

"Yes, Mr. Reeper?"

"Think about where you want to settle down soon as this is all over."

I broke into a run as I headed down the muddy street of Deadwood. The townsfolk had done what they could, using wagons, crates, and barrels to create a barricade, placing snipers on rooftops and in windows.

A dozen shooters stood guard in the street. As I walked towards them, they turned and waved to me, tipping hats and nodding.

"Howdy," I said. "I am very sorry for causing all this trouble for y'all, and much obliged to you for helping me out of it."

"Ah, shucks," Billy the Kid said. "Ain't no trouble. I've always wanted to get in a gunfight with dead folks."

"Truly, I have never seen its like," Wild Bill Hickok added.

"I met Frankenstein's Daughter once." Jesse James surprised everyone. "That was sure something."

"Stop flapping your fat lips and get ready!" Jennifer Chaos cried. "Here they come!"

Sure enough, Marie Laveua's Voodoo zombie army was coming straight at us. But they weren't shambling along like normal zombies, no sir. Marie Laveau had whisked up some of her Voodoo magic and given them all mounts: black, bristly Creole hogs, each one the size of a large horse. The pigs snorted and shook their tusks as they charged down on Deadwood. We all stared at the great beasts in terror.

"What are you waiting for? Judgment Day's already here!" Jennifer Chaos's shouts roused us, and with a whooping and a howl, every gunslinger drew their weapons and opened fire. Zombies went down, blasted right off of their pigs, and some of the hogs got hit as well. They fell to the ground, sliding ahead in the dirt before turning into thick piles of ash. The giant Creole pigs were Laveau's summoned creatures, and when they got shot up, they turned back to the dust of the earth.

The gunfire continued, but the zombies kept coming. Even after being shot down, the corpses simply got back up and kept on walking. They drew their own weapons and started shooting back, killing and wounding some of the townsfolk. Then, the pigs made it to the barricades. The great hogs smashed right through, trampling those not quick enough to get away, and the zombies hopped off and leapt into battle.

Franklin Franks, the masked anarchist bomber, fired away with his Volcanic Ten pistols, splattering zombie brains across the ground, before holstering his guns and hurling a bundle of dynamite into the oncoming enemy. The blast sent one of the giant pigs hurtling through the air, and the big animal crushed a couple of zombies when it came tumbling down. Trapper Jack fired a single shot as a big as a ninepins ball with his massive rifle, the bullet tearing through several zombies before it stopped moving. Bat Masterson struck out with his cane, bashing a walking corpse over the head and then blowing out its brains with his revolver. Little Napoleon dived under the legs of the zombies, blasting them from below with his little derringer.

I walked into the battle slowly, firing both of my Colts at once. Brimstone Brown stood by my side, plinking away with his long barreled pistol, and Jennifer Chaos was on my other side, firing with her Snider rifle. Zombies went down before us, blasted apart and falling to the ground. A giant Creole pig came charging at me, but I leapt out of the way and fired off my remaining revolver shots as it ran past. The pig squealed and turned into ash as it ran on. I could swear the air smelled like pork chops.

Armed with shotguns, Wyatt Earp, Cole Corbucci and Doc Holiday charged down the road mounted on war horses. They fired all their barrels at the zombies, one shot to knock them over and another to blow their heads clean off. The battle sprawled out through all of Deadwood as the townsfolk fired down from the rooftops. One by one, the zombies were blown to pieces and moved no more.

Before we knew it, the battle was over and done with, or at least it seemed that way. Every feller I had ever killed was dead again, lying on the ground and draining his guts into the dirt. I looked around for my Old Man, but he was nowhere to be found. I figured his corpse was rotting somewhere.

"Yee-ha!" someone shouted, and we all took up the cry. Guns were fired off in the air and hats were tossed up to celebrate our victory. I looked at my revolvers, wondering what it was going to be like not having them strapped around my waist.

Then, one of Al's henchmen came running down the street. "She's at the Gem!" he cried. "The Voodoo witch is there! But she ain't the good looking lady she was when she came in!"

I instantly thought of Charles. While we were fighting off the zombies, Marie Laveau had snuck around from behind and got into the Gem, and there was nothing between her and Charles. I started running down the street, reloading my pistols as I went. Some of the other gunslingers followed me, but I paid them no heed. As I got closer to the Gem, I saw of number of bodies littering the street. I hoped to hell I wasn't too late.

I kicked the door open and burst inside, only to get a blow to the head that knocked me to the floor. I looked up and saw my Old Man, holding his nock gun. He had bashed me with the butt of the weapon and now pointed the nine barrels of it right at me.

I looked around and saw Al Swearengen and Marie Laveau engaged in pitched battle in the balcony. Al wielded a shaving razor, trying to slash Marie's throat and bleed her dry, but Marie wasn't going down easy. She had changed too, looking less like a beauty and more like a nightmare. Her skin had changed from a creamy, coffee complexion to pure red; her hair was long, unkempt and tangled; and her hands were stretched and twisted into curved claws.

"Run for it, boy!" Al called and Charles, with Winston perched on his shoulder, jumped up from a hiding place and started running down the stairs, his dress shoes clicking on the wood as he breathed hard. Marie let out a primal hiss and batted Al aside with a single blow. It sent him careening off of the balcony and down to the floor.

Marie ran after Charles, running on all fours and swiftly catching the terrified boy. She held him aloft with one hand, and when brave little Winston tried to bite her, she swatted the armadillo and sent him skittering across the room. Charles cried out in rage.

"Marie Laveau, you done lost!" I shouted at her. "Let Charles go and we'll let you leave with your life!"

"That's not what's going to happen!" Marie's voice was raspy and cruel. "I'm going to kill this brat in front of your eyes, and then your Old Man is going to kill you."

I looked into the dead face of my father. He moaned and mumbled, but the nock gun didn't waver. Marie let out a cold laugh and held out one of her hands. Her nails grew into cruel claws the size of Bowie knives.

"I'm sorry, Clark!" Charles called to me, just as Marie prepared to stab her clawed hand right into my boy's chest.

My Old Man was mumbling, and I noticed the nock gun dipping as if he was trying to let go of it. "Come on, Old Man," I begged him. "You weren't never there when I was a boy. Please, I need you here now."

Josiah Reeper looked at me for what seemed like a long time. I think I saw the trickle of a tear from his eye. Then, he twisted the nock gun around, pointing it right under his chin and he squeezed the trigger, blowing his own head off. The nock gun fell to the floor and I was quick to pick it up. I aimed the gun at Marie.

"My love!" Marie Laveau cried, staring at my Old Man's headless corpse. "My one true love!" She let Charles fall to the floor.

I didn't give her any more time to mourn. I squeezed the trigger of the nock gun eight times, firing off all the remaining shots of the great weapon straight into her. The recoil nearly knocked me over, but I kept steady and kept firing. Soon Marie Laveau was blasted to bits. She had stayed alive for over a century, romanced and captured countless men, and probed the darkest levels of occult knowledge. But now and forever, Marie Laveau was dead.

Well, the Gunslinger's Ball did not become an annual tradition. Al Swearengen was pretty beaten up from his fall, but he looked like he was gonna pull through. To Charles's delight, Winston was fine as well, except for a bent tail. The other gunslingers all said their goodbyes and took a final drink before heading out on the trail, getting back to their lives of adventure and fast shooting. I said goodbye to all of them, and we parted friends. Even Jennifer Chaos and her girlfriend Lula didn't make me ornery, not when I was thinking on a new future for Charles and me.

That new future is gonna be a good one. Charles and I decided that San Francisco would be a good place to settle. We had been there before, helping Emperor Norton take care of a giant squid. We figured it would be a nice place for Charles to grow up.

I got all my money out of the bank, and it was quite a large amount. I figure I'll open up a dry goods store. It can't be that difficult, and I got enough cash to keep us going even if I turn out to be a terrible businessman.

The night before the stagecoach for the coast left, Charles and I went into the hills outside of Deadwood with a carriage carrying the bodies of my Old Man and Marie Laveau. We put them both in separate graves. Then, I tossed my two Colts into the grave and started shoveling the dirt.

"Thank you, Clark." Charles held my hand as I finished the burial.

"Much obliged, son," I told him. And I believe I was.

Acknowledgments

I would like to thank everyone who helped contribute to this book and took time out of their lives to make my dream come true. I'd like to especially thank my wonderful editors Pat Lynch and Michael Eldridge for sifting through my purple prose and picking out the typos; Elijah, Kai and the kids in my B'nai Israel Class who were the first to read the rough drafts, and my talented illustrator Jake Delaney who brought my characters to life. I'd also like to thank my parents and sister, for putting up with my pig-headed need to see this in print and who are responsible more than anything for making me want to be a writer and a decent human being.

-MPP

The Grentelman Author and Illustrator

The Gentleman Author—Michael Phineas Panush

Born in the highlands of Ohio, Michael Phineas Panush was the heir apparent to the impressive Panush Glove Factory fortune, until he squandered the entirety of the fortune on experimental back pain medication and a collection of exotic fezzes. He later joined the Peace and Harmony Commune in southern New Hampshire, and after several court cases, was cleared of any responsibility in the Commune's dissolution within the year of his joining. He spent several years wandering the west and was beat up by Wild Bill Hickok, buffaloed by Wyatt Earp and soundly drubbed by Al Swearengen. Following this formative experience, he drifted to Paris where he wrote most of his books under an opium-induced stupor, including the widely unknown *Phantasmo, Master Thief*, the remarkably ill-received *Why I should be Pope*, and the jingoistic piece of doggerel and early science-fiction entitled *Theodore Roosevelt Licks the Moon-Kaiser*. He was garroted to death by Paris gangsters circa 1902, and his body was destroyed in a particularly explosive Grand Guignol Theatrical Production.

The Gentleman Illustrator—Jacoby 'Lighting Jake' Delaney

After immigrating with his family from Ireland as an infant, young Jake acquired a fearsome reputation as a brickbat hurler and woodcut artist in the Five Points Neighborhood of New York. His violent attitude and habit of head butting those who disagreed with him led to his expulsion from several influential Fine Arts Academies. After a particularly brutal episode which left an entire class hospitalized, Jacoby Delaney headed west. He gained his nickname during an Oklahoma Range War in which he was struck repeatedly by lightning. He later returned to New York where he got in a fight with 'fighting cartoonist' Thomas Nast. Delaney joined Emma Goldman's anarchist circle in Greenwich Village; in the investigation of the McKinley Assassination, Delaney was suspected to be the rumored 'second gunman.' He fled to Europe and joined Madame Blavatsky's Theosophist Society, Aleister Crowley's Ordo Templi Orientis and Guido Von List's Rune Worshippers before becoming a militant atheist. In 1908, an anonymous psychic source told Delaney of an 'event' in the Tunguska region of Siberia. During his trip, he was caught in the Tunguska Explosion and never seen again. He is presumed dead, though Delaney Sightings sometimes occur on rainy nights.

5

Made in the USA